# SPINNING TALES, WEAVING HOPE

## Stories, Storytelling and Activities for Peace, Justice and the Environment

Edited by

ED BRODY, JAY GOLDSPINNER, KATIE GREEN,
RONA LEVENTHAL & JOHN PORCINO of
The Stories for World Change Network

Foreword by Holly Near  Illustrated by Lahri Bond

NEW SOCIETY PUBLISHERS

Illustrations and cover art by Lahri Bond.
Cover design by Diane McIntosh.
Book design by Greg Bates, Josh Bernoff, and Ed Brody.

Printed in the United States of America on partially recycled paper by Capital City Press, Montpelier, Vermont.

New Society Publishers acknowledges the support of the Government of Canada through the Book Publishing Industry Development Program (BPIDP) for our publishing activities, and the assistance of the Province of British Columbia through the British Columbia Arts Council.

BRITISH
COLUMBIA
ARTS COUNCIL
Supported by the Province of British Columbia

Paperback ISBN: 0-86571-447-9

**Cataloguing-in-Publication Data:**
A catalog record for this publication is available from the National Library of Canada.

Inquiries regarding requests to reprint all or part of *Spinning Tales, Weaving Hope* should be addressed to New Society Publishers at the address below.

To order directly from the publishers, please add $4.50 shipping to the price of the first copy, and $1.00 for each additional copy (plus GST in Canada). Send check or money order to:

New Society Publishers
P.O. Box 189, Gabriola Island, BC V0R 1X0, Canada

New Society Publishers aims to publish books for fundamental social change through nonviolent action. We focus especially on sustainable living, progressive leadership, and educational and parenting resources. Our full list of books can be browsed, and purchased securely, on the worldwide web.

NEW SOCIETY PUBLISHERS                                              www.newsociety.com

# Table of Contents

111000

## Living with Each Other: The Problems of Working Together

## Living with the Earth

"Linger on the details, the part that reflects the change. There lies revolution.
Our everyday lives, the changes inside, become our political songs . . ."

    —Holly Near

# Foreword

## by Holly Near

SONGS ARE STORIES PUT TO MUSIC, and stories, like songs, illuminate and sometimes change our lives. Stories, an essential part of our lives long before the written word, invite us to create and pass down our culture from generation to generation, to share our values, to question our assumptions, and to see our individual and collective futures.

In my life, the stories I have heard from my family, my friends, my community and from willing strangers all over the world have been the true source of my education. They have taught me humor, compassion and courage.

This book, with its carefully chosen stories, is designed to bring out the storyteller in each of us. But primarily, it is written for the teacher or leader. Each story is accompanied by carefully thought out exercises that "linger on the details," so we may be guided into discussion. As we think out loud, we feel the feelings, see the colors, understand the lessons. The teacher, the camp counselor, the therapist, the dramatist, will find hours of creative play and thought-provoking time. And as our abilities expand as storytellers, so will communication improve, as we strive to reach full human potential. Bring out the storyteller in you, for yourself . . . for all of us.

*Holly Near*

# Acknowledgments

We would like to thank:

Hanna Bandes Geshelin and Michael Punzak for helping to get the ball rolling;

Josh Bernoff for substantial assistance with the typesetting;

Phil Stone for legal advice;

Mayra Bloom for contributing to the activities for Gaura Devi;

Jane Porcino for advice on the publishing process;

Flic Shooter, Ellen Sawislak, David Albert and Annie Hanaway for their support at New Society Publishers;

Althea Boswell-Green, Margaret Boulden, Anna Brody, Deborah and Phil Brody, Dena Feldstein, Christina Porcino, Julian Césare Porcino, Jane and Chet Porcino, and Phil Stone for their love and patience during this process (and before and after it).

❦ ❦ ❦

A substantial part of the royalties from this book will be used to support the following organizations:

**Amnesty International** is a world-wide independent movement working impartially for the release of all prisoners of conscience, fair and prompt trials for political prisoners, and an end to torture and executions. 322 Eighth Avenue, New York, New York, 10001. (212) 807-8400.

**Creative Conflict Resolution with Children (CCRC)** was founded in 1972 and is affiliated with Fellowship of Reconciliation. CCRC provides workshops which help children and people who work with children to learn conflict resolution, mediation, problem solving and bias awareness. CCRC has two publications: a workbook, *The Friendly Classroom for a Small Planet: Children's Creative Response to Conflict Program* — available from New Society Publishers — and a songbook, *Children's Songs for a Friendly Planet.* Box 271, Nyack, New York, 10960-0271. (914) 358-4601.

**The Children's Rainforest** works with the Monteverde Conservation League in Costa Rica, which buys and protects rainforests in northern Costa Rica, and carries out local education and reforestation projects. El Bosque Eterno de Los Ninos (The International Children's Rainforest) is a 42,000 acre area of lush, remote tropical rainforest which is currently being purchased with funds raised by children (and adults) in Europe, Canada, Japan and the US. One hundred dollars protects one acre. P.O. Box 936, Lewiston, Maine, 04240. (207) 784-1069.

**The Lion and the Lamb Peace Arts Center** provides an opportunity for the study and promotion of peace and international understanding through the arts and literature for children. Art, literature, and other materials are available for loan. For more information write to: The Lion and the Lamb Peace Arts Center, Bluffton College, Bluffton Ohio, 45817. (419) 358-3207.

**The Stories for World Change Network** was a support and networking group whose purpose was the discovery, creation and sharing of stories that relate to the search for positive change in the world. These are stories that open windows on issues of war and peace, resolve conflicts creatively, affirm similarities and differences, build trust, find both inner and outer peace and look at and begin to heal some of the world's pain and injustice. The organization is now dissolved, but its members, including this book's editors, continue to pursue its goals.

# The Hermit and the Children

## retold by Susan Tobin

THERE WAS AN OLD MAN who lived alone in the woods outside a small town. He had little to do with the people of the village. All sorts of odd tales, stories, and rumors circulated around town about him. The children in the town delighted in teasing and playing tricks on this old man. It was said that the hermit was very wise, so the children were always trying to outsmart him.

One day, the children thought up a new trick. They snared a small bird and carried it through the woods to the hermit's cabin. One boy held the bird in his hands behind his back. The boldest of the children stepped up and knocked on the old man's door. When the hermit opened the door, the boy with the bird said rudely, "Old man, what do you think I have behind my back?"

Now, the children did not believe the old man could guess it was a bird. But if he did, they planned to ask him, "Is it alive or dead?" If he guessed, "Dead," the boy would show him the live and fluttering little bird. But, if he guessed, "Alive," the boy planned to crush the bird in his hand and show the old man the dead bird.

Living close to nature, the hermit was very observant. He noticed a small down feather float to the ground behind the boy's back, and he said, "You have a bird in your hand."

The children's eyes opened wide in amazement. He was smarter than they thought. They were ready with the second question, "Is the bird dead or alive?"

The hermit thought for a moment. He looked at the faces of all of the children, and then directly into the eyes of the boy who held the bird, and said, "The answer is in your hands."

❦ ❦ ❦

**Susan Tobin** is and environmental storyteller who is dedicated to recycling stories of lasting value. She has shared her program, *Earth Echoes: Stories For A Small Planet*, at museums, libraries, classrooms and celebrations coast-to-coast. Her love of story magic accompanies her in her other roles as therapist, clown, and bubble expert.

# Introduction to the Second Edition:
# Ten Reasons to Tell Stories in the Classroom

## by Rona Leventhal and Katie Green

WELCOME TO THE SECOND EDITION of *Spinning Tales, Weaving Hope.* We are pleased that the book is once again available. As with prior printings, most of the royalties will be donated to four organizations we think make a difference: The Children's Rainforest, Children's Creative Response to Conflict, The Lion and the Lamb Peace Center, and Amnesty International. Happily, all of these organizations are thriving in pursuing their respective missions. The Stories for World Change Network, on the other hand, has disbanded, its members spreading the messages of peace, justice, and environmental awareness in their individual work as storytellers, educators, and parents. This book is, perhaps, the group's legacy.

Since the book was first published in 1992, we have been contacted by numerous groups and individuals who have thanked us for creating the book, telling us how it has helped them. We have heard the experiences of classroom teachers, university educators, participants in nonprofit organizations working for peace, and we are even included in the Peace Corps manual for their environmental education program. What is it about storytelling that makes it such a powerful and effective teaching tool? Here are some of the reasons that we and other educators have discovered when storytelling in schools:

## I. Storytelling Is Fun!

*I find that oral lessons are more enjoyable for me. I have an opportunity to really be with my students. I can look at them, they can discuss things—I am so involved with the lesson. At other times of the day I am staring at a text or chart paper. I'm realizing a new connection to my class through storytelling.*

....

*Shawn thinks everything is boring lately. This is the one thing he likes! It's been worth every penny in the world to see that boy smile!*

As teachers, we are always looking for ways to capture the attention of students. The teacher quoted above discovered one of the primary benefits of storytelling: When you tell or hear a story, you capture the imagination and make learning fun! And who isn't motivated to learn when it's fun? Storytelling inspires learning—not only of academic skills but also of life skills. And when this happens, something else magical happens: the teacher's job becomes more agreeable as well.

## II. Storytelling Stimulates Learning

*Throughout the whole story my students were invested; all eyes were on me. I have worked with these kids for almost a year. I have children with severe reading disabilities and attention disabilities. No one was zoning out! I believe it had a lot to do with my voice, my eye contact, and my movement.*

Teachers are constantly amazed at how attentive students are, how much information is retained, and the excitement that listening to a story or creating one orally brings to their classroom. Listening to lots of stories provides us with a flexible framework in which we can develop a sense of story structure in an organic way, rather than memorizing a set of rules. Within that framework, we also define our world through the lives of the characters. All of this, combined with our "imagination muscle," often fuels an interest and improvement in reading and writing.

## III. Storytelling Strengthens the Imagination

*At the very end of the afternoon, we listened to a tale of a Tennessee Panther. It was so enthralling. For most of the story, it did not seem that the storyteller was even there. I saw the old woman and the hunter as if they were standing in the room.*

Stories capture us inside a bubble of time and place, transporting us on the breezes of our imagination and the currents of our experience. We each hear the same words, but the meanings we attach to them differ from listener to listener, and from teller to teller. As such, storytelling is a powerful tool for people to process emotions, viewpoints, events, and facts. As in a journey, we return from hearing a story with thoughts and questions and a desire to share those with others.

But the role stories play in developing the imagination is even more important, since without imagination, intellectual growth is limited. To be able to create our own images is essential to development and learning. If we can visualize a scene from history as we hear about it, it will be imprinted on our memories. If we can create a map in our minds of mathematical functions—or if we learn them via a story—the equations will make better sense. If we can envision molecules bouncing around faster as air is heated, we will remember what "temperature" really means. Remembering basic facts becomes a series of images rather than disconnected information. To make changes in the world—whether social, technological, or ideological—we need to be able to imagine something that doesn't exist: a life of freedom, a new kind of computer software, a new scientific model. But first children have to know that they have permission to have their own images, and become aware of them. The result is students who are engaged in their learning.

## IV. Storytelling Enhances Communication

*The kids discuss stories with each other now. That never happened before I started using storytelling! In the past, after reading them a story, they would direct a million questions at me before they would have any comments.*

When we provide opportunities for young people to tell stories, we are providing an opportunity for them to feel good. Everybody likes to be listened to. Telling stories builds self-esteem and self-confidence. Students improve their skills in attentive listening and critical analysis while coaching each other.

Today's fast-paced society has pushed personal communication out of many households. All too often, the bedtime story has been replaced by television shows or computer games. When most communication from parent to child is organizational or disciplinary, something important is missing. Storytelling is an effective and enjoyable tool to counter this trend.

Building community—living together and working toward a common goal—depends on effective communication. Inherent in sharing a story is an agreement between teller and listener: the teller shares, the receiver actively listens, and a natural form of communication is established in a way that does not happen when a story is read.

## V.  Storytelling Builds Cultural Awareness

> *You made me think twice about what I say to people and the way I look at them: their race, religion, size—everything.*

Storytelling also fosters another kind of communication: it speaks to who we are as individuals within a culture. The stories we tell—and what we take from them—reflect what is important to us. There is a reason why so many of the classic folktales involve concerns about having enough food or searching for a mate! Some of these cultural connections are universal, demonstrating our common humanity. Others highlight interesting features of specific cultures: an Eskimo tale might describe seal-hunting for food and clothing to survive the harsh winter; an Indian story can give a flavor of the humility and selflessness Buddhists hold in high regard. Storytelling enhances cultural awareness and tolerance of difference, celebrating diversity by exposing the listener to different cultures while addressing our common humanity.

## VI. Storytelling Enhances Empathy

> *As I was telling the story, I could tell the kids were starting to make predictions and conclusions about what was happening. When my character, Plug, was about to get in trouble, they would cover their mouths and giggle!  When another character was about to hurt Plug, my students would gasp!*

When a storyteller takes on the role of a character in the story, whether it is Prince Charming or the vines covering the castle walls, the listener experiences that character's emotions and intentions through the voice and gesture of the storyteller. As the listener is drawn in to the drama, both the storyteller and the listener can "become" the character for a time. This enhances understanding of another's point of view, and promotes empathy. Because the storyteller embodies all of the characters in the story, the listener is allowed to experience different characters' perspectives on the same event.

Stories often have universal concerns at their core—love and hope, rejection and loss, physical and emotional abuse, sibling rivalry and familial divisiveness—issues that can be played out safely through the characters. Storytelling provides a safe venue for young people to explore roles that may be emotionally charged. For instance, educators in the field of conflict resolution realize that violence is related to oppression. Storytelling provides a venue for young people to explore the roles of the persecutor and the persecuted. A story about a mistreated character may give an abused child permission to relate his own personal painful experiences by exploring the point of view of the oppressed character.

Through stories, students realize that conflicts are a natural part of living. They can recognize sources of conflict and what escalates and de-escalates conflicts. And they can create alternative resolutions. Storytelling makes a heart-to-heart connection.

## VII. Listening to Stories Encourages Critical Thinking

*The best part of this lesson was the fact that the students themselves were about to do all of the educating. Through listening to their stories, all of us were able to learn from them. Storytelling was an excellent way to communicate a lot of wonderful information!*

Peter Eppig, director of the Integrated Day Education Program at Antioch New England Graduate School, developed the critical skills program called Education by Design. He has identified a number of critical skills and attitudes that are important for children to learn. Many of them relate directly to storytelling and story creating in the oral tradition.

**Problem Solving:** A story cannot exist without a conflict at its center. Stories explore ways to solve these problems, promoting critical thinking skills and improving students' ability to resolve conflicts creatively. Problems in stories are identified, causal relationships are explored, and the perspective or point of view of each character is examined.

**Decision Making:** The stories that we tell and hear influence our thinking and decision making. When we hear about a character's decision, we instinctively evaluate it: Was it was a good choice? What consequences will it bring? How would we have reacted in the same situation? How did we actually react under similar circumstances?

Conversely, when we tell a story, there are many decisions that we encounter: Which story speaks to us enough to motivate us to tell it? Why is it an important story to tell? How much audience participation should we include? How should we balance narrative, characterization, movement, and sound effects? Telling a simple story can be a lesson in making choices and having the flexibility to improvise and change as needed.

**Organization:** In telling or creating an oral story, we need to use our organizational skills to sequence the images that we want to relate to our listeners. Otherwise, they will not be able to relax and simply soak in the story. Then we need to overlap that organization with our creative impulses in order to make the story interesting, humorous, or touching.

**Communications:** The very act of telling a story is an act of communication! There is a give and take between teller and listeners, and there are usually lessons and themes that we wish to emphasize. As coaches, we also need to be able to listen well and relate what we hear and see to the teller in helpful ways.

**Critical Thinking:** Both storyteller and listeners must consider how conflict is raised and resolved in a story and be aware of the narrative's intention. The class may agree or disagree with a story's resolution of its problem, but this can provide a springboard for discussion of the roots of such conflicts and how to avert or resolve them when they arise.

**Leadership:** A student who is willing to take the risk of sharing a story that he or she has worked hard to shape is taking a leadership role by being a role model for other students.

**Collaboration:** Performing artists often use the assistance of others to be successful with their work. We need fresh eyes to see our stories, to see what works and what needs adjusting. Through peer coaching, students can work collaboratively to help each other tell the best stories they can.

## VIII. Storytelling Builds Literacy Skills

*I always include fairy tales in my third grade curriculum. But this year, my kids were able to have stories told to them. Their original fairy tales have never been so beautifully written. Listening to a storyteller made all the difference!*

Listening to a story requires the listener to focus on only one thing—the storyteller. There is no "rewind" or "instant replay." This not only encourages concentration and recall, it also builds respect. The story is not to be interrupted. The continuation of the story is, at the moment, more important than the listener's commentary. Attention and memory are enhanced when we listen to stories.

Storytelling enhances all areas of language. A person's vocabulary expands when a story contains a word that may be unfamiliar to the listener. As storytelling often stresses and repeats the unusual, the listener is likely to remember the new word and seek out its meaning. Because the unfamiliar word was used more than once in a pleasant narrative context, the listener is apt to retain it. Thus, storytelling builds vocabulary skills.

Listening to stories improves understanding of grammar and literary devices. Some stories use language that is more formal than that used in normal conversation. Similes and metaphors appear more often in storytelling than in dialogue. Storytelling encourages an appreciation of language and develops rhetorical skills.

Listeners develop a sense of story structure. Story comprehension and the ability to formulate a story-narrative are learned. Storytelling rewards cohesive thinking.

When a child listens to stories, language comprehension improves. Children are better able to recall a told story than one that is read from a book. Auditory and memory skills are improved when young people listen to spoken narrative.

## IX. Storytelling Creates Classroom Culture

*One of the best things about the story I told is that it was easy to relate to. The moral—that being forgetful can get you into trouble—was interesting and my kids related to it immediately. They connected it to forgetting their homework or studying for a spelling test. This story automatically became part of our classroom culture. On Thursdays, homework packets are due. They changed the words from, "Soap, soap, don't forget the soap" to, "Homework, homework, don't forget the homework!"*

The students in the example above used their connection with the character in the story to build common ground and added some joy to their daily tasks. When a group listens to a story, a common experience is shared and community—often a "classroom culture"—is developed. This contributes to the group's identity and builds a sense of cooperation.

Similarly, a story can sometimes help students to understand human behavior within the context of their classroom. Once, after telling a story about a turtle whose constant urge to talk gets him into lots of trouble, one of us spoke with a boy who had been interrupting the lesson. We reminded him that he should share his thoughts at appropriate times rather than whenever he wanted to. The boy thought for a moment, and then said, "You mean, like the turtle in the story?" He got the point! Sometimes this special classroom knowledge comes from a student. But teachers can also use such gems throughout the year to remind a student or the whole class about how to live well and act well in the world.

## X.  Storytelling Changes the World

*When you tell stories, the world changes.*
— A girl in Crozet, Virginia, after attending a storytelling event at her library

Hearing and telling stories can make the world a better place. Stories provide the framework for the way we experience and define our world. Storytelling can build a community and create a safe, nurturing place where people are receptive to learning. All humanity has the urge to tell stories and to listen to them. Just note the appearance of so many small stories in our everyday conversations: tales of the workplace, anecdotes about children and parents, and even jokes. Even those of us who are not teachers by profession have the opportunity to educate in the course of our everyday lives. So we hope that, like the bird who tried to save the forest by putting out the fire a few drops at a time, you will take this book and—with your mind, your heart, and your words—change the world, one small piece at a time.

❦ ❦ ❦

**Katie Green** and **Rona Leventhal**, adjunct faculty at Fitchburg State College and Lesley University, respectively, tell stories to kids and adults, help students to tell and create stories orally, and encourage teachers to incorporate storytelling into their curriculum.

Two neighbors feuded for a long time over a plot of land. They finally took their bitter disagreement to the rabbi, for arbitration. After their mutually contradictory claims were stated, restated, deflated and negated, the rabbi said, "I have heard your claims on the land. I have not yet heard the land speak. Please be quiet, now, while I listen for the testimony of this witness."

Bending low to the earth, the rabbi remained silent for a while, then straightened his old back and said, "The land tells me it belongs to neither of you. You, she says, belong to her."

# Introduction:
# Stories Can Make a Difference

## by Ed Brody and Michael Punzak

The power of a story is unique upon the earth. What else can take your mind and heart to places they have never been, let you experience events and emotions far from your daily routine, tailor itself to your own moods and reactions, and leave you with new dreams and insights? What else comes from traditions so ancient, holds meanings so deep, and makes lessons so meaningful?

Those of us in the Stories for World Change Network have found that stories make wonderful teaching tools—not to moralize, but to empower people to clarify their feelings and values by helping them escape from the narrow viewpoints the world is always trying to thrust upon them. For years, we have been searching for stories that deal with peace issues: conflict resolution without violence, better understanding of our neighbors, appreciation of other cultures, and healthier relationships with the earth. We have looked for tales that stress empowerment and encourage the development of the individual's capabilities to make informed and compassionate decisions. We want to provide our children with metaphors they can trust and grow with, helping them lead lives which are more caring, loving, and thoughtful. Our goal is to unearth such stories and get them out into the world by telling them and sharing them freely.

The Stories for World Change Network is a support and networking group. Our purpose is the discovery, creation and sharing of stories that relate to our search for positive change in the world. To this end, we have compiled bibliographies, taught workshops, published newsletters, given performances, and now, produced this book. The book itself is the cooperative work of thirty or so storytellers, including a group of five dedicated members acting as an editorial board.

We have created this collection for teachers, parents, storytellers, and anyone who works or plays with young people. The storytellers who are sharing their work in this book all believe that storytelling shapes young minds and lives. We believe that the chance for survival of humanity in these difficult times may be improved by having stories grow in the hearts of the world's children.

Each story is accompanied by follow-up activities which teachers or group leaders may use to draw upon the story's wisdom to enable the children to explore their values and to come to their own conclusions. John Porcino expresses our beliefs, claiming, "A well-spun tale will bring to the surface a range of emotions. It is almost as though the listener has lived through the experiences of the story. By taking advantage of the feelings brought close through the story, a wonderful opportunity presents itself to explore our values around the issues that the story addressed."

How do we know that stories make a difference? Those of us who live in the Boston area have an excellent reminder, in the person of a street storyteller called Brother Blue. He performs on stage, in college classrooms, at parties, weddings and fairs, but most often he is in the streets, leaping about, bare feet punctuating his rhymes with jazzy staccato rhythms, ever improvising upon his unchanging themes of hope, joy, and love.

There's a crowd of fifteen or twenty gathered around him. Others stop and stare; some silently move on. Teenagers giggle self-consciously, afraid it's not cool to listen. The very young have no such concerns. You might think young children would be frightened by his animated energy, or his outrageous blue costume, festooned with bells, butterflies and rainbows—his symbols of our need to wake up, to change, to become a harmonious people. But children know no fear of Blue.

And how many times has he told his soulful parable of that lowly caterpillar, so slow, intimidated, humbled, fearful and oh, so worried? For years Blue has chanted this story, his eyes and feet dancing with his words. Listen to his story, but also spread your senses to take in the audience—what are they feeling? *There!* There it is! There, in that little girl's eyes, can you see it?

The children know! "That caterpillar—it's like me! I also hold the promise of the butterfly! I can—*I will*—fly! What joy!"

Let us remember the power of story! Let us bring stories back into the classroom and re-capture education as a stronghold for the empowered imagination, for change, and for dreams. The well-told tale will take root, like a seed, in the heart of a child.

Let us remember the power of story! James Stevens remembered, saying, "I have learned . . . that the head does not hear anything until the heart has listened, and what the heart knows today the head will understand tomorrow."

The contributors and editors of this anthology see a unity behind the concerns of those who call out for peace, for social justice, and for environmental sanity. Our relationships with our neighbors, our community, and our earth need to improve. Stories can help us see beyond our own concerns, and help us listen to the needs of others and gain the perspective we need to strike a healthy balance. Our conviction is that stories are wonderful tools for change, and we see this book as a collection of levers to help educators move the hearts of their students.

❧ ❧ ❧

**Ed Brody** has been telling stories for longer than he has been trying to make computers listen to what he has to say. A resident of Cambridge, MA, he is a founding member of the Stories for World Change Network.

**Michael Punzak** has been alive since he was a very small baby. He has been telling stories professionally since 1982, but, as a teacher, for a lot longer. He hopes that by the time you read this he will again be teaching. Besides being a highly paid professional storyteller, he also is an occasional actor and a hard-fiddling musician. He hopes that the love of story infuses his entire life, whatever the endeavor.

It is the story of all life that is holy and good to tell, and of us two-leggeds sharing
in it with the four-leggeds and the wings of the air and the fins of the sea and all
green things:
for these are children of one mother, the Earth, and their father is one spirit, the Sky.

—Alice Walker, quoting *Black Elk Speaks*

# Telling Stories: Bringing a Tale to Life

## by Jay Goldspinner

Heard a good story lately? A good story will bring people together, share dreams, get a point across, even change the world!

The stories in this book focus on the themes of Peace, Justice and the Environment. These are such large concepts that they have different meanings to different people; you will find this breadth reflected in the stories in this book. They have been shared with us by storytellers from across the country, who have been telling them lovingly, laughingly, movingly, to children, young people and adults.

The stories range from personal experience stories to passed-down myths and made-up fables, rap stories and ballads, creation stories and folk tales. These stories stir the imagination. They encourage the listeners to become the story characters, to see, hear, taste, and feel the events as if they were actually happening. Some of the stories invite the listeners to join in. All are powerful and moving in themselves. We hope you will enjoy these stories and share them with others.

## Sharing the Stories

There are many ways to share these stories. Reading them aloud to a group may be completely satisfying to you and your listeners.

However, as storytellers, we encourage you to try telling the stories. Telling a story brings it to life. When you tell a story you create another world for yourself and the listeners. You can tell it in your own words and your own way. You are not looking at the pages of a book; your eyes are on the audience. Storyteller and listeners are sharing a common experience. In some magical way you are creating the story together.

Some of you are already storytellers, looking for tales to tell. And some of you may think you have never told a story before, but that's not so. Everyone tells stories, if only of how you got a traffic ticket or why you were late for school. Anyone can be a storyteller. All it takes is the desire to tell, a story to share, and practice. You can begin now, with one of these stories.

## Choosing a Story

Perhaps the best way of choosing a story from this book is to read them all. Keep in mind the group you are telling to, their ages and interests, and especially why you are telling this story. Most importantly, choose a story that you really love and want to tell, because

5

your feeling about the story will empower you in the telling of it. You will put time and energy into it; your listeners will respond to your love of the story.

The stories in this book are grouped into four sections: *Living with Ourselves, Living with Each Other (Working Together to Solve Problems), Living with Each Other (The Problems of Working Together),* and *Living with the Earth.* These sections may help your search for an appropriate story.

If you are looking for a story that deals with a particular subject (for example, Apartheid, Conflict Resolution, or Old Age), check the Theme Index at the end of the book. You can also refer to the Age Suitability Index. Some of the stories, as written here, are better for younger children, some for older. However, a story may be adapted to tell to older or younger listeners than the suggested age: more about that later in this chapter, under "Changing The Story."

## Getting to Know the Story

After you have chosen the story, what next? The important thing is to connect with the story. Sometimes when I hear a story told, it sinks right in to my center, and I go and tell it to the next person I meet. But taking a story from a book (even a book of stories by storytellers) is harder because you haven't heard the story.

So here are some ideas for connecting with the story. Let's take "The Hermit and the Children," which introduces this book, to work with.

Read the story over, preferably aloud, until it becomes familiar. Do this whether you are planning to tell or read the story to the group. You may want to tape record it and listen to the tape, so you can hear how it sounds.

Ask yourself: What do I like about this story? What is the story about? What is the mood (dark, light, scary, dreamy)? Where is the climax? You may begin to "see" the story in your mind.

## Learning the Plot

To remember and recreate the story, learn the plot first and then think about the words. The plot is the order of events: this happened first, then this, and then that.

You may envision the story's plot as a series of images in your head, sort of like a movie or a set of slides. In "The Hermit and the Children," imagine the first slide showing the old man living out in the woods; the second slide, the children playing tricks on the old man; the third, the children snaring a bird; the fourth, the boy knocking on the hermit's door; the fifth, the old man opening the door, and so on. Let the images come into your mind in order, and describe them: that's the story.

You can make a simple outline of the story.

You can draw a "comic strip," a series of simple pictures with stick figures, to recreate the story. I use bright-colored markers for this.

You can draw a story map, or diagram of the story's events in their setting. A story map for "The Hermit and the Children" might show the town, the old man's house, the path the children took through the woods (using stick figures for the children), where they caught the bird, and so on.

Tell someone the one-minute version, the bare bones of the story.

Do any of these things that help you connect with the story.

## Beginning to Tell

Thinking about the story is different from telling it. Tell the story out loud when you're doing the dishes, tell it in the car, tell it to the mirror, tell it to a doll or the cat. Tell it to anyone who will listen: family, friends, the child next door. Tell it as long or as short as you like. Tell it to the tape recorder then listen to it. Have fun with your telling and your discoveries about the story.

Find the rhythm and the words to express the story your own way. See if you want to use your own words or those of the previous storyteller. In general we recommend, "Don't memorize," but there are exceptions. Usually tellers want to learn the beginning and ending sentences of a story by heart; it keeps our feet on the ground. There may be phrases and parts in the story you especially like and want to keep. Songs, chants, and poems are usually learned word for word, to keep the rhyme and rhythm. You would memorize stories written as poems, such as "Showdown at Pangaea Creek" or "The Snowflake Story."

## Exploring Characters, Setting, and Style

Get into the characters of the story. Play with them; become them. Discover who they are, how they act, how they feel. What kind of man is the hermit? What does he look like? How does he feel about the children? Imagine the children: How many are there? How old? Are they scared of the old man? Why do they want to trick him? Take the hermit's part: when he walks in the woods, when he goes into town, when the children come to his door. Imagine this in your head, or act it out.

Explore the setting of the story. If the story is from a different culture (as "Amaterasu" is from Japan, "The Image Maker" from India), you may need to do some reading and research to better understand its background and setting. With "The Hermit and the Children," picture the old man's place, the town, and the woods. The more vividly the story comes to life in your head, the more it will come across to the listeners, even if you don't describe it in words. If you see the old man coming to the door, your audience will too.

Different storytellers have different styles of telling, and you will tell different stories differently. Experiment with sitting or standing or moving around, with using gestures, with varied voices for the characters. Do what seems natural and right for you in that particular story. When telling "The Hermit and the Children," you might want to mime the boy holding the bird behind his back, or you might simply tell that part.

## Choosing the Place to Tell

When you are telling stories to a group, be aware of your listeners; without them the story cannot be told. Native people and country people have been telling stories informally for years: under a tree in the moonlight, sitting around a campfire, on the back porch; try to create that atmosphere of expectancy and community wherever you may be telling. Even if you are used to teaching children seated in straight rows of desks, try to make a special circle in the corner of the room for the storytelling time.

I like to have my listeners comfortably sitting in a semicircle, in chairs or on the floor, close to me with just enough room for me to move around. Choose your own place to be telling, sitting, or standing where you are comfortable and can be seen by everyone.

## Telling the Story

You have practiced and formed images and gotten into the story. You have told it in the car and to your best friend. Now you are telling this story for the first time to a group.

Tell the story as if you and the group are discovering it together. Tell it in your own way. Let your love of the story come through. Don't worry about getting it perfect. You will find that the story grows and changes each time you tell it, as it becomes more your own. Your listeners will help shape the story too. Responding to your audience, to nonverbal as well as verbal cues, you will tell it differently at different times and to different groups.

You might feel nervous standing up in front of a group; most of us do. Don't be afraid of the audience. A decade ago when I first decided that I had to tell stories, especially to women, I engaged to tell stories at a women's festival. I stood up that September day in front of fifty or more women seated on the ground, looked around and said, "This is the first time I've told stories." A woman sitting at my feet said, "Well, we're all with you," and I could feel it was true.

Remember you love the story and the group wants to hear it. Pause, take a breath and begin speaking from that deep place within yourself. Tell the story in your most expressive everyday voice and language, as you would share important news with a friend. You don't have to shout; just let your words reach out to the farthest person in the room. With your eyes and your words take in the whole group.

Your voice is the carrier of the story. Let it resonate from the center of you. Speak slowly and clearly; you needn't "hurry up to get it over with." The story itself will let you know when to whisper or raise your voice, when to speed up or slow down. Let yourself pause—for suspense, at a turning point in the story, or to give listeners a small break; they won't think you've forgotten what comes next. And if you do forget something (the best storytellers do, sometimes), just stop, take a breath, and let the story come back to you. Go on telling. When you finish, let the last words die away. Take in the listeners once more, and affirm your connection to them and to the story.

## Involving the Listeners

Your audience is already involved in the story, by their active listening. But sometimes you will want the hearers to participate in other ways. You may ask a question and expect an answer. "What can you make out of clay?" asks the storyteller in "New Pots for Old." The storyteller in "Amaterasu" tells everyone to call the sun goddess to return, "Amaterasu, come back!" The group will quickly take up a phrase that is repeated over, like "They pulled and they puffed and they puffed and they pulled but that stubborn turnip would not move," in "The Stubborn Turnip."

If necessary, you can teach a song or chant before the story begins, but often the group can just join in. Young children love to repeat songs and chants; I have found that older children and adults do too, when the atmosphere is comfortable.

You may also make up a song or chant to add to a story. You may encourage listeners to act out parts as you tell. You will find changes like this happening naturally in the process of telling and retelling the stories.

## Beginning and Ending the Story

Introduce the story before you begin telling. Give the title, some background, where in the world it came from, who told it to you (giving credit to the previous teller and the sources), and especially your personal connection to the story. Generally, keep the introduction brief and get on with the story.

"Once upon a time . . . ," "Long ago when the earth was new . . . ," "A long time ago . . . ," "Once there was . . . ." The very first words of the story set the scene in a different world; they give the listeners time to get used to your voice and go there with you before the action begins.

The ending wraps up the story and comes back to the beginning: the hermit, who was said to be very wise, was wiser than the children expected. The storyteller doesn't usually say (except as a spoof) "The moral of this story is . . . ," but you need to be clear why you have told the story, and the last line should have a sense of completion. It may be like the punch line of a joke; without it, the story wouldn't hang together: "The answer is in your hands." Or it may be a familiar formula, " . . . and they lived happily ever after." I like the African folktale ending: "This is my tale, whether it be sour, whether it be sweet, take what you wish and let the rest return to me."

## Changing the Story

Storytellers in all times and places have taken a story they heard and passed it on, changing it to reflect their own ideas and circumstances. In a remote village in Haiti, a woman who couldn't read told me a story that I recognized as the African folktale "Talk." The story as she told it had the same plot but the characters and setting reflected life in the Haitian countryside. In telling stories, you will take the story you find and make it your own.

When I was first telling stories to and about women, I often changed the hero into a woman, and I never ended with " . . . and they got married and lived happily ever after." There will probably be parts and attitudes in some stories that you will want to change, for your perspective on the world may be different from the last teller's.

Be careful, though, that you keep the essential truth of the story you are telling, especially if the story comes from a culture that is not your own. For instance, Coyote has certain attributes in Native American stories: he is arrogant, tricky, cowardly, brave, stupid, smart. If you change his character, he is no longer Coyote—no matter what you call him. You need to respect and pass on the story's tradition and meaning and specialness, while you tell it in your own way.

You may want to change a story in this book to tell to an older or younger group than the story is intended for. The story, "Gaura Devi Saves the Trees," was written for very young children, and so it is told very simply, leaving out some of the "roughness" and complexities of the real life situation on which it was based. These details could be added to make a more realistic story for older children.

You often don't have to change a story much to fit a different age group. Keep in mind that younger children like a simple plot, action, repetition and connection with their personal experience. Older children will respond to more "interesting" plots, realism as well as fantasy, and stories that stretch their imagination and their life experience.

"Talking without Words" and "Tree Planting in South Africa" are written as personal experience stories, in the first person ("I" stories). It may be more comfortable for you to retell these stories in the third person (using "he" or "she": thus, "He grew up in Johannesburg, South Africa"), as though the previous teller had told their experience to you and you are passing it on.

Brother Blue's story "The Rainbow Child" and Michael Punzak's "Half-Boy" are each created particularly in their own style of rhythmic word jazz; you might choose to use one as a model to create your own story in your own style and rhythm. And that could be the next step: to make up your own story.

Take an idea, a half-remembered tale, or a personal experience and create your own story. Make up a different story on the same theme as one of the stories in the book. With your class or group, create a story and tell it together. There are no limits to the possibilities of telling stories.

So enjoy the special world of storytelling. Tell a story, and you share a gift that will return to you over and over again.

❦ ❦ ❦

**Jay Goldspinner** started telling stories to women because "we don't hear enough of our own stories." She has told stories of women and men and wondrous creatures of the earth throughout New England and across the country, anywhere from festivals to people's backyards. She leads storytelling workshops, believing we all can tell stories. Her chapter on storytelling and ritual is in the book, *The Goddess Celebrates*, edited by Diane Stein. She has an audiotape, *Rootwomen Stories*.

# Stories, the Teaching Tool

## Using and Creating Follow-up Activities

### by John Porcino

Throughout human history, stories have been used to pass on the wisdom and values of society as well as to nourish and strengthen the minds and spirits of those listening.

A well-told story can be a dynamic and important teacher. It can touch common chords of hope, joy, and sorrow. It can help us understand the world and our place in it. In the simple act of telling a story we are planting a seed—a seed that may grow and blossom for a lifetime.

So why follow up a story? When you water and care for a seed, the seed is more likely to grow healthy and strong. The same is true with a story. With just a little extra time, a story can become a wonderful springboard toward deeper insight and understanding. A well-spun tale will bring a range of emotions closer to the surface. It is almost as if the listener has lived through the experiences of the story. By taking advantage of the feelings brought close through the telling, we have a unique opportunity to explore our values.

With this opportunity in mind, the editors of this book asked each storyteller to submit both a story and follow-up activities. We asked that the activities not moralize, but give young people the chance to use the story as a catalyst to explore, choose, and act on their own values. As a result, this book contains a wide variety of ideas and techniques for using stories as a springboard toward values exploration.

Unless otherwise noted, the activities after each story were created by the storyteller to give a few of the many possible ways the story might become a springboard. The tapestry of different techniques reflects the contributors' varied backgrounds. You will find a wealth of follow-up activities to challenge your students, for them to laugh and grow with. There are detailed classroom explorations, playful educational games, suggestions for direct community action, and much more.

Throughout the chapter I use the terms teacher, classroom, and students. Please reinterpret or generalize these to fit your particular kind of group and setting:

- Teacher = parent, counselor, therapist, educator, group facilitator . . .
- Student = daughter, son, young person, camper, client, participant . . .
- Classroom = home, camp, office, retreat center, natural world . . .

The rest of this chapter contains:

- suggestions on using the activities in this book;
- perspectives on values and beliefs;
- how to create a safe environment for risk-taking;
- a method for creating your own follow-up activities;
- a list of additional resources.

## Using the Activities in this Book

Teaching is a constant experiment! We do our best to create productive, nurturing and enjoyable learning experiences, yet sometimes even the most skilled of us fall flat. Most of the time, though, if we listen to our senses and find our own teaching style, we do very well. Facilitating learning by using innovative follow-up activities is certainly an experiment. Here are a few suggestions to help in that experiment.

After telling or reading one of the stories, pick one or more activities that seem appropriate to your group, and try them.

Decide how much time you have. Once the story has been told, just about any amount of time can be effective for follow-up. The class might spend fifteen minutes retelling the story, an hour with related activities, or a full semester working on some project that spins off from the story. Even a quick five-minute discussion can help young people deepen their insight into a story.

Choose activities to fit the allotted time. As educators, we know this is more an art than a science. Sometimes we find what we think will be a ten-minute activity actually takes a hour, or vice versa. It can help to plan for flexibility by preparing a few extra activities and prioritizing the ones you've planned.

Don't hesitate to adapt the activities in this book to fit your group. Some of them will work splendidly with your group as written, but others may need to be adapted. The changes you make may be just what is needed to make an activity fly. Nothing is written in stone! Also, you may want to develop new activities to suit a particular group or lesson. A model for creating follow-up activities to a story appears later in this chapter.

Also, feel free to use related stories, songs, games, poetry, movies, or other media that you already know. Susan Tobin suggests introducing or following up "The Hermit and the Children," which introduces this book, with the song "Two Hands Hold the Earth."[1] Susan also uses a two-word poem by M. C. Richards:[2]

Hands . . . . . . . . Bird.

## A Perspective on Values Clarification

Nearly every moment of our lives each of us is making decisions based on our beliefs and values: sometimes big decisions, other times less significant ones. When we're mad at someone do we hit, kick, talk, negotiate, or get the teacher? When we see a fellow student being mistreated, do we step in and help, find someone else to help, or not act at all? When we're serving ice cream, do we give ourselves the biggest scoop? Do we work to feed the hungry of the world, give a can of food to local food drive, or decide it's out of our control? These decisions, big and small, can often be very confusing. The process of taking a conscious look at our belief systems is called *Values Clarification*. Being aware of our values allows us to make these decisions in a healthy way.

Our hope is that the stories and activities in this book will give students the opportunity to spend some time looking at and clarifying their values. The goal is to give

1. By Sarah Pirtle on her album *Two Hands Hold The Earth*. Order from Sarah for $8, at 54 Thayer Road, Greenfield, MA 01301.

2. M.C. Richards, *Centering in Pottery, Poetry and the Person*, Wesleyan University Press, 2nd edition, 1989, pp. 68-69.

students the chance to explore, choose, and act on their values. When we try to dictate our values to young people, even if they come away believing us, it will most often be only with their words, not their actions.

> Young people brought up by moralizing adults are not prepared to make their own responsible choices. They have not learned a process for selecting the best and rejecting the worst elements contained in the various value systems others [parents, teachers, peer groups, government, etc.] have been urging them to follow. Thus, too often the important choices in life are made on the basis of peer pressure, unthinking submission to authority, or the power of propaganda.[3]

A selection of the many excellent books on values education and values clarification are listed in the bibliography at the end of this chapter.


## Creating a Safe Environment for Risk-taking

As the facilitator, look to create an environment where students feel safe to explore their feelings and values openly. This may mean choosing activities in the beginning that don't go too deeply, and then progressing toward greater risk-taking. Without this safety, none of the activities, no matter how well planned, can fully work. A safe environment is the foundation on which you can build trust, caring, communication skills, problem-solving abilities, self-esteem, and much more.

If a class is new to exploring feelings and values, take the time to develop with them a list of agreements that will facilitate healthy communication. This can be a fun and educational process if the concepts are then taught through role play, games, stories, songs, and discussion. Here is a list of five agreements I have used. Each is followed by one activity that can help facilitate understanding of the concept.

**Agreement:** One person talks at a time, with the others really listening.

**Activity:** "Bat and Moth" is one of my favorite listening games. It is a game of tag for two, where the "Bat" chases the "Moth." Children make a circle which becomes the boundary for the game. Two children are chosen to come into the middle of the circle. One becomes the Bat and is blindfolded, the other becomes the Moth. The object is for the Bat to tag the Moth. The Bat must use her sense of hearing to discover where the elusive Moth is hiding. The Bat is given approximately one minute to complete this task. During that time the Bat may "send out radar" by calling out "Bat!" five times. Each time the Moth hears this, he must answer the radar with a call of "Moth!" Stress the importance of the circle's total silence. If the Bat is about to head outside the circle, two taps on the shoulder is a signal to turn around.

Adapt the game to keep it challenging for both Bat and Moth by enlarging or shrinking the circle or by giving the bat more or less opportunity to use "radar." Try to give students the opportunity to play both roles.

Afterwards, talk about what really listening to another person means (i.e., listening as though you are the Bat).

---

3. Simon, Howe and Kirschenbaum, p. 16. (Item 3 in the resource list at the end of the chapter.)

Role play what listening well looks like and again what *not* listening looks like. Discuss the importance of listening well to people who are sharing their feelings.

**Agreement:** It's fine to be different. Try to say what you're really thinking or feeling.

**Activity:** Read the book *Molly's Pilgrim* (by Barbara Cohen, Lothrop, Lee & Shepard Books, New York, 1983), or *Oliver Button's A Sissy* (by Tomie de Paola, Harcourt Brace Jovanovich, New York and London, 1979), and discuss the importance of each person's feeling fine to be whoever they are. Talk about the courage to say and be whoever you are.

**Agreement:** Use "put-ups," not "put-downs" (both verbal and nonverbal). Try to think of ways to make others feel good. Be careful not to hurt others' feelings.

**Activity:** Choose two puppets to act out some typical scenes where children put one another down (making an error in a baseball game, reading out loud slowly, forgetting their lines in a play, sharing a feeling that is different.) After the scene has developed, stop and ask the children what the second puppet might say or do to "put down" the first puppet. Have the second puppet act out one of the put-downs; stop again, and ask how that put-down is likely to make the first puppet feel. Finish the play having the puppet show that feeling. Now repeat the play but this time ask for "put-ups" instead and watch how differently it ends.

Discuss how to make a classroom full of "happy endings."

**Agreement:** What someone shares or does in the classroom is confidential.

**Activity:** Develop a role playing scene in which "Joe" shared something important to him (how he felt when his dog died, the fight he had with his sister) or "Mary" did something that looked foolish (tripped during a running game, acted a character in a play in a strange way.) Now do a role play in which one character runs off and tells some friends. Stop here and ask the class questions like: How would it make you feel if this happened to you? Would you be likely to share again? Is there ever a time or way that it would be OK to tell others what happened in the class?

**Agreement:** Challenge yourself to take risks, but also know that it is fine to "pass."

**Activity:** "Cookie Machine" (from *More New Games*—see the bibliography). Imagine you have become a giant cookie, of your favorite kind. You are being passed down a conveyor belt of human hands with their voices chanting the name of your favorite cookie ("Chocolate chip! Chocolate chip! Chocolate chip! . . ."). You have the choice of what kind of cookie you want to be and what kind of ride you want (gentle, smooth, bumpy, bouncy . . .). If you have imagined all this you have imagined the cookie machine!

First, everybody takes off any watches and jewelry they might have on their arms. Then the group makes two lines facing each other, standing shoulder to shoulder, with elbows bent, forearms in front, palms up, and alternating forearms with the other line. Everyone is standing very close together making a wonderful, long, thin oven-conveyor belt with which to cook this cookie "just right."

Two strong "Bakers" help the "Cookie" get on the belt and then get off at the end. Now pass the Cookie (who has taken off glasses and belt buckle) down through the oven by gently moving everyone's hands in a circular motion and chanting the type of the cookie.

Those in the conveyor belt reach down and support the Cookie as soon as they can and keep supporting the Cookie until they can no longer reach. We can't afford broken cookies in this bakery! When the end of the oven is reached, the Cookie is well cooked and joins the conveyor belt so another cookie may be baked.

Generally, it is a good idea to start this game with a light-weight "Cookie" so the group gets used to the idea, but after a few good "cookies," groups can pass most people down. At 180 pounds, I was passed down by a group of fourth to sixth graders!

The teacher may find it necessary to occasionally stop the process and remind children of the importance of giving each Cookie total attention.

Afterwards talk about how it felt to take the risk and be passed down the line, or be part of the conveyor belt, or to have "passed." Try to validate everyone's feelings. Let the class know that you could play the game another day, if others wish to try becoming cookies.

## How to Create Your Own Follow-up Activities to a Story

The activities in this book are simply starting points. We hope they will spark creativity and lead toward yet-to-be-discovered activities that will foster insightful understanding of the stories and ways of translating the stories' teachings into our lives.

How do you create follow-up activities that truly add to your students' understanding of the story, capture their imaginations and hearts, and gently guide them toward exploring and acting on their own values? The approach outlined in this section of the chapter is a model I developed based on my own experience and some of the many sources, values education books, and human beings who have become teachers to me.

The challenge is to create activities that become tools for clarifying our values rather than tools for teaching students "right" and "wrong." With these activities, young people use the story's teachings to explore their own values, make their own choices, come to prize those choices and then act upon them. When this happens, students will truly develop their own values, which they will carry beyond the classroom into their lives and on down the road.

These same simple concepts are as helpful in exploring issues of self-esteem with five-year-olds as in examining racism with adults.

## A Model for Generating Follow-up Activities

When developing specific follow-up activities to a story, determine

- the *age level* you will be working with
- the *goal* of the activity

and one or more of

- the *viewpoint* the activity illustrates
- the *medium* you will be working with
- the *physical activity level* of the exercise.

## Age Level

For activities to be effective they must be focused toward the intellect, wit, and abilities of the participants' age group. A discussion on nuclear war with a class of kindergarten children would not only be beyond their grasp, but it would probably leave children feeling scared and helpless. The goal is to create activities that are empowering. Keeping empowerment for five-year-olds in mind, you can create an activity centered around issues at their level. For instance, the topic of resolving conflicts creatively in the classroom would be just right for a kindergarten class.

On the other hand, playing "Duck, Duck, Goose" as the first activity with a group of ninth graders could "sink the boat" for that day. However, many activities, if set in a positive, age-appropriate context, can be adapted to suit just about any age group.

## Goal

If time allows, a full spectrum of follow-up activities will include goals that give a class the opportunity to review the story, explore the story and then act on what they have learned.

*Review* the story: Students move closer to the story by retelling it in some form. Through reviewing the story, they will know the events of the story and have a deeper understanding of the characters and their feelings.

*Explore* the story: Students explore feelings as they relate to the characters and events of the story, define and explore the story's teachings, and begin to choose and affirm values based on these explorations.

*Act* on what has been learned: Students translate what they have learned through hearing, reviewing, and exploring the story into real and direct action in their lives. The scope of these actions can range from tiny to grand.

## Medium

Picking a stimulating medium with which to review, explore, or act on the story's teaching can be very useful in developing follow-up activities. By using media which require involvement and creativity of the students, they can gain first-hand experience of the issues the story touches on. While the traditional method of discussion is an important piece of the follow-up, there are many other tools to use in this process. Here are some ideas:

- Performance Arts:
  storytelling, drama, role play, mime, dance, puppetry, music;

- Visual Arts:
  drawing, coloring, painting, cutting and pasting, sculpture, folk art, crafts, batik, quilting, weaving, toy making, wood arts, pottery, photography, printmaking, silkscreening;

- Literary Arts:
  writing (fiction and non-fiction), reading, poetry, scriptwriting;

- Media Arts:
  video, audio, film;

- Games:
  movement games (tag, running, stalking, hide-and-seek, relay races, musical),
  cooperative games (trust games, old games with new twists, group challenge),
  nature games (night games, sensory awareness),
  party games (cultural festival, mixers, energizers),
  personal challenges (stunts, ropes courses, rock-climbing, obstacle courses),
  quiet games (paper and pencil, board, card, word, mental puzzles),
  competitive games;

- Discussion.

## Viewpoint

The teachings of a story can be thought of from many different viewpoints. The problems addressed in a story can be used as a metaphor for problems in the world at large. For example, the theme of individual responsibility presented in "The Hermit and the Children" (at the beginning of this book) could be thought of in terms of issues local to a child, like taking care of a pet, or in terms of global issues, such as environmental concern for wildlife in polluted areas.

In developing follow-up activities for a story, it is very helpful to narrow the scope to a specific viewpoint:

- Global: issues that are worldwide or international in scope;

- Country and State: issues that are specific to the part of the world the class lives in;

- Local Community: issues that concern life in local cities, towns or neighborhoods;

- Interpersonal: issues that look at our relationships at school, home, and work: interactions that occur in our day-to-day lives;

- Personal: issues that have to do with who we choose to be, both internally and externally.

## Physical Activity Level

Given the classroom setting and the size of classes teachers usually work with, low activity lessons are probably the most common teaching tool. But don't forget that the gym, the school's playing field, the patch of woods surrounding the school field, the park around the corner, the pond down the street, and even the classroom can become spaces for some amazing physically active learning experiences. A teaching game which uses lots of energy may be just the thing to "shake the brains" of your students or to keep their focus on a project. Activities that require little physical exertion can also challenge students in quieter ways. I've found units that cross between levels of activity to be very effective.

- High: Fast-paced, high energy games, reviews, challenges;

- Moderate: Activities with moderate physical exertion;

- Low: Discussion, writing, visual arts projects, and so on.

Put this all together and you get the "Follow-up Activity Form" on the next page. Fill in the age level, choose the appropriate goal, medium, viewpoint, and physical activity level and you are on your way:

# Follow-up Activity Form

**Age Level:**

**Goal (choose one):**

- Review the Story
- Explore the Story
- Act on Values

**Medium (choose one):**

- Performance Arts:  storytelling, drama, role play, mime, dance, puppetry, music
- Visual Arts:  drawing, coloring, painting, cutting and pasting, sculpture, folk art, batik, quilting, weaving, toy making, wood arts, pottery, photography, printmaking, silkscreening, crafts
- Literary Arts:  writing (fiction and nonfiction), reading, poetry, scriptwriting
- Media Arts:  video, audio, film
- Games:
  movement games (tag, running, stalking, hide-and-seek, relay races, musical),
  cooperative games (trust games, old games with new twists, group challenge),
  nature games (night games, sensory awareness),
  party games (cultural festival, mixers, energizers),
  personal challenges (stunts, ropes courses, rock-climbing, obstacle courses),
  quiet games (paper and pencil, board, card, word, mental puzzles),
  competitive games;
- Discussion

**Viewpoint (choose one):**

- Personal
- Interpersonal
- Local Community
- State
- Country
- Global

**Physical Activity Level (choose one):**

- High
- Moderate
- Low

**Activity:**

## Examples of the Model At Work

I used this model to developed three activities for "The Hermit and The Children" story, which appears at the beginning of this book. (For a more in-depth use of this model, see my follow-up activities to "The Difference between Heaven and Hell.")

### Example 1

Age Level: Fifth Grade
Goal: Review the Story
Medium: Drawing
Viewpoint: Personal
Physical Activity Level: Low

What comes to mind with these criteria? How about making up comic books of the story in full color?

### Example 2

Let's change the goal to exploring the story, the medium to video and the viewpoint to interpersonal:

Age Level: Fifth Grade
Goal: Explore the Story
Medium: Video
Viewpoint: Interpersonal
Physical Activity Level: Medium

Now what? Perhaps the children could use the school's video camera to take turns taping their answers to the question, "What do you think 'The answer is in your hands' means in our lives at school and at home?" When everyone in the class has been taped, they can watch the video and discuss what they see.

### Example 3

Suppose the class had decided while exploring the story that one thing "the answer is in your hands" means is that each one of us has an important part to play in keeping our town clean. You might fill in the chart like this:

Age Level: Fifth Grade
Goal: Act
Medium: Movement Game
Viewpoint: Local Community
Physical Activity Level: High

How would you satisfy these choices? Go to the local park and challenge the class to collect as much garbage as they can in a half-hour. Everyone's got to move fast! Measure the pile at the end, take a picture and post it on the wall of the school. Maybe you can get each class in the school to keep one section of the town clean in this way! Maybe you could invite the newspapers! Certainly you'll call for a trash pick-up! This could be a great introduction to a unit on garbage.

## Be Brave

Now try it yourself:

Let's use "The Hermit and the Children" story again. Try taking these two sets of choices on the "Follow-Up Activity Form" to create your own follow-up activities.

(By the way, I can hear all the little negatives running around in your mind: "I'm not creative enough to use this." "Too complicated." "Sounds like work . . . ." Don't give up just yet. Just imagine you've climbed all the way up onto a diving platform. You can't go back because there's a line of people on the ladder behind you. The only way is to take the leap. You'll be amazed at how creative you can be. And really, after you've safely splashed into the pool and come back up to the surface you might actually think it's fun.)

Here we go!

Age Level: Fifth grade (or your own grade or group)
Goal: Review the Story
Medium: Puppetry
Viewpoint: (when reviewing a story, viewpoint is irrelevant)
Physical Activity Level: Low

What did you come up with? OK, try another:

Age Level: Seventh grade (or your own grade or group)
Goal: Act
Medium: Painting
Viewpoint: Local Community
Physical Activity Level: Medium

The more you do this, the easier and quicker it gets. Challenge yourself to choose categories that you might not normally think of using in your class. You'll find your mind stretching in ways that you never imagined and the children learning in a most magical fashion. The worst that could happen is a belly flop. When I flop (and we all do), I've trained myself to say "Oops!", learn from the mistake, and try again.

This model is a tool meant to support our creative process as teachers. Use it to help create meaningful and exciting follow-ups to the story. Like any tool, use it only as much as it assists the process.

## A Selection of Values Activity Resources

### Books

*ABRIS: Adventure-Based Resource Index System*. Charles Learned. P.O. Box 25, Woodford, WI 53599. An easily accessible file box of over 800 games and values activities from many of the following books and more.

*Cooperative Sports and Games Book: Challenge Without Competition* and *The Second Cooperative Sports and Games Book*. Terry Orlick. New York: Pantheon Books. Good for young children.

*Cowtails and Cobras*, 1977 and *Silver Bullets*, 1984. Karl Rohnke. Hamilton, MA: Project Adventure, Inc. (P. O. Box 100, Hamilton, MA 01936). Cooperative "initiative" games.

*Creative Conflict Resolution: More than 200 Activities for Keeping Peace in the Classroom K-6.* William J. Kreidler. Glenview, IL: Good Year Books, 1984. Activities for keeping peace in the classroom.

*A Manual on Non-Violence and Children.* Edited by Stephanie Judson. Philadelphia: New Society Publishers, 1984. Games and activities.

*New Games* and *More New Games.* Available from the YMCA of the USA, 101 N. Wacker Drive, Chicago, IL 60606. Games with a twist.

*100 Ways to Enhance Self-Concept in the Classroom: A Handbook for Teachers and Parents.* Jack Canfield and Harold C. Wells. Englewood Cliffs, NJ: Prentice Hall, 1976. Activities that teach self-worth.

*Personalizing Education.* Leland W. Howe and Mary Martha Howe. New York: Hart Publishing Company, 1975. Values activities.

*Sharing Nature with Children.* Joseph Bharat Cornell. Nevada City, CA: Ananda Publications, 1979. Environmental games.

*Values Clarification.* Sidney B. Simon, Leland W. Howe and Howard Kirshenbaum. New York: Hart Publishing Company, 1978. Values activities.

## Groups

*Educators for Social Responsibility,* 23 Garden St., Cambridge, MA 02138, (617) 492-1764. Education information, workshops, and conferences.

*National Association of Mediation in Education,* 425 Amity St., Amherst, MA 01002, (413) 545-2462. Mediation trainings for students, teachers, community people, and others.

*20/20 Vision National Project,* 69 S. Pleasant St., Amherst, MA 01002, (413) 259-2020. Sends enough information to write informed letters, in less than twenty minutes, to our representatives in Washington.

❦ ❦ ❦

Each year **John Porcino** spins his colorful repertoire of tales and songs for thousands of enthusiastic people nationwide. His stories and songs celebrate our common humanity and build bridges of understanding between all people. They are sparked to life with warmth, humor, zest, and a playful touch of audience participation. Woven throughout is music played on folk instruments from around the world. Available for performances, workshops, and in-service trainings.

# Living With Ourselves

# Chew Your Rock Candy

## by Doug Lipman

ONCE, THERE WAS A TOWN that had a terrible problem: one day, quite unexpectedly, a *monster* appeared!

Can you imagine? Some people were walking down the street. When they rounded a corner—there was the monster! They ran home as fast as they could. They ran straight to their bedrooms, and slid under their beds. Oww! They skinned their knees!

If someone went out to get a loaf of bread at the store, that person would start walking down the road.

At the store, they'd get the bread, put it under one arm, then start walking back.

Suddenly, they'd see . . . the *monster!* They'd run home, slide under their bed . . . and skin their knees. Oww!

Things got so bad that people spent most of their time under their beds . . . with skinned knees.

Things got so-o bad, that the whole town ran out of band-aids.

But one day, one person thought, "We can't spend all day under our beds with skinned knees. This is no way to live. We have to go to the wise old woman, and get help—so we can get rid of this monster."

So this brave person opened her door, and peeked out. She looked one way down the street . . . no monster! Then she looked the other way . . . no monster! So she began to tiptoe down the road.

> *She tiptoed down the road.*
> *She went and tiptoed down the road.*

When she came to her neighbor's house, she rang the doorbell. The neighbor said, "It's the monster at my door!" The neighbor ran to his bed, slid under it . . . and skinned his knees. Oww!

The brave person said, "It's not the monster—it's me! We've got to go to the wise old woman, get help, and get rid of this monster."

It took some talking just to get into her neighbor's house. It took even more talking to get the neighbor to stay out from under the bed, but after quite a bit of talking, the two of them opened the neighbor's door and peeked out. They looked one way down the street . . . no monster! They looked the other way . . . no monster! So they both began to tiptoe down the road.

> *They tiptoed down the road.*
> *They both tiptoed down the road.*
> *They went and tiptoed down the road.*

It took an enormous amount of talking, and the better part of the day, but eventually they had the whole village tiptoeing down the road.

*They tiptoed down the road.*
*They all tiptoed down the road.*
*Everyone tiptoed down the road.*

When they had almost reached the home of the wise old woman, one of them accidentally kicked a stone. It made a loud noise. Someone else said, "I hear the monster. It's after us! Run for your lives!"

They began to run! The first one to reach the wise old woman's house threw open the door, ran to the wise old woman's bed, slid under it . . . and skinned his knees! Oww!

The next one ran in, slid under . . . and skinned her knees! Oww! The next one . . . the next one . . . .

The wise old woman watched all these people run into her house and under her bed—without even saying hello! "Excuse me," she said. "What's going on here?"

The people looked up from under the wise old woman's bed. "Haven't you heard about . . . the monster?"

The wise old woman sighed. "Come on out. Let's talk about it."

When the people had told her the story, she said, "That kind of monster was created by a magic spell. If you break the spell, the monster will disappear."

The people cheered. "Hurray! If we just break the spell, the monster will disappear! How do we do that?"

The wise old woman held up four fingers. "You must do four magical things."

The people cheered again. "Hurray! If we just do four magical things, the spell will be broken and the monster will disappear! What are the four things?"

The wise old woman shrugged her shoulders. "I don't know."

"You don't know?" The people sounded crushed. "But if we don't know what the things are, how can we do them?"

Now the wise old woman spoke quietly. "You must go to the middle of the town square, and listen very carefully."

The people cheered, once more. "Hurray! We just have to go . . . ." Suddenly they realized what the wise old woman was demanding of them. "To the middle of the town square? But the monster will get us there!"

At last the wise old woman smiled. "If you hold hands, the monster can't touch you."

In a short time, the entire town had formed one large circle in the middle of the town square. No sooner were they all holding hands than they saw it coming toward them: it was the scariest . . . the hairiest . . . the nightmariest monster they had ever seen! And the monster looked around for someone who was not holding hands—someone the monster could grab!

When the monster saw that everyone was safely holding hands, it got frustrated. Do you know what monsters do when they are frustrated? The monster started to . . . sing!

> *Oh, you can't pick cherries, I know you can't,*
> *Oh, you can't pick cherries, I know you can't,*
> *Oh, you can't pick cherries, I know you can't,*
> *Chew your rock candy.*

Someone said, "Did you hear what the monster said?"

[Note: If no one answers, say the following lines. If, however, someone answers correctly, say, "Oh, you saved us! I was too scared to listen, and I bet that's one of the four magical things!"]

Someone else answered, "I was too scared to listen."

"But we were supposed to listen very carefully, to learn the four magical things!"

Luckily, someone had listened. The smallest person there shouted out, "The monster said, we can't pick cherries."

"We can't pick cherries? Oh, yes, we can!" The whole town started to pretend to pull cherries down from above—as though there were a huge cherry tree right in the middle of the town square. But they kept holding hands, of course!

> *Oh, we can pick cherries, we know we can,*
> *Oh, we can pick cherries, we know we can,*
> *Oh, we can pick cherries, we know we can,*
> *Chew your rock candy.*

When they finished singing, they looked around at the monster. It had shrunk! It was shorter—and more upset! The monster walked outside the circle of people, singing to the backs of their heads:

> *Well, you can't count money, I know you can't,*
> *Well, you can't count money, I know you can't,*
> *Well, you can't count money, I know you can't,*
> *Chew your rock candy.*

"We can't count money! That's wrong! Of course we can count money." So, still holding hands, the people pretended to pull dollar bills toward them, one after another—as though there were an enormous bushel basket in front of them. As they reached out together, they all sang:

> *Oh, we can count money, we know we can,*
> *Oh, we can count money, we know we can,*
> *Oh, we can count money, we know we can,*
> *Chew your rock candy.*

When they looked at the monster this time, it was very much smaller—and very much more upset! It walked right up to one person after another, stared them in the face, and sang some more:

> *Well, you can't do the eagle rock, I know you can't,*
> *Well, you can't do the eagle rock, I know you can't,*
> *Well, you can't do the eagle rock, I know you can't,*
> *Chew your rock candy.*

Someone moaned, "The eagle rock? But we don't know what that is. How can we possibly do it?"

Puzzled, the people scratched their heads. Since they were still holding hands, they had to take turns scratching.

Suddenly, the oldest person there shouted out, "I've got it! When I was young, there was still a rock on the edge of town where the eagles nested. I used to watch the baby eagles learning to fly."

Someone else said, "Then we can be baby eagles." Without dropping hands, they pretended to be baby eagles, flapping their wings up and down. As they flapped, they sang:

> *Oh, we can do the eagle rock, we know we can,*
> *Oh, we can do the eagle rock, we know we can,*
> *Oh, we can do the eagle rock, we know we can,*
> *Chew your rock candy.*

When they turned to look at the monster, they could hardly find it. It was considerably smaller, and considerably more upset. As it sat, it sang and sniffed, still demanding of them:

> *Well, you can't dance, I know you can't, (sniff)*
> *Well, you can't dance, I know you can't, (sniff, sniff)*
> *Well, you can't dance, I know you can't, (I sure hope not)*
> *Chew your rock candy.*

By now, the monster was no bigger than a guinea pig. The people dropped hands, and immediately began to dance:

> *Oh, we can dance, we know we can,*
> *Oh, we can dance, we know we can,*
> *Oh, we can dance, we know we can,*
> *Chew your rock candy.*

When they were finished dancing and singing, they looked for the monster. They couldn't find it. The monster had disappeared! The people cheered and cheered.

The people were so proud of what they had done that they declared a holiday. Every year they still go back to the town square, hold hands in one big circle, and sing all four magical things:

> *Oh, we can pick cherries, we know we can,*
> *Oh, we can pick cherries, we know we can,*
> *Oh, we can pick cherries, we know we can,*
> *Chew your rock candy.*

*Oh, we can count money, we know we can,*
*Oh, we can count money, we know we can,*
*Oh, we can count money, we know we can,*
*Chew your rock candy.*

*Oh, we can do the eagle rock, we know we can,*
*Oh, we can do the eagle rock, we know we can,*
*Oh, we can do the eagle rock, we know we can,*
*Chew your rock candy.*

*Oh, we can dance, we know we can,*
*Oh, we can dance, we know we can,*
*Oh, we can dance, we know we can,*
*Chew your rock candy.*

By the time they are done dancing, they get so tired, they have to rest. They go home, sit down, and rest. They rest the way people do whenever they know they are safe, and have plenty of friends—and can solve any problem, together.

And no monster has ever been seen there, again.

## Chew Your Rock Candy

## Follow-up Activities for "Chew Your Rock Candy"

### Sources for the Story

I created this story to teach a song. As part of my music teaching, I had been researching songs in the Archive of Folk Culture, Library of Congress, that had been sung by children. One of the songs that attracted me was sung by Eva Grace Boone and a children's group at Brandon, Mississippi, in 1939 (recorded by Herbert Halpert). It had four striking verses:

> *Can't pick cherries, I know you can't,*
> *Can't pick cherries, I know you can't,*
> *Can't pick cherries, I know you can't,*
> *Chew your rock candy.*
>
> *Can't count money, I know you can't . . .*
>
> *Can't do the eagle rock, I know you can't . . .*
>
> *Can't dance, I know you can't . . .*

The song seemed to be part of a circle game in which the one standing in the center makes whatever movements the group sings. But these particular four verses seemed so mysterious to me! They seemed like part of a magic spell. In order to give a "rationale" for these four verses belonging together, I made up a brief story about a monster that disappears—inspired no doubt by Pete Seeger's "Abiyoyo" (a story which was, in fact, also created around a song—an African lullaby).

When I taught the song to a class of preschoolers via the story, they loved it. The next week, I reviewed the song with the class—omitting the story, which I felt had served its purpose. The children felt otherwise! They demanded to hear about the monster again. I tried the story/song out on other groups, and gradually expanded it to its present form.

My recording of the song and story can be heard on *Tell It With Me: Participation Stories with Songs* (Gentle Wind cassette GW1035). Pete Seeger's "Abiyoyo" was recorded on his *Abiyoyo and other Story Songs* (Folkways Records 7525 or 31500). The song alone is on *Bantu Choral Folk Songs* (Folkways FW 6912), with a short description of the original African folk-tale.

### Notes on Telling the Story

This story divides into two parts. I tell the first half (through the visit to the wise old woman) sitting down, with my audience sitting around me. I invite the audience to join with me as I mime "walking" and "running" (by slapping my hands on my legs), skinning my knee, opening the door, etc.

I tell the second part (which begins with the villagers forming a circle in the town square) standing up, with the audience standing up and holding hands. When the villagers head toward the town square, I just motion the audience to stand up.

If space allows, I have the standing audience form a single circle. In the role of the monster, I stand outside their circle, approaching people from behind, sometimes peering over their joined hands and singing the monster's song in a gruff voice to individuals in the circle. When the monster is smallest, singing, "You can't dance . . .," I sit on the floor in the middle of the circle. If space does not allow a circle, as in an auditorium performance, for example, I simply have the audience hold hands in rows.

## Dealing with Reluctance

What about those who do not hold hands? I find that young children don't hold hands for one of two likely reasons. Some are too shy. In this case, I may approach them in the voice and posture of the monster, saying, "The monster was looking for someone who was not holding hands, *so it could eat them!*" Usually, the humorous fearsomeness of the monster overcomes their shyness! If not, I can easily enough smile at them and then move on. I might even appeal to the group: "Can anyone help save this child from the monster?"

Some children, however, deliberately taunt the monster: "See! *I'm* not holding hands!" In this case, I have a few choices. I may decide to play along; after all, they are only continuing a game that I myself started. Often enough, once I get close to the taunting child, s/he gets scared enough to grab someone's hand. On the other hand, if the group is large and boisterous, I risk a chaos of taunting children. I have two strategies for such situations. To a relatively quiet taunter, I might say, "You're in mortal danger, little boy," before turning my attention to some other part of the group. To a loud taunt or escalating group of taunters, I say, "And when the *survivors* were all holding hands . . ." and go on with the story. If I won't play the game anymore, the game is over!

What about children who become frightened by the monster? In general, I recommend making stories less frightening the first time you tell them. Once children know that a particular story ends "okay," they will enjoy it if you make it scarier on subsequent tellings. If I inadvertently frighten a child, however, I just drop the character for a moment and smile reassuringly.

## Adapting the story

You can shorten this story by decreasing the number of "magical things" the townspeople must do.

You can also change the setting of the story. As I tell it here, it takes place in a non-specified village setting. If you wish, however, you can make it take place in almost any particular culture. For example, I tell a Jewish version that takes place in a Eastern European village. Instead of dollar bills, the townspeople count out paper rubles; instead of a "wise old woman," they consult their rabbi. With a similar change of details, you could set the story in Japan, or Ireland, or your own block.

## Follow-up Activities

I tell this story to children ages three to eight (sometimes with their parents). The following activities have been chosen with three to eight year-olds in mind.

The most important follow-up activity with young children is to tell the story again, another time. Children, like adults, usually need to hear a story more than once to fully absorb it.

After they know it well, you can ask, "Who'd like to be the monster today?" Then a child can act out all or part of the monster's actions. Another time, you can add more parts for children to act out: the brave person, the wise old woman, the neighbor.

After hearing the story, children may want to draw the monster as they imagined it—or sculpt it from clay, make it in collage, etc.

## Making Up Verses

The song, Chew Your Rock Candy, suggests a discussion about our abilities. This discussion can be like any other discussion, or it can be put in the form of making new verses to the song, or of a story game.

"What is something that you know how to do?"

"Ride my bike."

"Great! Let's sing it:

> *I can ride my bike, I know I can,*
> *I can ride my bike, I know I can,*
> *I can ride my bike, I know I can,*
> *Chew your rock candy.*

If children are slow to make suggestions, you can ask more specific questions:

"Have you learned how to do something new lately?"

"What's something new you learned in school? At home? From watching TV?"

If some children point out disabilities, this is an opportunity to discuss individual differences.

"But Meg can't walk."

"Good point! Does she have any other way of getting around?"

"She uses her wheelchair."

"She sure does! Let's sing, 'I can get around in my wheelchair, I know I can . . .'"

To further the theme of group cooperation, ask for verses about what we can do as a group. Again, if the children are unable to think of suggestions at first, try contrasting the children with a group of infants. Alternatively, suggest situations they have been in, or challenges they have met: "Do you remember when Jason got sick? We wanted to talk to him but couldn't all go to the hospital. What did we do together?"

## Story Game

This differs from "making up verses" in only two ways. First, children are encouraged to give longer answers, in story form. Second, the song is sung with its original words, to separate each child's story from the one before it. The stories told can be about individual abilities, or, as in the following discussion, they can be about group abilities.

The leader begins this activity by singing the verse, "We can do the eagle rock, I know we can . . ." All join in. The leader adds movements.

Then the leader says:

> When you hear me say the special words, "We can do the eagle rock," do you know what to do? What we just did! Let's practice. I'll say the special words. "We can do the eagle rock." That's it, let's sing it and do the movements . . . .

When the verse is over, the leader begins without pause:

> Well, I'm not sure I know what the eagle rock really is, but I'll tell something we *do* know how to do. We are very good at helping each other. Do you remember when Valerie fell on the playground? One of us went for the school nurse, one went and got me, and a bunch of us stayed and talked to her. Even the next day, people helped her carry things. We can do the eagle rock . . . .

After singing the verse, the leader says, "Who can tell us something you have learned how to do? Don't forget, when you want to stop your turn to speak, just say the special words, 'We can do the eagle rock.'"

When playing this story game, the example story (or stories) that the leader tells will influence the kind of stories that the children tell. If the leader tells one or two stories about helping people, the children will probably tell similar stories. If the leader tells about building things, or classroom manners, or sports, the children will be more likely to tell similar stories. The group skill mentioned in a story can be a physical skill, or an emotional, cognitive, artistic, communicative, or social ability. It can be a problem-solving skill, or one that forms a part of daily routine.

## Make your own story

Using the story "Chew Your Rock Candy" as a model, you can make up your own story about group cooperation. If the group makes up such a story, the story-creation process will itself be cooperative.

With young children, a few elements can be chosen from which to make a new version of this story. The most obvious element is the monster. The next most obvious is what things the people must do to make the monster disappear. Next might come who tells the people how to proceed, and who the people are.

Once the children have had a chance to draw or talk about their own monster, a group of them can be led through the process of creating a new version of the story.

> Leader: We're going to make up a new story about a monster. What kind of monster will we have in this story?
>
> Group: A scary one! One with scales! It has long teeth!
>
> Leader: Good! We'll have a scary monster with scales and long teeth. Is this a huge monster, or just medium sized?
>
> Group: Huge!
>
> Leader: Okay, how big is this monster?
>
> Group: As big as a house!
>
> Leader: Great! We'll have a monster as big as a house, with scales all over its body, and long teeth that come down to its chin. Where do the people live?
>
> Group: In apartments. In our city.
>
> Leader: And who helps the people? Do they go to the wise old woman, or to someone else?
>
> Group: To a homeless person on the street.

Leader: Great! Where does the homeless person tell them to go?

Group: Into an alley.

Leader: And what three things do the people have to do together?

Group: They have to clean up the garbage. They have to paint the walls of the buildings in the alley. They have to jump up and down.

Leader: Those are great! You know, two of them have to do with making the alley a nicer place. What else could they have to do together to make the alley nicer?

Group: Put in street lights! Fix the potholes!

Leader: Is there a motion we could do for fixing the potholes?

Group: Pretend you're digging.

Leader: I think we have it!

At this point, the leader tells the story, substituting the suggestions of the group for the corresponding details in the story.

Although first or second graders might be able to sustain interest in creating a list of suggestions and then telling them, as described above, preschoolers or kindergarten children might need an approach requiring more immediacy. In this case, the leader can just begin telling the story, then stop for each suggestion.

Leader: Once, there was a terrible monster that bothered some . . . Who should we make this story about?

Group: Rabbits!

Leader: Good! Once there was a whole meadow full of rabbits. They lived in peace in their rabbit holes. But then one day, some rabbits were jumping across the meadow. They suddenly stopped and looked up! There was a monster! What kind of monster do you think it was?

Group: It had a green head, and it was shaped like a bug.

Leader: Very good! The rabbits looked up and saw the monster! It was enormous. It had long legs like a bug. It had long wings like a bug. And on top, it had a green head and two long, floppy green antennae.

The rabbits hopped back into their holes, and squeezed down them so fast they got their fur all dirty.

They spent all day under the ground with dirty fur. But one brave rabbit said, "We can't live like this! We have to go get help, and get rid of that monster!" Who do you suppose the rabbit wanted to get help from?

Group: The snake.

Leader: Oh, yes. There was a wise and kind snake who lived deep in the forest. The brave little rabbit hopped to her neighbor's hole, and threw a pebble down it to let her neighbor know she was there. The neighbor said, "It's the green-eyed monster after me!" The brave rabbit said, "No, it's just me. We have to go to the wise snake of the forest, and get help getting rid of this monster!"

Using this method, the leader can incorporate each detail into the story as soon as the children suggest it.

## Making Your Own Story: Decision-Making

Since the process of creating a story together is itself an example of group cooperation, it helps to have some techniques on hand for low-friction group decision-making.

With preschoolers, the leader should probably make most of the decisions. To validate *every* suggestion, the leader can respond enthusiastically to each one, but choose to incorporate only certain suggestions into the story. For example, you might respond to a series of suggestions in this way:

Leader: A monster with long teeth! Great! What other kind of monster should we have?

Group: A monster that looks like YOU!

Leader: Great! A monster that looks like me. What other kind?

Group: A monster that looks like chocolate pudding.

Leader: Good idea! A monster that looks like chocolate pudding. I think our monster for today will have long teeth. Now, how big is this long-toothed monster?

The most commonly mentioned way of making a group decision, of course, is voting. Because voting is fairly uninteresting to such young children, however, a classroom of preschoolers can perhaps tolerate one vote per day. As a result, voting should be used only sparingly with young children, and then only for simple, clear-cut decisions. Other methods should be relied on more: decisions by the leader, consensus, turn-taking, etc.

Another drawback of voting, for any age, is that those who vote for the losing items may feel excluded or un-listened-to, or like "losers." When creating a story as a group, however, there may be less need to make exclusive choices than we think. Instead, the most popular ideas can often be combined:

> Can you imagine a monster that looks like chocolate pudding but has long teeth? Someone suggested that the monster look like me. What part of me would the monster look like? My glasses? All right, we'll have a big, blobby chocolate pudding monster, with little glasses like Doug's and two long teeth that reach all the way down to the ground.

Another decision-making technique that can work with older children resembles voting, but is more likely to result in agreement. Suppose we have generated a list on the blackboard of possible magic things for the people in our story to have to do:

*   clean up garbage
*   jump up and down
*   paint the walls of the buildings
*   spin around three times
*   put in street lights
*   eat a magic food
*   fix the potholes.

As facilitator, I might say, "Now, vote as many times as you want. In other words, raise your hand every time I say something you think would be okay for a 'magic thing' in our story." Once I've written down the number of hands that were raised next to each suggestion, I can cross out the suggestions that got the fewest votes. If this leaves me with four or five remaining possibilities, we might vote again—but this time, each person gets two or three votes only. Then we can vote again with one vote each, or I can choose the three highest vote-getters for our story. Alternatively, I can try to combine some of the four or five possibilities:

Leader: Well, what if they have to jump up and down while they paint the walls? Would that work?

Group: Yes, they could have to jump to reach the high parts of the walls with their paint brushes!

Leader: Great idea! They have to paint the walls, but can't use ladders! Is there any way they could help each other reach the highest parts of the walls?

Group: What if they climbed on each other's backs?

Leader: All right! The third magic thing is that they must paint the walls, but can't use ladders. They jump up to reach the higher parts of the walls, but when they get so high that even jumping won't work, they have to figure out something else. So they finally get the idea of climbing on each other's backs.

## Picture Books to Read

I chose this story because of its theme of group cooperation in conquering difficulties. The following picture books have similar themes:

*The Blind Men and the Elephant: an Old Tale from the Land of India.* Lillian Fox Quigley. New York: Charles Scribner's Sons, 1959.

*Harlequin and the Gift of Many Colors.* Remy Charlip and Burton Supree. Parents' Magazine Press, 1973.

*Swimmy.* Leo Lionni. New York: Pantheon Books, 1963.

*William, Andy, and Ramón.* Peter Buckley and Hortense Jones. New York: Holt, Rinehart and Winston, 1966.

## Cooperative Games

In the story, children imagine the experience of uniting as a group to solve a problem. In cooperative games, they can have the experience directly.

I recommend the following five books of games:

*The Cooperative Sports & Games Book.* Terry Orlick. New York: Pantheon Books, 1978. This is the best single source of cooperative games, conveniently divided by age group. Also includes a chapter on games from other cultures.

*The Second Cooperative Sports & Games Book.* Terry Orlick. New York: Pantheon Books, 1982. More games, extensions of games from the first volume, and extended chapters of games from several other cultures.

*Playfair: Everybody's Guide to Noncompetitive Play.* Matt Weinstein and Joel Goodman. Impact Publishers, 1980. Oriented more toward adults, but very useful. Excellent format gives actual introductions to each game.

*The New Games Book*, 1976 and *More New Games*, 1981. Andrew Fluegelman, editor. Dolphin Books. These two classic, useful books have much less emphasis on the non-competitive aspect of alternative games.

In all five books, you will find games in which a group of children solve a problem together; the two Orlick books have by far the greatest wealth of such games. Some of these games require cooperative strategies to evade or capture someone who, like the monster in our story, is chasing or otherwise menacing the group. Since they are so similar in concept to our story, they deserve a special mention:

"Fish Gobbler" (*Cooperative* , page 23). A special tag game in which there are special commands that put the "fish" at risk. But all are safe if they are touching another fish.

"Mush Mush" (*Second Cooperative*, pages 110-111). From the Innuit of Alaska comes this "hide the token" game in which the seated circle tries to outwit the person in the center.

"Red-Handed" (*New Games*, page 71). Similar to "Mush Mush," but without "swats" to the center player.

"Clam Free" (*More New Games*, page 113). A more complicated tag game in which the clams cooperate to defeat the "nuclear reactor."

A former pre-school teacher, **Doug Lipman** is a professional storyteller and musician who tours, teaches, writes, and records. A featured teller at the National Storytelling Festival, the Smithsonian, and numerous folk festivals, he has brought the joy of story and song to audiences of all ages. In addition, as a master teacher at the National Storytelling Institute and elsewhere, he has helped thousands of teachers, librarians, and other storytellers begin or advance their storytelling.

# Connor and the Leprechaun

## by Jay O'Callahan

ONCE THERE WAS A LEPRECHAUN that lived high in a tree. The tree was on the edge of a field called No Man's Land, for no one in the fishing village crossed that field. They knew the leprechaun was getting old and grumpy and liked his privacy. The wonderful thing about the leprechaun was that he made fine shoes. The strange thing was that he was always barefoot. You see, every time he made a pair of shoes he'd hear some human crying. The leprechaun would seek out the crying, give his shoes away, and the crying would stop.

Today the leprechaun lay high on a branch wiggling his toes in the breeze.

"Tree," the leprechaun declared, "I think I'll go down and see the butterflies."

"Good," said the tree in a deep voice that was rooted to the earth.

The leprechaun climbed freely down tickling the tree as he went. The village in the distance looked especially bright because the drying clothes were snapping on the lines and the fishing boats were bobbing in the sparkle of the sea.

The leprechaun swung around a last branch and jumped to the grass below. Slapping his friend the tree, the leprechaun said, "I'll be off now to romp among butterflies."

"I'll stay right here," the tree replied.

"You do that," the leprechaun said, laughing politely. It was the tree's only joke.

Soon the leprechaun was somersaulting in the field's high grass. He was bounding happily about among the flowers and butterflies when he cried out, "Owwwww! A bee bit me in the toe!"

His little toe was red and throbbing and swelling up big as a strawberry.

"Bee!" he shouted, "Why'd you bite me in the toe?"

The bee buzzed over, "Bzzzzzzzzz, wear shoes, wear shoes."

Furious, the leprechaun hopped back to his friend the tree. "Tree," the leprechaun called angrily, "What kind of shoes shall I make myself?"

"Make shoes so you can walk up my trunk, out on my branch and enjoy yourself."

"Good!" the leprechaun said, pleased. "Now I'm going down to the lake to see the bird."

"I'll stay right here," the tree said.

"I know you will," said the leprechaun.

Down at the lake the leprechaun saw his tiny friend. "Hey bird," he called, "What kind of shoes shall I make myself?"

The bird fluttered up saying, "Make shoes with a golden wing . . . no, two golden wings." The bird was suddenly excited. "Better still, make four golden wings. Then you could fly above and see the world as I do."

"Good!" the leprechaun squealed, and left. The leprechaun climbed his friend the tree and began to work at once. He carved the shoes out of a knob of wood he kept there for the job. The moment the shoes took shape, they became as soft as the finest leather. The sun was setting when he finished the first golden wing and it fluttered alive in the dying light of day. The leprechaun was weary so the second wing took hours. The moment he finished, it burst alive like a gold flame in the dark. He could do no more; his hands and arms ached and the leprechaun lay back and fell asleep upon the branch.

He did not sleep long before the night was pierced with a human cry of pain.

"Oh," he groaned awake, "someone's crying." The shoes weren't finished so he had to climb down barefoot. The tree called out, "I'll stay right here."

"I know you will, tree!" Stiff and aching the leprechaun went in search of the trouble. It didn't take him long to find it. At the far end of the forest, an eight-year-old boy named Connor sat weeping by a tree. He was lame and could not run well. Everyone knew Connor's story.

Connor and the other children would arrive early at the school and the master was often late. The boys and girls would race around, but Connor would pick up a stick and do the most wondrous drawings in the dusty dirt. But a ritual grew up around the drawings. The bigger boys led by a bully named Dirk would come over, stamp out Connor's drawings and pull him to his feet.

"Whyn't you be a man, Connor, and run? We're gonna have a race right now." Twenty boys would be lined up and Dirk would cry out "Go!" The race around the schoolhouse would begin and Connor would come in a sad last. "You're so slow, Connor," Dirk would sneer. Dirk's wild red face looked as if he had blown too hard on a stuck whistle. "Now we're racing up that tree, Connor. You better not be last. Go!" The climbing race began and Connor would be a sad last.

Connor was bitter sick of it and tonight he sat in the dark saying, "I know the drawings are good. They don't bother to look at them. I hate the school. I hate it!"

The leprechaun could see in the dark and, although Connor's tears were as bitter as lemon drops, the leprechaun turned his back sighing, "I cannot help the boy."

The leprechaun returned to the tree to sleep. At dawn the leprechaun woke and feverishly began to work, and soon the shoes with the golden wings were finished. The leprechaun put them on and walked down the trunk of the tree, and the tree cried out, *"Brave Shoes!"*

"Thank you, tree," the leprechaun agreed. "I'm going to show my friend the bird."

"I'll stay right here," the tree said. "I know you will, tree." The leprechaun ran down to the lake, "Hey bird, look!"

"Come," said the bird, "we'll go flying above the sea."

They flew above the field and village and now above the dazzling sea. "You live a wondrous life seein' sights like these," the leprechaun exclaimed.

"We all do," the bird replied. Just then there was a piercing cry of human pain.

"Oh," the leprechaun grunted angrily. "There's some trouble somewhere. I'll be back, bird." With that, the leprechaun flew swiftly over the village schoolhouse.

Dirk, the huge bully, and several others had just stamped out Connor's drawing and pulled him up. Someone cried, "Go!" and the race began. When Connor came in last, Dirk and two others pushed Connor into the bushes. Dirk said, "You were so slow we're gonna race around again and you better not be last. And when that's done, we'll race up the tree."

Connor was getting resignedly to his knees and he heard, "Shhhh." There was the leprechaun concealed in the bushes and looking none too pleased.

"I'm puttin' my shoes on you," the leprechaun said. The shoes stretched just right and the leprechaun laced them tight. "Now get up and race."

Connor stood up feeling as if he were standing on the waves.

"Ready," Dirk called. "Go!" Connor flashed out ahead and flew around the schoolhouse nine times like a stallion full of fire before any of them got around once. Connor stood lounging against a tree as they came panting in.

"Lovely day," Connor said, staring at the sky.

"Well," Dirk said, panting so he had to wait to get his breath.

"Keep at it," Connor said, "you'll get faster. Don't worry."

Dirk burst angrily. "Let's race up the tree."

"I'll show you how to climb the tree," Connor said. "Watch."

With his arms folded Connor walked up the trunk of the tree out onto the highest branch where he did a somersault and then he floated slowly down to earth.

"Come over here!" Connor ordered. "Come over here," he said severely. "Stop your gapin'. Close your mouths. Come here. You, too, Dirk, before I lose my temper!" Dirk and twenty wide-eyed boys came shyly forward as Connor picked up a stick. Connor knelt down and did a wondrous drawing of a butterfly in the dusty dirt. "Sit down," said Connor gently. "I'm gonna show you how to draw." And they learned a thing or two that day.

Late that night, Connor ran across No Man's Land to the leprechaun's tree. "Leprechaun," Connor called. "I know you're up there. Thank you for the best day of my life! Here are your shoes."

"What would you do if I let you keep the shoes?" the leprechaun called down.

"Well, I don't need them for running," Connor called. "I do that fine. But I could fly up and see fine things and then make a drawing of them."

"Keep the shoes," the leprechaun called down.

"Thank you!" Connor called, running back across the field. "Thank you, leprechaun!"

The leprechaun lay on the branch for hours and finally stretched out, saying, "Well, tree . . . I guess I was meant to go barefoot on this earth."

[Note: If you decide to tell this story to an audience, I'd appreciate it if you would write to me and let me know. I'd love to hear what draws you to this tale.]

## Follow-up Activities for "Connor and the Leprechaun"

### by John Porcino and Jay O'Callahan

In the story, the magic of the leprechaun's shoes helps to build Connor's self-esteem. So out of the story are activities spun to help create the magic: a safe environment where young people treat each other with kindness and caring. It is in this type of environment that young people develop a strong positive sense of self-worth from which to flourish.

### Glad to Be Me

Each of us has qualities that make us unique and special to the world. For Connor, one of those qualities was his ability to draw. Here is a way of celebrating those qualities in each student.

Each day choose a "student (camper, person . . .) of the day." Trace the student's head and upper body on a large sheet of paper. Write the person's name on the top, and below that write "things we like about you" and "things that you are good at." Hang the sheet up so that students can easily reach it. All during that day (or two days, or week) the class writes appreciations on that sheet of paper.

In the beginning this may be hard for students, but with practice they get better and the "student of the day" will take home a nourishing reminder of his or her uniqueness.

### Trust Walk

Students first pair off and then choose one of the pair to be blindfolded and the other to be the leader. The leader will take the blindfolded partner on a walk. The leaders are challenged to make the walk safe and fun for their partners. The leaders can guide their partners up and down over safe obstacles, have them touch different textures, listen to sounds, smell, and even taste things. Encourage leaders to be creative, have fun, and take care of their partners. After about ten minutes have the pairs switch roles. If students get to feel comfortable with this activity, challenge them to do it without speaking.

Give students time to share their feelings about both being blindfolded and being the leader.

## Inside, Outside Box

For fourth grade and older: You will need enough old shoe boxes so that each student in your class can have one. You will also need stacks of old magazines, glue, scissors, magic markers, crayons, and so on. Using these materials, have students make a collage on the outside of the box of how they think others see them. On the inside of the box have students make a collage of how they see themselves or how they wish other children would see them.

Have small groups of two to four students show their boxes to each other. Let them know that it is fine to "pass." After everyone has had time to show their box a discussion with the whole class may follow.

## Start a Connor Skills Cooperative

Once a week (or day, or month) devote 45 minutes for a student to teach others a skill, game, trick that they've learned. I have seen young people teach others everything from magic tricks, to juggling, to drawing, to writing Haiku, to string games, to origami. This is really "show and tell" taken one step beyond.

## Extend the Story

- Draw part of the story that you liked. Really enjoy the colors and the place you choose. What's important is not a great drawing, but spending time with a part of the story you liked.

- Imagine what you'd do if you had invisible shoes that let you fly. Write down a few of the things you'd do with these wonderful shoes.

- Make up a short story about the grumpy leprechaun when he was young. Where did he live then? What does he eat?

- Make up a short leprechaun song.

- Make up a very short story about where leprechauns come from.

- Imagine "Connor and the Leprechaun" were a book. Draw a cover to be used for this book.

**Jay O'Callahan** began telling stories in 1975. He found the stories he told to his children were fun and began performing in schools in Massachusetts. Since then he has performed from Lincoln Center to Stonehenge. He writes his own stories and has been commissioned to write and perform stories for the Boston Symphony Orchestra, National Public Radio, and cities, towns and museums.

I created this story from a "story-seed" given to me by a woman named Sita Akka Paulickpulle. Sita was born in India, and traveled in Germany during World War II. Educated as a nurse in England, Sita toured Nazi hospitals and concentration camps with the Red Cross. She bravely advocated for the hospitalized prisoners and questioned the German officers she met there.

I first met Sita in 1985 when she participated in a nonviolence training session that I was giving for participants in a civil disobedience action to protest the manufacture of nuclear weapons.

Sita believes that lasting social change must come from a place of love. She was last known to be living in Washington, D.C., where she was witnessing for peace at the Pentagon, and teaching peace to the children in her neighborhood.

# The Image Maker

## by Katie Green

ONE THOUSAND AND ONE YEARS AGO, in far-off India, there was an artist. He was an image maker who made small bronze statues of the god, Shiva. These images glowed like the setting sun, and all of Shiva's power and serenity radiated from them.

The images were known throughout the land for their beauty, and although they were very much in demand, the image maker never sold them. He gave the images away, to any and all who came and asked for one. The image maker believed, as did the monks who supported him and his work, that the images were a gift from the gods. To sell one of the gods' gifts would be blasphemous.

One day, there was a great royal procession. The king was touring the country with an entourage of many servants, elephants, and horses. Everyone hoped that the royal procession would come to their village, so they might have a glimpse of the king. The image maker was no different. He, too, wished to see the king.

The royal procession came to the image maker's village. Everyone crowded tightly along the road as the king's carriage approached. Just as the carriage passed the image maker, the curtains were pulled to one side, and the king peered out. There was an expression of bored curiosity on his fleshy, round face.

The next day, the image maker had a visitor. The king had sent a messenger to obtain an image of Shiva. The image maker was pleased and honored that the king himself wanted one of the images. However, his pleasure faded when the messenger offered him a purse of gold coins, which the king had sent for payment. The image maker attempted to explain that the images were not for sale, that they came to him as a gift from the gods themselves. But the king's messenger was more concerned about obeying the king's orders, and he could not listen to what the image maker had to say. The messenger placed the image into his saddlebags, and told the image maker, "You *must* take the purse." The messenger threw the purse to the ground, and galloped away.

The image maker was insulted to the core. No one, not even the king, could *buy* one of the images. He turned back to the image on which he had been working when the messenger had arrived. With anger and haste, he began to break the baked clay mold from around the bronze image.

To create the images, the image maker used a method called lost wax casting. This was a lengthy process which began with carving the figure out of wax, and then covering it with clay. Small openings called vents were placed in such a way that the wax could run out of the mold while it was baked, or fired, in the kiln. After the firing, the mold was filled with melted bronze. Once the bronze had cooled and hardened, the mold was chipped away. This process took several days.

The image maker furiously chipped away the mold which covered the image. He carefully examined the image before he began the arduous task of polishing it. Shiva was seated on a perfectly formed lotus blossom. His six arms were outstretched in sanctified dance. One arm was in the posture of teaching, one in the posture of acceptance. The remaining four hands held objects: a flute, a cup, prayer beads and a flower. Shiva's head was tilted slightly to the left, and there was a vague smile on his lips. Similarly, a vague smile crossed the image maker's face as he looked upon the flawless image.

The polishing brought a golden luster to the bronze. It was as if light were emanating from within the statue. Then a strange thing happened. As the image maker polished, he watched, incredulously, as Shiva's face changed into the face of the king. The image maker was horrified. He destroyed the image, and began a new one without hesitation.

Several days later, he began to polish the new image. To the image maker's horror, once again the face of the king appeared as he polished. The image maker could barely contain his rage and disgust. He destroyed the image, and set to work on a third one. The same thing happened. The polishing transformed the face of Shiva into the face of the king, with his expression of bored curiosity.

The image maker stopped working, and began to meditate. He felt confused. He had always been an image maker, had been born into the caste of image makers. But how could he be an image maker when he had no control of the images? How had he fallen into such disfavor with the gods? He grieved about the loss of his art, the loss of his life.

He left his home and went to visit the old woman who lived at the edge of the village. He described what was happening to the images, and told her how the King's face appeared on the image of Shiva when he polished the bronze. Together, they sat and meditated. Then, the old woman said, "Tell me, how do you feel about the king?" The image maker raged, "I *hate* the king." The old woman paused, nodded her head slightly, and reflected, "When your hate is stronger than your love, you will always create what you hate."

The image maker and the old woman continued to meditate. Then the image maker returned to his home where he continued to sit in meditation.

After several days, he knew what he must do. He left his home, taking only the clothes he was wearing, and carrying a small metal bowl. The image maker headed toward the city where the king lived, a place he had never been. During the long journey, the image maker slept beside the road. He begged for food. He was often hungry, for there were many people who had no food to spare. By the time the image maker arrived at the city, his clothes were ragged and he was streaked with dirt.

He walked through the crowded, unfamiliar streets. Everything was strange and disorienting: the noises, the smells, the people. At last, near the center of the city, the image maker came upon a high wall that he knew must be the one surrounding the king's palace. He followed the wall until he came to a heavy wooden door.

The image maker knocked, but no one answered. He knocked again, and waited. Still, there was no answer. The image maker continued to stand at the door, and knock, and wait for an answer. People came by and offered advice. "You can knock on that door all day, but no one will answer it," they said. "That door only opens for royal business."

Still, the image maker continued to knock and wait. He refused all offers of food or drink. When he became tired, he sat on the ground, and banged on the door with his metal bowl. The noise echoed throughout the hall, until the guard inside could stand it no longer. He opened the door. "Go away."

"I have come to do business with the king," replied the image maker, tiredly.

"The king will not see you," and the guard closed the door.

Throughout the next day, the image maker sat at the door. He pounded the door with his bowl, and he waited for the door to open. The following day he did the same. And he continued his fast.

The guard reported the presence of an insistent beggar to the king, stating, "He will surely remain there until he dies."

"Let him in. I will see him," the king said.

As the king watched the image maker approach, he realized that this man was not a beggar. Although he dressed like a beggar, and he carried a beggar's bowl, he did not carry himself like a beggar. "Who are you?" asked the King. "Why do you come?"

"Your majesty, I am a humble image maker. Some time ago, you sent a messenger to my home for an image of Shiva."

The king recalled sending for the image, and complimented the image maker on the beauty of his work.

"I am honored," said the image maker, "but the images come to me as a gift. Your messenger left this behind, by mistake." The image maker gave the purse of coins to the king.

The king took the purse, and exclaimed, "One of my messengers would never have been careless enough to leave a purse full of gold behind!" But when he examined the purse, he could see that it had come from his house.

The king looked from the purse to the image maker. Their eyes met. No words were spoken, yet at that moment, the king understood. The image maker's ability to create these images was a gift; a gift from the gods—perhaps from Shiva, himself, and as such, they were not for sale. The king quietly said, "Yes. A mistake was made."

The king sent a small caravan to return the image maker to his village. Once he was home, the image maker again sat in meditation. He fasted for several days. When his heart was easy, and his mind felt clear, he returned to his work.

He carved Shiva from the wax. He covered the wax model with clay, and vented it. The wax ran out as the mold baked in the kiln. He melted the bronze and carefully poured it into the mold. The metal cooled and hardened. He chipped away the mold, and saw the rough bronze form of Shiva: his six arms, his head tilted to the left, a vague smile on his lips. The image maker began the arduous task of polishing the image . . . . And . . . as he polished . . . the image began to glow like the setting sun . . . and Shiva's face radiated power and serenity.

&#x1F339; &#x1F339; &#x1F339;

Now, it is said that the king was a patron of the image maker for many, many years. And that the image maker produced numerous images for the king's household. However, I am sorry to tell you that none of these images are to be found today. Perhaps they were hidden away in monasteries during various invasions. Perhaps, over time, they were melted down, to be formed into newer, more popular images.

And so, no images that the image maker produced remain. What we have today is this story. The image maker.

## Follow-up Activities for "The Image Maker"

### Shiva

Shiva, a Hindu god, has dominated Indian thought and ritual for over 2000 years. He is the Creator and the Destroyer, and reveals himself to people as everything and its opposite. He is the all-pervading ruler of the life processes of the world. It is Shiva, the "Lord of the Dance," who brings forth the miracle of evolution, maintenance, and dissolution.

The worship of Shiva is central to the lives of over 250 million people today. Throughout the centuries, artists have attempted to capture the essence of Shiva.

The images of Shiva have shifted throughout time and history. Often, the bronze images were melted down to create newer, more popular images from this rare metal. During the late ninth century, the time that I have chosen for my story, some especially lovely wax casted bronze images of Shiva were made in Kashmir, in northern India. Many of these images were only recently discovered, twenty to thirty years ago, inside caves in hidden monastaries in southern Tibet. Some hypothesize that the images had been hidden away to protect them from looters invading from the north.

Very little is known about the artists who created the early images of Shiva. It is assumed that they were of a specific caste of image makers.

In this story, the image of Shiva has six arms. Each arm represents a value of the culture. Objects are held in four of the hands; a flute, prayer beads, a cup, and a flower. Two of the arms are positioned, one in a posture of teaching and the other in a posture of acceptance.

If you were to create an image of Shiva that would reflect the values of our culture, positioning some of his hands, and placing objects in others, what gestures would he be making and what objects would he hold? Your images may be written, drawn, or sculpted.

## Artists

The image maker felt that his ability to create the images of Shiva was a gift from the gods. This belief prohibited the sale of his art. How do artists fit into our society today? Discuss, with an artist, the relationship of money and the nature of art.

## Role Play

The image maker "hates" the king, although he does not actually know him. Communication between the two men changes his feelings toward the king. Have you ever had strong feelings of dislike, or "hate," toward a person that you have never met? What was it about that person that was disagreeable to you?

With a partner, role play a dialogue between yourself and that person whom you have never met, but have negative feelings about. After a few minutes, switch roles; your partner will role play *you,* while you role play the person you do not like. Share any changes in understanding that you may have had.

Begin this exercise again, with your partner choosing someone s/he dislikes.

## Media and our Perceptions

We often have strong, emotional feelings about persons from other cultures or other countries. How do we develop these opinions without personal experience?

Collect clippings from the media, and compare the ways that different publications describe the same international events. Also compare the photographs of national leaders. Use a diverse set of publications, such as *Time, U.S.A. Today, Newsweek, Mother Jones, The New York Times,* and your local newspaper. Make sure that you include publications that are not as well known, such as *The Guardian* (33 W. 17th St., New York, NY 10011), and those available from the American Friends Service Committee (2161 Massachusetts Ave., Cambridge MA 02140).

Educators for Social Responsibility has an excellent book that allows high school and college students to explore how media sources influence commonly held views. *The Other Side: How Soviets and Americans Perceive Each Other* offers comparisons of the same events as reported in Soviet and U.S. press coverage. Additional projects and an annotated bibliography are included. The book can be obtained from Educators for Social Responsibility (23 Garden Street, Cambridge, MA 02138, 617/492-1764).

## Nonviolence

Show the movie, *Gandhi*, and discuss the use of nonviolent actions as a response to oppression. What oppressive laws were in effect in India during this time? Martin Luther King was greatly influenced by Gandhi. Discuss the action at the salt mines and compare it to the civil disobedience actions that took place in the United States during the late 1950s and early 1960s.

## A Game

In the story "The Image Maker," tension, distrust, and hate are dissipated by communication. The following game is one that plays on nonverbal displays of negative feelings. The act of using nonverbal insults in a game tends to diffuse their power within that group, and helps participants become more aware of the effects of these communications by inviting laughter to heal past experiences that we all have had.

I have played this game with adults and with children over ten. I call it "Matches."

This game requires each person to have a partner. To play the game, partners are back-to-back and the leader counts to three. On "three," the partners jump around, face each other, and do one of three movements (see below). If the partners "match," or perform the same movement, they sit down, and continue to participate by watching the other pairs.

Demonstrate and have the group imitate three different nonverbal insults. I use the following:

- Point at your partner and make a "yucky" face. (Exaggerate it! Make a corresponding sound.)

- Put your hands on your hips and stick out your tongue.

- Put your thumbs in your ears and wave your fingers, and make a "raspberry" sound.

The last people to be standing "win the game," but they, too, must continue playing until they "match." This is a fast-paced game that has resulted in much laughter whenever I've played it.

## Bibliography

*The Hindu Tradition*. Minneapolis, MN: World Religions Curriculum Development Center, 1978. Argus Communications, Allen, TX 75002. (A division of DLM, Inc.)

**Katie Green** lives in Princeton, Massachusetts, with her family and their two cats. She is a founding member of Oak and Stone Storytellers, Worcester, Massachusetts. Katie is also a speech/language pathologist, and uses stories in her therapy with children and adults. Katie tells stories with the hope that they may connect people to each other and to the natural world.

Wait! Don't turn that page! Just give me a chance to explain . . . I know it looks like poetry, but it's really more like music, a song . . . oops! There, I've gone and frightened you even more.

Many teachers are intimidated by music. Some teachers also stay away from poetry. Possibly they were subjected to boring and inept presentation when they were in school. Possibly they don't want to experience the frustration of having their presentations rejected by the children.

Still, I hope that if you are a teacher of adolescents you will give this "rap" or "street"-style poem a try. My experiences with it in classroom situations have felt very powerful. It's a folktale from Borneo, considerably updated. Since beginning to perform it, I have felt that "Half-Boy" deals with powerful forces in conflict within our children. One warning: with mention of drugs and allusion to sex, this is not a story for young children. I have told "Half-Boy" to inner-city high school kids, though, and I believe that it "gets through" like no other story I know.

As you read it, don't worry if some sections don't seem to have the same meter, or any meter at all. It's written that way. In fact, the sections that aren't indented aren't in meter, but are delivered as narrative.

# Half-Boy

## by Michael Punzak

Now you folks out there might think it queer
You might think it strange, you might think it weird,
But a while ago, in this dirty old town
There lived a certain dude who just hopped around . . .
Just hopped around, on one strong leg . . . .

Now you folks out there, who are startin' to think
This old tale-teller's been hittin' the drink;
I got somethin' else to tell you, might give you alarm:
This boy only had himself one strong arm!

"Wait a minute now," you're startin' to say,
"Now I get the drift of this little word play!"
So let me just take you right down the path—
What we got, well, this boy got half!

Half-a-Boy they called him: Half-Boy!
      No father, no mother,
      No sister, no brother!
      One leg, one arm, one ear, one eye,
Half-a-mouth? You bet! I tell no lie!

Lie? That's just what he'd do, east, west, north and south!
Wherever he could hop to, he'd lie with his half-mouth!
The kind of lies he'd tell would chill your heart so cool:
"Hey son, ya know your brother Billy said ya was a fool!"
He'd run on with the insults, until he got it right—
Half-a-Boy weren't happy, unless he caused a fight!

> As a child
> He was wild.

Little girls, out havin' fun and skippin' rope.
He'd cut the rope with a knife—just for a joke!
And that's just the kind of jive
He did when he was five.

When he was six
He learned better tricks:
> Lady hangin' washing, out on a line,
> He'd splatter mud all over it, laughin' all the time!

When he was nine, he got caught one time. The old blind man who sat on the corner, beggin' for coin, he caught Half-Boy stealin' from his hat one time, when he was nine. The old feller rapped him with his cane, made his head mighty sore! Half-Boy hollered, "I'll be good! I'll never bother you no more!" So the old blind man let him go.

> But

Half-a-Boy went and caught a rat in a trap.
He tortured it a while, then gave its head a rap.
When the rat woke up, he was in the blind man's lap!

That old man was bit pretty bad, but comin' back from the hospital he found his home . . . burned down to the ground! Some folks thought they knew who did it, but they couldn't be sure . . . .

When he got to be a teen
He tried the drug scene.

He had a gift of gab, and he knew how to plan,
So he gave himself a job as a crack-pushin' man!

Half-Boy was pullin' in a mighty large buck
He got so greedy, he would push his luck!

So some deals went down in this dirty old town that gave Half-Boy a certain reputation. He could lie, I told you once, and he could jive with the best alive. But, ya know, a dealer's no dunce. He couldn't lie to one more than once.

So as time went on, the word got around.
The wild child had aggravated 'bout half the town!
And some folks said, the ones who ought to know,
That the time had arrived for the half-boy to go!
They didn't mean jail—he'd be let out, on bail.
They didn't mean leavin' on a bus or a train.
What they had in mind was to stop his breath.
What they had in mind was a cold, hard death.

Now, 'bout that time, Half-Boy was 'most a man,
And like a natural child, he'd see ladies 'bout the land,
And one caught his eye, me-oh-my!
And he hopped right up to her, sayin' "Hi!
There's only half of me,
That you can see,
But I can guarantee
I'll keep you satisfied!"

Now this lady didn't laugh, like some had, or spit in his face, or call him "mad." There was somewhere inside her a wise gentle place, and a voice within that told her just what she should do. She looked at Half-Boy and she said to him: "You are only half a man—that's right! And you're the bad half, sorry to say. But out there somewhere, a long way off, is your other side. Go, find him. Together you can be one."

"I sort of like you," she went on. "I get a glimpse of something deep in your soul. But until you get together, bro, and make yourself whole . . . .

"Your road is filled with pain,
With the wind, the cold and rain!
But no one else can help you—
It's for you to do.

"This other road you're travelin', hurtin' others, huntin' wealth—
You're hurtin' others, but you're also hurtin' yourself!
And sure as shootin' these words I say are true:
Someday, someone will catch up to you!"

Truth to tell, these words did not sit well with Half-Boy.

With a gesture of contempt and a rude word he was off, but she knew from his eye that he heard. So, after he got himself to his own place, what struck him then, like a blow across his face, was that she had talked to him with a voice that was kind. When had he last heard that? When was the last time?

> So when night came
> And some boys of the town
> Came with their guns, to shoot Half Boy down . . . .
> > He was out on the highway,
> > Had a sack on his back,
> > Hoppin' on one leg,
> > Plannin' to come back
> > After findin' the good part—
> > The one with heart!

Now, after thirty miles of hoppin', Half-Boy came to a town. Folks all stared at the stranger. He stared back and said: "I'm Half-Boy. Ever see anybody like me before?" "Nope," said a man, "But I heard of one like you, off in St. Loo." Half-Boy trotted on . . . .

> Well, my story's gettin' long,
> I don't want you to yawn,
> But truth to tell
> His journey felt like hell!
> The road was not short,
> But Half-Boy was the stubborn sort.
> Though his knee-bone would be achin'
> And his cold bones would be shakin'
> He kept a-hoppin' down that road, from town to town to town,
> And he kept on askin', if a half-boy was around.
> He got a load of advice. They called him fool, jerk, and clown.
> But on he went; he just kept a-hoppin' down
> That twistin' old road, that went from town to town,
> And always he'd be askin' if a half-a-boy was 'round.
> His knee-bone would be achin', his body would be cold,
> His cash down to nickel one, but still, if he was told:
> "I heard-a one, just like you . . .," he'd hop on.

Let me make a long story short. One day he found him. They looked the same. Some said: "It's clear they're brothers . . . of some sort!"

But one's eye was hard, and the other's eye was kind. Said the other: "It's mighty good you looked for me. I would have never looked for you!" They stared at each other, and wondered what to do.

> 'Til an old gypsy woman put down her violin,
> Wise eyes shinin' out, behind her wrinkled skin,
> Said they'd have to fight it out,
> To see which twin would win.
> > Good twin or evil twin:
> > "Let the match begin!"

So off they went, they left that neighborhood,
Went into a clearing, in a nearby wood,
They fought it out and wrestled the whole damn day!
"Gonna win!" sneered Half-Boy, "Cause I fight the dirty way!"

"Don't be too sure," said Half-Boy's twin.
"I got a strength inside, comes from deep down within.
All my life, helpin' others, doin' good,
Hasn't made me weak inside, like you thought it would!"

So they fought all the day, and they fought all the night
While all around them others joined in on the fight.
The south wind fought the north. The snow fought the rain!
It seemed to all the folks on earth that life was filled with pain.

Well . . .

> This battle goes on in other places too.
> It's a struggle that might occur
> *Inside* of a few.

But inside,
Or outside,
Who loses?
Who wins?
I wish I knew.

> Or is there a place in-between?
> That's an idea!—no one losing!
> An idea seldom seen!

So what happens next?
Well . . . that's up to you.

## Follow-up Activities for "Half-Boy"

In the "original"—I put that word in quotes because only rarely is it clear that a folk tale *has* an original, or correct, or primary version—Half-Boy and his Good Side are united: "they" live happily ever after. I was afraid this verged on the maudlin. You may feel my ending does, too. Please feel free, in the classroom, to experiment with other endings.

Speaking of experimentation, you might also consider adding percussion to this story. I perform it with a home-made drum set. I think it could work with the sort of electronic rhythm machine that is part-and-parcel of a lot of inexpensive electronic keyboards. Again, it is my style when performing it to stop the rhythm during the non-metrical sections. I think it focuses attention and builds appropriate tension to have periods of relative silence, then take up the rhythm again. If the story is effective within your classroom, you might perform it for other groups; your students have the rhythmic and percussive talent and imagination to figure out a good accompaniment.

It's an open question whether immediate discussion of a story after presentation elicits the best thinking. As a performer I never want to impose my meaning and interpretation on an audience. Sensitive handling of responses allows kids to think and hash the issues out on their own. It seems not to be a good time to moralize.

## Suggestions for Follow-up

- Since this can't very well be a factual story, in what sense can it still be, powerfully, true? What is the story about? Discuss this question, perhaps comparing with other stories, both fantastic and realistic.

- At what points in the story did characters make key decisions? What could have happened differently? This question and others like it can be used as creative writing topics. As well, they could be jumping-off points for dramatic improvisation.

- Try some confrontations between inner voices in various situations. It's sort of like the "good angel" versus "bad angel" (or conscience versus wicked impulse) scenario that might appear in a comic strip. These situations might also lead to other ideas; for instance, a mock trial of an aspect of one's personality. Don't be afraid to let it become comical.

- Write, create or tell your own ending to the story. You, as the teacher, might want to reassure the kids that in the folktale from which the author wrote this adaptation ("Half-Boy of Borneo" from *Old Tales for a New Day*, by Sophia Lyon Fahs and Alice Cobb, Buffalo: Prometheus Books, 1980), the "good" side is the "winner" in the wrestling match. Discuss why the author omitted this.

Finally, be advised that this story can bring out some pretty "heavy" material from the audience. I asked one group of inner-city kids if any of them had ever been in jail. In my previous visits this audience had seemed quietly appreciative of stories I told, but unwilling to respond with any personal revelations. But this time they answered with descriptions, some quite detailed. I was moved by the change, but I worried that the situation had the potential to get into risky areas. Nevertheless I feel talking about some of humanity's lower inclinations is healthier than denial.

I hope someday to hear that "Half-Boy" has made a difference in some classrooms.

ﾞ ﾞ ﾞ

**Michael Punzak** has been alive since he was a very small baby. He has been telling stories professionally since 1982, but, as a teacher, for a lot longer. He hopes that by the time you read this he will again be teaching. Besides being a highly paid professional storyteller, he also is an occasional actor and a hard-fiddling musician. He hopes that the love of story infuses his entire life, whatever the endeavor.

# The Snowflake Story

by Tracy Leavitt

One day I was a wondering,
Just pondering and questioning
Some things I did not know,
      Like: "From where does the wind blow?"
      or, "Who paints the rainbows?"
      and, "Why do those fuzzies grow between my toes?"
But what I was really wondering on that day
      was, "Who is it that makes the flakes of snow?"

So . . . I set off to my grandmother's house
Because whenever I have an impossible question—
      (That's what my mother used to call them)
Grandma was always the only one who would know!

"Grandma," I said when she had let me in,
"Who makes the snow?"
      "Why, child," she said,
      "Don't you know?"          [Grandma voice for indented
                                           quotations]

She picked up a stick by the fireplace
And poked the fire up to a roar.
Next she went and got a large sheet of paper
And scissors from her brown desk drawer      [get a sheet of paper and scissors]

Then she sat me down right beside her,
Poured me some cocoa in a cup.
She picked the scissors up from her lap
And started cutting the paper up.      [begin cutting a circle]

Saying . . .

      "There's an old, old woman,
      Much older than I,
      Who keeps a cloud full of paper
      Up in the sky."

Right then I ran to the window to look,      [stop cutting and look up as if
But Grandma said I'd never see . . .      out a window]
      "Cause the old woman is tiny—
      Just as tiny as can be.

      "She has a trillion pieces of paper      [resume cutting]
      Or maybe a trillion and three.
      She's made the paper of starlight
      Mixed with sparkle water from the sea!

      "Now, as I said, she is tiny.
      As are her scissors and paper and all.

She holds up her cloud carefully
To be sure that none will yet fall.          [circle is complete]

"In springtime she shapes them          [show circle]
Into circles of white.
She folds them all neatly,
Three times to be right.          [fold circle as in illustration, counting aloud]

"All summer she cuts them          [begin cutting snippets out]
Snip, snap; one by one.
Each one different, each one perfect
Until all are done.

"Then when on earth the grass is brown,
And the trees are all bare.
When there's not a single flower
Growing anywhere . . .          [continue cutting snowflake, enjoy yourself, take your time]

"The skywoman looks down and exclaims,
          'Things look dull, dull, dull!'
Round about that time
Her cloud is getting full.

"The time is now late in the fall
          'Oh goodie,' she says, 'it's time it's time!'
          My work at last is done,
          Oh, and isn't it fine, fine, fine!'          [open up snowflake and show it]

"So she takes up the edge
Of her cloud in her hand,
And she shakes it!
Papers fly—*Oh*, so grand!

"As each circle flutters
To the earth far below,          [guide your flake to the ground]
Her magic makes the paper change
Into fluffy flakes of snow.

"And now you *know*!"

Grandma then put away her scissors          [set aside scissors and snowflake]
And washed out my cocoa cup.
She helped me put on my hat and mittens,
And buttoned my coat all the way up.

"Thanks for the cocoa," I said with a grin,
"I'll think of the sky woman on my way . . . ."
          "Now wait just one minute," said my Grandma,
          "I've an important thing to say."

          "When you go out and catch a snowflake;
          Look at it glittering bright,

Dream of the sky woman's magic, yes,
Then think of your own sparkle and light.

"For there's something magic inside of you
A talent, a treasure so fine.
As you grow older you'll find it,
Then you'll polish it till it shines!"

Well . . .

All through the years I wondered—
What Grandma meant I just didn't know,
Because I tried to play the piano, but couldn't
And I couldn't dance on the tips of my toes.

My math skills are slightly below any third grader's
And as you can plainly tell                          [swish your snowflake around
My snowflake remains just paper                      so it rattles]
For I know no real magic spells.

But I did grow to understand.
Now, I have no more worries,
Because I know that my magic lies
In the way that I can tell stories!

Now, each of you has a magic
Something inside bright and shiny new.
And as you grow and learn
Your magic will grow with you!

## Follow-up Activities for "The Snowflake Story"

The relationship of self-concept and learning is well documented. Simply stated, the more positive the self-concept, the greater the ability to take the necessary risks that will make learning possible. Without the feeling of success within oneself, the willingness to risk will not be there.

In our society it is often deemed "boastful" to talk about the things we do well. We generally are quite aware and communicative of our weaknesses and problems: think how many times you've heard, "I can't do it" or "I don't know how" from children or adults or, perhaps, yourself. To be aware and confident of one's own strengths requires continuous internal questioning and discovery.

The activities are designed to help young people discover a sense of their own personal power and strength, as well as develop an appreciation for the unique experience and strength of others. Adapted to serve specific developmental levels, the activities can be used with any age group. They are part of a five-session workshop that has evolved with direct input from children.

As with storytelling, the ideal environment for the games and exercises is a comfortable, intimate space. The atmosphere needs to be one in which the children can be honest and open, and do not feel that they are being judged or graded. It may be that a special corner of the room or library is set aside for these story activities. All present must participate, including the leader; observers would inhibit the growth of trust and vulnerability among the members of the group.

## Snowflakes

With everyone seated in a circle, this first session of self-exploration begins with the telling of "The Snowflake Story." During the story the teller will make a snowflake and at the end extend an invitation to the group to make snowflakes of their own. Don't be afraid that older age groups will resist—I have found that they are excited to try this simple activity and that it puts them in touch with their younger selves.

Here is my recipe for snowflakes. (I got it from the Sky Woman, of course!):

1. Fold an 8 1/2" by 11" piece of paper as shown and cut on the dotted line, *or* draw circles with a compass and cut them out. For younger children you can already have circles cut out.

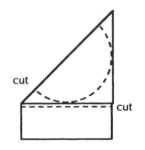

2. Fold the circle in half. Fold in the edges twice to make thirds, as shown. (". . .three times to be right!")

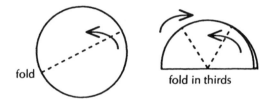

3. Cut or tear designs in the folded sides, being careful not to cut away all the folded edges, because then the snowflake will fall apart (not a very good move for a magic sky person).

4. The snowflake can be displayed by mounting it on a dark color of construction paper or by hanging it on strings from the ceiling or from sticks to form a mobile.

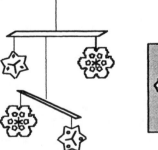

As the snowflakes are completed, facilitate a discussion about the unique qualities in each of the snowflakes. As you hold a few of the different flakes up, ask questions such as:

Are any of yours exactly like this one? Could any of these snowflakes be the same without having cut-marks printed on the paper? What is the meaning of the word *unique?* What is the meaning of the word *creative?* Like real snowflakes, each one of ours is different . . . . Let's talk about people instead of snowflakes. Can any one of us be exactly like another? Even twins—how are they different from each other? What is it about each of us that can be called unique? How about perfect—is any one of us more perfect than another?

Through discussion, guide the group to the gradual realization that each of us is special, each with our own strengths and weaknesses, each invaluable and impossible to duplicate. We each have a special gift to give the world. Ask students to tell about someone they know who is in some way special.

Go outside when it is snowing to allow your group to examine the diversity of real snowflakes. The use of a magnifying glass and black velvet or corduroy will encourage a realization that every part of nature has its own pattern and beauty.

## You, Too?

The purpose of the following activity is for the group to understand that we are all different in some ways and similar in other ways. Tell everyone to answer the following questions out loud and *to keep repeating the answer out loud* as they wander around the activity area. All those who are answering the question in the same way should gather together in a group.

- What color socks or stockings do you have on right now?
- Do you like vegetable soup?
- How many syllables in your name? Don't answer with a number, answer with claps for each syllable—for instance, Harriet would answer with three claps.
- What is your favorite animal? Which animal would you be most afraid of in the dark?
- In which month is your birthday?
- Do you have an innie or an outie? (belly-button, silly!)
- Don't answer out loud: open your eyes wide and find everyone with the same color eyes as you have.
- What did you eat at breakfast this morning?
  Ask if anyone can think of other questions.

## I'm Proud

Identifying the things we do well and have pride in may be difficult for many of us. Vocalizing and affirming the good in us helps it to be true, and helps us to keep it true. Hearing what is good in others helps us to appreciate them.

Instruct the group to think of something they do pretty well. It doesn't have to be anything earth-shattering, just something about which they feel pride. Stress the safety and comfort and openness of this special group of people. (In showing your confidence in them, they will live up to it!) This could be made into a writing project, but it is important for the dynamics of the group that each child verbally share his or her thoughts with the others. If it seems difficult for your group, help them out by suggesting some topics:

- Something you've done for your friends.

- Something you've done for your parents or siblings.

- A project you've done or a paper you've written.

- Something you do in your free time.

- Habits you have.

- Something you have shared.

- How you earn money.

- Some way in which you have helped others in school, church, or at home.

- (Older group) Something you have done in regard to world problems, like ecology, homelessness, racism, sexism, ageism, or other -isms.

## A Magic Box

In this activity, students are given the opportunity to tell about the roots of something that is important to them. They will discover new ideas and connections between their past and their present. This activity will often inspire great excitement for the student as feelings are verbalized and shared.

To begin this activity, stand up and walk to an imaginary wall, reach to an imaginary shelf and pull down an imaginary box. Tell the group . . .

> The box holds an object that will remind me about the beginning of some interest or hobby or fascination in my life. When each of you holds the box, your object will be inside. Reach inside and bring out the object. Give us a good description about how it looks, sounds, smells, feels or tastes. Show us how it is used. Tell us about how it led to a current interest of yours.

It is a good time to provide an example. Practice yours ahead of time. A detailed mime and verbal description from the leader will inspire a more elaborate response from your students. I will provide an example for you, but it would be best if yours really came from your life experience:

> This was my very first yo-yo. I love the color of red that it is. And do you see the sparkles inside of it? Look close! And watch this (mime the action of the yo-yo) . . . and here's "walk the dog" and "around the world"! My Uncle Pete gave me this yo-yo. You should see the tricks he can do. He gave it to me when I went to stay on his farm when I was eight years old. He had an apple tree farm. I was picking apples that summer. It was the first real money I ever earned—and I saved three hundred dollars. The only thing I spent money on were yo-yos. I had nine of them by the end of the summer—but this one, this red sparkle one was the first! I have a name for each one of my yo-yos: this one I call "Pete Pal."

## Bibliography

*Human Potentialities.* Herbert A. Otto, editor. St. Louis: Warren Green, 1968.

*Impro: Improvisation and the Theatre.* Keith Johnstone. New York: Theater Arts.

*100 Ways to Enhance Self-concept in the Classroom.* Jack Canfield and Harold C. Wells. Englewood Cliffs, NJ: Prentice-Hall, 1976.

*Values Clarification: A Handbook of Practical Strategies for Teachers and Students.* Leland W. Howe and Howard Kirschenbaum. New York: Hart, 1972.

❦ ❦ ❦

**Tracy Leavitt**, storyteller/writer, spreads her magic tales throughout the country with her storytelling theatre programs. Tracy's collection of tales communicate the richness of different cultures and the specialness of "just plain folks." She has produced a fine cassette tape of original and traditional stories called *Whispers of Light.* She also provides Artist-in-Residence programs at schools sharing the art of creative drama and storytelling with young people as well as offering teacher-inspiration workshops.

# The Artist's Search

by Peninnah Schram

THERE ONCE WAS AN ARTIST who was restless. Why was he so restless? Because every time he began to paint a scene, he discarded the unfinished painting, saying always, "No, this is not beautiful enough. This does not *touch* my soul."

He kept searching for what would be the most beautiful subject to paint. He walked along the river, which ran near his home, and painted the flowing water. But still dissatisfied, he put a new canvas on his easel and started over.

He walked all around the village.

He looked up at the sky and down at the earth.

He looked at the animals in the fields and at the workers in their workplaces— the carpenter, the shoemaker, the tailor, the butcher.

He would start to paint what he saw and then stop, just as quickly as he had begun. Nothing pleased him completely. Nothing seemed to be beautiful enough, satisfying both his senses and his soul.

One morning, as the sun was rising in the sky and the light spread a rosy glow across the village, the artist awoke and thought to himself, "I must find the most beautiful thing to paint. Since it is not here in my village, I will go out into the world and search."

With that thought, he quietly said his morning prayers and dressed as quickly as he could. Gathering up his artist's tools, he left his home, while his wife and family were still asleep.

Months later, the artist found himself in a beautiful park, sitting under a tree. He heard music, a beautiful melody, played on a violin. Looking around, he saw a young man and a young woman sitting at a table under a nearby tree, singing a love song to each other.

| | |
|---|---|
| *Papir iz dokh vais* | *As paper is white,* |
| *un tint iz dokh shvartz* | *and ink surely black,* |
| *Tsu dir main zis lebn* | *My heart yearns for you, dear love,* |
| *tzit dokh main hartz.* | *You're all that I lack.* |
| *Ikh volt shtendig gezesn* | *I'd sit three whole days,* |
| *drai teg nokh anand* | *all time I'd withstand,* |
| *Tzu kishn dain shein ponim* | *To kiss your sweet face,* |
| *un tzu haltn dain hant.* | *and to hold your dear hand.* |

Quickly, the artist began to draw the scene, capturing the love he saw in the lovers' faces and heard in the words they sang to one another. What could be more beautiful in the world? He felt happy that he had found what he had long been looking for.

He then started for home.

On the way home, he came to a bridge, where he was stopped by a guard in order to allow some soldiers to cross the bridge first. As the soldiers came closer, the artist asked one of them where they were going. "Home!" cried the soldier. "The war has ended, and the fighting is over. We are at peace, at peace!" Tears filled his eyes, and as he added, "Blessed be God, the God of *Shalom*," a look came over his face such as the artist had never seen before.

"*Shalom*. Peace! Yes, the feeling of peace, the look of peace—that too is a most beautiful thing in the world." And the artist began to paint, to capture on his canvas this feeling and the look he had seen on the soldier's face.

The artist continued on his way home, feeling satisfied that he had captured a second most beautiful thing in the world. But the story is not over yet.

One morning the artist got up especially early in order to start out for home. He was not far from it now. He left the inn where he had stayed and was walking along a country road, when he saw in the window of a small cottage an old man beginning his morning prayers. The artist watched as the old man put on his *tallis*, a beautifully embroidered prayer shawl, and pulled it around him. Then the old man put on his *tefillin*, which are small boxes containing holy words. He was completely immersed in his prayers. His face was beautiful to look upon, radiant in prayer.

Standing in the road, the artist worked quickly to paint the expression of faith that he was witnessing. "Yes, faith is a third most beautiful thing in the world," said the artist aloud to himself, as if committing it to memory.

It was just before the beginning of the Sabbath when our artist approached his home. Through the open door he saw his wife sitting with the children around the table. She was reading a letter she had received from him before they were married. And he heard her read, "'As paper is white, and ink surely black, My heart yearns for you, dear love, you're all that I lack.' And so, my dear one, write to me on Friday. In that way I will have something to read on *Shabbos*. Your friend, Moshe."

There was such love in the way she read the letter, holding on to the sweetness of their courtship days. The peace of the Sabbath and the joy of the blessing filled the house as he saw his wife rise from the table, take the children to her, and, placing her hands on their heads, bless each one in turn. Then she lit the candles to welcome the Sabbath bride.

The artist could no longer restrain himself. He opened the door wider and called out, "A good Sabbath, *A gut Shabbos*, my wife and children. I went searching throughout the wide world for beauty, only to discover that the three most beautiful things in the world—love, peace, and faith—are here in my own home. I did not recognize them before."

And the artist extended his hand for his wife's forgiveness. She took his hand and, together with their children, all in a close circle, recited a prayer of thanksgiving.

So the artist and his family were reunited, and from that day on they celebrated the Sabbath, and every day, with even deeper feelings of the three most beautiful things—love, peace, and faith.

## Follow-up Activities for "The Artist's Search"

"The Artist's Search" is a story that I first heard from my friends Rachayl and Hillel Davis. Hillel remembered hearing the story from his father, Rabbi Herman Davis of Chicago. With their permission, I have retold it and published it in my book *Jewish Stories One Generation Tells Another* (Northvale, NJ: Jason Aronson Inc., 1987, pp. 259-262). It is appropriate for junior high and high school students.

## Artists and Art

"You don't paint what you see; you paint what you feel," says Romare Bearden, the master of collage art. In order to do this, we have to first discover for ourselves what we feel. We are *all* artists, whether we paint our feelings through art, or music, or movement, or words, or just through living.

In this story, an artist is searching for the most beautiful thing. What he sees and paints does not "touch his soul." So the artist stops and leaves his canvas unfinished.

What might those unfinished scenes be? What would the artist have seen or not seen to cause him to say, "No, this is not beautiful enough"?

Look around you and respond to what you see. Is it the most beautiful thing you feel? Why? Why not?

## Discover Treasures at Home

Someone once said that, in order to have a story, either someone leaves town or someone comes into town. In this story, the artist leaves town to seek what he could not find at home. He searches and finds three most beautiful feelings. (The magical "three" occurs frequently in folktales.) The artist returns home and discovers that those treasured feelings were there all along, but he had never recognized them before.

How is that possible? What good things are there in your own life, home, family, community that you barely appreciate? How did you learn to appreciate them? Sometimes we go away to camp, or to college, or visit someone else's home and that new perspective can help us see what we could not notice before. Share some of these experiences and discoveries.

Reb Nahman once said, "The treasure is at home but the knowledge of it is in Vienna." By Vienna, he meant "far away, in the big city."

Reb Bunam would say to each of his new students; "Remember, the treasure, the one that is yours, is to be found only in yourself and nowhere else . . . ." How do these quotations encapsulate what the artist in the story learned? What do they leave out?

## Questions to Explore

Other questions can be explored using "The Artist's Search" as a springboard:

- Why must the artist leave home before he appreciates the treasure that he has at home?

- What are you dissatisfied with at home? In your community? In your school? In yourself? Do you think you would find the solutions to this dissatisfaction elsewhere? Where? Why or why not?

- If you were to choose what you feel is the most beautiful subject or feeling in the world, what would it be?

## Projects to Explore

- Create (with paints, collage, paper-cuts, etc.) your choice/treasure.

- Write about your choice/treasure (using poetry, haiku, narrative, etc.)

- Move or dance the way this choice makes you feel.

- Compose music or choose a song that has a musical feeling similar to what you choose.

## Love

Music and lyrics often express beauty and feelings we are embarrassed to say in our own words. The artist hears a love song, but what strikes him is the "look of love" on the faces of the young people. What does a "look of love" resemble? Have you seen two people in love look at each other? A parent's face looking with love at his/her child? A child looking at or hugging his/her pet animal? Draw someone looking at a person with a "look of love."

Tell about a time when you were in love or loved someone (a friend, grandparent, a pet, etc.) and how it felt? Share your stories of love and some good feelings that resulted. Do the same with peace and with faith.

Create a celebration or ritual to acknowledge these feelings (for example, falling in love or getting married) when they become part of your experience. What is a celebration? What do you need in order to have a celebration? A ritual? Usually a celebration is a festive occasion with a group of people in order to commemorate an event or day with some formal prescribed ceremony or ritual. It often includes feasting, such as at a Thanksgiving celebration. If you were to create a new holiday for love, it could be called "The Day of Love." Some of the set rituals you might celebrate on that day could be to:

- Give a hug and smile to everyone in your home three times during the day;

- Create and use a special greeting, such as "A love day to you," and a response, such as "A day of love to you too";

- Invite friends to a special feast where poems and letters of love are exchanged and read (either published pieces or original ones), along with prayers for love in the world (traditional or original);

- "Break bread" together which would show that you were all friends. Take a large loaf of bread, shake some salt on it, since salt is the ancient sign of friendship, and then have each person break off a piece of the bread. Before eating the bread, everyone, in a round-robin, completes the phrase, "To me, love is . . ." or "Love is a many-splendored thing and sometimes resembles . . . ." Then an international meal with other symbolic foods can be served.

## Love Songs

The lovers in the story sing a Yiddish love song, a folksong with no known composer. Love songs are among the oldest types of songs. Through the songs of a people, we can discover more about their hopes, dreams, values, traditions, aspirations.

What American love songs do you know? Learn to sing a love song from another culture. What common characteristics do you find in this type of song? Write a love song, poem, letter, story to or about someone you love.

## Peace

The feeling of peace is a second most beautiful thing the artist discovers as he sees the tears on the faces of soldiers. Why tears? Why not hurrahs and shouts of joy? What would you say when a war has ended? What song might people sing relating to peace? Three Hebrew songs come to mind—the music for them appears at the end of this section:

> *Lo yisa goy el goy cherev, Lo yilm'du od milchama*
> Nation shall not lift up sword against nation,
> > Neither shall they learn war any more.
> > (Source: Isaiah 2:4—Folk song)
>
> *Hine ma tov umanaim, shevet achim gam yachad.*
> Behold how good and pleasant it is for brothers
> > to dwell together in unity.
> > (Source: Psalm 133:1—Folk song)
>
> *Ose shalom bimromav, hu yaase shalom alenu,*
> > *v'al kol yisrael, v'imru imru, Amen.*
> May he who makes peace in the high places
> > Make peace for Israel and for all mankind
> > And say Amen.
> > (Source: Hebrew prayer—Music composed by N. Hirsh)

There are also many American songs for peace, such as "All We Are Saying," "Last Night I Had the Strangest Dream," and "We Are the World." Do you know of any other peace songs?

## Peace Speeches

There have been some powerful, dramatic and inspiring speeches promoting peace and harmony among people. Two examples are Abraham Lincoln's "Second Inaugural Address" and Martin Luther King's "I Have a Dream." Read the texts of these speeches or listen to them on a spoken word recording. Write a peace speech that you could deliver to your family, to your school, to the United Nations.

## Faith

The artist discovers a third most beautiful thing, faith, when he observes an old man praying.

What song might this person sing? What is prayer? Why pray?

In Judaism there are many prayers for peace. One of these prayers is:

> Grant us peace, Your most precious gift, O Eternal Source of peace, and give us the will to proclaim its message to all the peoples of the earth. Bless our country, that it may always be a stronghold of peace, and its advocate among the nations. May contentment reign within its borders, health and happiness within its homes. Strengthen the bonds of friendship among the inhabitants of all lands, and may the love of Your name hallow every home and every heart. Blessed is the Eternal God, the Source of peace.

Get into a small group of four to six people and discuss this prayer. Then have the group try to rewrite the prayer using simpler and more powerful language. What are some of your worries in the world? What do you wish could happen to make it a better world? Compose a prayer that expresses your concerns and hopes for peace.

## Sabbath

When the artist returns home, he watches his wife bless each child and light the *Shabbat* candles which signal the sacred time of the Sabbath. The Sabbath is a day of rest which allows us to put away mundane everyday concerns. The Sabbath creates a different sense of time to enter the person, the home, the community, the world. The Sabbath begins just before the sun sets on Friday evening, although the preparation begins much earlier, and leads up to welcoming the Sabbath Queen at sunset. At this time, everyone wishes everyone else "Shabbat Shalom," a good and peaceful Sabbath.

How can you achieve more of this sense of peacefulness and calm—to untie all the inner knots—in yourself? Try taking slow deep breaths whenever you feel upset, nervous, or have "stage fright." When you are feeling rushed because you have so much to do, it helps to make a list of all that you must get done the next day, and review the list in the morning so as to plan out your time schedule. What are some other ideas to help achieve a calmness? What can you do to achieve this sense of peacefulness in your home? In your school? In the world?

Why is it good to change the pace one day a week? How does it affect the body? The soul? What does rest mean to you? What would you do on a day of rest? How would the world be different if everyone observed such a day of rest? What one thing could you do to bring this sense of rest to yourself and your home at *one* dinner a week?

The Sabbath is central to Judaism as it is stated in the Bible: "Wherefore the children of Israel shall keep the Sabbath, to observe the Sabbath throughout their generations as a promise for all time. It is a sign between Me and the people of Israel forever for in six days the Lord made heaven and earth, and on the seventh day He ceased from work and rested" (Exodus 31:16-17). This seventh day of the week commemorates the creation of the world and acknowledges God as the Creator of the Universe. "The establishment of a seven-day week based on the regular observance of the Sabbath is a distinctively Jewish contribution to civilization" (Zerubavel). This seven-day cycle has also been preserved by Christians and Moslems, two other monotheistic religious groups. The

Christians chose Sunday as their day of rest, and the Moslems, Friday. How does a day of rest contribute to civilization?

People can become free from the slavery of everyday concerns on a day of rest. What are we slaves to during the week? What laws govern our human conduct? How do these operate differently on the Sabbath when, it is said, every man is a king in his home and every woman, a queen?

On the Sabbath, people prepare special foods, set a table with a white tablecloth, a special cup of wine over which a blessing will be recited, special white bread in a braided loaf (*challah*) over which a blessing will also be recited; we wear clothes other than our workday clothing, etc. And the special greeting is "Shabbat Shalom" (Hebrew) or "Gut Shabbos" (Yiddish) for the entire Sabbath from Friday evening until after sundown on Saturday. No one says "Good evening" or "Good morning," only "Shabbat Shalom." It is a greeting of warmth, welcome, good cheer, and can only be said with a smile. Can you create a greeting to use throughout the week that would do the same thing? What else has to change in order to make such a greeting work?

## Greeting for All Times

*Shalom aleichem,* the Hebrew words for "peace be unto you," is the traditional Jewish greeting. *Shalom* (peace) comes from the word that means "whole." How is peace connected with the concept of wholeness? In Hebrew sign language, *shalom* is signed by forming a circle with the hands:

1. Bring both hands up to meet in the air.
2. Then have each hand form half a circle.
3. Complete the circle by bringing both hands together in the down center position in front of you.

Create your own gesture, in your own sign language, which could symbolize peace.

## Pronunciation Guide for Yiddish Words

The spelling of Yiddish words and names are written phonetically so that each letter is sounded (including the final *e*).

| Letter | IPA | Examples |
|--------|-----|----------|
| *e* | [e] | Similar to *e* in bet; *lebn, teg* |
| *a* | [a] | Similar to *a* of father; *papir, shvartz, hartz* |
| *ai* | [ai] | Long I; Similar to aisle or high; *drai, main, dain* |
| *ei* | [ei] | Long A; Similar to grey; *shein* |
| *kh* | | Similar to *ch* in German *ach; nokh, ikh* |
| *i* | | Somewhere between the *i* of mitt and the long *e* of meet; *dir, papir* |

## Glossary for Story and Activities

*Reb* (Yiddish): A respectful form of address. A short form of Rabbi or Mister.

*Hasidic*: Belonging to the Jewish religious sect founded by Israel ben Eliezer, also known as the Baal Shem Tov (the Master of the Good Name), in the eighteenth century. The emphasis is on faith and joy in prayer through song, story, and dance.

*Reb Nahman and Reb Bunam*: Two Hasidic rabbis and storytellers.

*Tefillin*: Two black leather boxes containing parchment inscribed with Bible verses and connected to leather straps. One is worn on the left arm and the other on the forehead during morning prayers, except on Sabbath and festivals. By the act of binding and wearing the *tefillin,* the total self is bound together to worship God. They serve "as a sign . . . and as a symbol . . . that with a mighty hand the Lord freed us from Egypt" (Exodus 13:16). In other words, by wearing the *tefillin* during morning prayers, we are reminded of this event of freedom from slavery. In English, *tefillin* are known by an ancient Greek word, phylacteries, which means "amulets."

*Tallis*: A four-cornered prayer shawl with fringes worn in synagogue during morning services.

*Shabbos* (Yiddish): Sabbath.

*Sabbath Bride*: The spirit of the Sabbath is referred to as the Sabbath Bride.

*Gut Shabbos* (Yiddish): Good Sabbath. A greeting used on Sabbath.

*Shalom*: Peace. A greeting.

## Sources For "The Artist's Search"

*Nashir Shalom* (audio cassette of Jewish peace songs) and *Shiron L'Shalom* (book of Jewish peace songs), The Shalom Center, 7318 Germantown Avenue, Philadelphia, PA 19119.

"Sabbath." In *The Jewish Catalog.* Richard Siegel, Michael Strassfeld and Sharon Strassfeld, editors. Philadelphia: Jewish Publication Society, 1973.

*The Seven-Day Cycle: The History and Meaning of the Week.* Eviatar Zerubavel. New York: The Free Press, 1985.

*Souls on Fire: Portraits and Legends of Hasidic Masters.* Elie Wiesel. New York: Random House, 1972.

*Voices of a People: The Story of Yiddish Folk Song.* Ruth Rubin. Philadelphia: Jewish Publication Society, 1990.

# Papir Iz Dokh Vais

Translated from the Yiddish by Roslyn Bresnick-Perry

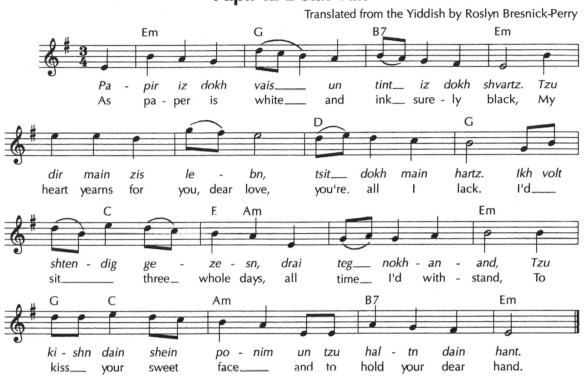

Pa - pir iz dokh vais___ un tint___ iz dokh shvartz. Tzu
As pa - per is white___ and ink___ sure - ly black, My

dir main zis le - bn, tsit___ dokh main hartz. Ikh volt
heart yearns for you, dear love, you're___ all I lack. I'd___

shten - dig ge - ze - sn, drai teg___ nokh - an - and, Tzu
sit___ three___ whole days, all time___ I'd with - stand, To

ki - shn dain shein po - nim un tzu hal - tn dain hant.
kiss___ your sweet face___ and to hold your dear hand.

# Lo Yisa Goy

Folk tune

Lō yi - sa goy el goy che - rev___ v'lō yil - m' - du ōd mil - cha -

ma.___ Lō yi - sa goy el goy che - rev___ v'lō yil - m' - du ōd mil - cha - ma.

Lō yi - sa goy el goy che - rev v' - lō yil - m' - du ōd mil - cha - ma. mil - cha - ma.

Nation shall not lift up sword against nation; neither shall they learn war any more.

## Hiné Ma Tov

Behold how good and pleasant it is for brothers to dwell together in unity.

## Ōse Shalom

May he who maketh peace in the high places
make peace for Israel and for all mankind and say Amen.

❧ ❧ ❧

**Peninnah Schram**, storyteller, author, recording artist, and teacher is Associate Professor of Speech and Drama at Stern College of Yeshiva University (NYC) and Founding Director of the Jewish Storytelling Center. As a storyteller, she travels presenting workshops and performances of Jewish folktales. Her CD, *The Minstrel and the Storyteller: Stories and Songs of the Jewish People*, was recorded with singer/guitarist Gerard Edery. Her books include *Jewish Stories One Generation Tells Another*; *Tales of Elijah the Prophet*; and *Stories Within Stories: From the Jewish Oral Tradition*.

# Living With Each Other:
## Working Together to Solve Problems

Although this story can be told successfully by one person, It works especially well when told by two. The version which follows is arranged for tandem telling. Parts for Storyteller #1 are in normal print. Parts for Storyteller #2 are in *italics*. Parts for both storytellers are in **bold print**.

# The Stubborn Turnip

A folktale from Russia
by Martha Hamilton and Mitch Weiss
Beauty and the Beast Storytellers

THERE WAS ONCE a very old man and very old woman. Everyone in the village knew them as Grandma and Grandpa.

*They had a big garden in their backyard where they grew all kinds of vegetables.*

They grew potatoes, tomatoes, cucumbers, and carrots.

*They grew green beans, and broccoli, and peppers, and pumpkins.*

One beautiful morning Grandpa woke up early and thought to himself, "I'd like to plant something different this year. Why, we've never planted turnips before." So Grandpa rushed out to the garden and planted a turnip in the ground.

*But Grandma happened to be looking out the window and she saw Grandpa plant that turnip. So she made sure to water it everyday. And both of them talked to the turnip because they had heard that all plants and vegetables like to be talked to.*

Grandpa would say, "Grow sweet and juicy!"

*And Grandma would say, "Grow big and strong!"*

And that turnip grew bigger and bigger.

*It grew sweet and juicy.*

It grew tall and enormous.

*It wasn't long before the leaves were almost as tall as Grandma.*

One morning Grandpa went out to the garden to look at the turnip. "Grandma! Come look quick, my turnip has gotten so big."

*"Ho, Ho Grandpa! Your turnip indeed. Didn't I water it everyday? It's my turnip."*

"Ho, Ho, Ho! I planted it, didn't I? It's my turnip."

*And Grandma and Grandpa got into a terrible fight.*

And the whole time they argued that turnip got bigger and bigger.

*One morning Grandma woke up early. When she looked out the window she saw a rabbit out in the garden. "Goodness, I'd better pull up that turnip before that rabbit eats it all up." So Grandma went out to the garden, bent over that turnip and grabbed a hold of the leaves. Then she pulled and she puffed and she puffed and she pulled, but that stubborn turnip would not move. So Grandma thought to herself, "I'll bet if I make up a song and dance around the turnip I can coax it out of the ground." So*

*Grandma sang and danced, "Turnip, Turnip, come on up! Turnip, Turnip, come on up!" Then she pulled and she puffed and she puffed and she pulled, but that stubborn turnip would not move!*

Later on Grandpa went out to get another look at his prized turnip. "I'd better pull up this turnip before it's too tough to eat." So Grandpa pulled and he puffed and he puffed and he pulled, and the whole time he decided to sing and dance: "Turnip, Turnip, come on up! Turnip, Turnip, come on up!" Then he pulled and he puffed and he puffed and he pulled, but that stubborn turnip would not move! He decided to call Grandma to help him. "Hey, Granny! Let's pull up our turnip together."

*Grandma smiled to herself. "Yes Grandpa, let's pull up our turnip together." So Grandma stood behind Grandpa with her arms around his waist and all the time they sang,*

**"Turnip, Turnip, come on up! Turnip, Turnip, come on up!"**

*"Oh Grandpa, this turnip is very stubborn. We need some more help."*

"Hey! Why don't you all sing that song with us. Maybe we can get it up that way."

**"Turnip, Turnip, come on up! Turnip, Turnip, come on up!" They pulled and they puffed and they puffed and they pulled, but that stubborn turnip would not move!**

*Grandma wiped the sweat from her brow. "Grandpa we need some more help. Why don't we call our grandson Alex to help us?"*

**"Alex!"**

"Oh, Alex must be asleep as usual! Why don't you all help us call Alex."

**"Alex!"**

That woke up that lazy good-for-nothing. Alex came running. He pulled behind Grandma, who pulled behind Grandpa who pulled at that stubborn turnip, and everyone sang:

**"Turnip, Turnip, come on up! Turnip, Turnip, come on up!" They pulled and they puffed and they puffed and they pulled, but that stubborn turnip would not move!**

Grandpa wiped the sweat off of his brow. "Grandma, this silly turnip is laughing at us! We need some more help. Why don't we all call our dog Ivan to help us."

**"Ivan!"**

*Ivan the dog came and pulled behind Alex, the grandson, who pulled behind Grandma, who pulled behind Grandpa who pulled at that stubborn turnip, and everyone sang:*

**"Turnip, Turnip, come on up! Turnip, Turnip, come on up!" They pulled and they puffed and they puffed and they pulled, but that stubborn turnip would not move!**

*"Oh Grandpa, no turnip's going to get the best of me!"*

"I'm not so sure, Grandma."

*"Now come on, Grandpa. Let's try one more time and this time why don't we all call our cat Sasha to help us":*

**"Sasha!"**

Sasha the cat came. She pulled behind Ivan the dog, who pulled behind Alex the grandson, who pulled behind Grandma, who pulled behind Grandpa who pulled at that stubborn turnip, and everyone sang:

**"Turnip, Turnip, come on up! Turnip, Turnip, come on up!" They pulled and they puffed and they puffed and they pulled, but that stubborn turnip would not move!**

*Just then a little mouse came along. And when she saw Sasha the cat pulling at Ivan the dog's tail, it was such an unusual sight that she couldn't resist joining in. And Grandpa and Grandma and Alex and Ivan and Sasha and the little mouse pulled with all of their might.*

Come on, give a big pull with us. [Note: Storytellers make pulling gesture and invite audience to join in.]

*UUUUUhhhhhhhhhhh!!!!!*

*And just then there was a very loud noise.*

*PPPWISSSSHHHHH!!!!!* [Note: Both storytellers make a loud uprooting sound together.]

**And the turnip came out of the ground so suddenly that they all fell down.**

Then Grandma, and Grandpa, and Alex, and Ivan, and Sasha and the mouse all got up from the ground.

*They were so pleased and surprised that the mouse was able to help them pull up the turnip that they invited her to have supper with them. Then Grandma and Grandpa picked up the turnip and dragged it into the house.*

It was the biggest

*The sweetest*

The juiciest

*The most delicious*

The most enormous

*The most beautiful*

The most remarkable

**And the most unusual turnip in all the world.**

## Follow-up Activities for "The Stubborn Turnip"

### Breaking Down Stereotypes

We once introduced this story by mentioning that it was a very old story from Russia and were dismayed to hear a first grader call out "Yecch!" It never ceases to amaze us how early prejudices are formed. However, we have been greatly encouraged by the development of "citizen's diplomacy" between the U.S. and the U.S.S.R. These cultural exchanges and face-to-face meetings of ordinary citizens hold great hope for breaking down the barriers built up by the animosity of our governments. The Americans who have been fortunate enough to travel to the Soviet Union and meet with people have found that despite the obvious cultural differences, the Soviet people share many of the same ideas, dreams, and fears that we do. When we begin to see the Soviet people as mothers, fathers, brothers, and sisters, we will be less likely to consider them as enemies.

Unfortunately, the majority of us will never have the opportunity to travel to Russia. Another way to learn about different cultures around the world is to study their folk stories. Folktales offer endless insights into a culture. By telling them to children we can make them aware of the many similarities between world cultures, and thus dispel some of their preconceptions. A perceptive fifth-grader once said to us after one of our storytelling programs in which we had told a Haitian story: "Haiti is an evil place. I know this because my Dad was in a cab in New York City, and the cab driver was from Haiti and he told my Dad a lot of bad things about the country and the government. But that was a good story you told from Haiti. Maybe the people aren't really bad."

Before telling "The Stubborn Turnip," brainstorm a list of the stereotyped ideas your students have of Russian people. For younger students you will want to discuss stereotypes and give them examples such as the evil stepmother in fairy tales or the evil witch. (For an example of a good witch, read or tell them Tomie de Paola's *Strega Nona* books.)

Once you've told them the story and let them know that it's from Russia, ask them if their view of Russian people was changed by the story. What do they think the people who made up this story and have told it for hundreds of years must be like? What does this story tell about them? Judging from this story, do the Russian people seem to be very different from us?

Some of the ideas which have come up are:

"I thought of Russian people as being mean and evil, but they didn't seem like that in the story."

"The story was funny! I never thought of Russian people as being funny before."

Continue the discussion by asking what some of the important ideas or themes are to be found in the story. This may lead to discussions on the following:

### Every Individual Counts

"The Stubborn Turnip" illustrates the idea that someone (or something) who is small can have an important effect. The mouse, in spite of her size, was the one who made the difference. This could lead into a discussion of how one small act can be either helpful or hurtful. For example, discuss what would happen if we all shrugged our shoulders and thought, "Oh, this one piece of litter won't hurt," pretty soon our playgrounds would look like garbage dumps. Little things do matter. Everyone needs to do his/her part.

You could brainstorm a list of things that kids would like to see changed in the world, and then decide on small things we can all do to work toward these changes. For inspiration, you may want to read them Miss Rumphius (by B. Cooney, Viking Press, 1982), the story of a woman who set out to do something to make the world more beautiful.

## Cooperation

Another theme in the story is the importance of working together. Everyone needs to do a small part, but we'll succeed only if we all join hands and cooperate. Plan a group project to benefit the community, such as cleaning up a local park, riverside, or nature trail. Arrange regular visits to a local senior citizen's home; have students sing, tell stories or read poems to the seniors. Encourage the seniors to share with your students as well.

## Citizen's Diplomacy

If you would like to get your class involved in some citizen's diplomacy there is an organization called *International Peace Lantern Exchange Project* that can get you started. Jim and Peggy Baumgaertner, the directors of the project, hook up American children not only with children in the Soviet Union, but also with children in twenty-five other countries. The vehicle they use is a four-sided lantern shade which becomes part of a floating lantern. They will send you a sample shade as a prototype. Your students will fill up three of the panels with their artwork. The fourth panel will include their names, addresses, ages, and a personal message of peace which they wish to send. This initial exchange of peace lanterns can lead to a pen pal relationship.

The project is culminated each year on the first Saturday in August with the "Lanterns for Hope" global lantern floating ceremony. In 1989 over three hundred cities world-wide took part in the ceremony. On that day, peace lanterns floated on the Volga River in the U.S.S.R., on the Rhine in Germany, on the Nile in Uganda, on the Mississippi in the U.S., on the Mukugawa in Japan and on many other rivers, streams, and lakes on the planet.

Jim and Peggy have dedicated their lives to promoting peace in the world. When we talked to Jim on the phone he said it is not only a fantastic class project but one the whole school can become involved in. Because they fund the entire project out of their own pockets they ask for a minimal fee. For more information, write or call: Jim and Peggy Baumgaertner, International Peace Lantern Exchange Project, P. O. Box 2876, La Crosse, Wisconsin 54602, (608) 787-0801.

ぎ ぎ ぎ

**Martha Hamilton and Mitch Weiss** have been performing together professionally as "**Beauty and the Beast Storytellers**" throughout the United States, Canada, and Europe since 1980. Their specialty is "tandem storytelling" where they combine their differing styles, swapping lines and impersonating characters to add an absorbing dimension to storytelling. In addition to a videocassette, "Tell Me A Story," and an audiocassette, "Tales of Wonder," they have written a book: *Children Tell Stories: A Teaching Guide* (Richard C. Owen Publishers, Katonah, NY, 1990. [800-336-5588]).

I found the story of Amaterasu in Joseph Campbell's book, *The Hero with a Thousand Faces*, when I was discovering goddess stories as stories of woman power. This ancient Japanese myth was first written down in the eighth century but had been passed down in oral tradition long before that. It is the sacred story of the beginning of things, a story of goddesses and gods who represent aspects of nature—the story of the struggle between the Sun Goddess and the Storm Wind God.

But I have come to realize this story is also about the whole community coming together to push back the darkness and bring back the sun. The community—the world, all of us—can bring back the light through joining together in festival and celebration.

# Amaterasu, the Sun Goddess

## adapted by Jay Goldspinner

WHEN AMATERASU ŌMIKAMI WAS BORN from the Mother of All, it was like the sun rising in the east. The golden radiance of the newborn baby dazzled all who were gathered at the birth. Izanami and Izanagi, the Mother and Father of us all, exclaimed, "She is the most wondrous of all our many children. We must not keep her here on earth. Let us send her up to High Heaven, so that she may rule in the sky."

Her father Izanagi gave her a necklace of five hundred curved jewels. The young Amaterasu put on the necklace. Then merrily she began to climb the Floating Bridge that arched between earth and heaven—for earth and heaven were not very far apart in those days.

From the Plain of High Heaven she shone down on the people of earth. As she grew, she taught the people how to grow rice and millet, to care for silkworms and to weave silken cloth. All prospered in her light, for she was the Sun— Amaterasu Ōmikami, Heaven Shining Great Woman.

Amaterasu had a boisterous younger brother named Susanowo. He was the Storm Wind, Brave Strong Impetuous Man. His father Izanagi gave the ruling of the seas to Susanowo. But Susanowo left the seas and raged across the earth, weeping and wailing and tearing out his long beard. His breath tore huge branches from the trees. His stamping feet made deep chasms in the ground. His fierce roaring leveled mountains, flooded plains, and killed multitudes of people.

The Father of All called Susanowo to him, and demanded, "What is the matter with you? I ordered you to take charge of the seas and instead you rage across the earth. Why do you weep and wail and cause such destruction?"

Susanowo answered, "I am wailing because I wish to go to the land of my mother who has died, to the distant Nether World." It was true that Izanami, the Mother of All, had died and gone to the Nether World.

But Izanagi grew angry and replied, "If you wish to go to the Nether World, then go! Be gone from here." And he banished Susanowo from the earth.

87

Susanowo left the earth. But instead of going down to the Nether World, he climbed up to see his sister Amaterasu. The seas shook and the mountains quaked as he stomped across the Floating Bridge toward the Plain of High Heaven.

Amaterasu heard him coming a long way off. She was alarmed. "Why is my brother coming here?" she worried. "He is supposed to rule over the seas. Is he coming to steal my realm?"

She unbound her long black hair and twisted it in two bunches like a warrior. She tied up her skirts into trousers. She bound her necklace of five hundred curved jewels around her headdress and around her arms. She slung her thousand-arrow quiver over her shoulder and brandished her catalpa bow. She stamped her feet and strode out to the Bridge of Heaven. There she stood, her feet planted deep in the ground.

"Why have you come to my realm?" she demanded. "You destroy all I have created on earth. Will you destroy the Plain of High Heaven too?"

Susanowo paused at the sight of Amaterasu, all ready for battle. He bowed deeply. "August Highness, Elder Sister," he said. "I come here with no evil in my heart. It is only that when our father Izanagi asked me why I wept and wailed, I told him, 'I wail because I wish to go to our dead mother's land.' Then he said to me, 'Be gone,' and expelled me from the earth. I only came to say goodbye to you, Elder Sister, before leaving on this long journey. I have no evil intentions."

Amaterasu was not convinced. She stood sternly in the way, her strung bow in front of her. "How do I know that you speak the truth?"

"August Elder Sister," he pleaded meekly. "I mean you no harm. Let us make a pledge of peace. Come, let us bear children together. That will be our promise of trust and love."

Amaterasu paused, then she relaxed and lowered the bow. "Very well," she agreed. "Give me your ten-grasp sword."

Susanowo held out the sword. Amaterasu broke it in three pieces as if it were a matchstick. She chewed the pieces and swallowed them. Out of her mouth came a fine mist that turned into three handsome goddesses.

Susanowo turned to his sister. "Give me your necklace of five hundred curved jewels," he asked. Amaterasu gave him the necklace. Susanowo chewed the curved jewels with gusto. Out of his mouth came a pale cloud, and five young gods stood there.

Amaterasu looked at the young gods and goddesses. "Those young men are *my* children," she declared. "They were created from my necklace. The young women were made from your sword; they are yours."

Susanowo shouted with glee. "Look at those delicate females—my daughters. It's obvious that my children are better than yours. Ho ho ho . . . ." Laughing uproariously, he turned away and rushed headlong across the sky, crashing and smashing everything in a wild spree.

He tore down gigantic trees. He tossed the piebald horses of heaven, the black-and-white storm clouds, down into the planted fields. He tore down the irrigation ditches and flooded out the tiny green plants in the rice fields. Worst of all he broke into Amaterasu's Temple of the First Fruits at harvest time and defiled it with piles of his own garbage. He roared at the people's dismay, "Ho ho ho . . . ." He was a gross fellow.

Amaterasu put up with Susanowo's destruction for some time, and even made excuses for him because he was her brother.

Then one day she was sitting and weaving with a woman friend in her sacred weaving hall. Suddenly there was a *crash* and the sound of Susanowo's roaring laughter, "Ho ho ho . . ." Susanowo had torn a huge hole in the rooftiles and hurled down the corpse of a piebald horse, skinned and rotting.

Amaterasu's companion screamed and jumped back. In her terror the woman fell on the sharp shuttle from the loom. The shuttle pierced her body like a dagger. She twisted and moaned on the floor, then in awful agony she died.

Amaterasu knelt wailing by her friend's body. "What a terrible violation!" she shrieked. "Even in my most sacred place my brother attacks me!" In her anger and pain her only thought was to leave the world forever. She fled from the hall and down, down into the Rock Cave of Heaven. She dragged the stone door closed and hid there.

The Sun was gone. The world was plunged into darkness. Day no longer followed night. Evil spirits roamed the earth.

Everyone missed Amaterasu and mourned for her. They called out, "Amaterasu, come back . . . ."[1] But she did not even answer.

The eight hundred myriads of goddesses and gods gathered beside the Tranquil River of Heaven to talk over how to persuade Amaterasu to return. Omohi Kane, the Great Wise God, thought long and hard and finally said, "Bring long-singing night birds to crow outside the cave so she will think it is day." They brought roosters and put them outside the cave, and the birds began to crow. The God of Strong Hands, Tajikarawo, hid himself beside the entrance to the cave.

Two gods traveled far away to the forests of Mount Kagu. They dug up the five hundred branched true sakaki tree and brought it back. They planted the tree in front of the Rock Cave. The Mountain God, Tama-no-ya, made a string of five hundred curved jewels eight feet long, out of jade and amber and rock crystal.

The goddesses and gods hung the jewels on the high branches of the sakaki tree. They hung shimmering banners of white and blue cloth around the tree's trunk. In the very middle of the tree they placed the eight-sided bronze Yata mirror, which had been made by the Metalsmith God, Ishi-kore-dome. Then all the goddesses and gods chanted and circled around the true sakaki tree.

---

1. Ask for audience participation.

Ama-no-uzume was there. She was the round-cheeked fun-loving Goddess of Mirth; she could make anyone laugh. Ama-no-uzume kindled fires in a circle to push back the darkness. She took leaves from the true sakaki tree and decorated herself with them. Then she jumped onto an overturned tub in front of the cave and began to dance—a riotous comical madcap dance. She stamped her feet and chanted and tossed off the shiny green leaves of the sakaki tree. The goddesses and gods clapped and cheered and stamped in time with Ama-no-uzume's wild dance. The sound of their laughter rocked heaven and earth.

Hiding in the Rock Cave of Heaven, Amaterasu heard the crowing of the cocks. She heard Ama-no-uzume's pounding feet and the riotous clapping and merry laughter. She was puzzled and called out, "It's dark out there—why is everybody all laughing?"

Ama-no-uzume answered her, "Because there's a brighter goddess than you out here."

Amaterasu was so curious that she pushed open the Rock Door a tiny crack and peered out. She saw her own bright face reflected in the mirror. Dazzled, she stood still and stared.

The waiting Tajikarawo, God of the Strong Hands, took her by the hand and gently drew her out of the cave. Two gods moved behind the goddess and stretched a plaited straw rope across the cave entrance. They said to Amaterasu, "This rope marks the boundary for you! We beg you—don't ever go back into the Rock Cave. Do not desert us again."

When Amaterasu emerged from the cave, the light of the sun returned to heaven and earth. Everyone cheered and shouted for joy.[2]

They summoned Susanowo before the divine council. Once again he was banished from the earth. But this time they watched to make sure that he went down into the depths of the sea.

Amaterasu Ōmikami returned to the throne of High Heaven. Everything was peaceful in heaven and earth.

## Follow-up Activities for "Amaterasu, the Sun Goddess"

### Storyteller's Note

This story came alive to me when I visited Japan in 1985. I found Amaterasu's story woven into the land and life of Japan. I visited the Great Shrine of Amaterasu at Ise, along with hundreds of Japanese people who daily throng the beautiful grounds and buildings by the Isuzu River. I visited another shrine on the island of Kyushu; there the priest told me the story of Amaterasu as if it happened in that very place. "Over there is the Rock Cave

---

2. Ask for audience participation.

of Heaven, where Amaterasu went to hide," he said as he pointed to a cleft in the steep bank on the far side of the stream.

I saw sakaki trees and "long-singing night birds" at the shrines. I saw the plaited straw rope with tassels hung over shrine entrances and tied around sacred rocks. I attended a sacred dance performance; masked and costumed figures of Tajikarawo, God of Strong Hands, and Ama-no-uzume, Goddess of Mirth, danced to the flute and drums, to entice the Sun Goddess to come out of the Rock Cave.

This ancient story of Amaterasu is part of Shinto mythology. Shinto is the native Way of Japan, which embodies a sense of harmony with the natural world and a connection with local places and historical events. The Emperor of Japan is believed to be the descendant of the Sun Goddess. The sword Susanowo gave to Amaterasu, the Yata Mirror and the five hundred curved jewels in the story still exist and are tokens of the Emperor's divine descent.

## Goddesses and Gods in the Shinto Pantheon

- Izanami (Ee za *nah* mee): the Mother of All Things
- Izanagi (Ee za *nah* ghee): the Father of All Things
- Amaterasu Ōmikami (Ah mah tehr *rahs* Oh mee *kah* mee) the Sun Goddess
- Susanowo (Soo *sah* noh woh): the Storm Wind God
- Ama-no-uzume (Ah ma noh *ooz* meh): Goddess of Mirth
- Tajikarawo (Tah jee *kah* rah *woh*): God of Strong Hands
- Omohi Kane (Oh *moh* hee *Kah* neh): the Great Wise God
- Ishi-kore-dome (*Ee* shee *koh* reh *doh* meh): the Metalsmith God
- Tama-no-ya (Tah ma noh *yah*): the Mountain God

  [Note: Japanese words are almost unaccented. Accent only slightly the italicized syllables.]

## Other Terms and Symbols

- curved jewels: comma-shaped stones carved of jade, amber, rock crystal; found in ancient burial sites.
- piebald horses of heaven: black and white storm clouds.
- Tranquil River of Heaven: luminous band of stars in the night sky, called the Milky Way by Westerners.
- long-singing night birds: roosters; still seen in Shinto shrines.
- plaited straw rope: made of rice straw, sometimes with tassels hanging down; hung at shrine entrances and doorways, around trees and sacred stones, along the streets at New Year's festival, to show the mystery of the boundary between the worlds of matter and spirit.

- catalpa bow: a weapon in the story, also used by shamans as a musical instrument of magical sound, a one-stringed zither calling the spirits. An arrow shot from the bow magically joins the two worlds.

## Discussion of the Story

The story can be interpreted on three levels: as a myth of gods and goddesses, as a legend passed down of historical people and events, and as a story of everyday people and their relationships. I have described how the story is seen as a myth in Japan. On a second level, it can be understood as the struggle for power and territory between rival leaders in ancient Japan. Amaterasu and Susanowo are the bigger-than-life counterparts of people who lived and fought in the distant past.

This is also and most obviously a story of human behavior and relationships to which we can personally relate: a family quarrel between a sister and her obstreperous younger brother, which escalates until it affects the whole community. Each of these three levels helps to explain different aspects of the story.

After telling the story of Amaterasu, it is important to discuss it with the group, to help students understand ideas and symbols that come out of the Japanese culture, and to clarify the meaning and feelings of the events.

For instance, the listeners can't really understand the scene on the Bridge between Amaterasu and Susanowo without recognizing the importance of politeness in Japanese culture: bowing, greeting, forms of address like "August Elder Sister," and the Japanese custom of giving gifts (the sword and the jewels).

Talk about the confrontation between Amaterasu and Susanowo at the Bridge. What was happening for each of them? What was the "pledge of peace" about?

Talk about Susanowo's behavior and the horrible dead horse.

How did Amaterasu's friend die? Help students understand the process of weaving on a large loom, and the dangerously sharp end of the fatal shuttle.

Why did Amaterasu run away and hide? Why did the whole community get involved?

Drawing pictures of the scenes in the story, putting them in sequence, then retelling the story using the pictures is a good follow-up to this discussion.

## Giving a Gift

An activity related to the Japanese custom of gift-giving, but on a symbolic rather than material level, is as follows:

Ask students to choose a partner; have them choose someone they don't know well. In the pairs, each one takes a turn telling the other person what s/he enjoys, how s/he spends time, etc. (not more than five minutes each). Then each person thinks of a symbolic gift for their partner, something intangible or imaginary (such as, "I give you a week at the beach," for someone who loves the ocean). In the circle of the whole group, each person says aloud their gift for the other person.

## Conflict Resolution

**Discuss and Act Out**: The argument between Amaterasu and Susanowo at the Bridge of Heaven provides an opportunity to talk about conflicts between siblings or friends. If you ask a group of children, "Have you ever fought with your sister or brother?"—you will get a strong reaction!

Ask the class to retell the argument between Amaterasu and Susanowo: what they think are the feelings of each, the offer and acceptance of the agreement, carrying out the agreement, the outcome.

- Bring out:

  What were they arguing about?

  How do you think Amaterasu was feeling?

  What about Susanowo? Why was he upset?

  Was the "pledge of peace" a good way to work out their differences?

  Was there something else that could have been done?

- Encourage students to go beyond seeing Susanowo as the "bad boy."
- With volunteers from the group, act out the scene on the Bridge.
- Act it out again, finding another scenario or solution to the problem.

**Role Play**: Divide the class into groups of two to four students. Give all the groups the same situation. Ask them to role play an argument between siblings.

For example: a brother broke his sister's bicycle (or tore up her books or tormented her cat) and just laughed when she got angry at him. His mother sent him to his room but he sneaked out and came to his sister's room where she was reading a book. What happened next?

Or make up your own scenario. Keep the problem simple and immediate, and relevant to the age group.

Each group works out a scene using the same scenario, choosing their own roles, making up a solution to the problem, and acting it out for the class. Larger groups have to create extra roles.

After all the groups have performed their scenes, discuss the scenes one at a time:

- What do you think was the problem in the scene? (Encourage them to look at the problem from different sides and different characters' points of view.)
- What was the solution? Did it work? Why or why not?

**Role Play Variation**: If you have a small class and you are comfortable with them, you might have the students (all together or in small groups) make up a conflict situation and act it out. The situation should be between siblings or friends, not between adult and child. Have them plan the scene, choose their own roles, work out a solution, act out the situation. Discuss these role plays with the group. Be aware that this exercise could bring up angry and unresolved feelings out of children's real life experiences: be prepared to deal with these if necessary.

## Celebration as a Way of Bringing Peace

"Amaterasu" is the story of the terrifying disappearance of the sun—perhaps during the rainy season when clouds and rain block out the sun, perhaps in solar eclipse—and her joyously greeted return. It is the story of festival in time of darkness, which European-American tradition recognizes in winter celebrations such as Christmas and Hanukkah, in the Carnival before Lent (celebrated in New Orleans as Mardi Gras); one boy in a class I taught even saw Easter in the opening of the cave.

**Discuss Festival**: Talk with the group about festivals, parties, celebrations, those mentioned above and others. Don't forget local festivals (town, river, harvest) that the children may know and take part in.

Ask: What do you need to have a party? What makes a celebration? Music, dancing, singing, building fires, decorating a tree or something else, dressing up (as Ama-no-uzume does with the leaves of the sakaki tree), feasting (a common element of festival not mentioned in this story). Discuss these elements of celebration. Talk about celebration as a way of bringing peace and solving conflict.

**Act**: Then have the class act out the end of the story, from where Amaterasu hides in the Rock Cave. "Call her back, everybody." All the children become goddesses and gods gathered by the Tranquil River of Heaven. Choose volunteers to be Amaterasu, Ama-no-uzume, Omohi Kane, Tajikarawo, the two gods who bring back the tree, the evil spirits who roam the earth. Rhythm instruments (bells, drums, triangles—a cymbal is great!) add to the effect and give everyone something to do. Children really get into miming the decorating of the tree. Props can be simple: chairs will work for the tree, the cave, the overturned tub on which Ama-no-uzume dances.

Acting out this scene becomes a celebration in itself. Children experience the power of rollicking festival to persuade the goddess to return, because she doesn't want to be left out. She comes out of the cave and everyone cheers.

## Make a Play

As a follow-up to these activities, one fifth grade class put on the story of "Amaterasu" as a play. With only two rehearsals and a few props and costumes (a stuffed bunny and penguin as the "long-singing night birds"—causing great hilarity in the audience, a homemade wooden sword, kimonos for Amaterasu and Ama-no-uzume, a raincoat for Susanowo, black shirts for the evil spirits, some drums and bells), this class put on the play for their whole school.

The students acted it out while the storyteller narrated the story. The play wasn't elaborate, it didn't take a lot of time, and it was a celebration for players, audience—everyone.

## Tell Another Story

The sun and the wind, in their very different natures, might be seen as opposing one another. A hurricane or any severe storm demonstrates the Storm Wind's power for devastation.

Tell Aesop's fable of "The North Wind and the Sun," to show another disagreement between the sun and the wind. Compare the contest in that story (of getting a man to take off his coat) with the confrontation between Amaterasu and Susanowo.

Another story about the struggle between the sun and the wind is the Gypsy tale called "Mother of the Sun." A Cherokee creation story about the sun is "How the Sun Came." An English tale, "The Buried Moon," tells how the moon rather than the sun is gone and then brought back by the community. Any of these stories may be told or read aloud, and compared with the story of "Amaterasu." (See *Sources and Resources* at the end of this chapter.)

## Japan

### World War II and the Bomb

The story of "Amaterasu," since it is a Japanese myth, reminds us of a time when Japan and the United States were enemies. In World War II (1941-45), American men and Japanese men, grandparents of children now in school, fought and killed each other. The United States developed the atomic bomb and dropped it on the Japanese cities of Hiroshima and Nagasaki, ending the war and beginning the age of nuclear power—with all its threats and consequences.

Two books written for older children about the horrible effects of the atomic bomb blasts are: *Sadako and the Thousand Cranes* by Eleanor Coerr, and *Hiroshima No Pika* (which means "The Blast at Hiroshima"), written and illustrated by Japanese woman artist Toshi Maruki. These books are valuable ways to explore the effect of war, especially nuclear war, and the need to prevent its recurrence. The teacher/storyteller should be aware that the pain and horror underlying these stories may affect children deeply, and be ready to help children deal with their feelings.

### Relations with Japan

Since 1945, the United States and Japan have been closely related through the postwar American occupation of Japan and ever growing economic relations between the two countries.

Children may know people who have been to Japan or are from Japan. Students in the class or school may be Japanese or of Japanese descent. Students may find stories of experiences that relatives or friends have had in connection with Japan. Students can be encouraged to seek out these stories and tell them in class.

## Sources and Resources

"The Buried Moon." In *More English Fairy Tales*. Joseph Jacobs. New York: G.P. Putnam Sons, n.d.

*The Hero with a Thousand Faces*. Joseph Campbell. Princeton: Princeton University Press, 1949, 1978, pp. 210-212.

*Hiroshima No Pika*. Toshi Maruki. New York: Lothrop Lee and Shepard, 1980.

"How the Sun Came." In *American Indian Mythology*. Alice Marriott and Carol K. Rachlin. New York: New American Library, 1968.

*Kojiki: Records of Ancient Matters*. Basil Hall Chamberlain, trans. Rutland, VT and Tokyo: Charles E. Tuttle, 1981.

*The Masks of God: Oriental Mythology*. Joseph Campbell. New York: Viking Press, 1962.

"Mother of the Sun." In *Sister of the Birds and other Gypsy Tales*. Jerzy Ficowski. Nashville: Abingdon-Nashville, 1961.

*Nihongi: Chronicles of Japan from the Earliest Times to AD 697*. W. G. Aston, trans. Rutland, VT and Tokyo: Charles E. Tuttle, 1972.

"The North Wind and the Sun." In *Aesop's Fables*, any edition.

*Sadako and the Thousand Cranes*. Eleanor Coerr. New York: Dell, 1977.

*Shinto, the Kami Way*. Sokyo Ono. Rutland, VT and Tokyo: Charles E. Tuttle, 1962.

"The Sun Goddess and the Storm God." In *Myths of the World*. Padraic Colum. New York: Grosset & Dunlap, 1972, pp. 245-248.

ʊ̈ ʊ̈ ʊ̈

**Jay Goldspinner** started telling stories to women because "we don't hear enough of our own stories." She has told stories of women and men and wondrous creatures of the earth throughout New England and across the country, anywhere from festivals to people's backyards. She leads storytelling workshops, believing we all can tell stories. Her chapter on storytelling and ritual is in the book, *The Goddess Celebrates*, edited by Diane Stein. She has an audiotape, *Rootwomen Stories*.

# Maushop and the Porpoises

retold from an old Wampanoag Legend
by Manitonquat (Medicine Story)

Now I want to tell you the story of Maushop and the Porpoises. First you should know that Maushop was a wonderful being, one of Creator's helpers, sort of a magician and a deity, who helped in creating all the good things that there are on this earth, the grass and trees and flowers, and all the little animals and birds and fish. Human beings were special favorites of his, and in the early days of the world he used to help them a lot. He taught them how to make their houses and canoes, their bows and arrows, how to fish with lines and hooks and spears, and how to make fish nets. He taught them how to make fish weirs, which are poles put down through the water into the ground with nets strung around them, so that fish would swim in and get caught. The people loved Maushop and always went to him for advice when they were in trouble.

Now Maushop had a twin brother, Matahdou, who also made things, but because he was so jealous of his brother, the things Matahdou made didn't turn out so good. When he tried to make pretty flowers and fruit, what he made were things like poison ivy and berries that are no good to eat. So he made all the things that are poisonous and dangerous on the earth. And all the things that scratch and itch and make you sick. And when they were making the fish, Matahdou made a huge fish with long sharp teeth and little beady eyes and a nasty disposition. This fish began right away to attack everything it could. It terrorized all the creatures of the sea, and when it found the people's fish weirs, it tore them apart and had a feast on the fish inside. And if any human beings were in the way, it didn't mind chewing on them too.

So the people went to Maushop and asked him if there wasn't something he could do about this terrible fish. The next time this big fish came into the bay looking for trouble, Maushop went down to the shore to talk to him.

"The people have sent me to council with you. They see that you are very hungry a lot, but they don't like it that you tear up their fish weirs and even tear up any people who may be in the water too. They wonder if they might not make some agreement so that you could get enough to eat and leave them undisturbed." Well, that's what Maushop tried to say, but before he could get very much of his speech out, that old fish just turned its back on him and began swimming out to sea where it didn't have to listen.

Now, you know, when you are talking to someone and they just turn their backs on you without listening, sometimes it makes you angry. It made Maushop so angry that he shouted at the fish.

"Hey! You! You . . . you come back—I haven't finished—Hey!" But the fish just kept on swimming, and that got Maushop so angry that he threw his spear at the disappearing fish. The spear sailed through the air and stuck right on the top of the fish's back. But that old fish was so tough and mean it didn't even stop, but

dived under the water. It managed to knock the handle off that spear, by rolling it on the sand, but the blade stayed stuck fast in his back. And that was a little help to the people, because at least they could see that fish coming by the blade that stuck up and cut through the waves as it swam into the bay.

Now Maushop went to the next largest animals in the sea around there. They were the porpoises, which are a kind of dolphin. They were playing together when Maushop found them, because all dolphins like to play all the time. When I was a little boy and sailed my boat in the bay, the porpoises always came and played around my boat. They were great fun, and good friends and teachers.

Maushop told them about the people's problem with this terrible fish, and asked them to help, because they could swim as fast as that fish. But the porpoises were doubtful.

"You don't want to mess around with that fish. It doesn't listen to anybody. It's just plain mean."

"Vicious."

"Nasty."

"Have you seen the teeth on that dude?"

"We don't have any weapons like that; besides, we're nonviolent."

"Yeah, we're into Peace and Love, that's our thing, man."

"Yes," said Maushop, "But you do have one weapon which that fish doesn't have, and that makes all the difference."

"What's that?"

"Brains. You are very intelligent beings, and that fish just doesn't have any smarts at all. In fact, it's stupid! So I know you can figure it out."

Well, the porpoises formed a circle to have a council and put their minds together. They began to think out loud. It was a regular think tank.

"Well," the first one said, "What are we going to do about this big ugly old fish? Let's kick around some ideas."

The second one said, "Well, we can't fight, that's for sure. It would just tear us apart."

"I think we should come from our strength, do what we do best," said another.

"Well, what is our strength?" said the next one. "What do we do best?"

"That's easy," said another, "what we do best is have fun. We are experts in play."

"That's it! We'll play him to pieces!" shouted another. They all got excited.

"Yeah, we'll get just keep playing with him till we drive him crazy!"

"He'll either have to loosen up and join us or get out!"

"All right!"

"Great idea!"

Because, you see, they knew that whenever you can solve a problem and do something you have to do and have fun doing it, you know you're doing right. In fact, if what I am doing isn't fun, I always stop and think about it, because probably I'm either going about it wrong, or it's not a good thing to be doing.

So the next time that big fish came slipping down into the bay looking for fish weirs, there came the porpoises! They came diving and rolling and splashing and whistling and laughing.

That mean old fish rolled its beady little eyes up at them. "Get away from me! I don't have time for your nonsense now! I'm busy! Go away and play! Idiots!"

Then the porpoises made a big circle around the fish and started singing and bringing the circle in closer and closer to him, keeping him from going where he wanted to go.

"Whatsamatter, didn't you hear me! I don't want to play. Get out of here, you clowns! Take your silly games somewhere else! I don't want any of your nonsense now!"

But now the porpoises began to run at the fish, swimming very fast, and jumping over him, landing splash right by his head, and running under him so that the point of their dorsal fins would run along his belly and tickle him. "Wooo eeee . . . *Stop that, you . . . ooo eeee!*"

And then some porpoises began to race at him and nudge him in his sides with their heads and tickle his tail. They swam over him and under him, spun around and around, and danced until he was dizzy.

Finally that big mean ugly old fish couldn't stand any more and he turned and swam as fast as he could for the deepest farthest part of the sea. And all the people who were on the shore watching let out a great cheer for the victory of the porpoises.

And you know, if you go down to the ocean even now, and you see the dolphins playing there, you know it will be perfectly safe to go in the water, because to this day there's not a shark that will hang out when the dolphins are playing because they will still drive him crazy. And that's the truth!

## Follow-up Activity for "Maushop and the Porpoises"

The teacher might have the students form a circle and address a problem, and try to solve it together in a way that might be a game and fun, as the porpoises did. Each person should speak only once until everyone has spoken, perhaps taking turns around the circle. The teacher can be part of the circle too, and help devise a game that would be fun. Then they could all play it together. This could be done with little local problems, and also with large scale problems, like creating world peace, cleaning up the pollution, or saving endangered animal species.

**Medicine Story**, elder, storyteller, and keeper of the lore, is the spiritual and ceremonial leader of the Assonet Band of the Wampanoag nation. Believing that stories can be a great force for healing, Medicine Story collects tales from many nations that illuminate common human values. He has told stories, lectured, and led workshops for many years throughout North America and Europe. Medicine Story lives in a little house in the woods of southern New Hampshire.

# The Archduke and the Wizards

## by Michael Parent

THE STAGE HAD FINALLY BEEN SET. Archduke Intrudio had pulled all the strings of influence this time. This would surely be the grandest of all the schemes he'd devised as High Councilor to King Herbert III of the Mountain Kingdom. Herbert, as he was referred to even by the peasants, had been easy for Intrudio to persuade, as usual. Queen Mavis of the neighboring Seacoast Realm had, at first, been reluctant to cooperate. Perhaps she had been unwilling to fan the still-glowing embers of hostility of the Twelve Year War—ended by treaty weeks before the Mountain Kingdom's inevitable victory and a decade before the present rulers would ascend to their thrones. When Intrudio implied that Mavis' wizard, Malcolm the Magnificent, would be no match for the great Ulric Graybeard of King Herbert's realm, Queen Mavis agreed to the convocation and to Intrudio's "agenda."

As High Councilor and organizer of grand events, Intrudio had much to be pleased with as he surveyed the scene in the royal banquet hall. His efforts had brought the great wizards to the convocation for the first time, and he gladly accepted congratulations from the gathering nobility. It was his fond wish that, after this event, his name and the wizards' names would forever be spoken in the same breath.

Archduke Intrudio smiled as he remembered his own eminent father's words. "There is no substitute for victory," Archduke Antonio had often said, and it was indeed he who had claimed victory for the Mountain Kingdom before the treaty was signed ending the Twelve Year War. Intrudio had often grown bored with the symbolic and diplomatic victories available to him as High Councilor in the tranquil era following the Treaty, which Intrudio privately referred to as "that foolish document." So he had decided to make all his victories more and more dramatic.

Queen Mavis and King Herbert were eager for the match between the great wizards, Ulric and Malcolm, that Archduke Intrudio had promoted to them as the event of their generation. Intrudio, however, had mentioned nothing about such a match in his invitations to Ulric and Malcolm. He had only requested that they present a brief talk on their recent "discoveries." It was now simply a matter of arranging things so that the wizards would do more—much more.

Archduke Intrudio, Queen Mavis, and King Herbert really wanted nothing short of a full display of the two great men's magical powers—a display they felt sure would answer the much-debated "Great Question": Which of the two wizards, Ulric or Malcolm, was indeed the most powerful? Left unspoken was Intrudio's belief that a decisive victory by either wizard (he was certain it would be Ulric) would also clearly show which of the two sovereignties was superior. In the absence of opportunities to display superiority in battle, Intrudio saw significant value in establishing potential superiority. "Even if our cannons are idle," he'd

103

often said to King Herbert, "it's best that we have the biggest cannons." Even King Herbert could grasp that a mighty wizard was far more valuable than even the best cannons.

The wizards, for their part, had come to the convocation for the opportunity to finally meet. Though each had admired the other's work from afar, neither Ulric nor Malcolm left his home or work except on rare occasions. And though they bore each other no ill will, the fact was not forgotten that the wizards' fathers had played key roles in the Twelve Year War. Most especially was it not forgotten by those who, like Intrudio, paid close attention to history. Ulric and Malcolm were gifted with many extraordinary powers, as their fathers had been, but there was little need for the more spectacular powers in these times or in the wizards' present work.

Archduke Intrudio had never understood why these great magicians, who could level mountains, puncture rain clouds, and make thunder roll, would be involved in such tame, though admittedly useful pursuits. He believed that power unused, like a muscle, quickly went to waste.

Many people had gathered that night outside the castle gates. Some had journeyed to the royal convocation to work as cooks, maids, or couriers. Most simply hoped to see one or both of the great wizards and tell the tale to their children.

Inside the banquet hall, Archduke Intrudio leaned over for a word with King Herbert when a rousing cheer exploded from the crowd at the castle gates. One of the wizards had arrived. In a moment, noble heads turned to watch the legendary Ulric fill the door of the great hall. Though the elder wizard was dressed in a flowing green robe, it was clear that he'd been given a woodsman's body. He was stocky, thick-necked, and, had he decided to pursue a career as a tree, would have made a fine oak. His thinning white hair accented a thick, bushy beard which seemed chiseled from granite. Ulric's voice had a rasping quality when he spoke softly and it burst forth thunderously when he raised it. He had long been known for spectacular feats of magic, but his genius had lately turned to the cultivation of more and better food. As Ulric approached the head table, he bowed to the King and Queen and was escorted to a seat near King Herbert.

Only moments later, the younger of the two wizards, Malcolm the Magnificent, arrived and inspired silent awe rather than raucous fanfare. He stood at least a head above most men and moved like a panther. His face would have been somewhat forgettable, had it not been for his eyes. They were deep-set and colored a striking blue that filled them with mystery and power. Malcolm had also been a phenomenal magician. But his recent renown stemmed from his discoveries of the healing powers of plants and weeds. As he walked toward the front of the hall, Malcolm's eyes met Ulric's and he extended his hand. One of Intrudio's assistants smoothly led Malcolm to the other side of the head table, near Queen Mavis, before the wizards could introduce themselves.

As soon as Malcolm was seated, Archduke Intrudio rose to welcome the gathered nobility and the two guests of honor. Then the feast began. The food was plentiful and delicious, but the meal ended rather quickly. Intrudio had eaten little and his impatience to get on with the proceedings seemed to dictate the speed of the meal. Intrudio rose to introduce Ulric Graybeard as the first speaker. King Herbert and Queen Mavis watched the wily Archduke closely to see how he would set about bending the wizards to his will. Would the great men indeed perform the wonders that Intrudio had all but guaranteed they would? If not, how would they sidestep the powerful and clever Intrudio?

The elder wizard stood and spoke in a voice that easily filled the room. He had lately been experimenting with new methods of fertilizing crops. He spoke briefly on that subject and concluded with these words:

"It is my dream, then, that one day all the good people in both realms will eat as well as we have tonight. Though perhaps a bit more slowly, I would hope. I shall conclude now as I am most eager to hear the words of my counterpart. Thank you."

Malcolm was introduced and spoke in a clear, quiet voice that seemed a whisper after the rumble of Ulric's. He scanned the room with his piercing eyes as he spoke of his research into the healing qualities of seaweed. Malcolm ended his presentation:

"This common substance, found in abundance on our shores, may well hold the key to many riddles we face in curing illness. I look forward to a blessed day when those children now dying in their mother's arms will live long, healthy lives."

Ulric joined the applause and began moving toward Malcolm when Archduke Intrudio abruptly stood to speak again.

"Fascinating, gentle Sirs, simply fascinating! I do have a small request to make, however. Though you are no doubt somewhat weary from your journeys, might it be possible to engage in a pleasant diversion for the good people here gathered before we draw the evening to a close?"

Ulric stared at the Archduke. Malcolm seemed puzzled. The air was flavored with tension and anticipation. "Perhaps," Intrudio continued, "our special guests would honor and inspire us with a display of their wizardly arts." Scattered applause added to the tension. Ulric signaled Malcolm and the two began to confer. The Archduke again drove a wedge between the wizards—"Surely, Graybeard, such a simply request hardly calls for a conference. You don't want to keep our honorable and beloved majesties waiting, do you?"

All eyes fixed on the elder wizard. "Your eminence and your majesties, since it does not please you that I confer with Malcolm, I will speak for myself alone. I will perform what your eminence refers to as a 'pleasant diversion' if the people outside the gates are allowed in to enjoy the program also. Malcolm?" The younger wizard spoke quietly and firmly. "An excellent idea, Ulric."

Intrudio had been High Councilor of the Mountain Kingdom for over two decades. He knew that it was not wise to push Ulric. A stalemate now would only mean embarrassment for everyone. "You do realize, my dear esteemed Ulric, that this room cannot possibly accommodate all those people." "Very well, then," Ulric replied, "let us stage the exhibition tomorrow, in one of the large meadows." Intrudio consulted the King and Queen and quickly turned to announce the time of the event—at the tolling of the second bell after the midday meal. The Archduke then retired to his chamber, confident that all would fall into place on the morrow.

The night was cool and windless. When the sun rose, it shone gently upon the large meadow where the grand event was to be held. It lighted the rolling hills which embraced the meadow like bulging arms and warmed awake the common folk who had spent the night outdoors. The royal platform was soon built and people began claiming their places on the ground as close as possible to the circle where the wizards would be performing.

Moments before the tolling of the second bell after midday, the Archduke, the Queen, and the King took their seats on the platform as the throng quieted. Ulric and Malcolm arrived within seconds of each other and were greeted with enthusiastic clapping and shouting. Ulric wore a maroon and gold robe and Malcolm a dark blue one flecked with orange. At a signal from Intrudio, the buglers blasted their instruments. The Archduke stepped forward. "Let this grand entertainment for the people begin."

Ulric Graybeard strode to the center of the circle, reached into his pocket and threw something to the ground. A huge cloud of blue and green smoke billowed and rose into the air. The people cheered heartily. Malcolm stepped forward, held up his right arm and produced a shrill, eerie noise. In the space of a dozen heartbeats, a large hawk swooped down, seemingly from nowhere, and alighted on his wrist. Enthusiastic applause filled the valley. Ulric waited for silence and asked Malcolm to remain there with the perched bird. Malcolm nodded and watched Ulric. The great Graybeard stepped back away from Malcolm, quickly waved his hand, and the majestic hawk disappeared. Malcolm then smiled and turned slowly with his empty hands upraised. He reached into the folds of his robe and pulled not one but two hawks out and sent them soaring over the hills and out of sight.

Intrudio smiled the confident smile of a man about to be granted his fondest wish. The wizards were surely building up to something wonder-filled and historic. Soon one of these masters of magic would do something altogether unmatchable—perhaps level one of the surrounding hills or cause thunder and lighting to split the sky. Intrudio would then secure his position in history as the man who had provided the answer to the "Great Question."

Intrudio's high spirits began to fade as the wizards continued with rather subdued manifestations of their powers. This lame display was not going to answer the "great question." Intrudio thought of the wonders and marvels his own father had described when speaking of the wizards' fathers' exploits. He became most thoroughly disturbed when he saw the wizards taking a bow and leaving the center circle. Intrudio had long known that history belongs to those who, like his own father, take hold of it. He stood and called loudly through the cheers of the throng: "*Wizards! Ulric! Malcolm!!!* (The people grew silent.) Surely you do not mean to close the exhibition without displaying the full range of your powers?!"

Ulric turned and glared at the Archduke. The elder wizard knew that Intrudio did nothing without considering every possible gain or loss to his power and reputation. "Your Eminence, you, of all people, are aware of how dangerous that could be."

"My dear Ulric," Intrudio said through clenched teeth, "I am quite confident that men of your skill, experience, and genius have complete control of your considerable powers."

"Your Eminence," Ulric replied, "there are those who would try to put a song in a bottle, the wind in a box. But the greatest powers cannot be bottled, labeled, or contained either for good or ill."

King Herbert clucked his tongue. Queen Mavis rolled her eyes. Intrudio whispered urgently to the King and Queen: "We must engage their loyalty or we will never see any marvels. Do I have your permission?" Their majesties nodded yes. Intrudio faced the wizards. "It has been decided that the greater good will be served with a full display of your powers. We are not, after all, asking you to reveal your precious secrets. Your King, Ulric, and your Queen, Malcolm, command you, as loyal subjects, to show us your best."

Ulric and Malcolm huddled in the circle and a hush rippled through the meadow. The wizards then reached into their robes and pulled out leather-bound books the size of a large man's hand. "So be it," said Malcolm, "we will now show you our absolute best. The source and secret of our most wondrous powers is contained in these." The King and Queen leaned forward in their seats. Archduke Intrudio folded his arms and waited. The people pushed in closer.

Malcolm and Ulric opened their books but did not read from them. No smoke or fire issued forth. Puzzlement creased many a noble brow, since the books contained only simple portraits. Both wizards had followed an ancient practice of drawing the faces of each of the persons from whom they had learned the world's wonders. The custom, when sharing the knowledge, was to tell a story about the person represented in the drawing. And that is what Ulric and Malcolm proceeded to do.

Ulric began by holding aloft a faded drawing of his deceased wife Margaret. He told how she had been the first to reveal to him the secrets and sacredness of the soil. Malcolm followed with a drawing of his grandfather Ferdinand and spoke of the countless times when the old man had shown him the miracles beneath the surfaces of things.

Intrudio glared sharply at the wizards, as though they were committing an act of treason.

Ulric and Malcolm continued with tales about people like Alvina the beekeeper; Andrew the planter of fruit trees; Alice the old woman who lived in the forest, cared for the birds and called them by name; Hiram, the fisherman whose love was the sea and whose genius lay in revealing its wonders. Ulric and Malcolm filled with new energy as each tale unfolded, and ended, and was greeted not with applause but with a sustained humming.

The Archduke could take no more and stood to call a halt to this "particular phase of the exhibition." This was no way to answer the "Great Question!" The wizards turned from the gathering to the platform as the royal trio discussed what might be done to get on with the "true wonders" and put an end to these "sentimental, useless narratives." Meanwhile, there was quiet movement taking place among the assembled folk. The Archduke and King and Queen ended their discussion and found only Malcolm and Ulric awaiting the results.

The people had by now huddled into groups of three and four and more. Some had made rough drawings on paper or cloth. Many had simply used sticks to draw on the ground. The stories accompanying the drawings brought forth frowns and laughter, tears and smiles.

Intrudio furiously called for his buglers. But they and the Sergeant-at-Arms had gone off to join one of the circles. He shouted for attention. But no one turned away from the drawings and the tales.

The Archduke then glared fiercely at the wizards. Malcolm calmly met Intrudio's gaze and Ulric simply returned the glare. Intrudio shook his fist at them both and stalked down from the platform. King Herbert and Queen Mavis followed him without looking at the wizards.

Ulric and Malcolm were each welcomed into one of the many circles that now filled the meadow. Darkness came and fires were lighted. Everyone, from the eldest to the youngest, had wondrous tales to tell. The earth was still and their words drifted into the cool night air.

"This is a drawing of my mother. My grandfather told me that once, when she was but fourteen years old, her quick thinking and courage saved her village from being overrun by marauders. The villagers had been warned of the coming of the brigands and were preparing for the worst. She waited, out of sight, at the well where she was sure they would dismount to drink their fill and water their horses. When they did just that, she ran toward the horse upon which the leader of the band had been riding, certain that the bags on its back held the most valuable booty. She could ride a horse as well as any man and, for the next half day, she led the marauders on a chase through the forests she knew so well until they were a very long ride away from her village and most thoroughly lost . . . ."

"My father told of a young woman he had known in his youth who was unable to make sounds with her mouth, but spoke the sweetest poems with her hands and eyes . . . ."

"I must tell you about a seemingly ordinary man who was like no other human I've known before or since. He was a shoemaker and he seemed to know every song the minstrels had ever sung. More than that, though, when he sang the sad, mournful songs, there was such a cleansing and refreshment of troubled souls that people brought him not yet worn shoes in the hope of hearing such songs . . . ."

The tales unfolded toward morning, and the moon, like a loving night mother, shone full and bright upon them.

## Follow-up Activities for "The Archduke and the Wizards"

### Questions about the Story

- Why did Archduke Intrudio arrange to bring the two great wizards, Ulric and Malcolm, to the royal convocation?

- And why did Intrudio make such an effort to keep the wizards separated during the evening of the banquet when he seemed to go to so much trouble to bring them together?

- At the beginning of the story, did you think Archduke Intrudio would get his way, provide the answer to the "great question," and thereby secure his place in history? Why or why not?

- One might easily think that Archduke Intrudio was the sort of person who was used to getting his way. How do you think he usually managed to bend people to his will?

- How about the story's ending? Did it surprise you, or disappoint you? Talk about, or write about, your reaction. Were there any clues earlier in the story that might have pointed to that kind of ending?

- Did you feel that the great wizards, Ulric and Malcolm, were weak or "wimpy" for not showing their full range of magical powers?

- What about their reasons for *not* showing their full powers? Did you "buy" those reasons or not?

- Were the characters in the story "true to life?" Were the wizards too clearly the "good guys" and Intrudio too clearly the "bad guy?" Do you think they represented certain points of view or ways of thinking?

### The Story and You

- Which characters in the story would you like to have as neighbors, as relatives, as friends?

- If you were telling someone about the story of the Archduke and the Wizards, how would you describe Ulric, Malcolm and Intrudio to them with one phrase—in your own words?

- If Ulric, Malcolm, Intrudio, Queen Mavis, and King Herbert came to your town and you could give a job to each of them, what would the job be? Explain why you'd give that job to that particular character. The job can be one that already exists or one that you create especially for that character.

- Are there people around you, or in your town, or in the news, that characters in the story remind you of? Who are they, and what are the similarities?

- Are there ways that any or the characters in the story remind you of yourself, of certain characteristics or qualities that you have?

## Circles

- Form circles of three or four people. Have each person on the circle answer the following question: "If you could invite anyone who ever lived into your circle, who would it be? Why?" Then discuss your choices and reasons.

- Within your already formed circle, draw a sketch of someone who has been important to you. Show the group your sketch and tell them something about that person. Describe their personality or talents, or influence on you. Tell a story about your sketched person that gives your group a clearer mental picture of the kind of person he or she is.

- Rotate around the room to form new groups and repeat the above activities.

## Interviews

Get a notepad and pen, or a tape recorder. Conduct interviews of classmates, friends, teachers, relatives, neighbors, people in your town, and even fellow interviewers. Remember that the following questions are only a starting point. You might think of and ask follow-up questions to clarify the initial questions you ask. You might also encourage people to answer related questions you haven't thought of asking. You could even follow a mental thread that is suggested by your interviewee's answers. You might even record your own answers to these questions. Or think of other, better questions to ask.

Some starter questions:

- What "powers" (talents, abilities, skills) do you admire in other people?

- What "powers" do you most resent or find distasteful in other people?

- What "powers" do you have that other people seem to notice? (Things you can do that not many others can.)

- Can these "powers" of yours be used in everyday life? Only in unusual circumstances? Only occasionally?

- Can a "power" you consider negative in someone ("He's a real con artist") possibly be used for a positive effect? For instance? By the same token, can a "power" you consider positive ("She's a really good leader") be used for negative effect?

- How do you feel is the best, most effective way to use your own powers?

- Do you think it's possible to fully use your own powers and not do any harm to other people? Tell of instances where this has happened or will happen.

After exploring the story and doing the above interviews, have students put together a book or a pamphlet called *Power: The Real Trip* (or the like). In this book would be essays, thoughts, poems, and stories by students on the use and abuse of power.

❦ ❦ ❦

**Michael Parent**, a Mainer of French-Canadian descent, has told traditional and original stories, in both English and French, in the US and beyond, since 1977. He has been featured at such events as the National Storytelling Festival in Jonesborough, Tennessee, and the Glistening Waters Storytelling Festival in Masterton, New Zealand. He is a 1999 recipient of National Storytelling Network's Circle of Excellence award.

Here are two classic stories about heaven and hell. To me they are wonderful metaphors for creating a strong, vibrant, healthy world.

# The Difference between Heaven and Hell

adapted by John Porcino

## The Monk and the Samurai

THERE WAS ONCE A SAMURAI WARRIOR who traveled to the distant home of an old monk. On arriving he burst through the door and bellowed, "Monk, tell me! What is the difference between heaven and hell?"

The monk sat still for a moment on the tatami-matted floor. Then he turned and looked up at the warrior. "You call yourself a samurai warrior," he smirked. "Why, look at you. You're nothing but a mere sliver of a man!"

"Whaaat!!" cried the samurai, as he reached for his sword.

"Oho!" said the monk. "I see you reach for your sword. I doubt you could cut off the head of a fly with that."

The samurai was so infuriated that he could not hold himself back. He pulled his sword from its sheath and lifted it above his head to strike off the head of the old monk. At this the monk looked up into his seething eyes and said, "That, my son, is the gate to hell." Realizing that the monk had risked his life to teach this lesson, the samurai slowly lowered his sword and put it back into the sheath. He bowed low to the monk in thanks for this teaching.

"My friend," said the monk, "that is the gate to heaven."

## The Farmer and the Angel

THERE WAS ONCE A VERY KIND AND JOYFUL OLD FARMER. He was ninety years old and, though his bones were a wee bit weary, his eyes still sparkled with love and laughter. He was the kind who seemed to know just what it took to make you smile, and when you needed to weep he'd sit by your side and hold you. He was the kind who noticed the dew sparkling on a spider's web and knew the taste of a juicy red strawberry. He was the kind who still at ninety worked hard every day on the land, and when you needed a helping hand his sleeves were rolled ready to go.

One day, because of his goodness, he was visited by an angel who granted him a wish. The angel said to the old man that anything he wanted would be his.

Now if you had one wish, what would it be? [*Note: Asked to the audience.*]

[*The teller picks audience members:*] "A million dollars!", "A castle by the sea!", "All the wishes I want!", "A Lamborghini!"

The farmer could have wished for any of these things, but instead he said to the angel, "I am happy with the bounty of food upon my plate and the love that

113

surrounds me daily, but before I die I should like just once to see heaven and hell."

The angel told him to take hold of her cloak and in an instant they arrived at the gates of hell.

To the surprise of the good man, when he passed through the gates he found himself on the edge of a beautiful open green surrounded by tall graceful pine trees. As he walked toward the middle of the green he saw many people seated around a great long table that was heaped high with the most magnificent and delicious foods the man had ever seen. Yet as he drew near he saw that the people looked sickly and thin, as if they were wasting away from starvation. How could this be? Then he noticed that the people's arms were locked straight so that they could not bend them. It was impossible for these people to feed themselves. "Achh," the man sighed, "this is truly hell."

Hastily he returned to the angel and took hold of her cloak. In another instant they arrived at the gates of heaven.

Here too the good man found himself on the edge of a beautiful open green surrounded by tall majestic pine trees. He walked toward the middle of the green and saw many people seated around a great long table that was heaped high with the most wonderful and delicious foods. As he drew near the man saw that the people's arms were locked straight so they could not be bent. Yet these people were smiling and laughing. Their eyes danced with a merry delight and their stomachs seemed joyfully content. How was this possible? The good man looked closer and he saw: the people of heaven were feeding each other! "Ah yes," smiled the good man with a knowing nod of his head, "this, this *is* truly heaven."

## Follow-up Activities for "The Difference between Heaven and Hell"

### Sources

The first is a Zen story. I learned it from the telling of several storytellers including Tim Van Egmond, whose version inspired me to add the story to my repertoire. I know of two written sources: *Zen Buddhism*, published by The Peter Pauper Press, Mount Vernon, NY, 1959; and *Zen Flesh, Zen Bones*, compiled by Paul Reps and published by Doubleday Anchor Books, Garden City, NY.

The second story, I think I first heard another counselor at Farm and Wilderness Camps in Vermont tell. I've heard it many times from many storytellers since. Sometimes instead of arms locked straight, the story will tell of a spoon or chopsticks too long to feed oneself. The written source I know of is in the book *Tales from Old China*, by Isabella Chang, New York: Random House, 1948.

## The Activities

To develop these activities, I've used the model outlined in the chapter "Stories, the Teaching Tool" at the front of the book. They are designed to work with older elementary and younger junior high, which is the youngest age I would be likely to tell these stories to. The activities are divided up according to their *goal*: *reviewing* the stories, *exploring* their teachings, or *acting* on values. At the beginning of each activity you will find the *medium*, *viewpoint* and/or *physical activity level* I used to formulate the idea.

I have used the terms teacher, class, classroom, student. Please adapt these terms for whatever group you are working with.

## Review the stories

*A) Medium: storytelling.  Physical activity: low.*

Pair up, each of you choose one of the stories. Now try telling it to your partner, taking turns being teller and listener.

*B) Medium: storytelling.  Physical activity: low.*

Try telling the story as if you are one of the characters (or a made-up character, animate or inanimate, who was present at the time). Tell the story as if it was really happening to you and you could smell, touch, taste, feel the feelings. How does it feel to be that character?

*C) Medium: drama.  Physical activity: moderate.*

In small groups define and then choose character roles for one of the stories. Put together a small play and perform it for others in the school, class, etc.

*D) Medium: drawing, coloring, painting, writing.  Physical activity: low.*

Create a full color comic book of one of the stories.

*E) Medium: puppet making, storytelling.  Physical activity: moderate.*

Make shadow-puppet characters for the stories. Then with one or more narrators telling the stories, do a shadow-puppet play.

## Explore the stories' teachings

*A) Medium: discussion.  Physical activity: low.*

Ask students questions like: What do you think is the message of the stories? How do these two stories relate to one another? Do you like what the stories teach? What does "feeding each other" mean to you?

Questions like these can be processed in many ways. Here are a few:

- Individuals can write or draw;
- Pairs or small groups can share responses with one another;

- What the individuals, pairs, or small groups have done can somehow be reported to the whole;

- A "values whip"[1] can be used, in which each person in a circle has the opportunity to give a short response to the question. The whole group hears those responses. Anyone can choose to pass;

- A "public forum" can be used where a moderator, who can be a young person, gives volunteers a chance to speak.

### B) Medium: drawing, discussion. Viewpoint: world, personal. Physical activity: low.

Have students draw two pictures: one of what "heaven on earth" looks like to them and the other of what "hell on earth" looks like to them. Let students know that they don't have to draw "well" to do this. When the students are finished, have them show their picture to one other person.

Students who wish can share their pictures with the class. The group can create a common mural with elements of "heaven on earth" from all the students' drawings. Try taking this activity one step further as described below in activity A of the "Acting on Values" part of these follow-ups.

For discussion ask, "How do we create heaven and hell in our day-to-day lives; at home, school, vacation . . .?"

### C) Medium: group challenge games. Viewpoint: personal, interpersonal.

One of the best ways I know to explore first-hand questions of community and of creating heaven or hell here and now in our lives, is to play initiative/group challenge games. These games bring many of the issues right to the surface. After a game is played, a wonderful opportunity for discussion presents itself. The playing of the game may lead naturally to the discussion of topics like: group support, trust, safety, fear (both physical and psychological), negativism, hostility, leadership, peer pressure, sexism, competition, joy, fun, or playfulness. Groups get better at playing "initiative" games the more they do them. The big challenge for students is in carrying what they learn in playing these games over into their lives. One way of doing this is by taking on a "real life" challenge for the group to solve (see activity C in the "Acting on Values" section below).

Here are three initiative games. I learned these at camp and from the books *Silver Bullets* and *Cowtails and Cobras*[2] (where you will find many more of these kinds of games).

**Touch My Can:** This is a simple, not too challenging starter game. The object is for a group of ten to fifteen participants to make physical contact with an empty soda can without making physical contact with one another.

Games like this can be adjusted to make the problem easier or harder so that they can be kept at a challenging level for different groups. If this game is too easy for a group, tell them that this first round was just a rehearsal and now they have to complete the

---

1. From *Values Clarification*, Sidney B. Simon, Leland W. Howe and Howard Kirshenbaum. New York: Hart Publishing Company, 1978, p. 130.

2. *Cowtails and Cobras*, 1977 and *Silver Bullets*, 1984 by Karl Rohnke, Project Adventure, Inc., P.O. Box 100, Hamilton, MA 01936.

task using a smaller object and/or having one person's nose touch the can. If it's a bit too hard or the group is larger, start with a bigger object.

**Diminishing Points:** The object is to have the entire group move a short distance, somehow connected to one another and with less and less "points" (hands, feet, bottoms, knees) touching the ground. (For instance, 12 people all standing on two feet have a total of 24 points.)

A good starting challenge for a group of 12 people would be to move across a small area with only 12 points (half the number of feet) touching the ground. (One possible solution for this would be to have six people piggyback six others—12 feet equals 12 points—with those being piggybacked holding hands.)

Once the group has accomplished this goal, challenge them to repeat the task with one or even two less points. Keep diminishing the number of points until the group seems to have reached its limit. Let the group's decision-making process take its own form. Only if a solution feels unsafe does the group leader need to step in.

**Bridge It:** You will need two groups. Each group will receive a box with the following props (feel free to substitute alternatives): 4 cups, 8 eight-inch-long small-diameter sticks, 1 roll of masking tape, 1 small box of Tinker Toys, Legos or blocks, 8 pipe cleaners of the same color, 1 terminology card. Also a sheet, two rooms or separate spaces, and a conference desk in another place with one chair on either side of the desk.

To set up, hang the sheet so it covers the doorway between two rooms and place props for each group on opposite sides of the sheet. The terminology cards (a different card for each group which will be used as each team's "dialect" during the conference meeting) should read something like this:

Card A: If you mean to say "tape," say "wide." If you mean to say "cross" or "crisscross," say "parallel." Instead of saying a number stick out your tongue that many times.

Card B: If you mean to say "top," say "bottom." If you want to say "side," say "under." Instead of laughing say "high, high, high . . . ."

How to play: Explain to both groups that the purpose of this game is for each group to build half a bridge on one side of the sheet so that their half-bridges meet in the middle and look as much alike as possible. Do not offer any guidelines except to say that only the props supplied can be used. Make up a story about two countries that are separated by a body of water and long-time fear and hatred. Now the two countries want to begin to establish a friendship. The first step is building a bridge across the river. The river is plagued by bad weather and almost constant fog (the sheet being the "fog"). The countries have a common language but the dialects are slightly different.

In order to establish the necessary dialogue between groups, three seven-minute meetings have been arranged (be quite strict on the timing) at a common meeting site in another room or space. As the members adjourn to the meeting room, remind them that they must not look on the other side of the sheet; offer blindfolds if necessary. Only one member from each group may talk at these conference meetings. Others watch, listen, and enjoy. These two individuals sit facing one another and attempt to communicate where and how the common bridge should be built.

The timing of the planning and building session should be:

• Both groups are shown the building props and are given seven minutes to talk over the problems of building the bridge (among themselves—not with the other group) and, if they choose to, begin constructing the bridge.

- Then the first seven minute meeting with the other group at the conference desk in another room will take place. At each meeting each group chooses a representative to act as its spokesperson. The group's representative is the only one to speak and must use the terminology card of his/her group.

- Seven-minute discussion and construction time back at the site.

- Second seven-minute conference of the two groups. (A new representative should be chosen each time.)

- Five-minute discussion and building time.

- Third and final seven-minute conference meeting of the two groups.

- Ten minutes to finish the building.

- Finally unveil the "fog" to see the groups' handiwork.

### D) Medium: role play, discussion. Viewpoint: personal, interpersonal.

Ask students to brainstorm a list of the times they've felt, as the samurai did with the monk, so mad at someone that they wanted to hit them.

Choose a few of these situations, have children choose roles, and act them out. Stop them at different points of escalation; ask students to come up with as many solutions as possible to creatively resolve this conflict. Challenge students to begin to look for creative solutions to their conflicts (The symbol for conflict in Chinese means both danger and opportunity.) See activity B on mediation in the "Acting on Values" section below.

### E) Medium: mixed. Viewpoint: world, nation, state, county, town. Physical activity: all.

Look back into history with students. Ask what peoples were forced to live in a kind of "hell on earth" (slaves, Jews during World War II . . .). To help bring young people closer to the experience of one of these populations, try creating an event with music, games, art, readings, or storytelling.

For example, let's look at the slaves in this country and their struggle for freedom. Below is a series of activities a group of us at a camp in Vermont spun together to make one indoor/outdoor evening event. Use them each separately or try the whole thing.

- Start by singing the song "Follow the Drinking Gourd"[3] and talking about the symbolism of the words in the song.

- Read a short reading from one of the slaves' lives.

- Explain and play The Underground Railway game: an outdoor night flashlight tag game.

The game is best played in a field with woods surrounding it with boundaries about fifteen feet into the woods. Players are mostly Slaves with one or two Slave Catchers.

The Slaves have to try to find their way to freedom by touching two objects at opposite ends of a playing field, which represent Safe Places along the underground railway. Once

---

3. "Follow the Drinking Gourd", traditional (arranged by Paul Campbell). Recorded on Pete Seeger's "I Can See a New Day" and Bright Morning Star's "Arisin'." In the song books *Carry It On*, *Children's Songs for A Friendly Planet* and *Rise Up Singing*.

they have successfully touched these two objects, they have to make it to a third object somewhere in the middle. This is Home Base and represents freedom. Once a player has reached Home Base successfully the game is over for that person.

Meanwhile the Slave Catcher has a flash light. If s/he points the flashlight beam directly at a Slave and calls out the correct location, the slave must go to a predesignated spot which represents the Jail. Slaves may be released from the Jail if one of the other Slaves (who has not yet reached home base) touches the Jail. The released Slaves now have 20 free seconds to move again into hiding. The released Slaves must start the game over, attempting to get to both Safe Places and then Home Base.

If most people have either made it to Home Base or are in Jail the leader rings a bell. Those still attempting to reach Home Base are given 60 seconds to get there.

The balance in this game changes depending on the number of players and the layout of the playing field. Play the game several times and adjust accordingly. If it's too easy to get to Home Base, try adding a second Slave Catcher; if it's too hard, maybe moving the Safe Places closer to the woods would help.

- Before going inside to debrief the game, look up at the stars. Find the Big Dipper and show how it points to the North Star. Talk about the North Star's importance to the slaves.

- Debrief the game by talking about how people felt playing it. Perhaps pair off students and give each five minutes to tell their story. Then bring the whole group together. Ask how they think it would have felt to be a slave trying to escape to freedom. Let the discussion flow as seems useful.

- Tell the story of Harriet Tubman and sing the song, "Harriet Tubman."[4]

- Move the discussion to the present day by asking questions like: Are there people in the world today who are facing similar struggles for freedom? Who? What are these people's stories? Can we do anything to help these people? What does this all have to do with our day-in and day-out lives? Do we behave at times in ways that put people down or keep them feeling powerless?

- Close the event as you started, by singing "Follow the Drinking Gourd."

## Acting on Values

There are so many ways to make these stories' teachings real. I like to hear the students' ideas as well as share a few of my own. Then together, if we choose, we can make one or two of these happen.

*A) Medium: painting.  Viewpoint: local community.  Physical activity: moderate.*

Take the group mural of "Heaven on Earth" you designed above. Work through the process of getting permission to paint it on a bare wall somewhere in town, and of cooperating to get it done.

---

4. "Harriet Tubman" by Walter Robinson. Recorded on Kim & Reggie Harris's "Music and the Underground Railway" and on John McCutcheon's "Gonna Rise Again." In the song books *Carry It On, Children's Songs for A Friendly Planet* and *Rise Up Singing.*

*B) Viewpoint: personal, interpersonal.*

Train a group of students to be peer conflict mediators, then start a mediators' club. Write the National Association of Mediators in Education.[5]

*C) Medium: media arts.  Physical activity: moderate.*

Create a film/video/slide show of one or both of these stories. Share it around.

*D) Viewpoint: local community.  Physical activity: high, moderate.*

Begin to make "heaven on earth." Take on a real-life group challenge that helps better the school or community: keep a park clean; collect food for the homeless; recycle all the school's cans and/or scrap paper; start a storytelling troupe that learns and tells stories in local classrooms; adopt a senior citizen as the class's friend; build a playground; paint the house of a needy family.

*E) Medium: literary arts.  Viewpoint: all.  Physical activity: moderate.*

Write a pamphlet or book called "The People Were Feeding Each Other." Students interview various people in the community, county, state, country or world who have done big or little things to help make "heaven on earth" and write about them.

*F) Medium: literary arts.  Viewpoint: all.  Physical activity: low.*

Create a book or pamphlet of collected essays, stories, poems, and thoughts that young people have written about creating "heaven on earth." Send it to children elsewhere in the world or to leaders of the countries of the world.

*G) Medium: literary arts.  Viewpoint: world.  Physical activity: low.*

Pen-pal with young people in another country. Send each other little gifts.

*H) Medium: literary arts.  Viewpoint: country, state, county.  Physical activity: low.*

Write to the President, Senate, Congress about what you like and what you'd like changed. Joining "20/20" as a class might help.[6]

❧ ❧ ❧

Each year **John Porcino** spins his colorful repertoire of tales and songs for thousands of enthusiastic people nationwide. His stories and songs celebrate our common humanity and build bridges of understanding between all people. They are sparked to life with warmth, humor, zest, and a playful touch of audience participation. Woven throughout is music played on folk instruments from around the world. He is available for performances, workshops, and in-service trainings.

5. National Association of Mediation in Education, 425 Amity St., Amherst, MA 01002 (413) 545-2462. They lead workshops and trainings on mediation for students, teachers, and community people of all kinds.

6. "20/20 Vision National Project 69 S. Pleasant St., Amherst MA 01002 (413) 259-2020. Sends information enough to write informed letters to our representatives in Washington.

# The Rainbow Child

## as told by Dr. Hugh Morgan Hill (Brother Blue)

ANGELS, ARCHANGELS, WHIRLING GHOSTS. Oh Maker, oh Shaker, oh Storyteller, Poet, Singer, Bringer, give us something wonderful, for the wonderful inside the people. Help us do something beautiful for the beautiful inside the people on this star called earth, so there will be no more war, no more hatred in the world. Oh Starmaker, oh Rainbow Shaker, we are gathered in a small room, children, a little baby, grown folks too, a yellow dog, and a cat, spotted black and white. The flames are dancing upward in the fireplace, to the stars. Oh stars, oh moon, oh night, give us a beautiful story for the beautiful inside the people. Oh people, do you know how beautiful you are? Do you know that you are jewels in the eyes of Heaven, so wonderful? Hear this story; the name of the story is "The Rainbow Child," or you can call it "Aaah," or you can call it "Oooh," or you can call it "Wonderful Times Wonderful."

Once, once upon a time ago, a rhyme ago, a nickel and a dime ago, tomorrow ago, now ago, far away, not far away on a particular star, something happened. I won't name the star, I won't name the people. They were fighting over the color of the skin, over race, over religion. So many people were crying and dying. Babies stopped being born on that star because there was so much fighting, so much killing, so much hatred. Oh, the sadness!

"Where did the babies go?" the people asked. Women became great with child, but at the end of nine months, suddenly the babies disappeared. "Where are the babies going?" the people asked, "they're not being born on this particular star." Some said the babies were flying away to a place where there is no fighting, no war, no hatred, the place where kites of many colors go when they escape in the summertime, where pretty balloons go when they fly away from children. Some said they go to the place where soap bubbles go when they fly upward in the summer air.

Oh the sadness on that star! Soon there were no children, no young people, anywhere on that star. Ah, aaah . . . . Little puppies were being born; a little yellow puppy was born. A little golden thing. A little spotted kitty was born. Little horses were born, little bunny rabbits, but no babies. Ah, ah, once more, aaah, the sadness on that star! All the doctors got together, and all the wise people, and they talked. "Where are the children going?" they asked. "Why don't they want to be born on this star? What can we do so the babies will not fly away from us?" Oooh, aaah, the sorrow!

Time went by.

On that star where there were no children, the grown folks would dream of children in the night. They would dream of children in the daytime too. They would hear music, a child singing, "Ring-around-the-rosie," you know, and "London Bridge Is Falling Down," and "Happy Birthday to You," all that sort of thing. Sometimes they heard the sound of a harmonica. Sometimes the music was soft

and sweet, sometimes loud—the way children play harmonicas. The people would reach out in their dreams, and there was nothing there. They tried to hug the air. "What shall we do?" they asked. They had meetings everywhere. People of all colors gathered, and wondered what they could do to bring children to their star. The people said, "We want to hear a baby laugh or gurgle. Oh please, please, even a sneeze, please." They all remembered when they were children. Grown folks walking down the street began to skip and hop like children at play. Sometimes they would hop on one leg. They played hopscotch and ring-around-the-rosie—all the children's games they could remember. The people played with children's toys, they jumped rope, they played with dolls, and rocking horses, and things like that. But the merry-go-round stopped turning, there was no point in merry-go-rounds without children, you know.

What to do, what to do?

Well, the wise ones gathered, and they thought, and they thought, and they thought. "What we need is more laughter," they said. "Maybe that will make the babies come to us." All the clowns gathered. They did all kinds of tricks, they fell down, and they laughed. They built pyramids, clown on top of clown. But no babies came to them. They had circuses, but no children came. Then they sent for the music makers. They brought harmonicas and flutes, whistles, all that kind of stuff, you know. And they played songs like "School days, school days . . ." and "Ring-around-the-rosie." But there were no babies, no children to hear them. They brought little ponies, and little bunny rabbits. The grown folks brought teddy bears that they had played with when they were children. "Oh please, please come to us," they said. "We'll love. We'll play. We'll laugh, there will be no fighting, no more wars." But no babies appeared, no children. In the night, in the day, the people, especially the old people, heard the sound of children laughing. But ah, ah, there were no children to hold, to hug.

And then oh, oh, once more, oh, something wonderful times wonderful happened. On that star without children there appeared in a small village a woman who was great with child. She was the color of night; she stood beneath a tree. The tree was the color of night. Her eyes shone like black stars. The people could hear a baby laughing inside the woman. Doctors came from everywhere to see this woman. They brought stethoscopes. They listened to the sound of the baby's heart inside the woman. Doctors with white hair danced to the heartbeat of the baby. Old men and women were jumping up and down like little children. They spoke to the woman. She did not answer. The old people danced around her in a circle. They played all the children's games. They sang all the children's songs. They made mud pies. They laughed.

The news went around that star.

People sent gifts for the baby, to this village. First they sent little gifts, like teddy bears, bunny rabbits, rag dolls, those kinds of things. Then the rich and the mighty sent gold, they sent diamonds, all kinds of jewels. They built a mountain of toys covered with jewels. On the top of this mountain of toys, there was a tricycle made of diamonds, for the baby. From all over, the rich and the mighty gathered to see the borning of a baby on a star where there were no children. So many came. The poor did not come; there was no room for them. The rich and the mighty spoke to the woman in many languages. She did not answer. She looked at them with her star eyes. They heard the sound inside her, baby sounds. The sound of a little harmonica. And then wonder of wonders, her body became transparent. Through the body they saw the baby, and oh, oh, the baby was changing colors. Red, white, brown, yellow, green, blue, purple. Aaah! The clowns danced around the woman and her baby. The people brought their harmonicas, flutes, and pennywhistles, and they played songs they remembered from their childhood, and they danced. They recited old nursery rhymes like "London bridge is falling down, falling down . . . ," "Little Jack Horner sat in a corner . . . ," "Old Mother Hubbard went to the cupboard . . . ." They said, "Once upon a time there were three bears . . . ." They spoke of "Alice in Wonderland," and stuff like that. But the poor were not invited.

At the top of this mountain of toys, on the top of the tricycle made of diamonds, someone placed a diamond that shone like white fire. It was the most expensive, most beautiful, most wonderful, biggest diamond on that particular star. When this diamond was put on this pile of toys, suddenly the people heard a little cry. All the light went out of the night. The stars stopped shining, the light of the moon went out. The light inside the woman who was great with child went out. The people could not see the baby inside the woman anymore. The doctors put their stethoscopes to the woman's body and they did not hear a sound. No heart beat. No music. Oh. The grief! The people began to cry. A dog began to cry. A little cat began to cry. The ponies began to cry. The stones began to cry. The stars, the sea began to cry. The woman beneath the tree, the woman with eyes like black diamonds was crying too. Her tears were the color of night.

"What to do, what to do? We've lost the baby."

Into the crowd of weeping people came a woman. She was poor. She was ragged. She had walked to this village from far away on bare feet. She brought bread to the woman. She put a piece of bread in the mouth of the woman who stood beneath the tree, the tree that was the color of night. And without speaking, she said, "I love you," with her body, with her eyes. And she broke the bread in little pieces and fed all the people who were crying. A light came into the eyes of the woman who stood beneath the tree. The stars began to shine in the night sky, and the moon began to shine. And the people heard the sound of a baby inside the woman under the tree of night. And they began to dance again. The woman who was great with child spread her legs and began to dance. And the stars danced, and the moon, and the wind, the trees, all the creatures beneath the stars. All night they danced. At the breaking of the day, at the first morning light, a baby was born. The baby was wrapped in many colors. The baby's skin was changing from white to yellow to green to blue to brown, to all the colors in all the rainbows. The baby's eyes were changing colors, too. The little baby gurgled. Out of the child's mouth came a rainbow bubble. Aaah! It rose up into the sky. The people said, "Oooh, oooh, we love you. You are so beautiful." And suddenly from the sky came babies, so many babies. They began to fall into the arms of the people, all the babies who had flown away before. They were many colors. Some were blue, some were green, some were striped, some were polka dot. Everyone caught a few. And all the pretty balloons that had flown away in the summertime fell into the people's arms, and the many-colored kites that had flown away. Ah, that was a borning, that was a rainbow morning, you might say. The people threw away all their weapons. No more war. How could they kill these beautiful, these wonderful babies, wrapped in so many colors. It's true, it's true. Once upon a time ago, tomorrow ago, now ago, not far away, on a particular star, people fell in love with life. They loved all babies. That was a rainbow borning, a new morning on that star. I won't name the star.

What should we call this story? "Wonderful Times Wonderful, Once More Wonderful"? Or should we call it "Aaah"? It could happen. Oh sweet ones, it's up to me and you, what we do. If not me and you, who? If not here, where? If not now, when? Let's fall in love with life, with babies of every color. A baby is a kiss from heaven wrapped in rainbows, don't you know. We'll catch them in our arms, in our hearts, too. Oh dear ones, every baby that comes into the earth is some kind of wonderful.

Once upon a time ago, a rhyme ago, a nickel and a dime ago, tomorrow ago, now ago, aaah . . . .

Dear little baby, we love you.

That's true.

That's true inside of true.

Aaah!

Oooh!

Peekaboo!

## Follow-up Activities for "The Rainbow Child"

### Review the Story

- Discuss the images brought to mind by the story, and make illustrations for the story. They could be drawings, water colors, paper cutouts, or whatever you like. Hang them up and use the opportunity to talk about "ways of seeing," and the use of different media for expression.

- Simplify the story to the key elements and turn it into a play to perform in your school or church or club. One person might narrate and the others act out the story, or you might decide to do it as a puppet show. If you don't have costumes, be creative: you might use water colors or different color stickers to indicate people of different skin colors, people of different economic classes, and the animals. Be sure to leave some time to talk about its meaning.

## How Do Small Differences Become Important?

- Split the students into two or more groups by an arbitrary characteristic, perhaps by the colors of their eyes or their hair or their socks. One group gets more, or different, privileges than the other—perhaps one group draws pictures with crayons while the other draws pictures only with black pencils, or in a game of kickball one team gets three outs while the other team only gets one. After playing, how do the kids feel about this? When we have conflicts due to differences, how do we solve them?

- Each student gets a balloon. The students are the "adults", and the balloons are the "children." Only "children" of the same color are allowed to play together. Select a King or Queen of Balloon Country. The Ruler wants to see a mixture of colors (children) playing together, so the Ruler takes all the balloons away since they will not play together. The people are unhappy. They miss the balloons (the children). The Ruler asks the participants to close their eyes and accept whatever balloon is given to them. When they open their eyes, how do they feel about having a different color balloon? How do they feel about the mixture that is now in their group? They will discover that all balloons are soft and wonderful.

- List on the blackboard or on a large newsprint pad the differences, external and internal, that separate people, e.g., wearing eyeglasses versus not wearing eyeglasses, being athletic versus not being athletic, being rich versus being poor, etc. How does it make you feel about these different kinds of people?

## The Meaning of the Story in Your Life

- There are questions about material abundance and luxuries versus what is really needed both materially and spiritually. Talk about what you have that you really need and some things that you like a lot, but don't really need. Relate this to how you are affecting the environment: energy sources, the trees of the rainforest, etc.

- What is a gift? What is the meaning in the story of the gift of bread and why is this gift different from the tricycle made of diamonds?

- How does the story relate to the issue of integrated housing, or even busing to school? How do you think about or talk about or relate to people, especially in other parts of the world, who look different or are culturally very different?

## Allegory

What does the story try to say about the ways in which people can behave? What does it try to show about people's desires and hopes for the future, and the ways people can feel about each other? What does it try to teach about how the different people sharing the planet must relate to one another? Do you think the metaphors in the story are apt?

## Celebrating Cultures

Create a fair or celebration of world cultures. Groups of students can be assigned, or choose, particular cultures. They can research food, clothing, arts, dance, traditions and other things that make their culture special. The students could create displays, food booths and performances. A class could do this for the school, or the school could do it for the community.

❧ ❧ ❧

**Brother Blue** (Dr. Hugh Morgan Hill) has been called "the world's greatest storyteller," "the father of modern storytelling." He holds degrees from Harvard, Yale, Union Graduate School. He tells Shakespeare, classics, and original stories in the streets, prisons, churches, schools, colleges, radio, television, and in many countries. He is the official storyteller of Cambridge, Boston, and the United Nations Habitat forum, the founder of the Harvard Storytelling Workshop, a member of the Oral History Association, and the first founding member of the Association of Black Storytellers.

# Nyangara

## as told by Peter Amidon

ONCE UPON A TIME a long time ago there was a Chief who was loved by everyone in his village. One day the Chief got sick. He took to his hut, he lay down on his mat. He got sicker and sicker. So he called the men of the village into his hut and said, "My men, I am so sick that I am afraid I will die unless you can get my doctor." "We'll get your doctor," said the men, "Where is he?" "Next to the village up on top of the hill is a cave. Inside the cave lives a python snake named Nyangara. He's my doctor." "A snake is your doctor? Well, we'll bring him to you. How do we do it?"

So the Chief told the men how they must fill a pot with beer and bring it up to the cave as a gift from the Chief. He taught them the magic song with which to sing the python out of the cave. He told them to let Nyangara drink the beer and then bring him down to the Chief's hut. The men did just as the Chief said. They filled a pot with the village beer and took it up the hill next to the village. On top of the hill they found the cave. They looked into the cave and saw nothing but dark blackness. The men stood outside the cave and sang the magic song:

> *Nyangara chena, Nyangara chena*
> *Nyangara chena, Nyangara chena*
> *Nyangara chena, Nyangara chena*
> *Nyangara chena, Nyangara chena*

They stopped singing and waited. Then, out of the mouth of the cave came the huge head of the python snake. He was all coiled up inside the cave. As he came out towards the men he uncoiled one coil, two coils, three coils. The men were so scared that the one who was holding the pot of beer dropped it onto the ground. The pot broke into a hundred pieces and the beer ran all over the ground. The men all turned and ran down the hill. They ran back to the village. They went into the Chief's hut. They said, "Chief, Chief, we couldn't bring Nyangara down from his cave on the hill. Is there anything else we can do to make you better?"

"No," said the Chief, "Only Nyangara."

The children in the village started wondering why the adults were acting so strange. The children noticed that the adults had stopped singing and dancing. The adults spoke with each other solemnly, in hushed tones. They hardly talked with the children at all. The children decided to ask the one person they loved the most. The children loved the Chief more than anyone else, because the Chief always answered all their questions. So the children ran into the Chief's hut and said, "Chief, Chief, what's going on? The adults have stopped singing and dancing and they won't tell us a thing."

"Ah, children," said the Chief, "It's because the men couldn't bring the python snake, Nyangara, my doctor, down from his cave to make me better, and now I'm going to die."

"What?" said the children. "The men couldn't bring you your doctor? We'll do it. We'll bring Nyangara down to you."

"No, no, children," said the Chief, "You have to be strong and brave."

"Strong and brave? We're strong and brave! We can do it! Just tell us what we have to do."

So the Chief told the children the same as he'd told the men.

He taught them the magic song. The children ran out of the Chief's hut and got another pot. They filled it with the village beer. They climbed up the hill; there was the cave. They stood around the cave and sang the magic song:

> *Nyangara chena, Nyangara chena*
> *Nyangara chena, Nyangara chena*
>
> *Nai-we Nyangara-we, We want to see you Nyangara*
> *Nai-we Nyangara-we, Our Chief is dying Nyangara*
>
> *Nyangara chena, Nyangara chena*
> *Nyangara chena, Nyangara chena*
>
> *Nai-we Nyangara-we, Ta zo ku wona Nyangara*
> *Nai-we Nyangara-we, Mambo wedu wofa Nyangara*

They stopped singing. It was quiet. Then out of the mouth of the cave came the huge head of the python snake. As he came out, he uncoiled one coil, two coils, three coils. The children were so scared that their bodies felt like turning and running down the hill. But they said to their bodies: "Be still! Be still." And they stood there as Nyangara looked at all those children and sang to them:

> *Kwire chinyere. Kwire chinyere.*
> *Some men came here yesterday.*
> *They broke the pot and ran away.*
> *Kwire chinyere. Kwire chinyere.*
> *They broke the pot and ran away.*
> *Will you also run away?*
> *Kwire chinyere. Kwire chinyere.*

The children stayed right there and sang back to the snake:

> *Nyangara chena, Nyangara chena*
> *Nyangara chena, Nyangara chena*
>
> *Nai-we Nyangara-we, We want to see you Nyangara*
> *Nai-we Nyangara-we, Our Chief is dying Nyangara*
>
> *Nyangara chena, Nyangara chena*
> *Nyangara chena, Nyangara chena*
>
> *Nai-we Nyangara-we, Ta zo ku wona Nyangara*
> *Nai-we Nyangara-we, Mambo wedu wofa Nyangara*

When the children stopped singing the second time, Nyangara continued coming out of the cave. He uncoiled four coils, five coils, six coils, seven, eight, nine, ten coils. He was completely out of the cave. He slithered right up to the children. Right onto the first little boy's feet. Right up his legs. Right up his chest and over his shoulder and onto the shoulder of the little girl behind him, and onto the shoulder of the little boy behind her, and on over all those children's shoulders. The children stayed absolutely still. Nyangara came to the last little girl who was holding the pot of beer, and she watched the python's huge head come right down into the pot and drink all that beer.

Then, slowly and carefully, the children carried Nyangara on their shoulders down the hill, back to the village, and right up to the Chief's hut. The Chief looked up from his mat and said, "Oh children, you've brought Nyangara."

Then Nyangara slithered off the children's shoulders onto the floor of the hut and up to the Chief's mat. And Nyangara licked the Chief's feet. And he licked the Chief's legs and body and arms. And he licked the Chief's head. And when he was done the Chief got up off his mat and stood up and said, "Thank you Nyangara. Thank you children, I feel much better."

Then the children took Nyangara back up on their shoulders and carried him back up the hill to his cave. And the children brought Nyangara a roasted ox, from the Chief, in thanks. And when the children came back to the village, the Chief ordered that another ox be roasted. "But this one," said the Chief, "This one is for the children, and only the children. For they are the ones who brought my doctor Nyangara down to make me better. The children. They are the ones who were brave and strong."

And that's the story of Nyangara.

## Follow-up Activities for "Nyangara"

### Source

I learned this story from my wife, Mary Alice Amidon, who'd learned it from Connecticut storyteller Sara deBeer. Sara learned it from a written source as collected from the Shona people of Zimbabwe and retold by ethnomusicologist and storyteller Hugh Tracey. The story has developed and changed, as stories do, through transmission, from storyteller to storyteller. Hugh Tracey's retelling and Andrew Tracey's music transcription can be found in the collection of world folktales entitled *The Singing Sack*: book and audio tape published by A & C Black, London.

### The Music

The song, transcribed by Andrew Tracey, is in the Karanga dialect. The men's song is the simple chant. The children's song can be done by having the audience sing the chant as the storyteller sings the other line over the chant, or the lines can be sung one after the other. "Nyangara chena" translates to "Nyangara, come out." You may choose to sing the song in just the Karanga dialect, or to sing in the alternating Karanga and English that I've notated.

## The Men's Song

## The Children's Song

## The Telling

Timing and pacing are important in this story. I leave a pause after the men sing their song and then I say, "They waited." I deliver slowly the lines about Nyangara coming out of the cave. I use my hands, one for Nyangara and one for the little boy, to help focus the scene where the python climbs up the first little boy. I give the Chief a sick and weak voice until he gets better. I had to practice a bit to come up with a python voice for the Kwire chant. As I chant it I look at all the children, snake-like, from side to side.

I have found some people concerned about the lack of women in this story, suggesting that I might, or asking if they may change the men to women, or at least have it be a mixed group in retelling the story. In the culture of the Shona people of Zimbabwe, the Chief would have been dealing only with the men of the village in this situation. I would suggest that you follow your conscience in changing genders in this and other folktales, balancing cultural and literary integrity against what you might perceive as sexism in a story. You can use the same standards in deciding whether or not to change the beer in the story to another kind of drink.

## Discussion

I try not to be directive in my facilitating the children's discussion of the story. If there isn't spontaneous discussion after the story I might ask an open-ended question like: "What was your favorite (or scariest, funniest, happiest) moment in the story?" (I learned these follow-up questions from Laura Simms.) Different children have different answers and all answers are correct. To each of their answers I respond, "Thank you," rather than "Great!" or "Oh really?" so children do not feel their answers are being judged. When the children talk about the men being more scared than the children I ask them why the men ran and the children didn't run. Any questions they ask me I put back to the group. They make wonderful connections and the story starts to become theirs.

I always tell the children to be sure to tell the story out loud sometime that day before they go to sleep. I ask, "Who can you tell it to?" The answers come tumbling in: "My parents, my sister, my dog, a tree, my pillow, myself." "Yes, yes, yes," I answer. If they say they won't be able to remember how the story goes I say, "Really? Let's see: Once upon a time there was a . . ." and let them fill in the blanks throughout the story. I help them remember the important elements, such as the pot of beer and the magic song. We practice the songs, but I give them permission to just say, " . . . and they sang the magic song," if they prefer.

## Activities

The most effective way I've found to make the story the children's own is to act it out as a group. I'll suggest two of the many ways to do this:

Divide the children into groups and send each group to a separate space to work out their version of acting out the story. Then have them come back together and perform each of the renditions for each other. These small group performances will be a celebration of different solutions to acting out the story. The narrating role may be taken by one child, shared by the group, or omitted. The children will come up with colorful variations in language, movement, use of props, and characterization.

You can also act out the story with the whole group at once. Everyone sits in a bunch on the floor as the audience, facing an empty floor space which is the stage. This is a good moment for discussion of the vital role of the audience. I like to bring out the audience's responsibility to be involved in the story. Then you choose volunteers for the beginning of the story: the sick Chief and the village men. Then you, the director, announce: *"The Story of Nyangara: Scene One. Once upon a time . . ."* and the children mime your narration. Since they already know the story, the children will often know just what to say and do. When you change scenes, inactive characters can rejoin the audience, and you can enlist new characters from the audience. Children can also be scenery, doors, gates, trees, and animals in the story. Once you've modelled the directing role, you might let children direct the group in a similar fashion.

Nyangara is a great story to include in a unit on Love and Bravery. You could act it out with the whole group as described above, but, when you come to the part where the men are scared and have dropped the pot of beer, you could stop the story and have a brainstorm. Put up a sheet of paper and have the children imagine themselves in the men's position. Then have them respond to one question at a time:

- What are the men thinking?
- How do they feel?
- What are their options?

The children should feel safe to say anything. They blurt it out and you write it down after a verbal thank you and no other comments. Repeated ideas get written down again. After the brainstorm you could facilitate a discussion, asking children to clarify any ideas you don't understand and letting the children make their own insights and connections. (Thanks to Devid Levine for this brainstorming technique.)

Then continue acting out the story until you come to where the children in the story are scared. Do the brainstorming over again with the same three questions followed by discussion which could now include similarities and differences between the men's and the children's thoughts, feelings, and options.

This activity could be a model for brainstorming/discussion sessions on fear, love and bravery as found in literature, local and national news, and in your own lives. You and your students could start collecting personal, literary, and news stories on bravery. Be sure to include "small" daily acts of bravery such as telling a friend that you don't like to be teased or confessing to an adult that you've scratched the finish on the new car. The brainstorming exercise might result in similarities between these daily acts and more dramatic examples of bravery.

To these activities of storytelling, story collecting, drama and discussion you can add the very important activity of the group doing loving and brave acts in the community: visiting a nursing home, acting on local environmental concerns, or learning and using real-life conflict resolution techniques for peer interaction in and outside of school.

❧ ❧ ❧

**Peter Amidon** left twelve years of elementary school music teaching in order to devote more time to telling stories, teaching and leading traditional dance, directing a children's choir, and performing with his family. He performs concerts of songs and stories by himself and with his wife Mary Alice Amidon and their sons Sam and Stefan in schools, libraries, teacher conferences, and at most of the major music and storytelling festivals in the northeast U.S.

# Living With Each Other:
## The Problems of Working Together

# Showdown at Pangaea Creek

by Michael R. Evans

In the small prairie town
Of Pangaea Creek
Life, it was hard
For the timid and meek.

> For there lived in this town
> Two outlaws so mean
> They could stare at chameleons
> And make them turn green.

Now the outlaw named Hank
Said, "I own this town,
And any fool who denies it
They'll find six feet down."

> But the outlaw named Frank,
> He said, "I'm in charge,
> And any fool who denies it
> Had better be large."

So they faced off on Main Street
One dark, chilly night,
To prove to the death
Which outlaw was right.

> Two hundred townsfolk
> Were lining the street
> To see which of the outlaws
> Would die in defeat.

Hank took a step forward
And Frank took one, too,
Then, smiling, Hank pulled
A small knife from his shoe.

> Frank looked at the knife
> And, still quite unafraid,
> He pulled out a dagger
> With a 13-inch blade.

Well, Hank moved in closer
And gritted his teeth,
And he pulled a long sword
From its black leather sheath.

> Frank smiled when he saw that
> And vowed to survive—
> And he drew from its holster
> A Colt .45.

Well, the distance between them
Was getting small fast
And the townspeople braced
For the opening blast.

> But Hank wasn't finished
> He still had some tricks
> And he pulled from his shirt
> Seven dynamite sticks.

He ignited the fuse
And he said with a hiss,
"OK, Mr. Outlaw,
Let's see you top this."

> Well, Frank didn't falter—
> He had nothing to lose.
> He pulled out eight more sticks
> And lit the short fuse.

Nose to nose, they just stood there,
Explosives held high,
And two hundred townsfolk
Prayed not to die.

> They were tall people, short people,
> Fat people, too,
> They were men, they were women,
> They were me, they were you,

They were neighbors and relatives,
And everyone knew
That their lifetimes would end
When that night was through.

> All because of two outlaws
> Too stubborn and blind
> To put down their greed
> And leave bygones behind.

But the fuses grew shorter
The end, it was near,
And neither old outlaw
Displayed any fear.

> They just stood there and scowled
> And stared, eye to eye,
> And somewhere in town,
> Someone started to cry.

Then, as two hundred townsfolk
Prayed in the dark,
Hank reached his hand up
And snuffed out his spark.

He threw all his dynamite
Down to the ground,
And he shouted to everyone
Standing around.

> He said, "Let it be known,
> If just one soul survives,
> It was Frank who destroyed
> All you townspeople's lives."

Well, Frank's face grew pale
As he looked up and down
At the parents and children
Who lived in that town.

> And the parents and children
> Just trembled and stared.
> They were white-knuckled, weak-kneed,
> Exhausted, and scared.

Well, he snuffed his fuse, too,
And he threw down his sticks,
And he said, "Listen up,
All you prairie-town hicks.

> If it's peace that you want,
> Well, I've hardly begun!"
> And he threw down his .45
> Caliber gun.

Well, Hank stared in wonder—
Then his sword hit the ground!
To the townsfolk, that clank
Was a heavenly sound.

> Then the two threw down bullets,
> And daggers, and knives,
> And the townspeople cheered—
> They'd escaped with their lives!

Well, the outlaws, they're gone now,
They left not a trace,
Those two men who started
Pangaea's Peace Race.

> And Pangaea Creek's thriving,
> And it's known all around
> That you leave your guns home
> When you visit that town.

All because of two outlaws
Who met long ago,
Who both had the wisdom
To simply say "No."

# Follow-up Activities for "Showdown at Pangaea Creek"

## Exploring Conflict I

1. The listeners name some conflicts that happen in real life. The conflicts could range in scale from two people wanting to be the pitcher on the softball team all the way up to military conflict. The conflicts are listed on a blackboard or piece of paper.

2. Two listeners come forward and select one of the conflicts. One takes one side of the issue, and the other takes the opposite side.

3. They act out their conflict—how it got started, how it escalated, how the two sides grew further apart and more aggressive.

4. They act out one possible ending: the result of continued escalation. It could end in refusal to speak to each other, it could end with blows, etc.

5. Then they act out the conflict again, but at some point one of them de-escalates the confrontation. They show how the dispute could be resolved in a cooperative way.

6. Other listeners do the same with other conflicts from the list.

## Exploring Conflict II

1. The same procedure is followed as in the first activity, but this time only the de-escalating version is presented.

2. The other listeners discuss and try to identify the "turning points"—the first step in the escalation and the first step in the de-escalation. How were they done? How successful were they?

3. In "Showdown at Pangaea Creek," what are the escalation points? What are the de-escalation points? At what other points could the showdown have been resolved peacefully?

4. Draw parallels between the conflicts acted out by the group and the conflict in "Showdown."

## Exploring Conflict III

1. A list of conflicts is prepared as in the first activity.

2. A pair of listeners selects one of the conflicts and secretly decides whether to present an escalating or a de-escalating version.

3. The other listeners watch as the two act out their conflict and try to guess out loud—and as quickly as possible—whether the conflict is escalating or de-escalating. The opinions are gathered as the action continues.

4. Once it is apparent whether the conflict is escalating or de-escalating, the action stops and the group discusses their opinions and what shaped their guesses. They also discuss how the action might have gone in the opposite direction.

## Cooperative Games

The group creates games that are based on cooperation rather than confrontation. Can a softball game be devised in which everybody's goal is to get as many people around the bases as possible? Can "tag" or "hide and seek" be done in a cooperative way? Can games be altered so that the object is to beat the clock rather than the other team? This activity could lead into the playing of "Blob Tag" or some other New Games.

## Mediation

1. Bring in a mediation team. Ask them how they work to solve conflicts. Talk about listening skills—how to listen actively, restate the other person's position in your own words, ask questions, etc. Talk about language and the difference between an information-gathering question and a reaction-provoking question. ("Could you explain that again for me?" vs. "What's that supposed to mean?") Talk about role reversal and other methods of bringing two sides closer together.

2. Form a mediation team within the group. Emphasize that the role of the team is not to judge or issue an opinion but rather to ask questions, clarify issues, and encourage communication. The team, which could be made up of different group members on a rotating basis, could consider conflicts that arise within the group and help both sides resolve the problem.

(Many communities have local mediation teams. For more information on mediation, contact the National Association for Mediation in Education, 425 Amity Street, Amherst, MA 01002.)

❦ ❦ ❦

**Michael R. Evans**, a writer and storyteller from western Massachusetts, wrote this story for a benefit performance that raised money for peace organizations. He enjoys writing the stories he tells, although he also tells some traditional favorites. A member of the Western New England Storytellers Guild, he lives and writes in a 200-year-old house that he is restoring with his wife, Joanna.

# The Gossip

### a midrash retold by Marcia Lane

THERE WAS ONCE, in a small village, a man who was a terrible gossip! He always had stories to tell about his neighbors. Even if he didn't know someone, he still had something to say about them.

Well, the New Year was coming, and the man decided to make a fresh start. He went to the Rabbi.

"Rabbi," he said, "I feel bad about the gossip and the rumors I've spread. I really want to make amends. Please tell me what to do to atone."

The Rabbi thought for a minute, and then he said, "I'll tell you what you must do in order to put right the damage you've done. But you must follow my directions exactly . . . no questions! Do you understand?"

"I promise, Rabbi. I promise I'll do just what you say."

"Good," said the Rabbi. "Now, go to the market and buy a fresh chicken. Then bring it here to me as fast as you can. But mind," warned the Rabbi, "that you pluck it absolutely clean. Not a single feather must remain."

Well, the man could not imagine what the Rabbi wanted with a chicken, but he'd promised not to ask questions, so off he went as fast as his legs could carry him. He got to the market, purchased the best chicken he could find, and started running back to the Rabbi's house, plucking off the feathers as he ran. Furiously he plucked until, when he got to the Rabbi's door, not a single feather was left.

Out of breath, the man handed the chicken over to the Rabbi, who turned it over and over until he was satisfied. Then he turned to the man and said, "Now bring me all the feathers."

"But Rabbi," gasped the man, "how could I do such a thing?! The wind must have carried those feathers so far, I could never find them all!"

"That's true," said the Rabbi. "And that's how it is with gossip. One rumor can fly to many corners, and how could you retrieve it? Better not to speak gossip in the first place!"

And he sent the man home to apologize to his neighbors, and to repent.

## Follow-up Activities for "The Gossip"

## Discussion

Discuss how it feels when someone spreads a story about you. How does everyone respond when you try to find out "who said that?" It almost seems that a rumor, once started, has a life of its own.

## Rumor Seeds

1. Give a deck of cards to one student (you can also use blank pieces of construction paper to make this activity go faster).
2. That student takes one card, splits the deck, and gives the two halves to the next two students. This continues until everyone has one card.
3. The first student then collects all of the cards. They must be collected one at a time, and s/he must ask each person for it. It is possible that some students may not want to give the collector the card.
4. Compare how quickly the cards were handed out to how slowly they were retrieved. How is this like rumors? If the cards were a rumor, what would have happened if someone didn't want to give their card back (i.e., didn't want to apologize or say that the rumor wasn't true)?

## Telegram

Have students sit in a circle. The teacher chooses one student's name at random (without telling the group who it is), and whispers a "rumor seed"—it should be something factual and innocuous; for example: Ellen is wearing red socks today. Then the student whispers it to the next child, and so on around the circle. The last child has to say the sentence out loud. The rules for this exercise are: 1) No repeating, and 2) Say what you think you heard—no changes.

Extension: You can take this activity one step further and make it more real for your students by verbally spreading a rumor during the school day. To ensure that each child gets a turn, each student will be assigned a number. At some point during the day, the teacher whispers something into a student's ear. S/he passes it on to the person with the next number until it comes back to the teacher. (You can start with any person. When the rumor gets to the last number, it goes back to number one).

## Integration Activities

You may want to have students act out small skits depicting how rumors are spread and discuss how people in the skit felt.

What are some ways to prevent rumors from being spread? Make a list. Students can make posters or cartoons depicting rumors being spread, how they affect people, and how they can be prevented.

## Fact or Fiction?

1. The teacher creates a list of statements, some of which could be rumors and some of which are statements of fact. For example, "Susan wore a red dress to school for two days" is a statement of fact. "Susan wore a red dress to school for two days, so she must be poor" is a rumor. "He is wearing an earring, so he must be gay" is also a rumor. Or simply, "He wears an earring" may be a rumor if it is not true, or if it was for a certain occasion, like a school play.

2. Go through the list and have the class decide which ones are fact and which are fiction.

3. Discuss what differentiates the factual statements from the rumors. A rumor may be a judgment added to a factual statement, something that isn't true, or something that is misconstrued. Discuss how gossip can hurt, even if it is not a rumor, for example, "Mary likes Joe" may be true, but the gossiping about it can hurt people's feelings.

4. Have the students make up their own list of fact versus fiction. See if they can think of examples in local, state, or world politics (e.g. "Russians hate Americans" as a rumor).

**Marcia Lane** has been telling world folk tales, myths, and legends since 1978. In 1987, she created The Amtrak Storytelling Odyssey, traveling to 22 cities and towns across the country! Odyssey II (1989) added another 17 stops to that total. Marcia has appeared at numerous conferences, festivals, and universities, and can be heard on two storytelling cassettes from A Gentle Wind: *Tales on the Wind* and *Stories from the Enchanted Loom.*

# The Four Wise People

retold by Gail Neary Herman

ONCE THERE WERE FOUR WISE PEOPLE who lived a long time ago in a faraway place in India.

Three of them read everything they found. They never talked to anyone. They never asked questions. They just read, morning, noon and night. They didn't put their books away until it was time to go to sleep.

But the fourth wise person often left in the late afternoon to walk and talk among the people. There was so much to learn from them. The fourth wise person would ask, "How do you make your garden grow so big?" For they knew the secrets of agriculture. "How do you keep your livestock so healthy?" There were also secrets of husbandry.

The other three wise people just laughed to think anyone would waste precious time in talking and asking questions.

After many years, the three wise people who never talked to the people or asked questions, decided they needed a test for their knowledge.

So they gathered together their most precious possessions and told the fourth wise person of their plan. They all journeyed to a faraway land. Once there they asked the people to give them a test for their knowledge.

The people directed them to a path and said, "Down that path, behind that tree, you will find the test that you are looking for."

The first wise person looked behind the tree and said, "A pile of bones! That's an easy trick. I can shape these bones into the tiger it once was."

And he began, one by one to shape and form the skeleton of the animal. When he was finished, he stood back and smiled. "Now I will become famous! That is a perfect reformation of a skeleton."

Then the second wise person began to work on the skeleton. He told the others, "I can transform the skeleton with fur to make it look exactly like the tiger it once was."

And he carefully set to work, using the knowledge of taxidermy to transform the skeleton with tendons, muscles, and fur.

When he was finished, he stepped back and grinned. "Now I will become the most famous of all wise people. Look at that creature. He is so real, he looks as though he could breathe."

The oldest of the wise people turned his face to the sun and his eyes lit up. "Wait a minute! I know how we can really test our knowledge and go down in history. With my knowledge and your help, we can breathe the breath of life into the creature. We must work very hard and very quickly, before dark sets in so that we don't have to waste another night."

By this time the fourth wise person was looking quite worried. "Wait a minute. I don't think that is a very wise thing you are doing—breathing the breath of life into a tiger!"

The third wise person laughed and said, "Of course it is. This will be a great scientific and technological discovery." And the third wise person set to work.

By this time the fourth wise person was climbing a tree to reach a safe limb. There was nothing to say which could stop them now. The three wise people set up their equipment, their chemicals, and used all of their knowledge to breathe the breath of life into the body of that inert tiger. After a time, the tiger began to move its legs, turn its head, and then it opened its mouth to *breathe*. All at once: *Whoosh!* In a quick three seconds, in a flurry of motion and dust, the three wise people were gone. Vanished.

The fourth wise person didn't move from the tree, but carefully watched as the tiger lumbered up the hill. Only then did the fourth wise person descend from the tree, taking with her the most important wisdom of all. And that, my friends, is the wisdom of our common sense.

## Follow-up Activities for "The Four Wise People"

### Creative Analogies

Analogical thinking is one of the most common tools people use to clarify thoughts. We compare one thing to another by looking for a relationship, such as when astronauts of today are compared to explorers of earlier times. Analogies encountered in testing involve relationships between relationships such as "large is to big as elderly is to old." Semantic relationships involving similarities or differences in meaning are only one type of analogy. Other types include symbolic, phonetic, class, functional, quantitative, and pattern relationships. The following activity illustrates a functional analogy because one item acts upon the other.

1. Write the following on the board:

Tiger is to the three wise men

as

_____ is to US?

2. Then ask the following:
    What did the tiger do to the wise men? Usual answers include: "The tiger ate them." "The tiger destroyed them."
    What did the Wise men do to the tiger? "The wise people put the bones together." "They brought it to life." "They created it."

3. Then draw an arrow with several student explanations, for example:

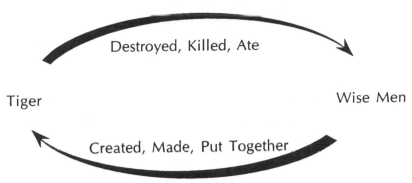

Destroyed, Killed, Ate

Tiger                                    Wise Men

Created, Made, Put Together

Explain that the second part of this complex analogy must have the same relationships as the first part. That is, to complete the blank we must be sure the item we choose is able to be created by us and that it can also destroy us if we do not use our common sense.

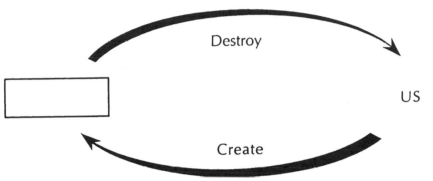

Destroy

US

Create

4. Ask what we create that could destroy us if we do not use our common sense.

5. List these ideas on a chart that has the analogy on top. Common answers have included the following: pollution, guns, drugs, bombs, nuclear power, knives, herbicide, pesticides, garbage and automobiles. Less common but creative answers have included the words "hate," "violence" and "greed."

6. If a student answers with words that do not hold the relationship, discuss it. For example, sometimes a student will answer with "sharks." To help them reason, ask "Do we create sharks or are they something in nature?"

7. I tell the students that one class thought up over fifty examples that fit the analogy.

8. Then I invite them to leave my chart on the wall and to add to the chart whenever they think of another answer. I also invite them to send me the results.

9. I purposely put capitals for "US" because it helps students think more on global terms rather than only on a smaller scale.

## Other Activities

• Divergent Thinking: Discuss the categories of the types of answers the students gave in the analogy activity.

   a. Count the answers and explain that this number shows how fluent in using analogies they were.

   b. Then count the categories, for example, weapons, transport vehicles, household articles, and industrial products. Explain that this number shows how flexible they were in their thinking. One group only thought of weapons, and they realized they were "thinking in a rut."

   c. Allow the class to discuss which of the responses surprised them. Explain that very unique responses are called "original" by creativity theorists.

   d. Ask if there were any detailed responses with many words or images. This type is called elaborate thinking. (Fluent, flexible, original and elaborate thinking are ways of diverging from the most obvious answers.)

- Ask the following questions and listen to student answers:

   a. What images will you remember about this story?

   b. What surprised you (if anything)?

   c. Did you expect something to happen that did not?

- Was the tiger doing anything abnormal for a tiger? Do you think wise people would have had knowledge about the normal behavior of tigers? How could the wise people have prevented their own demise? What precautions might the wise people have planned? How does this relate to our creation of dangerous inventions in the twentieth century?

- Think of other stories or create one that can be followed with an analogy.

- Write (in your journal) your first reaction when you found that the fourth wise person was a woman.
  Discuss several of the following questions.

   a. What assumptions did you make about the four wise people?

   b. Does it matter what gender they were?

   c. In the original story from India, the wise people were all men. Why do you think the author changed the gender of one wise person?

- A food-for-thought question to post in the front of the room:
  How common is common sense?

❦ ❦ ❦

**Gail Neary Herman**, the "organic storyteller," creates storytelling performances for schools and organizations across the US. She has performed in Germany, Jamaica, and most recently in Estonia. She teaches storytelling in many universities and colleges, including Garrett Community College, The University of Connecticut, and Lesley University and has published three storytelling tapes (one award winner), a cable TV show, and a book, *Storytelling: A Triad in the Arts*. She directed the Conference on Stories for Environmental and Global Awareness in Friendsville, Maryland and continues to direct the Tall Tale Festival in Oakland, Maryland. As a performer and teacher, Gail leads teachers and librarians toward an enthusiastic embrace of the art of storytelling.

Although the details in "The Sixth Day" are new, the ideas behind it are found in a 2,000-year-old Jewish book called *Midrash Rabbah* (mih'drahsh rah-bah'), a commentary on the Bible.

The Jewish Bible—what in Christianity is called the "Old Testament"—is known in Judaism as the Written Law. Judaism teaches that this is a summary of God's Word. The rest of God's teaching is found in the Oral Law. *Midrash Rabbah* is one important part of the Oral Law. Another part of the Oral Law is the *Talmud*. *Midrash Rabbah* and the *Talmud* include stories, explanations, and laws that were passed from teacher to student for many generations before they were written down. Jews still study these important books. As you can see from the story, "The Sixth Day," many of the ideas in the *Talmud* and *Midrash Rabbah* feel very modern even though they are thousands of years old.

# The Sixth Day

by Hanna Bandes Geshelin

GOD STEPPED BACK and looked at His brand-new world. Bees buzzed, birds sang, and cows lowed softly in green meadows. A gentle breeze carried the scent of flowers through the warm air. The angels looked around and smiled. "What a beautiful world!" they sang.

"It's a good world," said God, "but it's not done yet. My new world needs one more kind of creature—people. People to take care of it, the way I take care of the Universe. Help Me make them!"

"Watch," He said to the angels. He gathered clay from the corners of the world—red clay, yellow clay, black, brown, and white clay. Then He took one little bit of clay. He pulled and pinched it until He was happy with its shape. "Help me make lots of these to put in the world," He said.

The angels started working. "Look, this one's tall and skinny," said one angel. "Mine's short and fat," giggled another. "Oh dear, mine's crooked!" sighed a third. God looked at the different sizes and shapes and colors of people. "They're *all* beautiful!" He said with a smile. "Make me some more!"

"Look at the stick-out ears on yours!" teased one angel. "Stick-out ears yourself," snapped his friend. "This brown clay makes much nicer people than your ugly red!" "This red is beautiful!" shouted the first angel.

"Well," sniffed another angel, "I think the brown and red are both ugly. This black makes much prettier people!" "Black's too dark!" shouted someone else. "This yellow is best—it's bright and cheerful, like the sun!"

Another angel stood up and shouted, "The white is best! It looks like moonlight." Everyone took sides. Shouts of "Black!" "White!" "Brown!" "Yellow!" "Red!" filled the air. "Take that!" screamed an angel, throwing a lump of clay.

"Stop!" God's huge voice boomed through the heavens like thunder. The angels froze.

"I can't put all these people in My world," He roared. "What a mess that would be! They'd argue, just like you! They'd all scream, 'I'm best' and throw things at each other!"

He pulled all the clay people to Him in a heap. He slammed His fist into the heap. Smash! The angels shook with fear. Smash! Smash! God mashed the clay people together. After a long time God started to knead the clay.

Slowly all the colors blended together.

Slowly the clay became smooth and even.

And slowly God stopped being angry.

"Now," said God, "I'm going to make *one* person out of this yellowish-brownish-blackish-reddish-whitish clay." Carefully He pinched and pulled the clay until it looked just right. The angels nodded.

"I'm putting just this one person in the world," God explained. "It will make other people. Maybe someday, the colors will separate again. But the people will know that they are all from the same First Person."

"They won't argue about their colors," said one angel.

"They won't throw things at each other," said another.

God looked seriously at the angels. "We'll hope they won't," He said.

Then He breathed life into the First Person. Its chest rose and fell. Its toes started to wiggle, and then its fingers. When it was wiggly all over, God set it carefully in the garden of the new world.

The person stretched in the warm sunshine. It stamped its feet. It ran through the grass and waded in the cool water. It smelled the flowers. It looked at all the growing things and gave them names—
>    papaya tree and peach tree,
>    peony and petunia,
>    pepper, pea, and parsley.

It named the winged creatures
>    canary and cardinal,
>    chickadee and chicken,
>    kingfisher, killdeer, and coot.

The sea creatures it called
>    sunfish and starfish and swordfish,
>    shrimp and salmon and smelt.

It called the earth creatures
>    ermine and armadillo,
>    elephant and elk,
>    bear and beaver and buffalo.

God and the angels watched and listened so they could learn the new names for all the creations.

When the First Person had named everything in the world, it sat down. It leaned back against a tamarind tree, hung its head, and sighed.

"Oh, dear!" said an angel. "The First Person is sad!"

"You're right," said God. "Why are you sad, Person?" He asked. "You have a whole world to enjoy! Why aren't you happy?"

"I'm lonely," said the First Person.

"I tried making many people," said God. "It didn't work." He gave the angels a stern look. Then He continued, "In time, you'll make other people. Then you'll have company." The angels nodded to each other. It seemed like the best way.

"But I need someone *now!*" wailed the First Person. "Ponies and parrots are fine, but people need *people!* Can't you give me a friend?"

The angels looked at each other. They couldn't think of any way that God could give the First Person company without causing trouble.

God sighed. Then He said to the First Person, "I can take some clay from you and use it to make another person. Then you will both be from the same First Person, but there will be two of you. Close your eyes and sleep." Carefully He divided the clay into two people. He set them in the garden and whispered, "Wake up!"

The two people opened their eyes and looked at each other. The male person smiled at his new friend. "My name is Man," he said to her. She smiled and said, "My name is Woman."

God touched the heads of the people lightly with His huge hand. "See, here is your wonderful world," He said. "I've filled it with delicious foods to eat, and with bright flowers. With soaring birds and silvery fishes. Treasure it. Take care of it."

Then God gestured to His angels. "Come," He said, and they all moved away from the new world, toward the deep places of the universe.

Woman took Man's hand. Together they walked slowly around the garden of the world. They told each other the names of all the creations—skunk and squash, nighthawk and narcissus, coyote and cabbage and carp. Together they smelled some sweet roses and patted a soft, wooly sheep and brushed away a mosquito.

God looked back at everything that He had made.

He looked at the heaven and earth, and He smiled.

He looked at the sun, moon, and stars, and His smile grew.

He looked at all the growing things and creatures,
and at one yellowish-brownish-blackish-reddish-whitish Woman
and one yellowish-brownish-blackish-reddish-whitish Man
walking hand in hand through the world.

"Ah," He said to His angels. "Now, at last, My world is finished. Now, it is very good."

## Follow-up Activities for "The Sixth Day"

### Stories about Creation

Each culture has its own story or stories about how the world came to be. These stories answer many different questions. Some of the world's creation stories are found in the following books:

*Beginnings: Creation Myths of the World*, compiled and edited by Penelope Farmer, Atheneum, New York, 1979. An illustrated book suitable for children and adults.

*Origins: Creation Texts from the Ancient Mediterranean*, coedited and translated with an introduction and notes by Charles Doria and Harris Lenowitz, Anchor Books, 1976. A scholarly collection of creation texts; good resource material.

*Just-So Stories*, by Rudyard Kipling, gives many fanciful stories about the beginning of the world, including for example "The Elephant's Child" (how the elephant got its trunk) and "How the Leopard Got Its Spots."

### Sharing Creation Stories

Read a few creation stories aloud. Ask the class, "What stories do you know about how things were created?" Encourage your class to answer questions, such as, "How are these stories similar? How are they different? What do the similarities say about people all over the world? What interesting things do the differences say about different cultures?"

### Hands-On Activities

Provide modeling clay in several colors.

1. Give each child a little clay of at least two very different colors (e.g., yellow and green, red and blue). Have them make one figure out of each color. What qualities does each figure have that relate to the colors? Have the children imagine for a few moments that these two figures are family. Do they look related? Now have them smash up the figures, knead the colors together, and make a figure out of the new clay. Lastly, divide the last figure into two figures (this will take completely remodeling the first). Now imagine that these two figures are family. Does the fact that one was taken from the other make it easier to imagine that they're related?

2. Using several different colors for the class as a whole, give each child clay of one color without regard to the child's color preference. Have the children model several figures out of their one color of clay. After ten or fifteen minutes, have them group all the figures together by color (all the blues together, all the greens, and so on). Ask the children to think about which color of figure they like best. Then ask them which color they used. How many thought that the figures made of their color were prettiest? Why? Possible reasons are that they are familiar with that color, they've invested time and energy into that color. Does that make that color "better" or "better for them" or "just different"?

3. This is a three-part activity:

A. Talk about likeness and how people are comfortable with what's familiar to them. When they travel, does their family stop at independent cafes or fast-food chains? Do they like to wear clothes like their friends? Listen to the same music as their friends? Ask them to suggest things that they think should only be available one way (e.g., only rock music on the radio). Do other children disagree? *Do not try to make them see the advantages of difference.* If they start to talk about the advantages of difference, end the discussion and go on to Step B.

B. Now give out modeling clay. Have each child make one little person or animal (taking time to be somewhat careful and detailed). Now each child should try to make five more figures exactly like their first one. After they're finished, ask: "How did it feel to make the last few figures? Was it easy or difficult? Which figure was the most fun to make? Why? Did the job get boring?" Different children will feel differently; some will probably like the repetition while others will not. Neither viewpoint is right or wrong.

C. Now return to the discussion of difference. Did the exercise with the clay make a difference in their perception of like versus different? Did it add any new dimensions to the way they think of the problem? Now is the time to let them talk about the advantages of difference; be sure, however, that the discussion doesn't end up in a trashing of "like." Both are important in the total scheme of things.

## Story-Making Exercise

Have each child (or small groups of children) make up their own story that explains why people are different colors. Children can write their stories down or can draw a cartoon (one or several panels) illustrating their story. Now have them share their work with each other. Elicit constructive suggestions for improving the stories and cartoons. Finally, have the children incorporate any of the suggestions that they'd like into their work.

## Thinking Exercises

The object of these exercises is to give an awareness of the kinds of differences that exist right in the classroom or group. Exercise 1 deals with the visual differences in the classroom. People are sometimes very sensitive about these. If the class has scapegoats or tends to be disrespectful of each other, skip Exercise 1 and do only Exercise 2.

If at any time in these exercises anyone teases anyone else or says something disrespectful, stop the discussion *immediately.* Remind the class of the story, "The Sixth Day," and ask whether in the story God liked having the angels fight over which people they thought were best.

### Exercise 1

Explain that in this exercise you may be talking about things that the children have thought about but *have never felt it was all right to speak about.* You can set the tone by discussing some of the ways *you* are different. If you're comfortable talking about your size, religion, weight, color, ethnic group, age, physical handicap, etc., this will make the process easier for your class. (If you're not comfortable talking about this, then just skip this exercise.)

A. Tell your class, "Look around the room. Notice the ways people are different." After a few moments, say, "Some people are very sensitive about how they're different, so don't mention any names. Just tell us some of the differences you see." (For example, "Some people have straight blond hair and some have kinky black hair.") Answers will include height, weight, colors of skin, hair, and eyes, etc. White people often lump all people of color together and may never have noticed the many shades of brown and black, as well as the different shades of "white." This is a time to draw their attention to these more subtle differences.

B. Say, "Now look around again. This time look at how people are alike." After a few moments say, "Now share some of the similarities you saw." Answers will probably include color of eyes and other physical characteristics as well as clothing similarities.

## Exercise 2

Explain that physical differences are easy to see but that there are other differences that are not visible from the outside. Ask, "What do you like to eat when you're sick?" Some get jello and ginger ale, some get farina and tea, some get chicken soup, etc.

Choose a few people who answered (very verbal, outgoing kids who will give a strong "Yecch" are great for this). Ask, "How would you feel if you got 'X' instead of 'Y'?" (e.g., chicken soup instead of jello).

Tell the class, "These differences are *cultural*. There's no right or wrong. Different families and different nationalities and people from different places do many things differently from other people."

You might mention that one of the advice columns (*Dear Abby* or *Ann Landers*) once published a letter about whether toilet paper should be hung so that the paper comes off the front or the back of the roll. She received thousands of letters—about evenly divided—from people who felt there was only one right way to hang a roll of toilet paper.

Among the many differences are:

• What's packed in your lunch box?

• What is your morning routine—get dressed before breakfast or after? Bathe in the morning or evening? Brush teeth before or after eating?

• What do you call your grandparents?

Help the children see that many things feel "right" because they're familiar, not because they are higher on a universal rightness scale than other things.

🐛 🐛 🐛

**Hanna Bandes Geshelin** was a professional storyteller for ten years, using her art to transmit Jewish values to Jewish audiences and to teach non-Jews about her culture and religion. Author of two children's books as well as stories, articles and essays, she focuses now on writing. "Unfortunately, in every generation many people of good will fall victim to the poison of anti-Semitism, sometimes disguised as anti-Israelism. One way to reach them, I believe, is through stories," she states. Her other accomplishments include organizing the Jewish Storytelling Coalition and receiving the Association of Jewish Libraries' Sydney Taylor Manuscript Prize.

# Why People Speak Many Languages

A Seneca Indian Tradition
as told by Joseph Bruchac

LONG AGO, WHEN THE EARTH WAS NEW, all of the people spoke a single language. The people lived in peace and harmony then. They shared everything that they had and they had everything which anyone could ever need. They grew corn and beans and squash in their fields. They hunted the game animals in the forest. They gave thanks to the earth and the food plants, to the animals, and to their great Creator who had provided everything in such abundance.

In those days, in the big village by the wide river, there lived a woman chief. Her name was Godasiyo and she was a good chief. (Note: Godasiyo is pronounced: Go-dah-si-yo.) She was wise and generous and did everything she could to make the lives of her people peaceful and filled with harmony. There were so many people that the village was located on both sides of the wide river. Although the people did not know how to use boats in those days, they had built a strong bridge across the river. They had tied trees and branches together and woven them in such a way that it was easy for people to walk back and forth from one side to the other. This the people did often, for on the western bank of the river dances were held each night. There the people would come and bring whatever they had to trade. Some would bring skins and herbs from the forest. Some would bring dried corn or berries from the fields. Whatever was needed could always be gotten either in trade or as a gift, for if anyone truly wanted something but had nothing to trade in exchange, that man or woman had only to say, "Brother, I have need of that," or, "Sister, would you give that to me?" Then they would be given whatever it was that they needed.

One day, though, something happened. In those days, the people had many dogs. The small white dog which lived in the lodge of Godasiyo, which was on the western bank of the wide stream, had puppies. This had happened before and, as was the custom, whenever a dog had puppies they would be treated as members of the family and anyone who wished to adopt one of those new little ones had only to ask. This time, however, something was different. One of the four puppies in the litter was as white as its brothers, but it had two dark spots over its eyes. It looked as if it had four eyes. Such dogs are said to be wiser and better than all others, able to see things with those two spots over their eyes which make them great hunters and natural leaders. That little dog was so special that Godasiyo decided to keep it for herself. Thus the trouble began.

Soon the people on the western bank began to brag about the special dog which their chief had in her lodge.

"It is a dog like no other," they said.

"None of the people on the eastern bank of the wide stream have such a special dog in their lodges," they boasted.

It was the first time that such boasting had been heard in Big Village. Soon, something else appeared in Big Village. That something was envy. The people on the eastern bank began to envy their brothers and sisters who had such a special dog on their side of the stream.

Though Godasiyo was a very wise chief, at first she did not see what was happening. Then, one day, a group of people from her side of the village came to her.

"We are worried," they said. "Those bad people on the other side of the stream are talking about our four-eyed dog. We think they may try to steal our dog. We must make ready to fight them!"

Godasiyo was shocked. How could her people fight each other? She walked among them and listened and looked and she saw how bad things had become. The people were divided and none of her words could bring them back together again. She thought of allowing the people on the eastern bank to take the little four-eyed dog. Then she saw that it would only bring the jealousy over to the western side. The people on both sides were now making weapons and Godasiyo knew she had to act. She gathered together the people on the western bank and told them what to do.

"Destroy the bridge," she said.

They did as she said, setting fire to the bridge. Now the people were divided. But Godasiyo knew that another bridge might be built and that fighting might still happen.

"We must leave this place," she said. She had watched the way the pieces of wood from the bridge floated away as they fell into the water and she had an idea. She told the people to gather big pieces of bark from the birch trees and to sew them together in the same way they made baskets and cooking pots of bark. Then, using pitch to seal the seams, the people made the first canoes. They made a number of small canoes and also two very big canoes. The canoes were enough to hold all of the people on the western side of the river.

Then the people made ready to leave for a new place where they could find peace and harmony. But as soon as they started to get into the canoes trouble began again. The people began to argue about which canoe would be the special canoe which would carry their chief and her wonderful four-eyed dog!

Was there no end of this quarreling? Godasiyo felt very tired and sad. But she had another idea.

"We will tie saplings between the two big canoes," she said. Then, in the middle, we will make a platform. My dog and I will ride on that platform. That way we will not be in either canoe and there can be no jealousy."

So it was that they set out and all went well until they came to a place where the river divided into two channels. There, once again, the people began to quarrel. Those in the canoes to the right wanted to take the eastern channel. Those in the canoes to the left wanted to take the western channel. Godasiyo tried to stop them, but they did not listen to her. The people began to turn their canoes in the two different directions and those in the two big canoes, which had Godasiyo's platform suspended between them, also disagreed about which way to go. The lead paddlers in each of the two big canoes called for their people to paddle harder so they would pull the other canoe towards their side. As they struggled back and forth the two canoes pulled apart and the platform holding Godasiyo and the little four-eyed dog fell into the river.

The people leaned over the side of their canoes and looked down into the water. Their chief and the little dog had vanished. In their places were a big sturgeon and a little white fish. As the people watched in wonder, the fish swam away.

The people tried then to speak to each other about what had happened. But they could no longer understand each other. Those in each canoe spoke different languages. So the people separated and continued on their way. Each time the rivers divided, the people split again and more languages came into the world. So it is today. Jealousy and quarreling divided the people and brought many languages into the world.

## Follow-up Activities for "Why People Speak Many Languages"

A version of this tale, entitled "The Legend of Godasiyo" was collected in the autumn of 1896, by the Tuscarora Indian ethnologist J. N. B. Hewitt. It was published as part of the book *Seneca Fiction, Legends, and Myths*, collected by Jeremiah Curtin and J. N. B. Hewitt in 1899 as the 32nd Annual Report of the Bureau of American Ethnology. My own version of this tale draws on the Hewitt telling, though it differs in some details. Though I have heard versions of it from Iroquois friends in English, the story was given originally to Hewitt in Seneca. I mention this because people have remarked to me on the similarity of this tale to the story of the Tower of Babel from the Old Testament. Some have asked if this story really is an authentic Indian tale because it seems to have this similarity.

In many ways, though, this is a very different story. It presents us with a world in which peace and harmony are the natural order of things. It is only the introduction of jealousy and bragging which break that natural order. Among the Iroquois people of the Northeast, peace is still greatly valued. The five original Iroquois nations—Mohawk, Oneida, Onondaga, Cayuga and Seneca—were brought together a thousand years ago into a league of peace after many years of bloody warfare. The peace was brought to them by a special messenger from the Creator named The Peacemaker. The Peacemaker joined forces with a wise elderly woman named Jigonsaseh and a great orator named Hiawatha. Together they united the people and planted a great pine tree as the symbol of their peaceful union. Later, those five Iroquois nations were joined by the Tuscarora. The leaders of the Iroquois Great League had to be men of peace and could not serve as delegates to the Great League as "chiefs" if they went to war. To this day, the Iroquois chiefs speak for peace. Such men as Chief Oren Lyons of the Onondaga Nation and Chief Jake Swamp of the Mohawk Nation have taken the Iroquois message of peace throughout the world from the many nations of Europe to Australia. Decades ago, an Iroquois leader from the Tuscarora, Clinton Rickard, spoke of Peace and Native Rights to the League of Nations.

## Finding the Lessons in the Story

The story of Godasiyo is only one of many Iroquois tales about peace. It stresses certain important ideas, not by talking about them, but by showing them in action, showing the consequences of wrong actions. These important ideas include:

- The idea that community is more important than the individual.

- The importance of sharing and the dangers of being possessive.

- Women play important roles as leaders and thinkers. (This is so commonplace in American Indian culture that it is easy for someone immersed in that culture to forget the incorrect and stereotyped picture given of Indian women by the popular media. To this day, among the Iroquois, it is the women who choose the chiefs. Among the Mohawk, at present, two of their chiefs are women.)

- Animals are to be respected. The little dog is a member of the family, not just a possession.

As a facilitator, lead the group in a discussion of what lessons are to be found in this story. Do not tell them the four points mentioned above but try to see if the group can discover them on their own by asking the following questions:

- What ideas are stressed in this story?

- What lessons are taught by this story?

- What role do animals play in this story? Are animals seen differently than in our culture?

- What does this story tell us about the role of women? What roles do you think women played in Iroquois culture?

Further discussion may include personal experiences of the group members in their own attempts to find a peaceful life style. What things do they see as essential aspects of such a peaceful lifestyle?

## Communication and Conflict

The inability to communicate is one of the great causes of conflict—as this story shows. It is important for people to understand each other's languages. Bring a group of people together and brainstorm with them about ways in which breakdowns in communication give rise to conflict. Try the following:

Divide the group in two. Tell each group to choose or even invent certain words or phrases which only they understand and to use them in conversation with the other group without explanation of what those words and phrases mean. (For example, a made-up word such as "neyone" might mean "I do not agree," or the words in English "My hands are full" might actually mean "I cannot understand you.") It is very difficult to make up an entire language, so limit this to a few key words and phrases. Now have the two groups come together and engage in negotiations over some item which both claim to be theirs. Have both groups pay close attention to nonverbal cues such as tone of voice and body language.

After a few minutes of this, introduce a translator who has been given the key to the special languages of both groups. Continue the negotiations.

After doing this exercise, bring both groups together and have them discuss their experience. Use this as an opportunity for brainstorming about the ways in which break-downs in communication occur. Ask questions such as the following:

- How do our understandings or misunderstandings of each other's words affect our actions?
- What means of non-verbal communication do we use?
- Language and culture can affect international relations. What are some of the specific things which may differ from one culture to another and which may get in the way of communication?

## Problem Solving and Conflict Resolution

The story of *Why People Speak Many Languages* may also be seen as a lesson in problem solving. We see how Godasiyo tried to solve the problems brought to her people by their dispute over the dog. Her attempted solutions included:

- trying to talk with the two sides and mediate;
- dividing the two antagonists by destroying the bridge;
- moving away from the place where conflict might happen.

Without mentioning these attempted solutions, have the group define Godasiyo's attempts to solve the problem by asking these questions:

- What steps did Godasiyo take in this story to resolve conflicts?
- What things did she not try that you might try in such a situation?
- Imagine that you are negotiating between the two groups in Godasiyo's village. What would you say to either side? Do a role-playing exercise with a group of people on which you take turns being on one side, then on the other, and then playing the role of the mediator.

## Planting a Tree of Peace

When the Iroquois League was formed, a pine tree was planted at Onondaga and the weapons of war buried under its roots. That "Tree of Peace" is the symbol of the Iroquois League and has also been used as an American symbol. (One of the early American flags had a pine tree on it.)

Today, Iroquois people still view the pine tree as a symbol of peace and cooperation. Tree planting ceremonies take place at many locations each year. The story of the Founding of the Great League of Peace is told. Prayers of peace are spoken and a young tree is planted. Not only is the tree a symbol of peace and cooperation, it is also a gift back to the natural world, which is threatened everywhere by deforestation. Planting a tree is a gift to coming generations.

Devise your own "Tree of Peace" ceremony. Bring together a group of people to plant a young tree. Make up your own prayers of peace to speak when the tree is planted. Discuss ways in which the planting of a tree benefits the world and what symbolic actions might be taken during this tree-planting—such as the burying of weapons of war beneath its roots.

## The Many Towers of Babel

There are stories in other cultures which explain why people speak many languages. One of the best known of these can be found in the Bible.

- Read the story of the Tower of Babel. Compare and contrast it with this Seneca tale. Discuss the differences between these two stories and what those differences say about the world views of the two cultures.

- Try a role-playing exercise in which one group takes the part (and the world view) of the ancient Senecas and another that of the ancient Hebrews and the two groups discuss their differing versions of the tale of why there are many languages.

- Make up original stories to explain why people speak many languages. Examine these stories and see what lessons they teach or what messages they convey about a culture.

## Bibliography

*Tales of the Iroquois*, by Tehanteorens. Akwesasne Notes Press.

*The White Roots of Peace*, by Paul Wallace. The Chauncy Press.

*Indian Roots of American Democracy*, edited by Jose Barriero, Northeast Indian Quarterly.

*Keepers of the Earth: Native American Stories and Environmental Activities for Children*, by Michael Caduto and Joseph Bruchac, Fulcrum Press.

*Return of the Sun: Native American Tales from the Northeast Woodlands* as told by Joseph Bruchac, The Crossing Press. (This includes the story of Godasiyo.)

**Joseph Bruchac** is a storyteller and writer. He is of Abenaki, Slovak, and English ancestry and lives in the Adirondack mountain region of upstate New York. His books include *Return of the Sun, The Faithful Hunter,* and (with Michael Caduto) *Keepers of the Earth.* His audio-cassette from Yellow Moon Press, *Gluskabe Stories,* was selected for a 1990 Parents' Choice Honor. He and his wife, Carol, have been married for 26 years and have two grown sons.

A doko is a large basket used for carrying things . . . .

# The Doko

## A Nepali Story
## retold by Barbara Lipke

IN FAR-OFF NEPAL there was a small family of four: a man, his wife, their small son, and the man's very elderly father. The old man had worked hard when he was younger, climbing the high mountains to the terraced, stony fields to plant and harvest the small crop. Now he was too old to work any longer and so he was entirely dependent on his son and daughter-in-law. Much as he loved them, he didn't like being dependent on anyone. They loved him too, and they didn't mind his being dependent for he helped as much as he could, and for a time they left the little boy with him when they went off to work. The old man told wonderful stories to the little boy, and if he told the same stories over and over again, the little boy didn't mind.

But soon, the boy was old enough to climb the mountain and to help with the planting and weeding and harvesting. The family worked hard and, even so, had barely enough to feed themselves. They left the little house with the first light of day and returned just as it grew too dark to find the mountain path.

The old man sat alone in the house all day and by evening was eager for company. Because he was lonely, he complained a great deal.

"When I was young, I worked hard. I got a good crop. If you did as I did . . ."

The young man looked at his wife. "An old ox stumbles," he said, "an old man grumbles."

She nodded and they went on pretending to listen to the old man. Time passed and things grew worse. The old man complained more and the man and his wife were discouraged. Like a drop of water that wears away the hardest stone, the old man's complaints and grumbling wore their love and patience thin.

"You leave me alone too much. When I was young . . .," he'd begin.

As he grew older he often spilled his food. His shirt was stained yellow with curry.

"I don't want our son to see his grandfather eat like that," the woman said. "Let your father eat over by his sleeping mat." So they fed the old man on the other side of the room. Since there was little food and he wasted so much, spilling it, they gave him less.

The old man complained more than ever. He was hungry. He was cold away from the small fire.

"An old ox stumbles," said the man, "an old man grumbles." His wife nodded.

165

Sometimes in the evenings, the little boy would sit with his grandfather and listen to his stories again. Sometimes he tried to share his food with his grandfather. If his parents saw him they scolded him.

"Don't waste your food," they told him.

As time passed they began to worry about leaving the old man alone in the house with the fire.

"It's not safe," they said. "He could be burned. He could burn down the house." So they left him without a fire as they went off to work.

The old man grumbled and complained more than ever.

"I would like to help. If you do as I say I am sure you will have better crops. When I was young . . . ."

At last, the couple were at their wits' end. One night, thinking that everyone else was asleep, the man whispered to his wife. "Tomorrow I could go to the market and buy a *doko*. In it, I could carry my father far, far away, so far that he would not be able to find his way back. I could leave him by the side of the road, in the shade of a tree. Perhaps some kind people would look after him."

"Oh," said his wife, "it would be so good to be by ourselves, not to have the constant complaining." She smiled at the thought. "But what would I tell the neighbors? They are sure to notice that your father is no longer here."

"Tell them that I have taken my father to a place where kind people will look after him so that he may spend his last days in peace."

"Oh yes," said his wife. The more they talked, the more they believed that it was true.

In the morning the man went off to the market to buy the *doko*.

After a while the little boy asked his mother, "Mother, why are we throwing grandfather away?"

"Oh no," she said. "We are not throwing grandfather away. He has grown so old that we can no longer take proper care of him. We have to work very hard and he needs to have someone with him all the time. We are taking him to a place where kind people will look after him and he may spend his last days in peace."

"Where is that place?"

"Far, far away."

In the evening, the man returned with a new *doko*. He set it down in a corner of the house and said to his wife, "Let us eat supper. When it is dark, I will carry my father away."

When they had eaten, the man placed his father in the *doko*.

"Where are you taking me in this *doko*?" the old man asked.

"I am taking you to a place where kind people will look after you and you may spend your final days in peace."

But the old man was not deceived. "You are a wicked, ungrateful son! Is it for this I raised you and taught you everything I knew? Was it for this I nursed you when you were ill, for this I told you stories? You are wicked! I curse you! I curse you!"

The old man's railing only made the young man angry. He picked up the *doko* with a jerk and started out the door.

"Father," the little boy called, "Father, even though you have to throw grandfather away, please take good care of the *doko* and bring it back safely."

The man stopped. "Why?" he asked.

"Because," was the boy's innocent answer, "when it's my turn to throw you away, I don't want to have to buy a new *doko*."

The man could go no further. His knees shook. He turned and carried his father back into the house. He took him from the *doko* and set him down by the fire. Thereafter they all lived, perhaps not more happily, but with far greater understanding.

## Follow-up Activities for "The Doko"

Stories are not always easy—nor is life. This story is universal. It has many versions from many different cultures all over the world. The source for this version was published by the United Nations in a collection of stories from all over the world.

I have told this story to audiences of all ages, as well as to mixed-age and family audiences. Children love it because they understand that they are the heroes. The older generation loves it because it addresses, in a very straightforward way, a problem and a fear they live with. The middle generation is sometimes uncomfortable with it because they have to deal with the problem. It may be that the story gives them a special insight into the future of their parents as well as their own.

## Home Activities

These are things to think about and talk about within the family:

- What special things do you do with your grandchild(ren)/grandparent(s)?

- What special things do you do with your parent(s)/child(ren)?

- What family customs or traditions have been handed down from generation to generation? Do you still observe them? Would you like to institute new ones?

- Share family pictures with other family members. Find out about older people, including older people whose lives are unknown to some family members.

- Share family stories with other family members.

## Classroom Activities

- Arrange visits to local nursing homes. Be sure to prepare your students for what they will find. Arrange with the social worker there to have each child adopt a "grandparent" or "friend." Make this a more-than-one-visit activity. Follow through with letters, interviews, stories, pictures, and regular visits. If students interview their adoptee, they can make a book or tell a story from information they get from that person. The product should then be given to the subject. If it's a "told" story, an audio tape is a wonderful gift.

- Discuss with the class where grandparents live and find out whether any of the children have intergenerational living situations. Discuss the advantages and disadvantages of intergenerational living. Draw pictures, cartoons, write stories about these situations. Share them with the grandparent(s).

- Celebrate something special the class or class members have done with older people.

- Organize, with parental permission and support, volunteer help for neighborhood elders: chores (lawn mowing, dog-walking, shopping, etc.)

- Close your eyes and wish for the best thing that might happen between generations in your family. Write, draw, or tell a story about it. Share it with your family.

- Have the whole class brainstorm ways to see another generation's point of view. Fantasy may be a key to doing this. For example, ask students how they might view space travel, pre-packaged foods, video games, etc., if they were their grandparents or great-grandparents.

- Brainstorm a list of books, movies, TV programs that highlight intergenerational stories, and especially the remarkable accomplishments of each generation. Make up a bibliography. Read, review and share these with families and friends.

❧ ❧ ❧

**Barbara Lipke**, storyteller and educational consultant, was a classroom teacher for 24 years and is the author of *Figures, Facts, and Fables: Telling Tales in Science and Math*. She is a passionate advocate for the use of storytelling to teach and learn. She tells stories at festivals, in schools and anywhere people listen. She is a member of LANES, NSN and other storytelling organizations.

# King Solomon and the Otter

A Hebrew Folktale
words by Heather Forest

IT IS SAID THAT KING SOLOMON was so wise he could speak and understand the languages of all the animals. To set an example for people, he decreed there should be peace among the beasts.

> Peace Among the Beasts!
> Peace Among the Beasts!
> King Solomon Decreed
> Peace Among the Beasts!

"Death! Death! Death to the slayer! Death to the slayer," the otter cried. It's the fault of the weasel my children died. I came out of the water with their food (I brought them these little crabs . . . oh they loved little crabs . . .) and found that Weasel had trampled my children dead on the ground!
He broke the vow of Peace, agreed among the beasts. Peace is dead and death instead reigns without cease! I want Justice."

When the animals heard what the weasel had done to the otter's children, their outcry was immediate.
"Bring the weasel to the King!" cried the other animals.

"Oh, King," said the weasel, "what the otter says is true.
But my heart contains no malice when I do the things I do.
I heard the woodpecker drum a call to arms.
I never meant to do the otter any harm.
The drums . . . they thrilled me to the core
and I trampled her children as I marched to War."

   "Then bring the woodpecker before me," said the King.

"Oh, King," said the woodpecker, "be not alarmed!
I drummed the drums but I meant no harm.
I saw the scorpion sharpening her sting.
It frightened me so that I let the drums ring."

   "Then bring the scorpion before me," said the King.

Into the throne room came Scorpion holding her poison sting high above her head and she said,
"King, I made no offense.
I sharpened my sting in my own defense.
I saw the turtle climbing into her armor.
I did the same, but I meant not to harm her."

"Oh, King," said the turtle, "my armor is strong.
I climbed in for safety but I meant no wrong.
I saw the crab with angry claws,
She was charging across the ocean floors!"

Into the throne room came Crab
With tears in her eyes and claws outstretched she said,

"Yes, I confess. Yes, I confess. It's true what she saw.
With angry claws I *did* charge to war.
But I saw the otter dive into my home
and eat my children I'd left there alone."

"Well," said King Solomon turning once again to otter, "Otter, you're the one who cries 'Justice be done', when Otter, you're to blame!"

"One who sows the seeds of death shall reap the same."

Peace Among the Beasts!

# King Solomon And The Otter . . . *A Hebrew Folktale*

Words and Music by Heather Forest

Peace a - mong the beasts. Peace a - mong the beasts. King

Sol - o - mon de-creed. Peace a - mong the beasts. Peace a - mong the beasts.

*(Spoken)* "Death, death, death to the slayer! Death to the slayer!" the Otter cried. "It's the

fault of the weasel my children died. I came out of the water with their food.

(I got them these little crabs . . . oh, they loved little crabs . . .) and found that

weasel had trampled my children dead on the ground. He broke the vow

of peace a - greed a - mong the beasts. *Peace is dead and death instead reigns_ with-out cease!"*

*(Spoken)* "Bring the weasel to the King," cried the other animals. "O King," said the wea - sel, "What the

ot - ter says is true. But my heart con - tains no mal-ice when I

do the things I do. *I heard the woodpecker drum a call to arms.*

© 1982 NEW HARVEST PUBLISHING

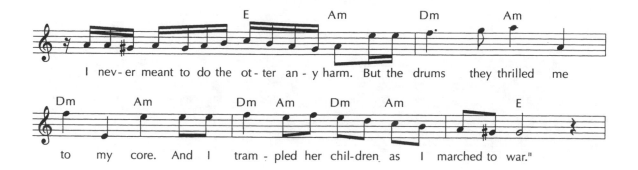

I nev-er meant to do the ot-ter an-y harm. But the drums they thrilled me to my core. And I tram-pled her chil-dren as I marched to war."

*"Then bring the woodpecker before me," said the king.*

"O King," said the wood-peck-er, Be not a-larmed.

*I drummed the drums* but I meant___ no harm. *You see, I saw the scorpion* sharp-en-ing her sting. It fright-ened me so that I let the drums ring."

**(Spoken)**

*"Then bring the scorpion before me,"* said the King.

*Into the throne room came scorpion holding her*
*poison sting high above her head. She said,*

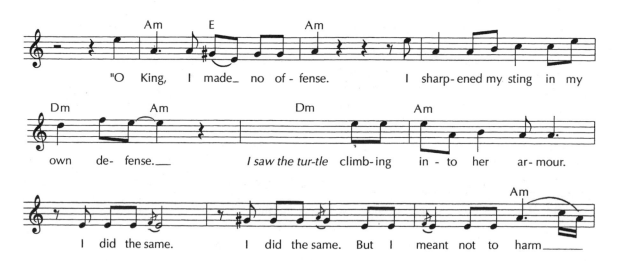

"O King, I made_ no of-fense. I sharp-ened my sting in my own de-fense.___ *I saw the tur-tle* climb-ing in-to her ar-mour. I did the same. I did the same. But I meant not to harm_____

her."    "O  King,"  said  the tur - tle,  "my  ar - mour is strong.    I

climbed  in here  for  safe - ty  but  I  meant  no  wrong. *You see,*    I  saw  the crab  with

an - gry  claws. *And she was* charg - ing  a - cross  the  o - cean__ floors."

*Into  the  throne  room  came  Crab.  And  with  tears  in*
*her  eyes  and  her  claws  outstretched,  she  said,*

"Yes,  I  con - fess.      Yes,  I  con - fess.  It's  true    what  she  saw.    With

an - gry  claws  I  did    charge    to  war.  But    I    saw  the  ot - ter  dive

in - to  my  home  and    eat__  my__  chil - dren  I'd    left__  there a- lone."

*"Well,"  said  the  King,  turning  once  again  to  otter,*

"Ot - ter,  you're    the  one    who    cries  'jus - tice    be done.'    When,

Ot - ter,  you're  to  blame.    One    who  sows  the  seeds  of  death  shall

reap__  the__  same."_____    Peace    a - mong  the  beasts.

## Follow-up Activities for "King Solomon and the Otter"

A recording of this storysong is available on "Songspinner: Folktales and Fables Sung and Told," from Story Arts, Inc., P.O. Box 354, Huntington, NY 11743.

### The Fable

Throughout history, storytellers have told stories about human nature by casting the characters in the story as animals who talk and act like people. This kind of a story is called a fable. Although fables are not based on true happenings, they usually have a ring of "truth" about them. There is often a wise moral at the end.

Ancient fables, as well as contemporary ones, can be found in most libraries in the folklore section (398.2). The most well-known fables are those of Aesop, but a scan of the shelves will reveal that cultures around the world have fables as part of their oral tradition. Aesop's fables, tales of Anansi the spider (Africa), Native American nature stories, as well as ancient Jataka tales (India) can be a source of inspiration for students to write their own fables about "human nature," describing human situations and predicaments, but featuring animals as the main characters.

The animals in "King Solomon and the Otter" use their characteristics in a "human" way. The turtle's shell becomes armor, and the woodpecker's hammering becomes the sound of war drums. All the animals speak and give excuses for their behavior in human terms, expressing their suspicions and their defensiveness.

### Story Origin

My storysong version of "King Solomon and the Otter" was inspired by a Jewish scholar named Hyman Nahman Bialik, who wrote a version in 1938 entitled "Whose Was the Blame" in his book, *And It Came To Pass*. His version was likely inspired by an earlier tale from *Kalima and Dimna*, a fable collection from India, which was the source for many Jewish adaptations. "The Cycle," retold by Peninnah Schram in *Jewish Stories One Generation Tells Another*, is yet another similar fable of repercussions from a chain of events.

In the way of storytelling tradition, each teller who shares the tale adds their own detail and personal vision.

I discovered this story in my reading during the war in Vietnam. I wrote the music and the poem to sing at peace rallies. Over time this storysong has not lost its current event relevance as, again and again, human beings go to war around the planet despite the best intentions for peace.

When I tell this story I end it as it begins, with a plea for peace. I feel that, even in the midst of destruction, we must hope and call for an end to war.

### Story Structure

The story of "King Solomon and the Otter" is a sequence of events in which the action of each character causes the action of the next. It also is a circle story since the flow of events initiated by Otter eventually affects her in the end. The tale uses a biological food chain as a metaphor for human behavior. In nature, an otter might indeed eat a crab for its own survival. The story is not a comment on the positive or negative results of food chains, an important aspect of biological balance in nature, but of individual human action as it touches the lives of others.

The motion of the story proceeds as each character defensively dons the posture or clothing of war because he or she sees another doing it. The animals in turn are suspicious and defensive and each assumes aggression from the character which precedes it in the chain of events. Each reacts in fear according to their suspicion of danger.

In our personal lives, everything we do, knowingly or unknowingly, affects something or someone. Becoming aware of our impact on the world around us, and taking responsibility for it, can help create a more harmonious and healthy environment for all.

## But What Happened First?

Diagram the sequence of events in this story as a circle:

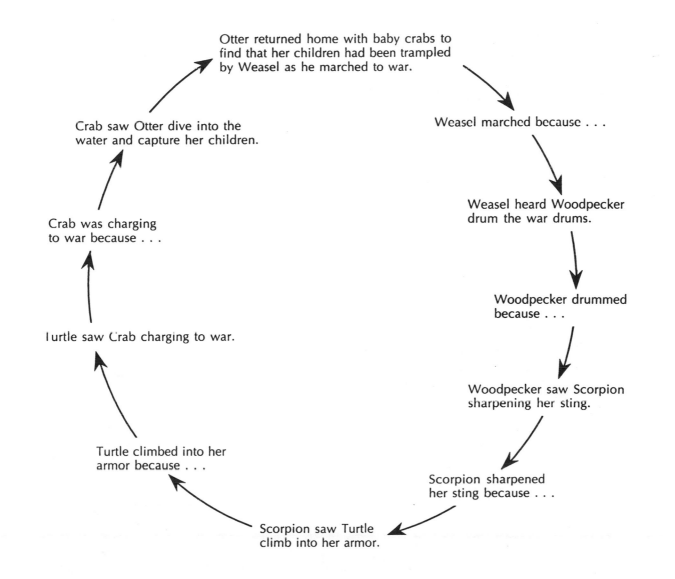

Otter returned home with baby crabs to find that her children had been trampled by Weasel as he marched to war.

Weasel marched because . . .

Weasel heard Woodpecker drum the war drums.

Woodpecker drummed because . . .

Woodpecker saw Scorpion sharpening her sting.

Scorpion sharpened her sting because . . .

Scorpion saw Turtle climb into her armor.

Turtle climbed into her armor because . . .

Turtle saw Crab charging to war.

Crab was charging to war because . . .

Crab saw Otter dive into the water and capture her children.

In my telling of this tale, I described first that Otter discovered her children had been trampled by Weasel. Otter blames this tragedy on weasel. But did the tragedy begin with Weasel alone? Like a detective, we can go to the scene of the crime and retrace the sequence of events around the circle to its start.

- Who saw Otter hunting? (Crab)
- What did Crab do? (Charged to war to protect her young)
- Who saw Crab charging? (Turtle)
- What did Turtle do? (Put on her armor)
- Who saw Turtle put on her armor? (Scorpion)
- What did Scorpion do? (Sharpened her sting)
- Who saw Scorpion sharpen her sting? (Woodpecker)
- What did Woodpecker do? (Drummed war drums)
- Who heard the drums? (Weasel)
- What did Weasel do? (Thrilled by the drums, he marched off to war and accidently trampled Otter's children)
- Who saw what Weasel had done? (Otter, returning from the hunt with captured baby crabs)

In retracing the chain of events we can see that it was Otter who started the chain of events. The *first* thing that actually happened was that Otter went hunting!

## Discussion Questions: Cause and Effect

According to the laws of physics, "change," or everything that happens in the universe, is a reaction to something else that happened.

Could the tragedy of Otter's children being trampled have been avoided if any character in the tale changed its action?

Can you remember a personal experience which involved a cause and effect? The effect could have been either positive or negative for you.

For example:

- Have you ever reacted in anger because you thought that another was angry at you?
- Has a rumor ever affected you?
- Has your good deed ever changed a difficult situation?
- Has a smile ever brought a friend your way?
- Has learning about different cultures ever helped you to become tolerant of differences?

## Flow Charts

A flow chart is a simple way to diagram a sequence of events.

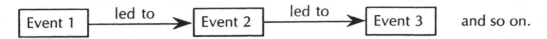

Can you find a cause and effect story in the newspaper and diagram your findings as a flow chart? (Use pictures or words.)

For example:

- Clip articles about a pollution problem and try to order the events that led to the problem.

- Can you continue the flow chart and include some solutions to the problem?

- Can you identify the point in the flow chart where the course of events could have been changed and the problem avoided?

Can you trace the history of something that ends up in a garbage dump?

For example:

- Diagram the autobiography of a piece of paper from tree seedling to garbage dump.

- How would the sequence of events be different if the paper was recycled?

Our growing awareness of the effect of our garbage on the environment has resulted in greater conservation and recycling to help change the course of events.

## Social Action

Individuals *can* have an impact on the world at large. And, since there are so many of us, our collective impact can be very great. Even small gestures in a positive direction can help to make a better world.

Can you think of some actions you could take that could start a constructive chain of events considering:

- Your personal behavior to others . . .
  . . . in your family?
  . . . in your community?
  . . . in your school?
  . . . among your friends?

- Your personal behavior with regard to the environment . . .
  . . . in the disposal of your own garbage?
  . . . in the conservation of water and electricity at home?
  . . . in purchasing environmentally safe goods?
  . . . in learning more about how to protect the Earth?

❦ ❦ ❦

**Heather Forest** is a professional storyteller, recording artist, and author of children's books. She has toured her repertoire of world tales told in a minstrel style of storytelling blending original music, guitar, poetry, prose, and the sung and spoken word for audiences throughout the United States.

# A Tree Planting in South Africa

by Gavin Harrison
edited by Sarah Pirtle

I GREW UP IN JOHANNESBURG, SOUTH AFRICA. Our home was very beautiful and filled with treasures that my parents had accumulated from all over the world. It was also surrounded by a great big wall, as were all the homes in the area where we lived.

At the back of our property behind the garage was a series of little rooms. A black man named Shadrak lived there in a room that didn't have electricity, hot water, or heating. Each morning he came out of his room at half-past-five and knocked on my parents' window. My father got up, went to the back door, opened the burglar alarm—which was a series of knobs and keys and buttons—and let Shadrak in.

Shadrak brought tea into my parents' room on a tray and then took a bucket of hot water back to his own room so that he could wash. During the day he looked after the garden, cooked the meals, and did anything else that my parents directed.

Each month he came to my father with his passbook for my father to sign. This was his permission to live in a white area. If he didn't have his passbook with him, it meant that he was illegal and could be arrested.

I was forbidden to have any real relationship with Shadrak. I was much closer to my pet dog than to him. He was just there to work for us, and he was treated as a sort of nonperson who lived in the backyard.

Once a week a woman came to our home from the black township of Soweto. She appeared every Monday to do the washing and the ironing and then she disappeared back to Soweto. To get to our house from hers was very difficult because there is only one road running out of the township. She had to leave at four o'clock in the morning, travel twenty miles by train and bus, and arrive for work at our house by seven o'clock.

As I was growing up, the 18 million black people in South Africa were hidden from me. The boarding school I attended was for white boys of English-speaking background only. Black men and women cleaned the rooms and the swimming pool and the tennis courts and did the cooking, but our lives were kept completely separated.

I also had nothing to do with the white Afrikaners in my country, the people of Dutch ancestry. Though I had to learn Afrikaans in school, I never spoke to an Afrikaans person. They went to different schools and were always our opponents on the rugby field, on the tennis court, and in cricket games.

I never had an Afrikaans friend until I was drafted into the army. There the Afrikaans-speaking people and the English-speaking people were all together. Some of the Afrikaners in the army were particularly vicious with us English-speaking kids because they saw us as liberals, the greatest threat to apartheid and the status quo. In their minds we were in some weird way a part of the enemy, and they made our basic training as rigorous as they could to break us down.

When I finished my time in the army, I studied to be an accountant. I used to go to the university every evening after work and often would chat with the liberal arts and divinity students who were deeply involved in political activities.

This was in 1972. I talked to white students who were involved in a nationwide protest campaign to make people aware of the appalling disparity between black education and white education in our country.

One evening I arrived at the university to find out that the police had just arrested some students. Something in my heart snapped. I knew that this was the moment—I had to make a stand. I picked up a sign and took my place on the picket line with several hundred white students. I was absolutely terrified, and also exhilarated.

Day after day we stood holding up placards on the pavement at the university. One read: The government spends $120 a year on the education of each white child but only $4 a year for each black child. Some of the people driving by flashed their car lights or honked their horns to show they were in agreement with us. But most of the white people ignored us, or screamed at us, and sometimes even threw rocks, or tomatoes, or eggs.

One day during rush hour traffic, everything suddenly went dead quiet. Armored cars drove up and policemen piled out. They lined up on an island in the middle of the road facing the group of us, about 200 students.

Looking at the faces of the police, I knew that they really wanted to hurt us, maybe even kill us. They were standing there joking, reading the placards, pointing at who they wanted to get.

Then the whistle blew: there was smoke and teargas, and they went for us. When they caught us, they beat us up with the truncheons, women as well as men. Some of us managed to get away, but it was like our campus had turned into a war zone.

From that point on, I began to see things I'd never seen before. I had relied on everything being okay and orderly, but when I looked a bit deeper, I saw that so much about my country was unfair. Such a rage came through me.

I had a falling out with my parents. I blamed them for the sense of betrayal I felt. The country I grew up in had promised me everything—wealth, the chance for success, and the enjoyment of what I believe is the most beautiful land in the world. But now it seemed to me that all of this was founded on oppression and violence, anger and ignorance.

I left South Africa and vowed never to return. I wanted to live where I wasn't surrounded by this nightmare. I lived in Europe, England, the Middle East, and finally America.

But there were immigration problems, and I had to go back to South Africa to live for two years. It was the lowest point of my life when I had to go back. What I saw was worse than I remembered. There was such pain and denial around me.

I decided to go to a meditation center in Zululand at a place called Ixopo. At the end of my first meditation retreat, they asked me to stay on staff.

Our neighbors were a black village on the next mountain in a place called the Valley of a Thousand Hills. You could hear the people singing there every morning, especially Sunday. Here for the first time in South Africa I felt connected to the black people. Sometimes people from the center and people from the village would work together chopping trees and cutting them into slices, all to the sound of our singing together.

If there was an emergency in the village, a woman having a difficult birth or a child bitten by a snake, they came to us for help. We went over in our truck, picked them up and took them to the hospital. Once we had a huge fire in the forest by our center; villagers poured down the mountain to put out the fire threatening our buildings. Living there, my heart began to heal.

I went to America where I was ordained as a Buddhist monk. There I realized that one of the hardest things I needed to do, one of the pains I most needed to heal, was my separation from my father. I went back to South Africa to stay with my parents.

By this time my parents had moved south to Warner Beach which is down in Zululand. Every day I took long walks in the mountains through fields of sugar cane. I needed to walk because my back hurt continually. I believe that this pain came from the beatings I was given in school as a child.

On one of these walks I met Armstrong Zulu who is a black man, a Zulu. I liked his huge smile, and I stopped to talk. It didn't take him long to find out I was a chartered accountant. He told me he was having trouble with his bookkeeping. He said we were brothers for life and he really needed me to help him. I was only too happy to help him. I felt useless just hanging out at home.

I asked my Mom and Dad if Armstrong could come around so I could help him with his bookkeeping. My father said, "No way will I have a black person in my home." So when Armstrong called, I suggested that I come to his house.

To get to his community of Umgababa, I had to catch a train, a ten-minute trip. At the station I said, "Could I have a ticket to Umgababa?" The ticket agent said, "You must be making a mistake." I said it was no mistake. He replied, "Well, Umgababa is a black town." I said, "Yeah, I want a ticket to Umgababa."

He asked, "What are you going to do there?" I said, "It's none of your business." He got up, went to the railway policeman nearby. The policeman took a pointed look at me and said, "Okay, give him a ticket." The agent gave me the ticket and I took the train.

I got off the train in Umgababa. I was the only white person in sight. Not even policemen were there. I was petrified. Since I arrived early in the morning, thousands of people were all leaving for work in the white area. On the way I was jostled and punched a couple of times. The women cringed from me, terrified. I stood at the bottom of Umgababa Mountain, and I knew that I had about two miles to go.

In that moment all the fear I had from being kept away from black people in my country just poured through me. I knew then that I could either run away or I'd have to climb that mountain.

I kept on going. Every step was a step away from all the things that had kept me from doing this for so long. When I reached the top, I was elated.

Armstrong greeted me, and I began working at the local school, helping him and his friends with bookkeeping to prepare them for examinations. The headmaster of the school asked if I would work with the rest of the pupils to help them with bookkeeping and economics and also the English language. I said I'd do that.

That night I went home, and over dinner I told my Mom and Dad that I'd accepted a voluntary position at the school.

My father threw a tantrum. He said, "Those bloody 'Kaffirs' are gonna burn the school down. You see it on television . . . look what they're doing in Soweto. You're wasting your time! It's dangerous. You're just doing this to embarrass me."

I exploded. I told my father, "Don't you ever, ever, ever say that to me!"

He retorted, "You've been overseas too long, you communist."

That was the first time we had open warfare in my family. After that my father and I didn't talk. I got up every morning and made a pot of porridge, enough for both my father and me. Then I went to the station to get my ticket to Umgababa and off I would go. I always left him the porridge I made for him.

I had been really scared that first day when I went to Umgababa, but after a few days when I arrived at the station in the morning, all the kids came pouring down to join me, and we'd all walk up the mountain together. Going to the school became an absolute joy. In about three days, everybody in the town knew who I was and what I was doing. They'd all wave and shout and I always went home with bags of papayas, bananas, avocado pears, and guavas.

The students were so excited about learning. We had conversations in English, and all of a sudden they became radiant when they could make themselves understood in a language they had learned but never before spoken to an English speaker. One by one the children in the class began to develop confidence and proficiency in English. Teaching at this school was really wonderful for me. At last, after thirty years, I felt I was doing something worthwhile in my country.

It was embarrassing for my father because many of the people from Umgababa worked in Warner Beach, and a lot of them knew who my father was. Every now and again my father would be walking down the street and somebody would come up and say, "Hello, Mr. Harrison. You've got a great son! He's teaching my daughter!" And then my father was mortified.

He lived in an apartment building where fifteen women and ten men from Umgababa worked. Because of me they developed a very friendly feeling for my father. He was very embarrassed, especially when they spoke to him in front of his friends.

I learned a lot about education for blacks in South Africa. Our school had nothing. The students were expected to learn three languages: English, Afrikaans, and Zulu. Most of them had never read a book. When I asked them why they didn't read, they said it was because they had no library and no money to buy books. Even with no textbooks at our school, they were made to write examinations in those subjects.

After two weeks I was furious and frustrated. I phoned up all the headmasters of white schools in the area. I went to the first one and said, "Hi, I'm Gavin Harrison. I'm a teacher at Umgababa High School. You know about us, don't you?" He said, "No, I don't know about you." I said, "We're up on Umgababa Mountain. We're a high school with 550 pupils. While you're concerned about how many video terminals you have and your second swimming pool and your rugby field, we don't have electricity or running water. We have to drink the water that runs off the asbestos roof. That's all the water we have. We don't have a library, much less tennis courts. What are you going to do about it?"

The response at every school, English or Afrikaans, was the same. They said, "We didn't know this was going on," and gave us all their surplus books. They asked me to speak at staff meetings, and I began to drive truckloads of books up that mountain.

An article was written about this project in a local newspaper, and people started phoning me at home. In the article we said we needed sets of encyclopedia; the sets started pouring in.

One day when I got home, my mother told me a phone call had come that morning and my father had answered it. He didn't know that my mother could hear him. He said, "Hello. No, it's not me you want to talk to, it's my son. He's the teacher at the school. What is it you want? Oh, yes, that's very nice. Yes, we definitely need sets of encyclopedia for the school. You know, it's really terrible. This school where my son works doesn't have electricity. They don't have running water . . . . Yes, yes, I'll come and pick up those books. Just tell me where you live." He went off and got the books, brought them back, and he put them into the garage with the others. I told my Mom not to say a word that she knew about this.

Some days later, I was very late for school. My father offered to drive me there. This was the first time in his 65 years that my father had been into a black area. On the way there I told him I'd been given $300 to buy wood for library shelves. I asked him, "Will you tell me what kind of wood to get?" He said, "No, I'm not getting involved. Once you put one foot in, before you know it, you could have a full-time job."

We got up to the school and he said, "Well, look, maybe I'd better come in and measure for the wood because you'll only make a mess of it." I took him to the library. I told him I had to go teach class, but that I'd send some pupils over to help. He looked at me with big wide eyes and said, "You're leaving me here?"

At break, the headmaster made some sandwiches and invited my father and me to eat with him. My Dad said to the headmaster, "Look, I think I'd better build these shelves for you. If I leave it to Gavin, they probably won't last a day. I think I'm going to do it. Is that okay?" The headmaster said, "Yes, that will be great." So my father built the shelves in the school library at Umgababa.

I was getting so excited about this project that I started going everywhere I could think of. I met a Methodist minister. I told him some of the students had to walk twelve miles to get to school, and by noon some passed out because they hadn't eaten anything all day. The next Sunday he mentioned it from the pulpit and within two weeks we started a lunch program with money from that congregation.

I went to the local white municipality and told the garden nursery supervisor that at the black school we didn't have a tree where the kids could get shade; we didn't have any flowers so that the school could be beautiful. He said to bring a truck down. We took a truck and filled it up with trees and manure. We planted a garden on one side of the school.

I was introduced to a Hindu swami, an Asian man who lived in Durban, north of Warner Beach. I explained we were so overcrowded that often three little kids would be squashed onto one tiny bench sharing one desk. The swami invited us to his ashram in the area where Mahatma Gandhi had lived; we went, staff and parents from Umgababa. He was a wonderful, open man. He asked questions about the school and then offered $25,000 to build four new classrooms.

We decided we needed to celebrate this outpouring of gifts so we planned a ceremony for the opening of the new library. We kept a record of everybody who helped us and sent out invitations to every person.

The big day came. Our choir had been practicing. All the students brought fruit and vegetables as a thank-you for the people who were coming. We had huge piles of papayas and bananas, potatoes and guavas and avocado pears. It would be the first time that all of these white people had ever been in a black area.

The party was set for nine o'clock. At quarter-to-nine our parking lot was full. At five-to-nine our students came flying out of the classrooms to watch several buses coming up the mountain, filled with white students and teachers. I wondered what was going to happen.

The buses stopped and all the black kids surrounded them. The white teachers in the buses just looked down and didn't move. I could see the terror in their faces. The doors opened. I went forward and welcomed them, and cautiously out they stepped.

There was silence for a few moments, and then everyone started talking and went together into the school. The white kids and the black kids talked about math and science and where they lived and all that. The white teachers went to all the classrooms and chatted a bit with the black kids, asking them about their school, and how they were doing.

We had the opening ceremony. The headmaster spoke, the choir sang and danced and then I spoke. There were fifty or sixty white people there. My father was in the back of the crowd. He was crying, deeply moved by the whole experience.

Then we walked together to a spot outside the library where a tree from the nursery was ready to be planted. We lowered it into a hole that we'd dug, and each person put a shovel of soil on the tree. All of us there committed ourselves to continue to make changes in our lives and to overcome what had kept us apart. There were white parents, black parents, black kids and white kids, Asian people, all together.

We sang a song in Zulu, a song that many people have been jailed for singing: the African National Anthem, *Nkosi Sikelel' iAfrika*, that says, God Bless Africa.

❧ ❧ ❧

Four years passed. I returned to the United States. When I went back to visit my parents, I also returned to the school in Umgababa. I saw the completed classrooms and some of the teachers. It was wonderful to be back on the mountain again. A number of pupils who I'd taught came up to me on the street both in Umgababa and in Warner Beach. Taller and older, they were as happy to see me as I was to see them.

I was staying with my parents again. One evening I was playing cards with my mother, when my father cried out from the bedroom. We rushed in, and it was clear that he was having a massive heart attack.

My mother began to panic. She said, "Who should I call? What should I do?"

I held my father in my arms. I said to her, "Why don't you come here right now and be with him? Don't lose this precious opportunity. He's starting to go." I suggested she hold him on the other side of the bed.

Through her tears she joined me whispering in his ears how we loved him and how we wished him well on the journey he was taking. He died in our arms. The look on his face in the moment of his passing was peaceful and contented.

I picked branches of bougainvillaea blossoms in the garden and brought them into the bedroom. During the two hours before they came to take his body away, my mother and I prayed together and shared memories of him. We each spent time forgiving him for the things he'd done which hurt us. We also asked him to forgive us.

I had never told him that I'd shared the story of him and the school in Umgababa with my friends in America, but I told him as he lay there. I said this story had helped me leave South Africa and had helped me come back again with none of the anger that had originally taken me away. I told my father how proud I was of him and how grateful I was that I could be there at the moment of his death to help him on his way. I said I knew that he loved me very much.

A memorial service was held for my father at the Methodist Church in Warner Beach. My mother asked friends and acquaintances not to send flowers but rather to make a donation to the school in Umgababa. Eight typewriters were bought with that money.

At his memorial service I told this story again. Teachers from the Umgababa school were there. When I finished, the children from the school choir came up to the front of the church and sang the song in Zulu,

> *Nkosi Sikelel' iAfrika.*
> *God Bless Africa*

It was the same song we sang before, my father and I and all the others, on that day on the top of the mountain in the hot sun, when we planted a tree together.

## Follow-up Activities for "A Tree Planting in South Africa"

## by Sarah Pirtle

### Preparation for the Story

- This is a long story. Rather than learn to tell it, you may want to read it aloud, perhaps in two sessions. Or you can make copies for the students to read themselves and then discuss together.

- If you are telling or reading the story, prepare the pronunciation of the song, "Nkosi Sikelel' iAfrika." It is pronounced: Ko-see See-ka-lay-lee Africa.

- Clarify that the story they will hear is true.

- Ask students beforehand, "What do you know about South Africa?"

- **What is apartheid?** Explain that apartheid is an Afrikaans word for "separateness." It refers to a social, economic, and political system whereby the South African government representing the white people, a small minority of the total population, exercises totalitarian dominion over the black people, the vast majority. (The term "black" encompasses people of color who are African, Asian, and "mixed-race").

- Find South Africa on a map and point out the locations in the story: Johannesburg, Soweto, Warner Beach and Ixopo.

### Discussion and Further Exploration

- Begin by allowing the students the opportunity to express their own meaning. Ask them: "What stays with you from the story?"

- Make a list of the questions they have after hearing the story.

- Choose the directions you want to explore from the five areas which are provided below:
  1. Exploring the Theme of Reconciliation
  2. Overturning Prejudice and Oppression
  3. Understanding South Africa through Music
  4. Taking Action
  5. Going Further with a Study of South Africa.

- Make use of this quote from Nelson Mandela as an introduction:

  > I have fought against white domination, and I have fought against Black domination. I have cherished the idea of a democratic and free society in which all persons live together in harmony and with equal opportunities. It is an ideal which I hope to live for and to achieve. But if need be, it is an ideal for which I am prepared to die.
  >
  > —Nelson Mandela, at the Rivonia Trial in 1964 and again in 1990 after his release from prison.

Background: In February 1990 Nelson Mandela, who is widely regarded as the leader of Black South Africans, was freed after 27 years in prison. He and President F. W. De Klerk, who is an Afrikaner, and other members of the white government are exploring the possibilities of political accommodation and coexistence. Although it is unclear what the outcome of these negotiations will be, it is very significant that these people are meeting and talking together seriously for the first time after 42 years. De Klerk has disavowed apartheid, and Nelson Mandela is working to create a broad coalition including Africans, Indians, people who are classified by the government as mixed descent, and friendly whites.

## Exploring the Theme of Reconciliation

### Discussion questions:

These can be approached not only in group discussion, but also through written responses and by talking in pairs before convening the whole group.

- Why did Gavin feel estranged from his father?

- How did Gavin and his father mend their relationship? What did each of them do to help make this possible? Gavin mentions that he was ordained as a Buddhist monk. One of the vows he took was to practice loving-kindness. How does he carry out this vow in the story?

- "Escalation" is the word which describes the process of making a conflict more heated. Yelling, accusation, and blaming are some things which increase a conflict. What else might escalate a problem? What helps ease or de-escalate a problem? What did Gavin and his father do to de-escalate their conflict?

**Topics for poem or essay writing:**

- "Recipe for Making Up with Friends"

- "Seeing Things from Your Eyes"

  Choose a person, where they live, and what they are doing. You could pick a person in the Umgababa school, a child living in Soweto, or a person you know, such as someone with whom you have a disagreement. What words might they use to describe their viewpoint?

- "A Person I Don't Understand"

- "Building Bridges"

- Humorous writing—"How to Make Things Worse"

**Idea for symbolic line drawings:**

- Make a line drawing where the lines represent you and someone you know, perhaps a friend of yours. Show the changes in your relationship during the last year.

## Overturning Prejudice and Oppression

The work of Equity Institute in San Francisco has informed this section. Here is the vocabulary the trainers of Equity Institute use in talking about oppression.

- The group which has the greatest economic, political, and other resources is called the "dominant group" in respect to a specific type of oppression.

- "The targeted group" is the one treated unfairly just on the basis of who they are.

  For example, looking at racism in the United States, the dominant group refers to white European-Americans, and the targeted group refers to Americans who are people of color: Asian-Americans, Black Americans, Latino-Americans, Native Americans, Pacific Islanders. In South Africa the dominant group is only 14-18% of the population, tremendously smaller in number than the targeted group, but maintains its dominance through the system of apartheid.

- "Acting as an ally": A person from the dominant group can intervene and interrupt the oppression of the targeted group. For example, when a man stops another man from deciding not to promote an employee because she is a woman, he is acting as an ally against sexism. Or in school if a person speaks up to interrupt namecalling, this is being an ally to the person called a name.

- The ally draws a wider circle to see how another's struggle is actually their own as well. They stand with the targeted person.

**Discussion of the story:**

- We saw Gavin's father change his attitudes and his behaviors toward people of color. What helped him change?

- How did Gavin, a white person, act as an ally with people of color in South Africa?

- In what ways do Americans act as allies with South Africans who oppose apartheid?

**Extension:**

- Give students a chance to talk in small groups about their own ethnic, religious, and class backgrounds and affirm their own identities.

- Describe a time you intervened, or wish you had intervened, when someone was being targeted.

- What are the different kinds of oppression? As you list each one, delineate which is the dominant and which is the targeted group. For example, in respect to the oppression of homophobia, the dominant group is defined as people whose sexual preference is heterosexual and the targeted group are those people whose sexual preference is lesbian, gay, or bisexual.

- Pick one form of oppression and discuss how people in the dominant group can act as allies to people in the targeted group.

Equity Institute points out ways in which each oppression interlocks and reinforces the others. They emphasize feeling proud of one's own identity, learning how to be an ally, and interrupting name-calling of all types.

For further information, contact Equity Institute, 6400 Hollis Street, Suite 15, Emeryville, CA 94608.

"Sticks, Stones, and Stereotypes" is their highly recommended curriculum resource guide and video. It addresses homophobia and racism using interviews and dramatic enactments by teenagers.

**Multicultural Education Resources:**

*Anti-Bias Curriculum: Tools for Empowering Young Children* by Derman-Sparks and the A.B.C. Task Force, and *Teaching Young Children to Resist Bias: What Parents Can Do* are available from the National Association for the Education of Young Children, 1834 Connecticut Ave. NW, Washington, DC 20009.

*Council on Interracial Books for Children.* 1841 Broadway, New York, NY 10023.

*Multicultural Education: A Selected Bibliography* is available from Bank Street College of Education, 610 W. 112th St., New York, NY 10025.

*Open Minds to Equality: A Source Book of Learning Activities to Promote Race, Sex, Class and Age Equity,* by Nancy Schniedewind and Ellen Davidson, Prentice Hall: Englewood Cliffs, NJ.

## Understanding South Africa through Music

The African National Anthem: Many people have been imprisoned for singing the song mentioned in the story, "Nkosi Sikelel' iAfrika." It was composed in 1897 by Enoch Sontonga, a Xhosa teacher, and was popularized by the concerts of the Ohlange Zulu Choir. The leaders of the African National Congress adopted it as a closing anthem for their meetings in 1925, and it became an integral part of the movement of "Africa for the Africans." When the Barwa chorus of South African students introduces this song to contemporary U.S. audiences, this is what they say:

"We who have no power to control the government regard this as our national anthem. They have their own national anthem which is based on conquering Africa. But we have ours which is based on lifting Africa. The lyrics speak for themselves:

Lord bless Africa. Let her horn be raised.
Listen to our prayers. Lord bless we, her children.

Come Spirit, come Holy Spirit.
Lord bless we, her children.

God bless our nation. Do away with wars and trouble.
Bless it, Lord, our nation.
Let it be so, forever and ever."

Here are three sources for this song and other important South African freedom songs:

- "Let Their Voices Be Heard: Traditional Singing in South Africa" from Rounder Records, One Camp Street, Cambridge, MA 02140. Lyric sheet included with the record.

- *Amandla*, a forty-member community chorus from western Massachusetts, sings songs of freedom and struggle from South Africa and the U.S.: "We sing to free ourselves and our nation from the racism and injustice around and within us." To order a teaching tape or concert tape, or for more information about Amandla, contact Lisa Limont, Route 1, Box 340, Colrain, MA 01340. (413) 624-3791.

- *Freedom is Coming* songbook has the words and music for many South African liberation songs. Contact: Walton Music Corp., 170 NE 33rd, Fort Lauderdale, Florida, 33334. Tape: $9, Book: $5, Postage: $3.

Here is music which can be purchased through most record stores:

- Miriam Makeba, "Sangoma," Warner Brothers, 1988.

- Ladysmith Black Mambazo, Shanachie or Warner Brothers. This men's a cappella group worked with Paul Simon on "Graceland." They have four recordings of their own.

The following recordings can be ordered from the Ladyslipper Catalog, P.O. Box 3130, Durham, NC 27705. 1-800-634-6044.

- "South African Trade Union Worker Choirs"—11 different all-female and all-male choirs recorded secretly at union meetings and churches. $8.95.

- "Soweto Never Sleeps"—Zulu Jive tracks by four women's groups from South Africa. $9.95.

- "Poppie Nongena"—Award-winning South African musical based on the actual story of a Black woman living in South Africa today, music by Sophie Mgcinas. $8.95.

- "Welela" (1989), "Country Girl," "Pata Pata," "The World of Miriam Makeba" and "Myriam Makeba (The Click Song)" by Miriam Makeba.

## Taking Action

Gavin Harrison illustrates in this story that each person has his or her own way of working to change what is felt to be wrong or unjust. Gavin struggled to change what he saw around him: joining the university demonstrations, speaking out in his family, allying with the school in Umgababa, speaking out among the people whom he encountered. He grew in awareness of the problems, he found other people at the Ixopo meditation center who shared his concerns, and later he drew others together and organized a common effort in support of the Umgababa school.

Students can discuss these questions:

- Is it true that one person can make a difference?
- What were all the different ways Gavin worked to make change?
- Did he do it alone?

For Gavin, taking action began inside him with his own personal motivation. How can we as teachers give students a chance to explore ways in which the story ignites their own concerns about the world without imposing our directions upon them? How can we give them the chance to listen to themselves and not presuppose what the outcome will be? One process is for small groups of three students to work with this question:

How does the story bring up for you the ways in which the world isn't working the way it could?

Then if they do have a personal investment in proceeding with this, you could ask:

Do you want to work further to take action on any of the concerns you've raised?

Some students may want to focus upon the racism in their own school. As teacher you can help identify avenues for action on this. If students ask, "What can we do about apartheid in South Africa?" these examples and resources illuminate directions other students have taken which they could take as well. More news of student efforts is listed in the newsletter: Educators Against Racism and Apartheid, 164-04 Goethals Ave., Jamaica, NY 11432. This groundbreaking group provided most of the information found in this section.

## Boycotts and Divestment Campaigns

Foreign investments, loans, and trade agreements as well as foreign companies located in South Africa strengthen the white South African regime. The Africa Fund publishes the *Unified List of U.S. Companies Doing Business in South Africa* by Richard Knight. The third (1990) edition and other updates are available from The Africa Fund, 198 Broadway, NY, NY 10038. (212) 962-1210.

As of 1990 about 160 U.S. corporations do business with South Africa and pay taxes to the South African government. Anti-apartheid groups (African National Congress, the Congress of South African Trade Unions, and others) have called for full divestment by all foreign corporations so that economic support for apartheid is withdrawn. When a company divests, it strips off all the ways it is economically linked to South Africa.

Here are examples of how students have expressed their concerns to some of the U.S. companies who haven't divested:

- Students at some New York City schools have sent coupons to the President of Kellogg's cereals which state, "While Kellogg's Company makes profits in South Africa, half of all Black children die from malnutrition and disease before the age of five . . . . I will not buy Kellogg's cereal until you divest fully from South Africa." Kellogg has a factory in Springs, South Africa, pays taxes to the South African government, and sells cereal to the South African military. Address: President, Kellogg's Company, 1 Kellogg Plaza, Battle Creek, MI 49016-3599.

- Coca-Cola is another company that has received extensive pressure from national boycott efforts. As of 1990 it had divested $60 million of its South African holdings, but still licensed its name and formula for use in South Africa. In 1989 students at Mt. Greylock Regional High School in western Massachusetts led the school in a Coke boycott. The Coca-Cola Company responded by offering the school a free electronic scoreboard, but they turned it down and kept up the boycott.

What can students do? Educators Against Racism and Apartheid provides these ideas:

- Writing an information leaflet for your school.

- Collecting signatures on a petition to remove the product from vending machines, the school cafeteria, or a local supermarket.

- Making pledges not to buy the product until the company divests from South Africa.

- Writing letters to the company.

- Contacting a local TV or radio station.

- Writing an article for a school or local newspaper.

Besides boycotting specific companies, groups also ask that their money not be *invested* in companies that do business with South Africa. An example of this is the effort by some teachers to research where their retirement system invests. The Teachers Retirement System Board of Trustees in New York City divested over $300 million from corporations doing business with South Africa after a five-year effort which included letter-writing, a leaflet campaign, and sending speakers to monthly board meetings. Other sources of information on economic sanctions:

- American Friends Service Committee, Southern Africa Project, 1201 Cherry St., Philadelphia, PA 19102, has a list of U.S. companies that export goods to South Africa. They can tell you if a company in your region is involved.

## Working Against the Commerce of Poisons

Greenpeace has a Waste Trade Project which is trying to stop a U.S. company, American Cyanamid, from exporting ten tons of mercury wastes each year to a mercury reprocessing plant near Cato Ridge, South Africa; these wastes affect the Mngeweni River. This river provides drinking water for Zulu villagers living downstream. For more information, write Greenpeace, Waste Trade Project, 1436 U Street NW, Washington, DC 20009. Letters of concern can also be sent to: George Sella, CEO, American Cyanamid, 1 Cyanamid Plaza, Wayne, NJ 07470.

## Expression Through the Arts

Here are examples of ways schools have focused this expression:

- In Teaneck, New Jersey, first grade students learned about apartheid and wrote a play called "Bryant School Goes to Soweto" with their teachers Jay Friedman and Diane McNeil. They presented the play at a Dr. Martin Luther King Jr. Celebration.

- An Apartheid Awareness Contest held by the For Our Children's Sake Foundation provides a model which can be used locally. They posed two questions: "How can we as global citizens work with the United Nations to end apartheid?" and "What does apartheid mean to you?" Responses could be in the performing, the visual, or the communication arts.

- Springfield Gardens High School in Queens, New York asked teachers of the humanities and all school clubs to help create a presentation where each segment heightened awareness of apartheid. Music from South Africa was sung, and dramatic presentations of the life of Nelson Mandela were performed.

- South African writers can be studied. Poems of Mzwakhe Mbuli can be heard on *Mzwakhe: Change is Pain* from Rounder Records, One Camp St., Cambridge, MA 02140. The American Friends Service Committee produced the video, "Voices from South Africa" which includes Mbuli and other writers and focuses on the cultural movement in South Africa.

Whatever way your group takes action, take time afterward to celebrate and appreciate your efforts. "A Tree Planting in South Africa" emphasizes having hope and never giving up. Give people a chance to speak on this subject, "I have hope because . . ."

## Going Further With a Study of South Africa

A wealth of resources is available to deepen understanding of life under apartheid:

### Curriculum Materials

*Apartheid Is Wrong: A Curriculum For Young People*, Paula Rogovin Bower, Co-Chairperson of Educators Against Racism and Apartheid and a New York City public school teacher, has authored hands-on, multidisciplinary materials for grades one through twelve. The lessons provide social studies, math, writing, drama, art, and science activities. For example, the social studies unit develops research and critical thinking skills using topics such as the Freedom Charter, population registration, forced removals, unequal education, and housing. The second edition of the curriculum has 308 pages. It can be purchased for $17 plus $5 postage (bulk purchases discounted) from: Educators Against Racism and Apartheid, 164-04 Goethals Ave., Jamaica, NY 11432.

- Here is a quote which provides background about the South African educational system:

    The deliberate creation of a 'permanent underclass' composed of the non-white racial groups in South Africa was propagated and perpetuated by the white minority class through, among other things, education. From the Cape School Board Act of 1905, which established separate schools for the different racial groups, through to the Bantu Education Act of 1953, up to the bill that led to the Soweto riots of 1976, Act after Act was promulgated to entrench a vicious circle of educational deprivation for the majority of the South African population. This was done for the purpose of creating and perpetually maintaining a privileged white minority class whose assumed superiority and supremacy over the other racial groups would, as such, be unquestioned.

    —Xoliswa Skomolo, *Thoughts on Education in a New South Africa*, in *Sechaba*, the official publication of the African National Congress, September 1990.

## Videos about South Africa

Two distributors have extensive catalogues of videos:

- California Newsreel, 144 9th St/420, San Francisco, CA 94103. (415) 621-6196.
- Cinema Guild, 1697 Broadway, New York, NY 10019.

Available videos include:

"Spear of the Nation: History of the African National Congress";
"South Africa Belongs to Us" (about the impact of apartheid on women and the family);
"Biko: Breaking the Silence";
"The Cry of Reason" (about Rev. Naude, anti-apartheid leader).
(Educators Against Racism and Apartheid makes the above videos available to the New York region for only the cost of shipping.)

"Mandela in America" is a ninety-minute video documentary of Mandela's 11 day tour to eight cities. Contact: South Africa Now, 361 W. Broadway, NY, NY 10013.

The American Friends Service Committee, 2161 Massachusetts Ave., Cambridge, MA 02140, (617) 497-5273, also inexpensively rents videos including, "Forget Not Our Sisters: Women Under Apartheid."

International Defense and Aid Fund for South Africa has not only films and videos, but also books and a photo library. P.O. Box 17, Cambridge, MA 02238. (617) 491-8343. Write for their fifty-page catalog.

In addition, "A Dry White Season" (starring Donald Sutherland, Zakes Mokae and Marlon Brando, directed by Euzhan Palcy) is available at many commercial video outlets.

## Literature for Young People

Cathi MacRae, young adult columnist for the *Wilson Library Bulletin*, has recommended the following books for middle school, junior high, and senior high school readers. The descriptions are developed from MacRae's reviews:

*Biko*. Donald Woods. Revised and updated edition. New York: Holt, 1987. 448 pp. A compelling portrait of Steve Biko, who originated the Black Consciousness movement in South Africa. Biko was only twenty-six when banned to his small town, yet his vision influenced thousands.

*Crossing the Line: A Year in the Land of Apartheid*. William Finnegan. New York: Harper and Row, 1986. 418 pp. paperback $8.95. While teaching in a Capetown secondary school, Finnegan realizes that his career counseling project for black students is doomed because the system guarantees most students' failure.

*Filming with Attenborough: The Making of Cry Freedom*. Donald Woods. New York: Holt, 1987. 163 pp. This book is about the film made from the novel. It goes behind-the-scenes in the making of the film and also reviews South African background.

*Kaffir Boy: The True Story of a Black Youth's Coming of Age in Apartheid South Africa*. Mark Mathabane. New York: Macmillan, 1986. 244 pp. Stirring bestselling book testifies both to the cruelty of life in a Johannesburg ghetto and the unshakable determination of a family to survive.

*Makeba: My Story*. Miriam Makeba with James Hall. New York: New American Library, 1987. 249 pp. An honest, personal view in Makeba's strong and eloquent voice.

*Nelson and Winnie Mandela* (Impact Biography Series). Dorothy and Thomas Hoobler. New York: Franklin Watts, 1987. 112 pp. Both biographies aim at Young Adult audiences and quote extensively from Winnie Mandela's autobiography.

*Promised Land.* Karel Schoeman. Translated by Marion Friedmann. New York: Summit Books, 1978, reissue, 1987. 205 pp. A 1978 novel prophesying that future South Africa will be under black rule.

*Somehow Tenderness Survives: Stories of Southern Africa.* Hazel Rochman, editor. New York: Harper & Row, 1988. 160 pp. Ten tales with distinct perceptions, including work by Doris Lessing and a section of Mark Mathabane's autobiography, *Kaffir Boy*.

*South Africa: Coming of Age under Apartheid.* Jason and Ettagale Laure. New York: Farrar, Straus & Giroux, 1980. 180 pp. Eight young South Africans of various racial groups speak in their own words alongside their expressive photographs.

*"They Cannot Kill Us All": An Eyewitness Account of South Africa Today.* Richard Manning. Boston: Houghton Mifflin, 1987. 288 pp. Penetrating observations informed by the heart written by an American *Newsweek* correspondent.

*Voices of South Africa: Growing up in a Troubled Land.* Carolyn Meyer. New York: Harcourt, Brace Jovanovich, 1986. 244 pp. An American visiting South Africa combines travelogue, conversations, and historical background. Very accessible for young adult audiences.

*Waiting for the Rain.* Shelia Gordon. Granville, OH: Orchard Books, 1987. 224 pp. Winner of the 1988 Jane Addams Children's Book Award. A story of boyhood pals Frikkie, who is Afrikaans, and Tengo, who is black, as they grow apart.

*Winnie Mandela: Life of Struggle.* Jim Haskins. New York: G.P. Putnam's Sons, 1988. 192 pp.

## Other Resources

*Harriet Tubman, Apartheid is Bad, and Other Plays for Young People.* Paula Rogovin Bower. To order, send $8 plus $1.50 postage and handling to Paula Bower, 625 Linden Ave., Teaneck, NJ 07666.

*A History of South Africa.* Leonard Thompson. New Haven: Yale University Press, 1990. A penetrating, comprehensive history by a leading scholar, lauded by Archbishop Tutu for its accuracy.

*Move Your Shadow: South Africa, Black and White.* Joseph Lelyveld. New York: Random House, 1985. 390 pp. A New York Times correspondent in South Africa gives a searing indictment of the apartheid system.

*Waiting for the Barbarians.* J.M Coetzee. New York: Viking Penguin, 1980. 156 pp. An allegory of the war between oppressor and oppressed which shows a magistrate living through a crisis of conscience. For mature readers only.

*Why Are They Weeping? South Africans Under Apartheid.* David C. Turnley. New York: Stewart, Tabori & Chang, Workman Publishing, 1988. Stirring photographs draw in the viewer, with text by Alan Cowell, and foreword by Allan Boesak.

*Winnie Mandela: The Soul of South Africa.* Milton Meltzer. New York: Viking Kestrel, 1986. For junior and senior high.

## Closing

An American United Mine Workers song says:

> Step by step the longest march can be won, can be won.
> Many stones can form an arch, singly none, singly none.
> And by union what we will
> Can be accomplished still
> Drops of water turn a mill, singly none, singly none.

As you end your work, share these lyrics and discuss how they encapsulate what you have studied.

**Gavin Harrison** is a writer, artist, musician and teacher of Insight Meditation in Hawaii, where he lives. He is the author of *In the Lap of the Buddha*. Gavin is actively involved in efforts to protect the endangered Hawaiian green sea turtles off the beaches of the Big Island.

# Living With The Earth

This is a wonderful little story that can be told without much practice. In my environmental education work, I usually tell it before a night hike, during sensory awareness activities, or as a "thought of the day."

# The Cricket Story

## adapted by Rona Leventhal

ONE DAY, WHEN I LIVED IN THE CITY, I was going to eat with a friend. It was lunch hour, and we were walking down one of the busiest streets. There was all sorts of noise in the city . . . cars were honking their horns, you could hear feet shuffling and people talking! And amid all of this noise, my friend turned to me and said, "I hear a cricket."

"No way," I said. "You couldn't possibly hear a cricket with all of this noise. You must be imagining it. Besides, I've never seen a cricket in the city."

"No, really—I do hear a cricket. I'll show you." My friend stopped for a moment, then took me across the street, and found a big cement planter with a tree in it. And there beneath the leaves there was a cricket!

"That's amazing!" I said. "You must have super-human hearing. What's your secret?"

"No, my hearing is just the same as yours. There's no secret—really. Watch, I'll show you." She reached into her pocket, and pulled out some loose change, and threw it on the sidewalk. And amid all the noise of the city, every head within twenty feet turned to see where the sound of money was coming from.

"See," she said, "it's all a matter of what you're listening for."

# Follow-up Activities for "The Cricket Story"

## Recommendations for Telling the Story

I have found that this story is best told in the first person, although it can be told in the third person (i.e., "One day two friends were walking down one of the busiest streets in the city"). The story as I originally heard it used a Native American as the wise friend.

I usually include some audience participation by dividing the listeners into three sections: one group makes noisy car sounds, one group makes noises like people talking, and one group makes feet-shuffling noises. During the telling, when the first group hears me say, "Cars were honking their horns," the first group makes their noise, and so on.

I have used the following activities both in residential environmental education work as well as on public school grounds. They include both indoor and outdoor activities, and can be done with approximately ten to twenty-five students. Most can be adapted to either rural or urban settings.

201

## Sensory Awareness Activities

The story speaks to the need for us to be more aware of our surrounding environment, whether in the woods or in the city. Below are some activities that use our various senses to heighten awareness.

## Stalking

This activity addresses several areas: listening awareness, sound localization, and predator/prey relationships.

- Participants stand in a circle.

- One person sits blindfolded in the middle of the circle, and a stick is placed approximately six inches away, to his/her side. S/he can't hold or grab the stick at any time.

- When everyone is ready, the leader selects someone in the circle to be the stalker (by pointing or tapping on the shoulder) and says, "Someone's coming." The stalker's goal is to get the stick and get back to the circle without getting caught.

- The person in the middle "catches" the stalker by pointing at them. The teacher responds to their pointing with either "yes" or "no." Let several stalkers try before switching the middle person.

### Notes on facilitating this activity

As the judge, you need to decide the accuracy of the pointing. Some children try to point all over the place at once. Explain that the blindfolded person should only point if s/he thinks s/he has detected the stalker. You might need to add a rule limiting the number of times the blindfolded person can point.

Because the blindfolded person is depending on the sense of hearing to determine where the stalker is, the people in the circle should be instructed to keep their feet still, and be totally quiet.

This can be played on gravel or in a wooded area with leaf litter to make it more challenging. It is interesting to try it on different terrain, such as grass or cement, as a comparison.

Between rounds of the game, it is worth taking a moment to discuss the methods different stalkers tried in order to avoid being heard, comparing them to the ways real animals behave in the wild. (Keep in mind that in nature, the predator can also become prey.) If no one has tried a technique that you would like to illustrate, take a turn or two yourself as a stalker. Different stalking methods include going very slowly (like cats), stopping if you've been heard (like rabbits and deer), going very fast, distracting the prey (throw pebbles), and walking on padded feet (taking shoes off).

## Visual Cues

- Participants stand in two lines, facing each other. Arrange the lines so that each person is standing across from another; they will be partners.

- At a signal, both lines turn their backs to each other. Each person changes three things about the way he or she looks. (You might use five things for older children.) Discuss the idea that a subtle change, like removing a belt, rolling up a sleeve or putting your hair behind your ears, will be harder to guess (and therefore more fun) than a major change, like taking off a shoe or a jacket. Behavioral changes, such as crossing your legs, are not allowed.

- At the leader's signal, the lines turn to face each other again. One at a time, each partner tries to guess which things the other person changed. It helps to designate one of the lines to be the first to guess what their partners have changed.

### Notes on facilitating this activity

It is a good idea, especially with young children (first and second graders), to quickly demonstrate this activity as part of the instructions.

This is a good activity to do before going out for a nature walk. At the end of the activity, I like to briefly explain that we often are not aware of details around us, both natural and non-natural. I encourage them to really notice things around them on the walk, or any time they are outside.

## Colorful Observations

While on a nature walk, there are several trail activities to focus children on things they might otherwise not notice. Below are several ideas:

A. Give each student a color card. These can either be small pieces of construction paper, or samples from a fabric or wallpaper store. Instruct each student to find something in nature that has a similar color. Encourage them to think expansively. For instance, a blue color in winter could be the sky, or a yellow could be a shade of tan on a winter tree bud.

B. Give each child a card (or tell each child secretly) something which you want them to find on the trail. These should be things that expand the way that they look at things in nature. For instance, you might ask a child to find:
  - something that is as old as s/he is,
  - something that is fuzzy or furry when you look closely,
  - something that is slimy,
  - three shades of the same color,
  - evidence of an animal,
  - three things in pairs,
  - something that looks lonesome,
  - something that smells good,
  - or something with the texture of sandpaper.

## Human Camera

This activity is best done outside.

- Students need to be in pairs. All pairs start at a centralized location. One will be blindfolded, the other sighted (the leader).

- The leader *gently* directs his/her partner to any spot outside (it doesn't have to be far away from the class meeting place) so that their partner is looking very closely at something (e.g. bark, grass, a flower, a fern). When they are situated, have them lift their blindfolds for five seconds—just long enough to get a quick, close look at something (like a camera shutter). You might want to go on a longer walk and take several "snap shots" as you go.

- The leader then takes the blindfolded person back to the starting point, where the blindfold can be removed. The "camera people" can then discuss, draw, and/or write a description or a fanciful story about what they saw.

## An Ant's Eye View

I have always done this activity in fields that have tall grass, but other habitats can be used.

- Have all of the students lie on their bellies in the grass—it is best if they wear long pants and shirts. With index cards and pens in hand, students use their imagination to look into the grass, and write five or six sentences that describe what they see. For instance, one person may see a jungle with 1000-foot trees; another may see a leprechaun village, and so on. (Alternatively, this could be done verbally with each student sharing one or two thoughts.)

- Take these sentences back to the classroom or meeting-place and write poems or a story, using the sentences.

- Try a bird's eye view for the opposite perspective. Have the children look down from a picnic table or a tree they have climbed.

## Peek-a-Boo

- Place a selection of natural objects that have interesting patterns under a kerchief. Some examples are a shell (curved lines or a spiral), a mushroom (patterns of dots or circles), lichen, bark, a rock, a bird's nest, and a snake's skin. Arrange this before the children arrive, or while they are out of the room.

- Gather the students around you and the objects on the floor. Explain that you will be lifting the kerchief for just five seconds, and that their challenge is to try to remember as many objects as they can.

- After you have done this part of the activity, ask the students what objects they saw. Discuss what each object is, focusing on its special pattern. Let a few children demonstrate drawing some of the patterns on the board (e.g., spirals or zigzags).

## Pattern Tic-Tac-Toe

This exercise works well with young children. I always prepare the children for this game by playing the "Peek-a-Boo" game above first.

- Set up a blank tic-tac-toe board (a blank piece of tagboard covered with contact paper, and an erasable marker are terrific, though a blackboard and chalk work just fine). Now, explain that they will soon be going outside to look for and draw patterns they find in nature. In the blank tic-tac-toe squares, have some children draw patterns they think they may find when they go outside.

- Before going out, give each student three small square pieces of construction paper (approximately 3" x 3") and a crayon or marker. Once outside, verbally establish boundaries to mark an area in which it's OK to explore (for example, a sidewalk or stream beyond which they're not supposed to go). Also establish a signal that will indicate that they need to re-assemble—I use a barred owl call.

- Now, each student goes exploring to find at least three of the patterns, and draw them on the squares of paper. If more than three are found, the backs of the squares can be used. Ask the students to try to remember what object they found each pattern on.

- Inside again, have children share their patterns and what objects they were from. See if the class succeeded at tic-tac-toe. (They almost always do!)

- You might end by commenting on how many beautiful things there are in nature that we have to take time to look closely at in order to see.

## Poems from Patterns in Nature

This pattern exercise is good for upper elementary and older students. It is done outside.

- The "Peek-a-Boo" game above is a good way to prepare the students for this game. Or you could simply ask them to think of different patterns in nature, show them some "treasures" (like a mushroom, a shell, and a snake's skin), and discuss what each object is, focusing on its special patterns.

- While gathered in a group, and with paper and crayons in hand, explain that everyone will be finding a spot in the surrounding woods by themselves, but within eye contact of you. Explain that everyone is going to look for patterns in nature. Half the group will be drawing five patterns that they *see*. The idea is to simply draw the pattern, not the whole object. The other half will be drawing five patterns that they *hear*. They can use both natural and non-natural sounds. These are abstract concepts, so it's important demonstrate them. For example, a squiggly line might represent the sound of a brook trickling, or scribbles might indicate leaves shuffling. Have the children return to your meeting spot when they are done.

- When everyone has regrouped, have them write a sentence from each of their five patterns. The sentences do not have to be about the object they drew the pattern from. For instance, a zigzagged line may have been drawn to represent a bird chirping, but the sentences may be about lightning, or an animal running across a field. I have found it more productive to wait until this point to let them know they will be writing sentences about their patterns. This way they won't worry about writing sentences while they are choosing and drawing patterns.

- Next, ask them to write a poem using their sentences (again, wait until this point to let them know they will be composing poems). I encourage the children to be minimalists in this sort of writing exercise, that is, to stay as true to the original sentences as possible, and to add only what is absolutely necessary to the sentences to create the poem.

- Have the children share their poems with each other. I've always been impressed with the quality of the poems.

## Alone Sit

- This is a very simple and very special activity to many children, because it gives them an opportunity to stop, be by themselves, and really notice things around them.

- Explain that each person will be sitting by him or herself for a predetermined amount of time (five to fifteen minutes, depending on the group). Their challenge is to notice as many things as possible around them, both big and small, using all of their senses. A discussion of the senses is good preparation for this activity. This is a quiet time, away from their friends, to really be with the environment.

- Establish a call to let people know to regroup (again, I use an owl call). When everyone is together, discuss some of the things they noticed or that were special to them. It's nice if the group can gather quietly for a few moments before starting the discussion. Often, I don't have a formal discussion—the children usually do that naturally with each other on the walk back to the meeting-place!

### Notes on facilitating this activity

It may be necessary to establish verbal boundaries as to how far the kids can go to sit alone. It's nice if you can find a location that has several different habitats, for instance, a forest and a stream, or a lake and a meadow. This allows participants to choose an area that is special to them. A more structured way of dispersing the children is to have them stand in a circle, facing out. Each person takes fifty steps (or however many is good for the particular area), and that is his or her spot.

It is also nice to do a pre-sit activity with the group to set the tone for the alone sit. Sometimes I tell "The Cricket Story." Other times I bring an object, or find one on the way to the place we'll be sitting, such as a fern. Sitting in a circle, the object gets passed around, and each person asks a question about the object. It is not necessary to be able to answer the question, only that it is something that you are curious about. For example, "I wonder why it has so many lines on it," or "I wonder why the dots grow in a circle," or "I wonder why green is the color of chlorophyll." People have the option to pass, though I usually go back and give them a second chance to participate.

If you have the opportunity to work with children at night, a night walk or alone sit can also be very effective and special. It can also be a good vehicle to talk about nocturnal animals, as well as not being afraid of the unknown and the darkness. However there needs to be a lot of work with the children beforehand in order to develop trust within the group. I usually do night alone sits on a trail. As we are walking in a line, I drop off one person at a time along the trail, spacing them within calling distance of each other. By the time I drop everyone off, it is usually almost time to go to the beginning of the line and pick people up. Emphasize the need to be very quiet, and only to call to your neighbor if you are truly scared.

## Values Clarification Activities

"The Cricket Story" also speaks to our values—what we think is important enough to give our attention to. The following activities deal with exploring value judgments in our life.

## Paper Dolls

This activity not only helps individuals explore their values but also can help build a sense of community and trust within a group. It can be done with any age participants—from very young through adult.

- Cut out a series of simple body shapes or have the students do it as a class. The paper dolls should be large enough to allow the kind of writing and drawing described below. (You could also adapt this exercise to use drawings or cutouts of coats of arms, backpacks, globes, or whatever is effective for you.)

- Before beginning the exercise, lead a brief discussion on the importance of respecting each other's thoughts and feelings. This should be a time when people openly share information about themselves without being criticized.

- Associate a question with each part of the body of the doll. Some questions should help the participants think about their values. Other questions should allow the group to share personal information that will create a sense of communication, community, and trust.

  **For example:**

  On the head, write one wish for this planet;

  On the left arm, write three words that you hope people would use to describe you;

  On the right arm, draw or write about a place you like to go when you want to be alone;

  On the stomach, name an environmental problem you want to see changed;

  On the left leg, draw or name your favorite food;

  On the right leg, name one thing you really like to do outside.

- Other ideas are: to draw a picture of your family, your favorite food, or a pet you have or would like to have; to write about a nice thing that someone did for you today, or that you did for someone else. The possibilities are endless. Consider the group make-up, age level and the areas you are working on with them when choosing questions.

- Encourage the group to get as colorful and creative as they like, using words, pictures, or symbols.

- When the dolls are finished, have each person share the thoughts and dreams s/he has recorded on the doll. The paper dolls can be hung on the wall.

## Values Auction

This follows the "Paper Dolls" activity nicely, but can certainly be done on its own. This activity is for upper elementary and older children. The goal of the activity is to take a closer look at some of the values we think are important, and what they are worth to us.

- Make a list of things that people think are important and of value to them. (Make sure there are more items than there are participants.) Before doing the activity, you may want to get some ideas from the class for the final list. Examples include money, preserving old growth forests, a happy family, a vegetable garden, a popular toy, saving endangered species, a chance to eliminate sickness and poverty, a close friend, a world without war or prejudice, a television, the ability to speak many languages, a car (or mini-bike, depending on the age), a long life, a cure for cancer, a trip to Florida or an amusement park, the chance to talk to the president, elimination of pollution, the knowledge of the future, a chance to go back in time . . . the possibilities are limitless, and depend on the age and group make-up.

- Give each student a certain amount of money. You can use something to represent money, or just tell them the amount they each have, and to keep track of how much they spend. This is how much they have to bid with. You may want to have a minimum and maximum bid.

- As the teacher, you become the Auctioneer. Go through the list, auctioning off each item, and have the class bid on them. If there are some students who have difficulty participating, you may want to establish a minimum amount of money that each student must spend.

- After the auction, discuss the results without placing judgments on their decisions and values. Which items were most and least important to each individual and to the group? Why? Ask each individual to think about what his/her choices express about what is important to him/her. Have another class or group do the auction and compare results. Have a group of adults do it and compare the results. Make a chart comparing which things were most and least valued.

## Thematic Murals

As a group, create a mural on pertinent themes, such as diversity, cooperation, world peace, environmental awareness, etc. You can use crayons, markers, or recycled or natural materials. Discuss how to expand the definitions. For instance, diversity can be thought of in terms of ourselves, our families, schools, neighborhood, towns, states, country, world, universe, or in nature.

## Resources

*Acclimatization, Sunship Earth* and many others. Steve Van Matre. The Institute for Earth Education, P.O. Box 288, Warrenville, IL 60555. (509) 395-2299.

*Hands-on Nature.* Jenepher Lingelbauch. Vermont Institute of Natural Science, Woodstock, VT 05091.

*Keepers of the Earth: Native American Stories and Environmental Activities for Children.* Michael Caduto and Joseph Bruchac. Golden, CO: Fulcrum Press, 1988.

*Nature with Children of All Ages.* Edith Sisson. Englewood Cliffs, NJ: Prentice-Hall, 1982.

*The Sense of Wonder.* Rachel Carson. New York: Harper and Row, 1987. Her thoughts on helping young people develop an innate love for the earth. She also wrote and is most famous for *Silent Spring*, an account of the devastating effects of pesticides on wildlife.

*Sharing the Joy of Nature*. Joseph Bharat Cornell. Nevada City, CA: Dawn Publications, 1989.

*Sharing Nature with Children*. Joseph Bharat Cornell. Nevada City, CA: Ananda Publications, 1979.

❦ ❦ ❦

**Rona Leventhal** is a storyteller, movement and drama specialist, arts integration specialist, certified teacher, and environmental educator. She is deeply committed to using storytelling and other art forms to develop imagination. She tells stories, does residencies, gives keynote addresses, and leads workshops internationally, and teaches "Storytelling in Education" for Lesley University. She performs the story-theatre piece "Degas and the Little Dancer," and will be producing a tape of environmental stories and songs and a first person living history show on abolitionism.

# The Tailor

## by Nancy Schimmel

IN A VILLAGE ONCE LIVED A POOR TAILOR. He had made overcoats for many people, but he had never made one for himself, though an overcoat was the one thing he wanted. He never had enough money to buy material and set it aside for himself, without making something to sell. But he saved and saved, bit by bit, and at last he had saved enough. He bought the cloth and cut it carefully, so as not to waste any. He sewed up the coat, and it fit him perfectly. He was proud of that coat. He wore it whenever it was the least bit cold. He wore it until it was all worn out.

At least he thought it was all worn out, but then he looked closely and he could see that there was just enough good material left to make a jacket. So he cut up the coat and made a jacket. It fit just as well as the coat had, and he could wear it even more often. He wore it until it was all worn out.

At least he thought it was all worn out, but he looked again, and he could see that there was still enough good material to make a vest. So he cut up the jacket and sewed up a vest. He tried it on. He looked most distinguished in that vest. He wore it every single day. He wore it until it was all worn out.

At least he thought it was all worn out, but when he looked it over carefully, he saw some places here and there that were not worn. So he cut them out, sewed them together, and made a cap. He tried it on, and it looked just right. He wore that cap outdoors and in, until it was all worn out.

At least it seemed to be all worn out, but when he looked, he could see that there was just enough left to make a button. So he cut up the cap and made a button. It was a good button. He wore it every day, until it was all worn out.

At least he thought it was all worn out, but when he looked closely, he could see that there was just enough left of that button to make a story, so he made a story out of it and I just told it to you.

❦ ❦ ❦

Now I didn't make that story out of a button, but I did make it out of a song. A long time ago, I heard someone sing a Yiddish folk song at a concert and explain in English what the song said, which was the same as the story except that the person in the song made a song instead of a story out of the button.[1] I didn't remember the song, but I liked the idea, and years later I tried it out as a story, first on a first grade class and later at a convalescent hospital.

I was working at a library just a block from the hospital. I told stories once a month at the hospital, and each time, after I did my stories and songs, we would

---

1. The song, in English, is available on *Songs of the Holidays* sung by Gene Bluestein on Folkways FC 7554. It is called "I Had a Little Coat."

sit around at tables and have tea and cookies. About the third time I went there, I told "The Tailor." Afterwards, I sat at a table with a man and a woman. The woman said, "You know, it's funny you told the story about a tailor today, because my father was a tailor. He was in Germany and he wanted to come to this country but he didn't have enough money, so he stowed away. When the ship had gotten out to sea, he poked his nose out of his hiding place and went out to see if it was safe. He overheard someone saying they were looking for a tailor, so he went right back to his hiding place and stayed there. At the end of the trip, he found out that they were just looking for a tailor to do some tailoring, they weren't looking for a stowaway at all, and he had missed out on a job."

I said, "That's funny that you're telling me this story about your father who was a tailor, because my grandfather was a tailor. His family scraped up enough money to send him to this country, but he didn't like it. He had been a tailor's apprentice in Budapest, but in New York he was working in a sweatshop, and the streets weren't paved with gold after all, and he was homesick. He was living with his uncle, but it wasn't home. On the Sabbath, on Saturdays, he would go down to the docks and look wistfully at the ships and think about Budapest. One day a man who spoke Yiddish came up to him and asked why he looked so sad. He said he was wishing he could go home on one of these ships, but he didn't have the money. The man said, 'Well, I can take care of you. You just sign on as part of the crew, and work your way across. When you get to the Old Country, you jump ship and find your way home. And since I speak English and you don't, I can get you on a ship going in the right direction.' My grandfather thought that was a fine idea, and he followed the man into an office, and he signed his name here, and he signed his name there, and he was in the U.S. Navy for four years.

"Luckily, he liked the Navy, so much so that he re-enlisted twice, and at the end of his service he became a naval tailor, which he was until the day he died. And since he was on a ship with a crew of New York Irish, this Jewish tailor from Budapest spoke English with a bit of an Irish brogue all his life."

After the woman and I had this little exchange, the man, who had been just sitting there not saying a word, said, "What did you say the tailor made out of the button?"

"A story."

He said, "What?"

I said, "A story. Out of the button he made the story I told you."

"Oh!" he said, "I thought you said buttonhole."

The man had a pretty good story there. Not the story I told, but one that makes sense, because after the button wears out you've got nothing left, and what do you make out of nothing? You make a hole. And what kind of a hole does a tailor make? A buttonhole.

And indeed this is the way stories and songs change. A word goes through a change of time or place, or through a hearing aid, and comes out nonsense. The listener, who becomes the next teller, changes the word so it makes sense again.

# Follow-up Activities for "The Tailor"

## Storytelling Activities

"The Tailor" is a recycled story and a story about recycling. Suggest to children that they can recycle the story too. After they have heard it once or twice, they can try telling it to family or a friend. It can be told to audiences from kindergarten to adult.

Ask your listeners if they know anyone who makes good things out of worn-out or thrown-away stuff. Maybe someone in your town makes sculpture out of junk, or makes dolls from odd socks. What they do could be a story for telling. Your listeners can tell a story about themselves, if they save things and use them again or make new things out of them.

A student could read "The Journey" aloud (in *Mouse Tales*, an I-Can-Read book by Arnold Lobel, Harper, 1972), and the class could discuss how it is the same as "The Tailor" and how it is different. "The Journey" can be fun to act out.

Another story you or children can learn and tell is "The Rainhat" in *Just Enough to Make a Story: A Sourcebook for Storytelling* by Nancy Schimmel (Sisters' Choice, 1982). Instead of using new paper for this paperfolding story, use paper that has been written or printed on and is ready to throw away.

## Papermaking

Find out if there are other ways that waste paper from your school or homes can be recycled. Some recycling centers take only newsprint, but some take used writing paper as well. Even using both sides of the paper will help save trees. Children can use the library to find out how paper is made from trees, and use these directions to make recycled paper of their own.

You will need used paper, a blender, water, a dishpan, and a piece of screen about 6 x 9 inches. Either tape the edges of the screen (to avoid cuts) or tack screen onto a wood frame. Papermaking is a wet process, and is best done outside on tables that don't mind getting wet, or on the ground.

Begin by tearing up used paper into tiny pieces. This can be boring, but not if your teacher or one of the students tells a story while you work, or if you listen to a story or ecology songs on tape (See bibliography). You might want to have different groups, one using only newspaper, one only white paper, and one using mixed, and compare the results.

Place a handful of paper shreds and 2 cups of hot or cold water (hot is faster) into a blender. Mix until it has a watery-creamy consistency, which means the paper fibers have broken down. Repeat, being careful not to overload the blender.

Fill a dishpan with four to six inches of water and pour the paper "slurry" from the blender into the pan. Mix by hand. Dip the piece of screen to the bottom of the dishpan, then, keeping it horizontal, raise it up out of the slurry, lifting pulp up on the screen. Let it drip for a few seconds, then turn it onto spread newspapers or a large screen (pulp side down), leaving the small screen on top of the pulp. Gently place a sponge on top of the screen to soak up excess water. Squeeze water into the pan and repeat until you've soaked up as much water as possible. *Slowly* remove the small screen. (It might be necessary to let it dry for a few minutes first.) Set in a warm place to dry for one to two hours.

Ragged edges are part of the "look" of handmade paper, but if you really want to, you can trim them. Using a rolling pin on the paper while it is lying flat on the drying rack will give it a more ragged edge. Alternatively, adding a wooden frame will make it look more "manicured."

Options: add food coloring or bits of grass, leaves, dried flowers, or other natural materials either directly to blender or into slurry. Can you make paper out of blended dried grass or straw only?

If at any step, the paper isn't working right, just crumble it back into the dishpan of slurry and try again. Experiment with different colors and thicknesses. Thicker slurry is easier to work with. Look for books in your library that give you different ideas for making paper. (Think about libraries. Do they recycle books?)

Two books that have pictures to help you figure out papermaking are: *Paper by Kids* by Arnold Grummer (Dillon, 1980) which has photographs and lots of ideas, and *Making Things, Book 2*, by Ann Wiseman (Little Brown, pp. 4-6), which has good drawings. A different set of instructions, but no pictures, is in a nifty little book called *Recipes for Art and Craft Materials* by Helen Roney Sattler (Lothrop, 1987, p. 141).

Did you know . . .

- Paper makes up at least 50% of the nation's municipal waste by volume.
- To publish a typical big-city Sunday newspaper uses 10,000 trees.
- Recycling about 120 pounds of newspapers will save a tree.
- Making recycled paper takes 61% less water and produces 70% less pollution than making new paper.

## Puppetry

If restaurants near you are still using styrofoam boxes for take-out food, children can wash the boxes, let them dry, and make them into puppet heads. Pie boxes make good birds, sandwich boxes make animals and people. Egg cartons make crocodiles, or cut them up to make features on the box puppets. Glue or tape paper eyes on, leaving room behind the eyes for the puppeteer's fingers.

Children can find out why styrofoam is so bad for the environment, and write a play about it for their styrofoam puppets to act out. Maybe they can persuade the restaurants to stop using styrofoam. The puppets could sing this song to the tune of "Little Boxes" by Malvina Reynolds:

Little boxes at the restaurant,
Little boxes made of styrofoam,
And we use them by the squillions
For our fast food every day,
Then we take those little boxes
And we throw them into bigger ones
But because they're made of styrofoam
They will never go away.

## Little Boxes

Malvina Reynolds

Lit - tle box - es at the res - tau - rant, lit - tle

box - es made of sty - ro - foam, and we use them by the

squil - lions for our fast food ev - 'ry day, Then we

take those lit - tle box - es and we throw them in - to

big - ger ones, but be - cause they're made of sty - ro - foam they will

nev - er go a way.___

You have probably already made puppets out of paper bags. If not, there are lots of books that will show you how. What else can people do with paper bags? Some re-use them in other ways, recycle them at a recycling center, or refuse them (politely) and carry purchases in pockets, book bags, or canvas shopping bags.

## Recycling

Some schools and clubs have raised money by collecting newspapers, aluminum cans, and glass bottles. At least one school used the money to hire a storyteller!

Take a field trip to a recycling center, or invite someone who works at one to come to your class or club to answer questions.

## Invention Convention

In this critical thinking activity, the teacher and students bring in items that are normally thrown out (broken toys or kitchen gadgets, springs, empty containers, scraps of cloth, odd-shaped styrofoam packing) and make something useful with them. This could be done in several ways. One suggestion is to give each group of four or five students a bag of five or six items with which to create an invention. You may add a rechargeable battery and wire to one or two of the bags to see what the students can do with it, even though it is not an old item. The inventions should be something useful or fun, such as a time-saving gadget or a toy. When the inventions are done, each group explains and demonstrates their creation to the class. Writing an explanation of what it does and why it is useful would exercise more skills.

Extension: To take this activity further, have the groups try to convince the class of the need to have/buy their invention. Students could write or draw advertisements, then talk about how ads try to convince people to buy things they don't really need, which uses up resources unnecessarily.

Note: Some localities have places where manufacturers donate waste that can be used for projects like this. You can find tubes, whistles, buttons, wire, etc. sorted into bins. Ask around at recycling centers, children's museums, toy stores or arts organizations.

## Bibliography

*Oscar Options*, Rhode Island Dept. of Environmental Management, Providence, RI 02908. Has many fact sheets as well as activities on recycling.

*Piggyback Planet* (RRR 301, Round River Records, 301 Jacob St., Seekonk, MA 02771) has a terrific song about garbage (called "Garbage") sung by Sally Rogers and a bunch of children. The tape also has "The Junk Round," "The Recycle Song," and other good ecology songs.

*All In This Together: 15 Ecology Songs for the Whole Family* (Sisters' Choice 467, Sisters' Choice Recordings, 1450 Sixth St., Berkeley, CA 94710) is an award-winning tape with singable songs.

❦ ❦ ❦

**Nancy Schimmel** has been telling stories on the road and teaching storytelling workshops since 1975. She has a storytelling book available through her own publishing company, Sisters' Choice. The book, *Just Enough to Make a Story*, includes a list of peace stories and sources. The third edition also has a list of ecology stories. For updates, check her website at: www.sisterschoice.com. Nancy lives in Berkeley, California with a friend, a dog and a redwood tree.

# What Now, Cloacina?!!

## by Diane Edgecomb

**Storyteller:** The old stories tell us that every body of water, every stream, every lake, every pond has a water spirit all its own. This water spirit is a living part of every stream or lake, and it watches over the water and cares for it like a guardian. Now remember, water spirits are usually invisible to human beings. Sometimes, if you're lucky, you can catch a glimpse of one out of the corner of your eye and sometimes, if you have the "second sight," you can tell where they are just by looking with your heart.

The story I have for you right now is the story of a water spirit from a little pond right near here. And her name . . . Well, her name is rather peculiar, her name is Cloacina *(Klo/a/chee'/na)*.

You know, taking care of a pond isn't always easy. All kinds of things can happen that Cloacina doesn't expect. And whenever something goes wrong, Cloacina always says, "OH NO!!" When you hear her say "OH NO!!" let her know you're there to help by saying, "What now, Cloacina?!!" Let's try that all together. (**Storyteller:** "OH NO!!" **Audience:** "What now, Cloacina?!!")

Wait . . . I think I hear her coming down the path right now . . . .

*(Storyteller becomes Cloacina entering the space, humming, enjoying the day. Then she stops short, looks carefully at the ground and looks all around.)*

**Cloacina:** OH NO!!

**Audience:** *(responds to this, led by the Storyteller)* What now, Cloacina?!!

**Cloacina:** *(Looking up and taking in the audience)* I just went into the woods for a minute and I came back and now my pond is gone. It's completely missing. I don't know where in the world it could . . ." *(Cloacina finds a pebble and picks it up.)* OH NO!!

**Audience:** What now, Cloacina?!!

**Cloacina:** This is a pebble from the bottom of my pond, but there's absolutely no water left. There's only these pebbles here and . . . *(Cloacina sees something and stops.)* OH NO!!

**Audience:** What now, Cloacina?!!

**Cloacina:** There's a big pipe right here and a sign, it says . . . *(spells)* R-e-s-e-r-v-o-i-r. What's a Reservoir? *(Cloacina gets the information from the children that the word is reservoir and that a reservoir is a place where people get their water from. If the children don't have enough information adults can be asked to chip in their knowledge or Cloacina can come up with a hunch.)* So that's where my pond went, down that pipe to homes and factories and schools. Wait a minute!! My pond is very big. Nobody could use that much water!! Everybody must have forgotten to put back the water they don't need. *(Cloacina calls down the imaginary pipe.)* Yoo hoooo! Don't forget to give back all the water you don't need!! *(Nothing happens.)* I guess they can't hear me . . . . Why don't you help me this time?

**Audience:** Yoo hooo! Don't forget to give back all the water you don't need.

**Cloacina:** Well how do you like that!! Nobody's answering. I'm gonna go down that pipe and get my pond back myself. Here goes nothing!

**Storyteller:** And so, Cloacina went into the big, dark, damp, pipe. *(Mime walking into one of the large water pipes.)*

**Cloacina:** Boy this is huge! Hello!!! . . . hello! . . . hello . . . *("hellos" trail off as if they are echoes.)*

**Storyteller:** Well, that big pipe divided into two smaller pipes and those smaller pipes divided into still smaller pipes and those still smaller pipes divided into even smaller pipes and those even smaller pipes divided into the smallest pipes of all. And at the end of those smallest pipes of all Cloacina could see light.

**Cloacina:** I'm going to go through that smallest pipe of all. *(She tries to squeeze through the pipe.)* MMmmmpfh!! Oouuhhhhk!! MMMmmmmpfh!! Oooooooooooff!!! *(She pops out the other end and begins slipping and sliding around.)* Whoops!! Wooooo!! Woooooooooo!! Where am I? I'm in a slippery white bowl. Whhheeee!! Whooooooooups!! How . . . how did I end up here? You mean I just went through miles and miles of pipes to end in a tiny white bowl? This tiny white bowl couldn't hold my pond. Whhhhoooooaaaaa!! *(She slips again.)* I'm going to climb up the sides of this bowl and see where I am. *(She climbs up the edge and sees herself in the mirror.)* Aaaaaaaaaah! Oh my goodness, it's only me. There's a mirror there. Whew! *(Peers over the edge of the sink.)* The floor is a long way down. And there's another white bowl down there with water in it. I wonder where I am. Do you know?

**Audience:** A bathroom!

**Cloacina:** A bathroom!!!! Wait a minute . . . . Someone's coming!

**Mother's Voice:** All right children. Time to go upstairs and wash your hands for dinner.

**Children's Voices:** *(They are rushing into the bathroom, tumbling over each other. These following sentences come quickly, one on top of the other.)* Last one to wash up is a rotten egg!!

**Storyteller:** And the children rush into the bathroom and turn the water on full force. Sshhhhhh! *(Sound of the water running down the drain.)*

**Children's Voices:** "I got the soap first!" "I got the soap first!" "I got the soap first!" *(Good-natured teasing back and forth.)*

**Storyteller:** And all the time the water was running.

**Children's Voices:** "No, I got the soap first!" "I got the soap first!" "I got the soap first!"

**Storyteller:** And all the time the water was running.

**Children's Voices:** "I got it!" "I got it!" "Oh-Oh! Here comes Mom!"

**Mother's Voice:** *(Take stance of the mother—very still, arms folded.)* Children.

**Child's Voices:** Yes, ma.

**Mother's Voice:** What did we talk about at breakfast this morning . . . that we were going to do together as a family?

**Child's Voice:** I don't know.

**Mother's Voice:** *(Laughs.)* No, it wasn't "I don't know." Don't you remember? Let me show you.

**Storyteller:** And the mother went over to the faucet and turned off the running water. *(Mime that action and imitate that sound as well.)*

**Child's Voice:** Oh, yeah. We weren't going to leave the water running.

**Mother's Voice:** That's right. Remember I said that all of our water comes from some pond or reservoir. If we leave the water running like that we might not have enough when we really need it. Let's remember to turn it off when we're not using it, all right?

**Child's Voice:** Yeah. Sorry. We forgot. And Mom, we're gonna remember that other thing too about the drains . . . . What was it?

**Mother's Voice:** We're not going to dump anything poisonous down the drains. No toxic paints or other chemicals that are harmful to living things.

**Child's Voice:** Right! No poisons down the drain.

**Cloacina:** Down the drain! That's where my pond went—down the drain. Hold on pond, here I come!! *(She slides down the drain.)* Whooooooops!!

**Storyteller:** So Cloacina went down the drain pipe. And that small drain pipe merged with another pipe and another larger pipe and another still larger pipe and Cloacina was whisked along with tons of water from hundreds and thousands of houses—with waste water from schools, factories, and stores. Let me tell you it was not always very pleasant! Finally the pipes took her to a place where people did all kinds of different things to the water to try to take out those things which would be harmful. And then at last Cloacina and the rest of the water were spewed out right into the harbor.

**Cloacina:** OH NO!!

**Audience:** What now, Cloacina?!!

**Cloacina:** I'm never going to find my pond out here! The ocean is too big and too all mixed together. Now I'll never know where my little pond went.

**Storyteller:** And Cloacina sat down on the ocean floor and began to cry . . . . Just then, the strangest creature happened along. He had two powerful claws. He had eight spindly little legs. He had a long pointy nose, a complete covering of blue and green armor and beady eyes on stalks. He was . . . do you know what kind of sea creature he was?

**Audience:** *(They give answers until they guess right.)* A Lobster!

**Storyteller:** It was *General Lobstah*!! And as he walked along, he rolled a gigantic ball of trash in front of him.

**General Lobstah:** Out o' my way!! Out o' my way, now!! You!! You over there! *(He points to Cloacina.)* Don't just sit there like a bump on a barnacle!! There's work to be done.

**Cloacina:** Work? What kind of work?

**General Lobstah:** Any kind of work you please!! Just look around you. I'm swimmin' in garbage!! It's quite a fishkettle, I'm tellin' you. Not just a little garbage here and there, there's tons of it. We've got every kind of junk imaginable, old cars, wood, metal, and just look at this . . . these plastic things and this stuff called sty-ro-foam. Plastic and styrofoam never dissolve, they stay around forever just to cause trouble. Not a day passes without some horror story caused by plastics or styrofoam of one kind or another.

**Cloacina:** Oh, General Lobstah, I know things will change, don't worry.

**General Lobstah:** Worry? Of course I'm not going to worry! Do you think I'm going to sit around and wait for somethin' to happen like some mollusk?! Not a one of it!! Do you see that pipe you just came out of? Every day all kinds of waste water comes out of that pipe, from houses, schools, factories. Now I don't mind most of what comes out of those kind of pipes and of course I don't mind water . . . . I love water! I'm a Lobstah! But . . . sometimes poisonous things are dumped into the sewage systems and then I'm tellin' you, what comes out of that pipe is very dangerous. Some of those poisons are even starting to eat through my thick hide. So, I'm going to completely plug up that pipe with this ball o' garbage and let's see what happens when the entire sewage system backs up!! *(He laughs uproariously.)*

**Cloacina:** Before you leave, General Lobstah, can you tell me if you've seen my pond? You see, it's disappeared out here and I really need it back. I mean, what's a water spirit without her pond?

**General Lobstah:** I can't answer a question like that! I'm an engineer, not a philosopher! You'd better ask Queen Surge, Queen of the Ocean. There she is! Coming in on the tide, now!

**Queen Surge:** *(With her voice rising and falling in volume like the sea.)* Cloacina, Cloacina, the only thing that will bring your pond back now is a little help from nature. What you need is some good old fashioned preeeeecipitation and eeeeeeevaporation.

**Cloacina:** What's preeeeeecipitation and eeeeeevaporation?

**Queen Surge:** Oh, those are fancy words for things like rain . . . but why don't you float up to the surface of the ocean and you'll see what I mean.

**Storyteller:** So Cloacina floated up to the surface of the ocean. And when she reached the top, the sun's rays warmed her through and through until . . .

**Cloacina:** OH NO!!

**Audience:** What now Cloacina?!!

**Cloacina:** I feel all tingly. Like I'm separating and floating and flying and . . . Wow, this is it!! I'm Evaporating!!! I'm becoming water mist . . .

**Storyteller:** And Cloacina became so light that she floated up, up, away from the ocean, back towards her pond. And as she floated, she gathered more and more pieces of mist around her, till when she arrived over her pond she was part of a big rain cloud that began to rain K-K-k-k-k-k *(thunder sound)* and rain and fill up her little pond again.

**Cloacina:** My pond! My pond! It's filling up again, filling up with rain water. How wonderful!! But how am I going to keep from losing it again?

**Storyteller:** And as Cloacina asked that question, she looked back over the miles and miles of pipes, and the places she had been, and what she saw was the best present in the world. She saw that people were conserving water in every way they could. They were remembering to turn the water off when they didn't need it. Remembering not to dump any poisons down the drain. Remembering to think about a little pond and the many living creatures of the sea. And Cloacina was so happy that, for a moment she looked like a rainbow right over her pond.

## Follow-up Activities for "What Now Cloacina?!!"

"What Now, Cloacina?!!" is designed to teach basic facts about water conservation and water pollution. During the course of the story, how our usage of water impacts other living worlds of nature becomes apparent. Simple and effective ways to help reverse this trend are also explored.

When researching how best to teach about water issues, I became aware that most people don't know where their clean water supply comes from or where the poisons flushed down their drainpipes go to. Few have ever seen these places and most have no sensory or emotional connection with them at all. Because of this lack of connection, there is an empty space in the minds and hearts of people where there used to be thankfulness for the cleansing gift of water. This is especially true in places where water is available on demand and where the wastes created are whisked out of sight instantly, flushed with more water down pipes and tubes. "Cloacina" is designed to counteract this lack of knowledge and to teach elementary facts about water systems.

Older folkloric beliefs in water spirits were an important source for this story. These beliefs, common to so many cultures, speak of a living essence in bodies of water; an essence with a life cycle; an essence with symptoms of health and disease. Cloacina, the water spirit I chose to be the heroine of this story turned up in an odd list of Roman deities. She was the little known and long forgotten Deity of the Aquaducts, the first Spirit of the Sewage Systems and it was with her in mind that this story was dedicated and built.

## Notes to tellers

**A general note**: This story explores the cycle of a water system, from reservoir to town and then, ultimately, to the sea. This is a basic model of a water system for many large cities and towns. If this story is being told in an area where a river is the source and is the major place of discharge for the water supply, the story can be altered by having Cloacina be a River Spirit (instead of a Pond Spirit) who is looking to get back *her* part of the river, and by changing the names and localities of the other characters. For instance, Queen Surge becomes Queen of that River and General Lobstah becomes General Crayfish or Crawdad. By using the follow-up activities supplied at the end of this story, the water system in each region and town can be explored in even greater detail.

**Audience Participation**: The audience will be able to participate in the story as it is told. They will learn the refrain, "What now, Cloacina?!!," to join in with at various points in the story, and will also be asked to help Cloacina figure things out along the way. Directions for audience participation are in parentheses in the text.

**How to tell the story**: The style of this piece involves the telling of the main body of the story using a simple and straightforward speaking voice which I will call the Storyteller. The rest of the tale comes to life with the "Storyteller" play-acting scenes between the other "characters." Each of the characters should have a distinct voice and body language. Below you will find a brief description of some of them.

*Cloacina* (pronounced Klo/a/chee'/na) is a very refreshing, youthful, and hopeful numen (spirit of nature). Her body movements are flowing and slightly wavy, her voice and laughter light.

*General Lobstah* has two large claws, eight legs, a full suit of armor, and the determination of an entire battalion! He is incredibly opinionated and full of bluster. For fun give him a regional accent!

*Queen Surge* is representative of the spirit of the Ocean. She is the "Ruler of the Tides." A strong and powerful force, her voice surges in volume like the waves.

## Explorational questions

- What do you think the ancient peoples meant when they spoke of the existence of a water spirit? Do you think a water spirit could be something that is real that we don't know how to be in touch with anymore or do you think it is an idea that only exists in people's imagination?

- Why is it that water is so often wasted?

- Do you think that families are starting to behave like that family in the story—living differently so that they can help the environment?

- Why was General Lobstah so upset about the plastics in the ocean? (This can lead to a discussion about biodegradable products versus nonbiodegradables. Also see Resource List.)

- How many ways can you think of to conserve water? What are some things that towns are doing to conserve water? (This can lead to a discussion of not watering during certain times of the day, having a hazardous waste pick-up day, etc.)

- How is your reservoir and sewage system similar to the one in this story? How is it different?

- What happens when water evaporates as part of the water cycle? Where do the toxins and other wastes that the water has carried go to?

## Exercises

- Finish the rest of the story of General Lobstah. What happens to him after Cloacina leaves?

- Go on a field trip to visit your reservoir or reservoirs. Imagine what the water spirit for that particular place would look like and sound like. What would her or his name be? Draw a picture of her.

- Go on a field trip to the sewage treatment plant. Study what happens to the water there and where it goes to after that. Find out what the most common problems at the treatment plant are and what can be done to help. (If the area you live in uses mainly septic tanks and/or leech fields to contain and process wastes, explore how these wastes are rendered harmless. Also trace the path of these wastes to see if there is potential danger to groundwater supplies at any point in their journey.)

- Interview someone from your town's water and sewage commission to find out about the history of the water systems in your area. Why do you have the water system you have? How was it created? And by whom? Interview elderly residents of your area to find out their stories about water availability in the past. Interview people from different cultures to see whether there are differences in the way water is valued. When is water looked at as a precious resource and when is it looked at as something to be taken for granted?

- Make a chart of how much water you use during a day. Chart what you use the water for and chart the amount you use. Then try to reduce the amount you use for one week. Have a class discussion at the end of that time. Why was it difficult to conserve water sometimes?

- Make up your own story about a water spirit that lives in a reservoir or well near you. Have this water spirit journey through the water system of your town to visit you.

- What are some common household hazardous wastes? What can you look for on the labels of products that can tell you whether the product is poisonous or not? (Hazardous products are not just those with the skull and crossbones on the container! Here are some common examples: ammonia, drain cleaners, most cleaning agents, fertilizers, gasoline, charcoal lighter, oil-based paints, bleaches, starches, photographic chemicals, and so on! Look for label words such as: Warning, Poison, Caution, Harmful, Flammable, and Caustic.)

## Resources

*Clean Water for Today: What is Wastewater Treatment?* Prepared by the Water Pollution Control Federation, 2626 Pennsylvania Avenue, N.W., Washington, DC 20037. This pamphlet is an excellent source of information on wastewater treatment plants.

*The Magic School Bus (at the Waterworks).* Joanna Cole. New York: Scholastic, 1986. A teacher takes her students on a journey through the interior of a waterworks system.

*Nature Scope Magazine.* A collection of educational activities published by the National Wildlife Federation, 1412 16th St. NW, Washington, DC 20036-2266; Their issue *Diving Into Oceans* (order #75042) is a collection of activities centered on marine life. In this issue there is a section on plastics in the ocean.

*Paddle to the Sea.* Holling Clancy Holling. Boston: Houghton Mifflin, 1941, 1969. Story of the journey of a boy's toy boat from the Great Lakes to the sea. Good for a study of natural and artificial waterways.

*Underground.* David Macaulay. Boston: Houghton Mifflin, 1976. A pictorial adventure beneath the streets of a city.

The New England Water Works Association, 42-A Dilla St., Milford, MA 01757, (508) 478-6996. A professional organization of water works personnel, specializing in education of the public. "The Story of Drinking Water" teaching guides and coloring book, contact Education Coordinator.

Water Resources Program, National Wildlife Federation, 1400 Sixteenth St. NW, Washington, DC 20036-2266, (202) 797-6833. "Citizen's Guide to Water Conservation," and free newsletter on upcoming legislation.

Water Works Division, Mass. Water Resources Authority, Charlestown Navy Yard, 100 First Ave., Bldg. 39, Charlestown, MA 02129, (617) 242-SAVE. Contact Neil Clark. Teaching guides: "Water Wizards" up to third grade; "Water Watchers," grades three and up. *Excellent* source of hands-on exercises. Supply may be limited to Massachusetts residents only. This material is worth trying to obtain.

❦ ❦ ❦

**Diane Edgecomb** has been creating and touring seasonal and environmental performances for children and adults for over ten years. These performances range from Solstice and Equinox evenings rich in music and mythology to environmental concerts for school children and families. Her vivid performance style has won her a Year's Best Performance Award from the *Boston Herald* and a Storytelling World Honors Award for her children's audiocassette: *Pattysaurus and Other Tales.*

"New Pots from Old" is the story of a family of potters, who build a village with clay. When they deplete their source, the villagers threaten the potters with exile. A young potter learns the secret of recycling in return for championing the differences in an old witch.

This version is a composite of many tellings. It is never the same twice. Several parts of the story require input from the audience. There are footnotes where I encourage joining in and corresponding notes following the text.

In general, repeat the response from your audience for all to hear. Use what they give you. Your attitude should be that they're always right. This will make for a very interesting and personal story.

# New Pots from Old

## A recycling tale by Papa Joe
### dedicated to Josh

A LONG TIME AGO, before your parents were born, before your grandparents were born, even before your great great great grandparents were born, there was a village near a river. It was so far away that we would never have known of it if not for the old storytellers.

In the village, by the river, lived a family who dearly loved to play with mud. There was a large bank of grey mud behind their house. At first the family just squished it between their fingers or patted it into pies. One day, however, they realized that this was special mud. It was different than the mud taken from other places on the river. This mud kept its shape when it dried.

What do you suppose it was? Can you imagine? That's right. It was clay.[1]

So what do you suppose they made with it?

Well, the first thing they made was a bowl. It was a fine bowl, a little rough around the edges, but they were just starting out.

Next they made a spoon. The bowl was great for putting soup in, but they needed a spoon to get the soup out.

Oh, boats! They made the most wonderful toy boats to sail in the river.

Jugs! The day the family learned to make jugs was a happy day for the whole village by the river. For that was the day that everyone could start storing water in their homes. Imagine that! Before that day, everyone had to walk to the spring every time they needed water.

Oh yes! They made pipes! And valves too! Pipes to carry the water from the spring into the homes.

---

1. Sometimes you might have to answer this question yourself. However, this is a good place to get the audience involved with the interaction.

And shirts. It became quite the fad, wearing clay mural shirts. Each little clay square stitched together to form the clothes and clicking and clacking with every step.

But mostly they made pots.[2]

Well, years went by and years went on and the family made better and better pots, fancier and fancier pots! Everyone in the village bought pots from them. In fact, the villagers called them the Potters.

But the Potters didn't just sell pots. They made and sold anything you could want and they made it all from clay. They made toys and tables, tiles for walls, floors, and roofs. They made bricks for streets and buildings.[3]

Well, years went by and years went on and the village by the river used more and more clay for more and more things. If you were to look at the village you might think it was all made of clay. And maybe it was. For now everyone lived in clay houses with clay roofs. They sat on clay chairs and slept on clay beds. They ate from clay plates on clay tables with clay forks.

From the beginning they found that they needed a hot fire to dry the clay hard. Each day the Potters had to cut trees to fire the clay. They cut the trees until the woods near the village were gone and only a few scattered trees were left. When the woods were gone the animals left. They walked, flew, or crawled until they found new woods so far away that the villagers knew nothing about them.[4]

But the clay! Aha! Everywhere you looked, anything that could be made with clay was. And you know about clay. If you drop it, what happens?[5]

It breaks! No one really worried about breaking anything. If something broke they would go to the Potters and have a new thing made. A new thing, a better thing, a thing with new colors and new designs, not last year's colors or scenes of trees and animals, no one wanted trees and animals any more.

And what did they do with all the bits and pieces? What did they do with all the old clay shards? They hauled them out of the village to a big hole and threw them in. As the years went by and the years went on the hole filled up with shards.

---

2. Use whatever the audience gives you. They should give more than enough items for the story. I use between ten and twenty items for most tellings. I give each item a story as illustrated in the text. If the audience doesn't offer any items you can start them off by pretending someone did, e.g.: "A bowl you say? Well, the first thing they made was a bowl. It was . . ."). Some items may be strange, but anything will work including shirts or current cartoon heros. The closing line that I use, "But mostly they made pots" brings the story back into the narrative.

3. Here is a good place to bring in the members of the audience who didn't get a chance to participate before now. I usually keep this section short (ten to twenty items), chanting out the items like a street peddler.

4. This section can be opened to deal more with the animals. You can use local animals to bring the story home to the audience.

5. Sometimes I bring in a small sun dried clay bowl and drop it at this point. It doesn't make much noise, but it has a powerful effect.

As the years went by and the years went on the hole became a pile, then a hill, and finally a mountain of clay shards. The people called it Shard Mountain.

As the mountain grew bigger and bigger, the clay bank by the river grew smaller and smaller until it became a pit that grew deeper and deeper. Finally the day came when the Potters could find no more clay.

"No clay! What are we going to do?"

"I don't know. What can we do?"

What could they do? They had never bothered to learn anything but making things with clay. For generations the Potters had used this clay and now they were helpless.

At first the villagers thought nothing of the used-up clay pit. But soon everyone was thinking of it. For whenever something broke it was gone and it could not be replaced.

The day a strong wind came and tore clay tiles from the roofs, people thought of the empty clay pit. They thought of the clay pit every time it rained.

The day a village elder tripped on a chair, fell on his table and broke two of its legs, he thought of the empty clay pit. As all of his clay dishes and cups crashed to the floor he thought of the clay pit.

Each time a thing broke people thought of the empty clay pit and knew the thing could not be replaced.

One day the villagers had a meeting.

One cried, "This is terrible! I don't have a single pot left."

The second said, "We must do something!"

A third called, "What can we do?"

Then they all began shouting ideas.

"Look for a new clay pit." "We tried that"

"Get a new Potter family." "That won't help."[6]

"How about replacing the broken things with something else?
Something different than clay." "Like what?"

"Wood?" "There is no more!"

"Paper?" "That's made from wood!"

"Animal skins!" "They left with the trees."

"Glass!" "Wonderful, how do you make it?"

"Sand!" "We don't have any."

---

6. If you can get the audience to suggest solutions here, that's great. If they go into the next section, that's fine. If they come up with the solution, I ask them if they know the story, smile, then I go on with the story.

| "Rocks?" | "None around here." |
| "Steel!" | "Steal what?" |
| "Plastic?" | "It hasn't been invented yet."[7] |

Finally someone said, "This is all the Potters' fault. We should be making them find the answer. We wouldn't be in this mess if it wasn't for them. I vote we tell them to find the answer or get out of this village."

The village elders went to the Potters and told them what had been decided. Do you know what the Potters did? They sat around and cried, "I don't want to leave."

But one little girl wasn't crying. Her name was Penny. Of all the people in the Potter family, Penny Potter was particularly perceptive. Penny Potter perceived that if no one in the village knew the answer to the problem, then she would need to go out of the village to find the answer. The only person she knew outside the village was the Witch of Shard Mountain.

In a cave on the far side of Shard Mountain lived an old witch. She had lived there as long as anyone in the village could remember. She only came into the village about once a month to do her shopping. When she came the children would laugh at her and call her names. They threw clay shards at her and sang terrible songs.

> Witchy, witchy, witchy
> Lives in the ditchy.
> Skin like dry clay.
> Hair like dry hay.
> Witchy, witchy, witchy.[8]

Penny thought of these things as she walked down the path to Shard Mountain. It was a long and hard climb around and up the far side of that mountain. She stood at last at the gaping hole that was the entrance to the witch's cave.

Penny was shaking. She thought, "Ohhh! What if she turns me into a frog." And then, "Well, I don't remember anyone really being hurt by her."

Still shaking, she called out:

| "Hello" | (Hello, Hello, Hello) |
| "Hello" | (Hello, Hello, Hello) |
| "Is anyone home?" | (Home, Home, Home)[9] |

From the back of the cave came the sound of a boot scraping across the floor. Scrape. Thump. Scrape. Thump. Scrape. Thump.

Penny shook harder and harder. The witch stepped into the light.

---

7. I use anything the audience offers here and sometimes I suggest things that they don't mention.

8. I teach this song as a chant.

9. I do this section as a echo game asking the audience to be my echo. Sometimes I play this before I start the story to build rapport.

"I know you. You're one of those village children. One of those children who throw shards at me. What are you doing up here? Did you come to call me names?"

Penny was still shaking. "Oh no! I never threw anything at you. I never called you names."

"Maybe you did and maybe you didn't, but you haven't answered my question: What are you doing up here? Tell me now."

Penny was almost sobbing. "I came because we need help and I was hoping you could give it to me." The witch fixed her eyes on Penny. "What kind of help could an old one like me give to you?"

"You've seen how our village is built of clay?"

"I've noticed," returned the witch bitterly.

"We've run out of clay. There isn't any more. I was hoping that if you really were a witch, then you could make more clay for us."

"Ha!" scolded the witch. "Why should I help you, little one? Why should I help your village? After the way your people have destroyed the woods? After the way your people have treated me, I'd rather punish you than help you!"

Penny was in tears. "But we need your help."

"Your village never helped me! I never did anything to those children. Why do they treat me so ill?"

"Well," stammered Penny. "Perhaps because you're different."

"Is that a reason to hurt me?" screamed the witch.

"No," Penny whispered. "I am sorry the children hurt you."

The witch looked at Penny for a long time. "Listen, Penny Potter. I do know you. You are particularly perceptive. I can help you. I don't like being disliked. If you can bring the children of the village here and if you can help me stop them from being so cruel, then I will help you and your village. Bring the children to me."

So Penny went back down and around the mountain. Down and around she ran as fast as she could. At last she came to the village. "Come out, come out wherever you are," she called. "Olly olly in free!"

All of the village children came running up to Penny.

"If we want to get new clay we need to get help from the witch. But the witch won't help because you've been so mean. Come up to her cave and tell her you're sorry. Come up to her cave and ask to be friends."

But the children began with "Ohs!" and "No!" They were afraid to go to the witch.[10]

"I'm not going!" said one. "Nor I," said another. "None of us will go. She'll turn us all into polliwogs!" claimed a third.

Penny shook her head. "I was just up there. She didn't do anything to me. She is just upset because you are so hateful. If you don't come with me to the cave, I'll go back alone. But you'll never see another new clay toy or game or anything again."

Penny turned and headed back for the cave. At first the children watched her walk away. Then someone said, "We have been cruel. The witch never did anything to us even when we threw shards at her. I'm going."

As the first child walked forward another followed. Slowly, one by one the children headed up the path to Shard Mountain. Up and around they went until they came to the gaping black hole near the top. Now it was the children's turn to shake as Penny called into the cave.

| | |
|---|---|
| "Hello" | (Hello, Hello, Hello) |
| "Hello" | (Hello, Hello, Hello) |
| "Are you home?" | (Home, Home, Home) |

From the back of the cave came the sound of a boot scraping across the floor. Scrape. Thump. Scrape. Thump. Scrape. Thump.

The children were shaking harder and harder.

Out came the witch. "So! You're all I here, eh? All the nice children who enjoy torturing an old lady? Have you had your fun? Do you think I like it? Would you like me to treat you like that? Well? What have you got to say for yourselves?"

| | |
|---|---|
| "We're sorry." | "What? I can't hear you." |
| "We're sorry!" | "What?" |
| *"We're sorry!"*[11] | |

"Will you think it's fun to mistreat people like that again?"

| | |
|---|---|
| "No, ma'am." | "What?" |
| "No, ma'am!" | "What?" |
| *"No, ma'am!"* | |

"Then off you go. Penny, come with me."

If you think Penny was brave to come to the witch's cave, can you imagine how brave she was to walk into its dark entrance? Deeper and deeper they walked

---

10. If I have a responsive audience, I let them be the children and they tell me why they won't go. Sometimes I let one of them talk the rest into coming up the mountain.

11. Let the audience play the children's part, saying "I'm sorry" louder each time.

through the dark tunnel until they came to a small room lit by one red candle with a green flame.

"Let's see. It's around here somewhere." The witch began tossing books off her shelves.

"No, not that one.
  Not that one.
    Nor that one.
      Or that one.
        No, no, no!
          Yes!

"Here it is. Now which page? Hmm, hmm, hmm. Yes, that's right. Yes! Just as I thought."

The witch turned to Penny. "Now you start by taking the old clay . . ."

"What?" Penny was confused. "I thought you were going to make new clay. I thought you'd say a spell and the clay pit would be full again."

"Ha! A spell to refill the old pit! You want something from nothing? You've been wasting clay and wood for years. Do you want to do it all again? Penny, your village needs to start saving things like clay and reusing them. You have a whole mountain of clay here and a whole village below. You'll never run out of clay again if you just stop throwing it all away."

"As I was saying," the witch continued. "Take the old clay and grind it into a fine powder. Add a little of this and a little of that and here you go: new soft pliable clay!"

Penny began to leap with joy. "Oh! Thank you! Thank you!"

"Wait, you silly little goose! What good is all this new clay now? You've used up nearly every tree for fire wood to bake your clay."

Penny sat down. She had been so worried about the clay she had forgotten about the wood. Ah well. So had everyone else in the village.

The witch continued, "If your people will promise to leave the trees alone and, more than that, if you will help replant the woods, I will help you build a new kiln to bake your clay. A kiln that doesn't burn wood."

Penny's eyes went wide and her mouth dropped open. "You really are magic!"

"Maybe I am and maybe I'm not, but the sun has all the power you need to fire your pots. The sun will heat the new kiln we'll build."

"The sun?" Penny was amazed. "That's wonderful!" And with one last "thank you and good-bye," she was gone. She was running down and around the mountain back to her home.

"Mother! Father! Everyone! Potters, one and all! Look what the witch has given to us. We can make new pots from old. Just take the old shards and grind them up. Add this and that and look: new clay. But that's not all. The witch is coming to help us build a new kiln, a kiln that is heated by the sun instead of burning all the wood."

The Potters were so pleased that they invited the witch to stay and live with them. And since they were so pleased with what she could do with all her strangeness, she was glad to become part of their family.

From that day on and from that day since, the Potters have wheeled their wagons through the streets collecting old shards to make new clay. And every year they go to the woods, plant young trees, and pray that the animals come back.

Now in the streets of the village you can hear the children sing:

> New pots from old,
> New pots from old,
> The witch and Penny Potter
> Gave us new pots from old.[12]

## Follow-up Activities for "New Pots from Old"

Note: This is just a story. It was written to help children see how important each person and thing is to each other. At the time of this writing, technology has not been able to recycle kiln dried shards to raw clay. I hope someday it will. In the meantime, it is possible to use recycled clay in other ways. Some people are already doing just that. Please have fun telling this story. I certainly have.

1. On the blackboard, have the class make a list of things that live in the woods. The list should be as long as possible, including all classes of plants and animals. Make a diagram showing how each plant and animal is related to the other as either food or shelter. Discuss how the loss of one member hurts the others. For another example, see a game called "Webbing" in *Sharing Nature with Children* by Joseph Bharat Cornell, Ananda Publications, 14618 Tyler Foote Road, Nevada City, CA 95959, 1979.

2. On the blackboard, have the class make a list of things for which people are made fun of (ridiculed) by other people. Divide the list into groups (for instance, things people do, how people look, where people live). Ask the class to discuss how they would feel if they were treated that way. Have the children share any experience in which they have felt discrimination.

3. Plan ways to set up a household or a school to recycle as much of its waste products as possible. Discuss plans for businesses and camps to recycle. Discuss how a town, state, or the federal government might be involved in recycling. Plan a global solution.

4. Try the previous activity using other environmental issues such as conservation and hazardous waste.

---

12. I teach this song as a chant.

5. Assuming ecological feasibility, have the class dig clay from a river bank. When the clay is dry, have them grind it into a fine powder. Add water slowly until the clay is the consistency of peanut butter. Have the class make anything they want with their clay. Allow the clay to air dry. This clay can be ground up and re-used as often as desired.

6. Have the class research and build a solar still to take water from the air. Or build a solar dryer for preserving fruits.

7. Play a game of differences. Have each child think of something that makes him different than the others in the class. Have each child make up a rhyme to show how special their differences make them (e.g., "I can tap dance. To the store I can prance.")

❧ ❧ ❧

**Joseph P. Gaudet** has provided over five thousand storytelling programs as **"Papa Joe"** for schools, libraries, civic organizations, businesses, and museums. He has worked with children, teens, adults, and seniors in the US, Canada, and Europe. Joseph writes original stories which he tells along with folktales, fables, tall tales, and historical stories. He has written two entertaining concerts about dragons and ogres. Papa Joe teaches oral communication skills to children and adults throughout New England.

# Gaura Devi Saves the Trees

## by David H. Albert

GAURA DEVI IS EIGHT YEARS OLD. She lives in India, near very high mountains called the Himalayas. The tops of the mountains are covered with snow all year round. When the sun hits the mountain tops, they shine like diamonds.

Gaura Devi lives on a hillside below the mountain tops, in a house made of stone and slate. It is a good house. In summer, when the sun is hot, the house is very cool. In winter, when the snow is very deep, the house is very warm. Gaura Devi is poor, but she is happy.

Every morning, Gaura Devi takes her two goats down to the valley so they can eat the grass there. On some mornings, she goes up to the forest above her village with her aunt. The forest has many big trees. In the forest they pick special plants and flowers and berries. Gaura Devi's aunt uses the plants, flowers, and berries to make medicines. She takes care of all the people in the village when they are sick, and usually makes them well again.

In the afternoons, Gaura Devi goes with her mother to collect broken branches and twigs and dried grass. They use branches and twigs to make a fire for cooking. The fire also keeps the house warm in winter. The cow eats the dried grass and gives them milk every morning and evening. Gaura Devi and her mother walk very far every day to collect enough for the family.

Gaura Devi wondered why her mother does not go up to the forest nearby and cut down the trees. She asked her mother, "Why do we walk so far for wood every day, but leave the trees in the forest?"

Her mother replied, "Gaura Devi, you listen to me. The trees are our brothers and sisters. They provide shade for the plants and flowers and berries that your aunt makes into medicine. They are houses for the birds and animals."

Gaura Devi's two goats stood still as if they were listening too.

"The roots of the trees are like hands. They hold the earth to the side of the mountain. They also hold the water from the big rains and from the melting snow. If anyone ever cuts down our brothers and sisters, our village will be washed away."

Gaura Devi told all her friends what her mother said.

One day, Gaura Devi and her two goats walked up the mountain trail toward the forest. Suddenly she saw a truck parked by the side of the road. Many men, wearing caps and carrying axes, were walking toward the forest. Gaura Devi went up to the leader. "Why are you going to the forest?" she asked.

The man said, "We are going to cut down the trees."

"My mother says the trees are our brothers and sisters. They are not to be cut down," Gaura Devi said.

The man replied, "We have orders from the people in the city to bring the wood to them. Now we have to go to work."

Gaura Devi thought. She began to walk down the mountainside. Then she began to run. She ran as fast as her legs would carry her. The goats ran behind her.

She ran to the big gong in the open space in the middle of the village. She picked up a stick and beat the gong as loud as she could. Again and again she beat it until her arms got tired. All the women in the village came to the open space. The men were away working. Gaura Devi told them what she had seen. The women began to walk quickly up the mountain side. Gaura Devi's mother was the leader. Gaura Devi ran behind. The two goats followed.

Soon they reached the forest edge. They saw the men preparing to cut down the trees. The women ran up to the trees and began to hug them. Gaura Devi's mother said to the leader, "We come as your friends and do not wish you any harm, but we cannot let you cut down the trees."

"Get out of the way," said the leader of the men.

"The trees are our brothers and sisters," replied Gaura Devi's mother, "If you cut down the trees, our village will be washed away when the rains come. We are hugging the trees. If you cut the trees down, you will have to hit us with your axes first."

The men looked around at the women hugging the trees. They knew they shouldn't cut down the forest, even though they were told to do so by the people in the city. They were ashamed. The leader said, "You have taught us a lesson. We will not cut down the forest. We will go back home with our axes."

The men walked slowly back to the truck. Some of the women ran back to the village and brought some tea. The men were thankful, for they were very thirsty. "We will tell others not to cut these trees down," they promised.

That evening, Gaura Devi's father and the other men from the village returned. When they heard what the women had done, they were very happy. The whole village had a big celebration. They ate fruits and sweet cakes and sang songs and danced.

Gaura Devi was a hero. Her friends put a necklace of sweet-smelling jasmine flowers around her neck. She was a hero! The women in village gave her a string of little silver bells.

Gaura Devi was very happy. Her two goats jumped to and fro as if they were dancing. The birds sang beautiful songs as the sun went down. The snow on the mountain tops glistened.

Soon Gaura Devi felt very tired, so she went to sleep. But in the nighttime the forest was not asleep. The animals talked about what had happened, and how brave Gaura Devi and the women had been. Her sisters and brothers the trees did not talk. But they too were very happy. They did not sleep. They smiled.

# Follow-up Activities for "Gaura Devi Saves the Trees"

## by Mayra Bloom, Jay Goldspinner and John Porcino

## Source of the Story

"Gaura Devi Saves the Trees" is based on a true story which took place in the village of Reni, in India near the Tibetan border, on March 26, 1974. The story was written simply by David Albert to be told to very young children—five and six year olds. It is part of a much larger story of the Chipko ("Hugging Trees") Movement in northern India: the story of mountain villagers, women and children, stopping big lumber companies from clear-cutting mountain slopes by issuing a call to "hug the trees."

Using information written by David Albert and Mark Shepard, I am giving you an expanded version of the story of "Gaura Devi," which you could incorporate into your telling for an older group of listeners.

The Chipko Movement has been growing in northern India in opposition to the devastating tree-cutting which was causing terrible floods and landslides, as well as destroying the trees that people depended on for many things in their daily lives: for fodder, fruit and fuel, for flowers, even water and soil. The local people in many places really were hugging the trees in the face of the lumbermen's axes, putting their bodies on the line to save the trees.

When the forest department auctioned 2500 trees in the Reni forest, the leader of the Chipko movement warned that the lumbermen would have to face the resistance of the Movement. But he was not taken seriously. Over the next few months, meetings and rallies were held throughout the Reni area to prepare the people for the coming struggle.

In mid-March of 1974, lumbermen arrived in a town close by the Reni forest. The villagers and Chipko workers waited tensely for the confrontation. Then government officials tricked the men of the village into leaving for a distant town, by saying this was their one chance to collect money that had long been owed to them.

The men of the village left, and that morning the lumbermen with Forest Department officials and a company agent were driven in a rented bus toward the Reni forest. They were dropped off outside the village of Reni, and took a roundabout path to avoid being seen by the villagers.

But a little girl ("Gaura Devi") spotted the men marching toward the forest. She ran to tell an elderly leader of the village women, who called the other women away from their cooking, and within minutes about thirty women and children were hurrying toward the forest.

They caught up with the men, who had made camp and were preparing lunch. The women pleaded with them not to cut down the trees, saying that if they did, the mountain would fall on the village. They asked the lumbermen to come back with them and wait to talk with the village men.

Some of the men seemed ready to listen to the women, but some others had been drinking. The drunk men tried to take liberties with the women or cursed at them for obstructing the work. One drunken man staggered toward the women brandishing his gun. The elderly woman stood in his path, saying he would have to shoot her for she would never allow the forest to be cut.

At this moment the sober men decided to leave, and started back down the path. The women kept on appealing to the drunken ones. Then they spotted another group of laborers coming up the path, carrying bags of food. Some women ran out to meet them and pleaded with them to go back. The men agreed to leave, after they had eaten—and they did.

Finally the drunk men realized they were the only ones left, and they started back. The women were helping to carry the workers' tools—some distance behind. They came to a concrete slab bridging a gap left by a previous landslide. The women crossed over the slab, then using the workers' tools, they pried the huge slab loose and sent it crashing down into the gorge below, cutting off access to the forest.

All night the women sat by the gap in the trail, guarding the entrance to the forest, and the laborers huddled by their ration bags below. The next morning, the village men and Chipko organizers arrived, and the women told the story; they didn't tell about the drunkenness and the gun because they hoped to win the laborers to their side. The laborers, after all, were poor working people like themselves. The Chipko organizers assured the company men and forest officials that the villagers meant no harm but only wanted to save their forest.

The story of the mountain women and children spread all over India and created an outcry for the protection of the Reni forest. Eventually, the lumber company withdrew their men. Two years later, after an investigation by a committee of experts, the government put a ten-year ban on all tree-felling in a large section of the Alakhnanda River watershed of which the Reni forest is a part, an area of over 450 square miles. It was a victory for the people, the trees, and the Chipko movement.

## Activities for Preschool and Elementary Children

**Puppet Show**: Have the children break up into groups of about five children. Have those groups design paper bag puppets to represent Gaura Devi, Gaura Devi's mother, other village women, the woodcutter's leader, other woodcutters, the village men, and of course the trees. Have each group develop a puppet show of the story using their puppets.

These puppet shows could be put on for other children in the class, for other classes in the school, for the parents, etc.

**New Musical Chairs**: The women of Gaura Devi's village worked together to save the trees. Here's a game that challenges young children to work together.

Play musical chairs with a different twist. Instead of taking out a person each time the music stops, take out a chair. More than one child will have to sit on each remaining chair. By the end of the game all the children will somehow be sitting on as few chairs as possible!!

Challenge the class to quickly get onto chairs when the music stops, and at the same time, to be the game's "referees," taking care to see that no one gets hurt. If you think the class is ready, try and make it to one chair. Two, three, or four chairs would also be a fine place to end the game.

**Exploring Trees**: Discuss why the trees were important to Gaura Devi's village. Go on a hunt around the classroom (don't forget lunch bags, or other less obvious things) and see how many reasons you can find why trees are important to your class. For instance, think about apples, nuts, desk tops, paper, air, glue . . . .

Have students hug a tree! Help them discover this tree by saying things like: Close your eyes. How does it feel against your cheeks. Smell the bark and leaves. How big is it? Can you put your arms around it? Think of the tree as your brother or sister like Gaura Devi's mother described. If you knew the tree could hear you what would you say?

Plant a tree or two or three or more (!) in the school yard or someplace else and care for them. See the book *The Simple Act of Planting a Tree* by Treepeople with Andy and Katie Lipais, Tarcher, 1990.

**Everyone Can Help**: First brainstorm (really encourage students to put out all the ideas that come into their minds without judgment) and then develop a list of ten simple things children can do (like Gaura Devi) at school and at home to conserve and protect their environment. Turn out the lights before recess, use the back sides of paper . . . . Practice these in the classroom. See the book *50 Simple Things Kids Can Do to Save the Earth* by the EarthWorks Group, Andrews and McMeel, 1990.

## Creating a Play from the Story

"Gaura Devi Saves the Trees" can be transformed into a wonderful play. It can be expanded or simplified to fit time and space, and children's ages and abilities. Whether put together on a rainy afternoon or expanded into a whole-school project integrating language arts, history, area studies, music, drama, art and conflict resolution, the story breaks down naturally into a series of scenes, each with accompanying songs. Rather than provide a written script, we offer scenes which can be improvised by the children as they come to understand the meaning of the play.

### Scene I: Gaura Devi's Village

To the sound of "A Ram Sam Sam," children set a morning village scene. Pantomimed actions can include: building fires, making chapatis, sewing, rocking babies, chatting, grinding meal. Background research or projects can include learning where northern India is on the map; how people live; what the trees and mountains look like; how houses are built; what language is spoken; what children learn and do.

### Scene II: Gathering Firewood and Herbs

Sarah Pirtle's zipper song, "My Roots Go Down" is a fine accompaniment for a scene in which Gaura Devi and her friends learn how and why the village is dependent on the forest. They learn that the trees provide shade and protection; roots prevent erosion of the mountainsides; dead trees provide firewood; plants and herbs grow on the forest floor. Teachers can write verses in advance, or the children can devise their own lyrics as they learn. The play will gain in power if the children have had the opportunity to *really* hug *real* trees; to experience the feeling and closeness of the bark and trunk; to write and draw what it feels like to think of trees as brothers and sisters.

### Scene III: Gaura Devi Sees the Woodcutters

This is an opportunity for the woodcutters to vent some energy by stamping, chopping, chanting. The teacher can provide rhythms and words, or these can be developed by the children as they get into chopping trees. "We're from the city, we're from the city, we're from the city and **we need wood!**" might be a place to start. It's important, after all, to realize that the woodcutters are not enemies or bad people; they need fuel and jobs; they may have few choices in their lives; they may not understand the villagers' position. Then, too, there's a part of each of us that exults in the power to knock down trees. This needs to be acknowledged, so that the power can be released and redirected toward more positive pursuits.

### *Scene IV: Gaura Devi Beats the Gong*

It takes conviction for a child to tell her village that something is very wrong. We warn our children not to cry wolf or raise false alarms, but then we expect them to act when an emergency arises. In its simplest form, this scene includes beating on a pot lid, gathering the villagers, and rushing off into the forest to protect the trees. Extended, the scene might include debating about what to do, expressing fear, or joining hands to strengthen one another. Preparation might include reading "The Boy Who Cried Wolf," the humorous "Rikki Tikki Tembo," or Japanese tales of children who have saved villages from tidal waves, as well as discussion of children's experiences trying to let grown-ups know when something is not right.

### *Scene V: Gaura Devi's Village Hugs the Trees*

Elementary school children are often (very understandably) embarrassed about hugging one another onstage, so the power of this central scene may depend upon finding the right "technical" solution. A group of children may be comfortable forming a circle and hugging a single, central tree; or the trees could be props or children in costume. This is an example of nonviolent direct action, and as such can be accompanied by the civil rights song which says, "Just like a tree that's planted by the water, we shall not be moved." Or, the audience could participate in a chant developed by the Paper Bag Players, in which all shake their fingers at the offending woodcutters and say, "Stop, stop, stop right there, don't, don't, don't you dare." The meaning and intensity of the scene will be enhanced if the children have had the opportunity to hug real trees ahead of time.

### *Scene VI: Conflict Resolution*

Tree hugging is a dramatic preface to the real work of conflict resolution. Preparation for this scene can include brainstorming responses to questions such as, "How can we resolve this problem so that the woodcutters *and* the villagers *and* the trees get what they need?" This might be an opportunity to stop the action and turn to the audience for suggestions. Because, like all real conflicts, this one is complex and difficult, it might be most realistic for the villagers and woodcutters to agree simply to negotiate; to decide not to cut down any trees while all think and talk together. Sarah Pirtle's "There is Always Something You Can Do" provides encouragement for the mediation process. A wonderful follow-up activity would be for the children in the audience to write and draw their solutions to the conflict, and then contribute these to a newsletter or bulletin board for further consideration.

### *Scene VII. Celebration/ Reconciliation*

In the last scene, villagers and woodcutters return to the village to share food and celebrate their commitment to conflict resolution. This might be an opportunity to put on some contemporary music and have everybody dance; or it might be a more solemn occasion when Gaura Devi is honored for her courage, and "A Ram Sam Sam" is sung again. John Bell's version of "Deep Blue Sea," which emphasizes the presence of peace after the threat of war might also be a good way to conclude.

# My Roots Go Down

Words and Music by Sarah Pirtle

# A Ram Sam Sam
## 2-part Round

Morocco
Collected by Piet Kriethof

**Round I** F

A ram sam sam, a ram sam sam, gu - li

C7         F     II    F

gu - li gu - li gu - li gu - li ram sam sam. A ra - fi, a

      C7               F

ra - fa, Gu - li gu - li gu - li gu - li gu - li ram sam sam.

# Chipko Song

Sarah Pirtle
Based on the words of Ghyansham Sailani

1. Where will we go if the green trees fall? What will we eat? _____
2. Where will we go if all In - dia is flood? Where will we walk? _____

What will we wear? Where will we go if the green trees fall?
Where will we live? Where will we go if all In - dia is flood?

***Chorus:***

Where will the poor go then? } Come with me now and em -
Where will the poor go then? }

brace the trees, feel their heart beat next to yours. Come with me now and em -

brace the trees, feel their heart beat next to yours.

# There Is Always Something You Can Do

Words and Music by Sarah Pirtle

# We Shall Not Be Moved

Derived from an old Spiritual

**Chorus:** We shall not, we shall not be moved, We shall not, we shall not be moved, just like a tree stand-ing by the wa - ter,

We shall not be moved.

**Verses:**
1. We'll stand and fight to-geth - er;
2. We're march - ing with the un - ion;
3. U - ni - dos ven - ce - re - mos;

We shall not be moved.___ We'll stand and fight to-geth - er;
We shall not be moved.___ We're march - ing with the un - ion;
Fuer - tes so - mos ya;___ U - ni - dos ven - ce - re - mos;

(1.,2.) We shall not be moved. Just like a tree stand - ing by the
(3.) Fuer - tes so - mos ya. Co - mo un ár - bol jun - tos cer - ca al

wa - ter, We shall not be moved.
rí - o, Fuer - tes so - mos ya.

## Resources

"Chipko: North India's Tree Huggers." Mark Shepard. *The CoEvolution Quarterly*, Fall 1981, pp. 62-69.

*The Lorax*. Dr. Seuss. New York: Random House, 1971. A delightful story in Dr. Seuss's whimsical style, about use and misuse of our environment and the importance of individual action in solving these problems.

*The Man Who Planted Hope and Grew Happiness*. Jean Giono. Friends of Nature, Brooksville, ME 04617. Also in *Sharing the Joy of Nature; Nature Activities for All Ages*, Joseph Cornell. Nevada City, CA: Dawn Publications, 1989. A true story of a man who spent the last 40 years of his life planting trees, single handedly reforesting a section of southern France. He worked through two world wars, restoring the region to life and living.

*Staying Alive: Women, Ecology and Survival in India*. Vandana Shiva. London: Zed Press, 1988.

❦ ❦ ❦

**David H. Albert** is a writer and publisher, and one of the founders of New Society Publishers, the nation's only trade publishing house specifically dedicated to fundamental social change through nonviolent action.

# Coyote and the Sleeping Monster

## by Cheryl Savageau

COYOTE WAS WALKING ALONG ONE DAY when he saw some men digging in the desert. He stopped to watch what they were doing, and what he saw was this. They were digging into the lair of a huge sleeping monster. They were bringing the monster up bit by bit and putting it into a truck. This monster's breath was so poisonous that even after they'd left, the rocks and air around the entrance to its lair were poisoned. All the plants died. Children who were born near there often got sick and died. Some were never born at all.

Coyote decided he wanted to know why the men would dig up such a monster, with such poison breath, when all the monster wanted to do was sleep in the earth. So he followed the truck.

The truck drove to a big building. The men got out and took the sleeping monster out of the truck and brought it into the building. Inside the building people were working. They wore special clothes to protect them from the monster's terrible breath. The people were pulling the monster out of the soil where it had spread itself out nice and thin, and they were squeezing the monster closer and closer together, so it wasn't very comfortable. But somehow that monster kept right on sleeping.

Then they took that monster and put it into tin cans, and into each tin can they put an alarm clock, so they could wake the monster up if they wanted to. At the other end of the building, men took the tin cans and loaded them onto another truck. Coyote followed the truck until it came to a big white train, and he watched as men took the tin cans out of the truck and put them onto the train. Then the train started to go. Coyote hopped right on top and he rode that train to see where they were bringing those tin cans. He rode all over the country, through cities, forests, over plains and mountains. Even to the ocean, and everywhere he went, that train stopped and men took tin cans and loaded them onto white trucks, and he watched as they put some of the tin cans onto big boats.

Coyote was curious. He wanted to see what they were going to do with that sleeping monster. So he followed one of the trucks. This truck drove out through the countryside, through the trees and into a valley between some hills, with Coyote following right behind it, until suddenly Coyote ran right into a steel fence that closed behind the truck. Some men came out and chased Coyote away, but he didn't go far. He ran up to the top of the hill so he could watch what was going on.

Inside the fence, men were taking the tin cans off the trucks, and putting them into the ground, and at first Coyote thought that was a good idea, even if it was kind of stupid to spend all that time and energy moving the monster from one place to another. But then he realized that inside those holes in the ground, there were giant sling-shots, so that the men could throw the tin cans anywhere they wanted to.

249

These men must be crazy, Coyote thought. Don't they know how poisonous this monster is? Don't they know how it will roar if they wake it up?

When the men were done putting the tin cans into the sling-shots, they began to do a dance, a tin can dance. Every day Coyote watched as the men polished the tin cans and then marched around doing their tin can dance.

Coyote decided to go down to the bar and talk to some of the men who worked at the tin can place. Hey, Coyote said. Don't you know that monster is poisonous? Don't you know what'll happen if he gets out of those cans?

Sure, we know, the men said proudly. Our enemies tremble just thinking about that monster's roar.

Then Coyote said to the men, You think that if you wake that monster up he'll only roar in your enemy's direction? Where do you think you're going to hide from that terrible breath?

But the men wouldn't hear him. Don't be such a drag, they told him. Here, have a beer. You wanna know about this stuff? Don't talk to us, we don't make the decisions.

These men are even crazier than I thought, Coyote said to himself.

So Coyote decided to read the newspaper to find out what the reasons were for putting the monster into the tin cans with an alarm clock, and what he read was this: We have to have lots of tin cans and lots of alarm clocks to make sure that monster never wakes up.

Coyote went back up to the top of the hill and he watched those men doing their tin can dance. These men can't listen and they can't think, Coyote said. That night, Coyote climbed over the fence.

The next morning, when the men woke up, they found Coyote droppings all over the tin cans. Now they'll know what Coyote thinks of that, said Coyote. But the men just took rags and shined up those tin cans and danced their tin can dance even harder. Coyote was so mad he ran down the hill and killed a sheep to eat, something Coyote doesn't do that often. There was a lot of blood from that sheep. That night Coyote climbed the fence again.

The next morning, when the men woke up, they found their tin cans covered with blood. Now they'll get the point, said Coyote. But the men just took their rags and shined up those tin cans and danced their tin can dance even harder.

Coyote got so mad he said, Hey, what do I care what these stupid two-leggeds do? And he took off. He rode his motorcycle all over the place, down to Albuquerque and over to Boston. He chased pretty young women. Then he went out into the woods. And while he was out there he started to think. It wasn't just the two-legged that would be poisoned if the monster woke up. The four-legged people, the people who fly, the people who swim in the water, all his green relatives, the air, the rocks, the water, all would be poisoned. So Coyote went back to that hill and he watched.

Now one of the things the men did with the tin cans was to take them out every once in a while. They put the tin cans onto the white trucks and then they drove around the countryside for a while, then they drove back inside the fence, took the tin cans off the trucks, polished them, and put them back into their slingshots. Coyote figured it was part of their tin can dance.

One morning while Coyote was watching, the men took the tin cans and put them onto the trucks. Coyote watched as they opened the gate and began to drive down the road. Then Coyote ran down that hill as fast as he could go. Coyote jumped on top of one of the trucks. And, because Coyote is magic, when Coyote jumped on one of the trucks, Coyote jumped on all of the trucks. And that truck started to run backwards. Backwards down the road that led back to the white train. Pretty soon trucks were rolling backwards to the white train from all over the country, like streams into a river, and on top of every truck was Coyote.

When the trucks got to the train, Coyote took the tin cans off the trucks and put them onto the train, and that train started to run backwards. Coyote rode that train all the way back to the white building, and when he got there, he took those tin cans off the train and sent them back into the building.

Inside the building, Coyote very carefully opened the tin cans and took out the alarm clocks. He took the sleeping monster and mixed it gently back into the soil. And then Coyote loaded that monster back onto the white truck and drove that truck backwards all the way out into the desert. And then he took the monster and put it back into its lair. And when the monster felt itself safe again in the earth, it stretched itself out as thin as could be in the soil and it took in a deep breath, drawing back all the poison, and fell into a very sound sleep. Coyote watched as Mother Desert filled over the place where the hole had been. And then Coyote heard the voices of children saying, it's safe now, we can be born.

When Coyote told me this story he told it as if it had already happened. But time looks different to Coyote, so you see, this story is still going on.

## Follow-up Activities for "Coyote and the Sleeping Monster"

### Notes on Coyote

Stories about Coyote are told by Native American people throughout North America. Coyote is a powerful spirit-person. He is known as Trickster, Imitator, Old Man, and Changing Person. Some say it was Coyote who created Indian people and taught them how to live.

Coyote has powerful magic. He can change shape and make things happen. But Coyote is also very foolish. He likes to play tricks on people, and sometimes he goes too far. Coyote has died many times as a result of his foolish tricks, but he never stays dead for long.

Coyote shows us the limits of acceptable behavior by acting in ways that are so far outside those limits, so outrageous, that we can only laugh and shake our heads as

Coyote gets in trouble one more time. In times of real danger, however, Coyote shows remarkable wisdom as he "puts things right." His magical powers as Trickster and Changing Person, even his otherwise "unacceptable" behaviors, are then used for the good of the people. (And people, in American Indian terms, includes not only human beings, but all creatures, including animals, plants, rocks, water, clouds, stars, and of course, earth herself.)

Coyote stories are traditionally told in wintertime, between the times of first and last frosts. Please honor that tradition by telling this story during your winter season. If you choose to tell it out of season, please acknowledge to your audience that it is a tale for wintertime.

## Activity I: Discussion

It's important that the students understand the story before doing Activity II.

• What do you think the sleeping monster is? The tin cans? The alarm clocks?

• American Indian people believe that the world is in balance, but that sometimes people do things to upset that balance. What is out of balance in the story? How does it affect the environment?

• Coyote tries to talk to the men and when they don't listen he climbs over the fence and leaves them "messages." What is Coyote trying to tell the men? What do you think of his actions?

• American Indian people believe that everything, including air, water, and rocks, is alive in some way and that all of them, as well as animals and plants are our relatives. How are we related to the animals? the plants? What connections do we have to the air? the water? the soil? the rocks?

• What finally convinces Coyote that he has to go back to the tin can place and do something about it?

• What do you think is out of balance in the world? What effect does it have on the environment? On "all our relatives"? What effect will it have on you? On your children? Your grandchildren? What needs to happen to put things back into balance?

## Activity II: Writing and Telling

Write or tell a story about an environmental problem. Let your story take this form:

• Start with the world in balance.

• Something happens to make it go out of balance.

• Show what effects this would have now and for your children or grandchildren.

• Show what effects this would have on "all our relatives."

• End the story by things being put back into balance.

### Use Symbols in Your Story

Using symbols is a little bit like using code, where one thing stands for another, but it is more than that. A symbol should tell a truth about something, and help us to see and think about it in a new way. For example, if I said "Men dug up uranium and built missiles," the reaction would probably be, "Yeah, so what?" There's no power in it. Maybe because we've heard those words so many times before. Maybe because words like "uranium" and "missiles" don't really describe what they are. But if I say "There was a monster with poisonous breath sleeping below the desert," then, we have the beginning of a story! With a symbol, you have the power of naming something, of giving something its true name, as *you* see it.

## Suggestions

It can be useful to model this activity once by having the whole class make up a story about an environmental problem that particularly concerns them. Then once they've gone through the story-making process, they can work in small groups, or on their own.

Oral stories can be taped for future listening and to keep in the library. Students can practice their stories and share them with other classes.

Written stories can be posted on bulletin boards or "published" in handmade books.

Some students may prefer to tell the stories, tape them, and then write them down. Other children may prefer to write the stories first, then read or tell them.

**Cheryl Savageau** is of French-Canadian and Abenaki heritage. She is a founding member of Oak and Stone Storytellers, Worcester, MA. Coyote whispered this story in her ear a few years ago, and she has been telling it every winter since then. Her first book of poetry, *Comes Down Like Milk*, will be published by Alice James Books in March, 1992.

# Talking without Words

### by Sarah Pirtle

I WAS OUT IN THE WATER ALONE. I knew I shouldn't be, but my friends didn't want to go scuba diving that day. I'd waited all winter for this trip to the Florida Keys, so when they said they were going sightseeing in Miami, I said, "You go without me. I'll meet you back at the motel at dinner time." That's how I ended up out there by myself.

It's a basic rule of scuba diving never to dive alone, but I felt very sure of myself. I figured I'd dive down to the same place we'd gone the day before, a deep reef that we'd named the Stone Flower Castle because of the coral that formed in lacy clusters and rose to the surface.

I pulled out in the motor boat we'd rented, let down the anchor, and set up the dive flag. I put on the equipment: first, the buoyancy compensator that goes on like a jacket. I made sure the straps weren't tangled and inflated it slightly. Next came the scuba harness, the air tank, and the regulator. I buckled on the weight belt and then positioned the face mask that pulls my hair in the back and narrows my vision. I wet the long black clumsy flippers and slipped them over my feet. I set my underwater watch that tells how much air is left. Finally I reached for the tube that goes from the air tanks to my mouth. I chomped down on the rubber mouthpiece as it pressed against my gums. For each breath, I'd have to suck in air from the tanks.

I went in feet first with a giant stride. The water was warm. I didn't need a wet-suit. I dropped ten feet, twenty feet, thirty feet, forty feet down.

There was that forest of sponges and peacock-colored sea fans attached to the coral. I saw parrotfish grazing on the algae and went after them to get a closer look. You don't see fish like that on the surface.

I spent a long time following fish of all different colors and shapes—yellowtail damselfish, thick schools of copper sweepers, and electric blue angelfish that glided like butterflies. I went deeper and deeper into the caves and hollows and didn't even think about what time it was.

I was following a school of green-striped porkfish and hurrying to keep up with them, when all of a sudden I got a stomach cramp. It hurt with white heat. I doubled over with pain, and tried to stay calm.

I concentrated on breathing regularly. In, out. The cramp didn't ease up.

I remembered what I'd been taught to do: release your weight belt. I started to do that. I wasn't worried. But then I realized my belt had twisted around, and I couldn't get the clasp to unhook. I felt like I was sinking. The noise of my own breath sounded strange and spooky. I panicked.

The worst part was when I checked my air gauge. It said the tank was almost empty. In just a few minutes the air in the tank would run out. "I can't die now! I'm not ready! Someone help me!"

Something poked my arm. Hard. It wasn't like a fish brushing against me. This was strong and insistent. "Shark!" I thought.

Terror ripped through me like lightning. I waited for the awful feeling of teeth ripping. Instead something strong but velvety moved against my right side, lifting my arm.

Then I saw its eye. It was dark and round, and it was looking at me. A friendly brown eye. A dolphin eye. I was safe.

The dolphin moved under my arm and started to pull me up through the water. I held on and hugged it, and it carried me to the surface, fast but not too fast. My stomach relaxed as if the dolphin was helping that cramp, too.

When we reached the surface, I tore off my mouth piece and took in gulps of air, still holding on to the dolphin. I wasn't ready to let go yet. The dolphin must have known that; it supported me all the way back to shore.

Finally the water was so shallow that I could touch bottom. As we moved closer, I was worried that the dolphin might be pulled in by the waves and get hurt on the hard limestone beach. I loosened my grip and wished I could speak to it. I gestured with my hand and even pushed its nose, trying to say, "Turn around before you get stuck in these shallows."

It stayed there watching a little way out from shore as I stood in the water. I guess it wanted to make sure that I was really okay.

I walked backward to the shore in the clumsy flippers and then took off all my equipment as fast as I could. I jumped and danced on the beach. I was so glad to be alive.

But I kept thinking about the dolphin who had saved me. I looked over in its direction. It was still watching me. I had to go back into the water. I dove in and swam right to it.

Immediately the dolphin began rubbing against me. I stroked it and noticed that it felt soft and smooth, like the thick white skin of a peeled hard-boiled egg. I looked closer at its silver-gray back and noticed scars. And its dorsal fin had a half-moon shape cut out of it like a bite had been taken. "You must have tangled with a shark," I said.

It rolled onto its belly, and I saw a vaginal line. She was a sister dolphin. I decided to call her Half Moon.

I rubbed the scars on her back, and she seemed to like that. Then she popped up higher in the water. She rolled sideways and deliberately placed her fin in my right hand.

I don't know how, but I guessed what she was trying to say to me. With my thumb down I closed the fingers of my right hand around the front of her fin and placed my left hand against her side to steady myself. I held on tightly.

Sure enough she began to tow me through the water, fast. I felt the water rush past me and swirl over my body. We streaked far away from shore. I loved the speed. We came near a group of dolphins who were leaping in the air, and she stopped.

One of the dolphins came whizzing over to us. It swam around in a circle and then rushed right toward me. Just inches in front of my nose, it stopped short. I stayed still, staring at it, trying not to flinch. I didn't want to show I'd been afraid, for then maybe the dolphins might stop playing with me.

The second dolphin paused for a moment. It had a narrow bony jaw. Its head looked so ancient. It circled away and rushed at me again. This time it opened its mouth wide, right in front of my nose; I was looking directly at its rows of tiny needle-like teeth.

I put my hand up automatically. It dipped its head and took my hand in its mouth like a dolphin handshake. My fingers were resting on top of its sharp teeth. But I could tell how careful it was being with me, because it stayed very still. I began to laugh. "I'll call you The Teaser," I said.

The two dolphins swam in wide loops going away from me, and then doubled back. They got up speed and whizzed past me on either side. They slid so close against me that I felt like the middle of their sandwich.

Suddenly the two of them dove down deep and disappeared. I wanted to follow, but without my equipment on I was stuck at the surface. I held my breath and tried to kick my feet and go below, but I came up sputtering.

Half Moon reappeared and tapped me under my chin with her beak. I felt as if she were saying, "You're fine right where you are. I'll stay with you on the surface."

She looked me in the eye and rolled over. Her underside was soft pink and shimmering. She slipped under me, upside down, and guided me to rest on her. She took me for a ride on her belly, and then rolled me off again.

I looked out at the horizon and noticed that the sun was low in the sky. I thought my friends might be worried about me.

The Teaser swam back to join the others. I saw where my boat was anchored, but I didn't want to go get it yet. I wasn't ready to say goodbye to Half Moon.

I stayed in the water with her, rubbing her velvet back. I massaged her scars, and she nuzzled me.

Half Moon began tapping my shoulder hard with her flipper. Tap, tap, tap. She was leaning against me, insistent. What was she trying to say? Her flipper felt rubbery against my skin. I didn't like the way those taps felt, and I moved away.

She dove underwater and disappeared. I waited for her to come up again, but she didn't. I was afraid I wouldn't see her again, that the day would end like that. I waited on the surface, treading water, but she didn't come back.

I decided to keep waiting. Still she didn't appear. The sun was getting lower in the sky, when suddenly she shot up right in front of me and remained straight up in the water.

I could see the lovely folds of skin around her neck. She looked all silvery and pink. She placed one flipper on my left shoulder, and her other flipper on my right shoulder.

I put my arms around her. I held her and she held me, for an instant, as long as a full breath. Then she folded back into the water.

She came back one more time and tapped with her beak at my heart. And then she was gone, out into the water to join her friends.

# Follow-up Activities for "Talking without Words"

## Recommendations for Telling the Story

Try gesturing to describe the events in the story. For example, pantomime putting on the scuba equipment in the beginning. When the teasing dolphin opens its mouth, show this with your hands in front of your nose. When Half Moon taps with her flipper, show this on your shoulder.

## How to Answer Questions about the Story

### "Is it true?"

Unlike some stories, this is a story where discussing which events could really happen is an important part of the understanding. Everything told here could and did happen.

This story is a composite of true events. Elizabeth Gawain was rescued by a dolphin while she was scuba diving (as described in her book, *The Dolphin's Gift*); many people have had tow rides with dolphins while gripping their dorsal fins; and all the interactions in the second half of the story—including the belly ride, the "handshake," and the hug—happened to me as I played with two dolphins in Key Largo, Florida.

### "Where can people meet dolphins?"

Frequently dolphin "shows" at aquariums and places like Sea World in Florida are a young person's only reference point for experiences with dolphins. There are many *different* environments where people can encounter dolphins.

On one end of the spectrum are the marine shows. Trained dolphins are rewarded for producing the behaviors their trainers have selected.

Other dolphins in captivity are in organized swim programs, such as at "Dolphins Plus" in Key Largo where I had the experiences described in the second half of the story. In these situations dolphins are given free choice in their interactions with humans: they are fed before they play with humans rather than using food as a reward, they can choose not to interact, they can enter areas where only dolphins can be, and their daily contact with visiting humans is limited to one or two hours. Dolphins Plus also sponsors zoo-therapy programs where children with cerebral palsy and autistic children can meet dolphins in the water.

Some wild dolphins have encounters with humans in their ocean home. A herd of dolphins have come close to shore at Monkey Mia Beach in Shark Bay on the western coast of Australia ever since fishermen started to feed them in 1964. Also newspaper stories about Monkey Mia relate how dolphins have rescued surfers from sharks in that region.

Historically, a dolphin that followed steamships in New Zealand for twenty-two years, who was called Pelorus Jack, seemed to be guiding the boats through the jagged rocks. His story is chronicled in *Nine True Dolphin Stories*.

Several cultures are said to have had a unique relationship with dolphins who chased fish into their nets, helping people bring in food for their villages. These cultures include Australian aboriginal peoples and the Imragen tribe of Mauritania in Northeast Africa. The book, *Sandro's Dolphin* describes one such fishing village set in the Mediterranean Sea region.

In modern times, some boats like the Dolphin Watch sailboat in Key West bring people out with snorkeling equipment in the hopes that they'll have a chance to swim with wild dolphins.

## Discussion Questions for Teachers

### "Keeping dolphins in captivity has become a controversial practice. Why? What do you think about this issue?"

When dolphins are kept in tanks the water is chemically treated and the small space may create a condition of sensory deprivation. Also, trainers for dolphin shows sometimes withhold food beforehand so that hunger will produce greater activity. Such practices are currently under criticism, and in some cases lawsuits have been brought on behalf of the dolphins.

In contrast, organized swim programs try to create a natural environment for captive dolphins. Dolphins Plus was commended by the International Dolphin and Whale Conference for trying to "create the ideal environment, setting an example globally for marine parks to follow." Dolphins live in an extension of a canal that runs between the ocean and the bay at Key Largo, and the dolphins regularly have a chance to swim in the canal and then elect to return.

Give students a chance to explore their own feelings about dolphin captivity.

### "In what ways did the narrator and the dolphin speak to each other without words?"

From the first moment the narrator sees the dolphin's eye, she feels safety. Talk about the wordless understanding—for instance, when she knows that the dolphin will stay with her all the way back to shore.

Later she realizes that the teasing dolphin, the second one, is being playful rather than threatening when it rushes close to her nose and halts. She senses the intent of the dolphin despite her initial instinct to be afraid of a sudden charge. In her name for it, "The Teaser," she interprets its behavior as friendly. In fact, when the dolphin places her hand in its mouth, it is trying to taste her skin and become better acquainted with her.

Talk also about the ways in which the dolphin and the woman make sense of each other's gestures. The dolphin waits in the shallow water without going closer to land. The woman understands that when Half Moon puts her fin in her hand, she is signalling to hold on. Later she interprets the tap at her chin as a message that she doesn't have to try to go below the surface.

Bring out these points in the discussion of communication. Note that the dolphins' movements appear not to be accidental but highly purposeful.

The story describes much contact the woman has with her hands. However, if you ever have a meeting with a dolphin, keep your hands at your sides and wait to see if the dolphin invites you to have further contact.

### Dolphins and world change: "Do you think that people who have been close to dolphins might look at the world differently?"

These words come out of my experience with dolphins: "To be in the presence of a dolphin is to change. They are teachers of peace." Ask students why I might say this. Ask how they react to this statement.

Dolphins have the ability to thoroughly scan individuals. Scientists report that dolphins can tell when a woman is pregnant, what a swimmer has had for lunch, and how much air a person has in their lungs. One dolphin even detected a tumor in a swimmer at Dolphins Plus. This close regard from the dolphins communicates a feeling of recognition and acceptance.

As the discussion progresses, ask also, "Why do you think the dolphin tapped her on the heart right at the end? Was this accidental or intentional? What might the dolphin be saying?"

After they have had a chance to discuss this, it might be interesting for them to know what I felt was being communicated when a dolphin tapped me on the heart at the end of my third and final swim with her.

I felt the dolphin's message was two-fold. First she said that even though our swim together was over, we could remain connected. She seemed to say: "If you stay close to awareness from your heart, if you stay inside your heart more than in your head, you will remember."

Secondly, I felt she was indicating that by living more from my heart I would find I was being more fully myself, more fully human. Several times during the swim, I thought that she urged me not only to find the dolphin species wondrous but also to appreciate the human species more.

How do I know what it was saying to me? I can't know for sure. But that was what I sensed.

### The impulse to help: "Why did the dolphin rescue the person in the story? Do humans also have a natural impulse to help?"

## Telling Stories Related to the Themes of the Book

Here are topics that can be used for students to tell their own stories. I have found that it's helpful to begin first by having young people tell their story in small groups of two or three, and then give them the option of repeating the story to the whole class. Here are some questions you can start with:

### Humans Close to Other Species

• Have you ever stood very close to an animal? What did it look like? What did you think about? Which of you moved first?

• Think of your favorite animal. What would you say to it if you could speak to each other in some way and each of you could understand what the other is saying?

### Stories About the Impulse to Help

• Think of a time someone in your family or school needed help. Who helped them? What did they do?

• Think of a time someone in your neighborhood, town or city needed help? Who responded? What happened?

• Think of a time you wanted to help somebody or felt concerned. Why did you think they needed help? What did you do?

### Telling Stories without Sound

Experiment in your small groups with telling a story using your whole body to express what happened—using hand gestures, pantomime, whole body language—but not using any words. Then show your story to the whole class and see if the others can understand what you are conveying.

Provide a beginning for the story, the same beginning for each group, and then let them finish the story in their own way:

• Sample Beginning #1: We were lost in the woods. We were very cold and hungry. We looked everywhere for food, but we found none. Finally a giant bird flew down and signalled for us to follow it.

• Sample Beginning #2: We were swimming near an island when a humpback whale came right up to us. It said . . .

## An Interspecies Council

This is an opportunity to imagine that species from the ocean are speaking to humans. In this council, the humans are the listeners. They sit in the center while the ocean animals, plants, and other life forms make a circle around them.

Step One: Each student selects an ocean life form they feel close to. They spend fifteen minutes intensifying this connection. This can be done by listening to appropriate ocean-related music while writing about the life form, by drawing a picture, by creating a paper bag mask using markers and colored paper, or by decorating a stone to symbolize it.

Step Two: The whole group meets in council. The teacher acts as ritual leader. Many embellishments for the ritual are described in *Thinking Like a Mountain*, by John Seed, Joanna Macy, Pat Fleming, and Arne Naess, from New Society Publishers, Philadelphia, 1988.

Step Three: Each person has a chance to speak: "I am seaweed and I feel clogged when litter people throw into the ocean gets tangled in me," or "I am sea otter and I love to play in the waves," or "I am right whale and I am few in numbers because humans considered me the right whale to hunt."

Step Four: When everyone has spoken, members of the group take turns coming into the center of the circle and listening as humans. The humans are encouraged to listen nondefensively, eager to hear the information. They respond, "We hear you, seaweed," "We hear you, sea otter," "Thank you for your words."

Step Five: The ocean life forms describe gifts they would like to give the humans to help them with protection and care of the ocean.

## Resources for Further Information

### Dolphin Information

*Dolphin Connection.* Joan Ocean. P.O. Box 275, Kailua, HI 96734.

*Dolphin Dreamtime: The Art and Science of Interspecies Communication.* Jim Nollman. New York: Bantam Books, 1987.

*The Dolphins and Me.* Don Reed. San Francisco: Sierra Club Books / Little Brown and Co., 1989.

*The Dolphin's Gift.* Elizabeth Gawain. Mill Valley, CA: Whatever Publishing, Inc., 1981.

*Falling for a Dolphin.* Heathcote Williams. New York: Harmony Books, Crown Publishers, 1988.

*The Friendly Dolphins.* Patricia Lauber. New York: Random House, 1963.

*Nine True Dolphin Stories.* Margaret Davidson. New York: Scholastic Book Services, 1974.

*A Ring of Endless Light.* Madeleine L'Engle. New York: Dell, 1980.

*Sandro's Dolphin.* Karen Winnick. New York: Lothrop, Lee, 1980.

### Thinking about the Impulse to Help

The story of Elizabeth Gawain's rescue by a dolphin begins the book, *How Can I Help?* by Ram Dass and Paul Gorman, Alfred A. Knopf, NY, 1985. This is a book of stories and reflections on service. They speak about the natural compassion the dolphin exhibited and the innate capacity for generosity we humans have as well.

### Dolphin Swim Programs

*Dolphins Plus*, Box 2114, Key Largo, FL 33037, (305) 451-1993. A ninety-minute format includes half-hour unstructured swims after a one-hour training for ages ten through adult.

A three-day workshop format including three swims at Dolphins Plus is led by trainer Carolyn Brooks, 680 Rio Del Mar Blvd., Aptos, CA 95003. (My encounters with dolphins occurred when I attended her workshop).

In addition a six-day Dolphin School program is offered several times a year which includes course work in anatomy, communication, and social structure, and unstructured swims with dolphins as well as field trips to coral reefs and to the everglades.

*Dolphin Research Center*, P.O. Box 2875, Marathon Shores, FL 33052. A one-week course is offered. (305) 289-1121.

## Dolphin Protection

The protection of dolphins is another important aspect related to the story. It is speculated that ocean pollution may be poisoning dolphins or altering their ability to navigate which might explain why some groups of dolphins are found stranded on beaches. Over six million dolphins have been killed since the 1960's by the purse-seine fishing technique. Schools of yellowfin tuna swim just below herds of dolphins; both are trapped and suffocated in purse seine nets. The problem continues although some U.S. tuna companies are no longer buying tuna caught in such nets. As the Environmental Research and Education Foundation explains, "If only one foreign country will buy tuna caught by setting on dolphins, it will be more than enough to encourage the practice." Work continues to bring international pressure to stop the slaughter of dolphins.

One action students can take is to decide not to eat tuna unless they are sure it was not caught with dolphins and to express their opinion to families, stores, and school lunch programs.

Here are sources where classes can obtain current information on dolphin protection and learn more activities they can engage in:

- Greenpeace, P.O. Box 3720, Washington, DC 20027.

- Earth Island Institute, Save the Dolphins, 466 Green St., San Francisco, CA 94113. Earth Island Institute set the guidelines for tuna canneries and now monitors tuna brands to verify they are "dolphin safe."

- The Environmental Research and Education Foundation which publishes the "Dolphin Dialogue" newsletter is developing an acoustic signalling system to encourage dolphins to exit nets once they have been encircled. This could save the lives of thousands of dolphins. E.R.E.F., P.O. Box 2728, Key Largo, FL 33037.

❧ ❧ ❧

**Sarah Pirtle** is an educator on peace and ecology through the expressive arts of music, storytelling, and literature. She is the author of *An Outbreak of Peace* (New Society Publishers) which received the Olive Branch Award for the outstanding book on world peace in 1988. Her recordings for children include "Two Hands Hold the Earth," winner of the 1985 ALA Notable Award, and "The Wind is Telling Secrets."

# Bibliography of Tellable Stories

This is a selection of other tellable stories which deal with the issues explored in this book. They are organized alphabetically by the name of the story, and are divided into two sections: Peace and Justice Stories, and Environmental Stories. There are also listings of Storytelling Books and Indexes, Activity Resource Books, and Organizations.

## Peace and Justice Stories

*The Angel with a Mouth Organ*. Christobel Mattingley. New York: Holiday House, 1984. Just before the glass angel is put on the Christmas tree, the mother describes her experiences as a little girl during World War II, when she and her family were refugees, and how the glass angel symbolized a new beginning.

"The Battle." In *Elderberry Flute Song*. Peter Blue Cloud. Trumansburg, New York: Crossing Press, 1982. Coyote stops the battle by giving his life, over and over and over.

*The Blind Men and the Elephant*. Lillian Quigley. New York: Charles Scribner's Sons, 1959. A delightful Indian tale about six blind men all touching a different part of an elephant and arguing about what elephants look like. The argument continues until they come to understand that you must put all the parts together to know the whole.

*The Boy Who Could Sing Pictures*. Seymour Leichman. Garden City, New York: Doubleday and Co., 1968. A young boy learns to sing images of peace, beauty and happiness for the delight of the poor. He dares to sing images of the injustice, hunger, and sorrow that he sees in the kingdom to the king himself.

*Brothers*. Florence B. Freedman. New York: Harper and Row, 1985. In a drought year, two brothers separately decide that the other should have more of the year's share of the harvest. For several nights, each takes wheat from his grain store and puts it in his brother's. Confused to find the same amount of grain each day, the brothers run into each other late one night—and, with joy, realize what has happened.

*Cellist*. Gregor Piatigorsky. Garden City, New York: Doubleday and Co., 1965. From the introduction. A true story about Piatigorsky's encounter with the master Pablo Casals and how Casals teaches him to "leave it to the ignorant to judge only by counting faults. Be grateful for one beautiful note, one wonderful phrase."

*Clancy's Coat*. Eve Bunting. London: F. Warne, 1984. An Irish tale about how Clancy the tailor uses the delayed repair of an old coat to mend a broken friendship with its owner.

*Evan's Corner*. Elizabeth S. Hill. New York: Holt, Rinehart and Winston, 1967. Evan's mother helps him establish a place of his own in their crowded apartment, and also to understand his little brother's need.

*Everybody Knows What a Dragon Looks Like*. Jay Williams. New York: Aladdin Books, 1989. When the city is threatened by war, everyone argues about what a dragon looks like and then runs away—but the small boy believes the old man who says he is the dragon, and for his sake the old man saves the city.

*Ferdinand.* Munro Leaf. New York: Viking, 1964. The story of a Spanish bull who would rather sniff the flowers than rough it up with the other bulls. When Ferdinand is accidentally picked for a bullfight, he just sits in the arena sniffing the flowers. This greatly frustrates all the bullfighters and Ferdinand is sent home to his peaceful orchard.

*First Snow.* Helen Coutant. New York: Alfred A. Knopf, 1974. The story of a small Vietnamese girl's relationship with her grandmother and the experience of her coming to understand her grandmother's death. A story full of gentleness and warmth.

*The Fools of Chelm.* Isaac Bashevis Singer. New York: Farrar, Straus and Giroux, 1973. The "wise" leaders decide that only war can save the economy of the city. What follows are the follies that occur in the city of Chelm.

*The Friendly Story Caravan.* Anna Pettit Broomell. Wallingford, PA: Pendle Hill, 1962. A whole book of stories, almost all on relevant themes, for school age children.

"The Gift of the Magi." O. Henry. New York: Macmillan, 1978. The moving story of a poor couple who sell their most cherished things (he, his watch and she, her hair) to buy the other a Christmas gift (she, a gold watch chain and he, a set of pearl brushes for her hair).

*Gluskap the Liar and other Indian Tales.* Horace Beck. Freeport, ME: Wheelwright Co., 1966. Gluskap creates the creatures of the world. He teaches Loon a special call, and Loon becomes his messenger. Gluskap leaves the world after becoming disenchanted with all the fighting. Loon still calls for his return. In the cry of the loon, we are reminded of our own calls for a more harmonious existence.

"Hafiz, The Stonecutter." In *The Art of the Storyteller.* Marie L. Shedlock. New York: Dover, 1951. The moving circular tale of a "lowly" stonecutter who comes to discover the wonder of who he is.

*Hiroshima No Pika.* Toshi Maruki. New York: Lothrop, Lee and Shepard, 1980. A little girl and her parents are eating breakfast when the atom bomb is dropped. A very real and vivid story of the struggle and desperation of this family because of the flash. This story, though very tellable, needs follow-up discussion, so that listeners can be left with some hope that this tragedy will never be repeated.

*Horton Hears a Who!* Dr. Seuss. New York: Random House, 1954. Horton, the elephant, becomes the defender for a group of people so small that they fit on a speck of dust. He is persecuted for his efforts, because others don't believe these small people exist. Only when all the small people together make as much noise as possible are the doubters convinced.

"How the Beldys Stopped Fighting." In *Folktales of the Amur: Stories from the Russian Far East.* Dmitri Nagashkin. New York: Harry Abrams, 1980. Two wise and respected twins stop war by pretending to favor it—but change the rules to make war impossible.

"How the Sun Came." In *American Indian Mythology.* Alice Marriott and Carol K. Rachlin. New York: Mentor Books, New American Library, 1968. A Cherokee Indian story about how Grandmother Spider brought back the light. Sometimes it is the smallest rather then the fastest, strongest or bravest who succeed.

"I'm Tipingee, She's Tipingee, We're Tipingee, Too." In *The Magic Orange Tree and Other Haitian Folktales*. Diane Wolkstien. New York: Knopf, 1978. A little girl organizes her friends to wear red dresses so that the old man who has come to take her away won't be able to pick her out. On a level understandable to young children, this introduces the story of the nonviolent resistance of the Danes to the Nazis, when the German invaders ordered all Jews to wear yellow stars, and the gentiles wore them also.

*It Could Always Be Worse*. Margot Zemach. New York: Farrar, Straus, Giroux, 1976. This humorous Yiddish tale is about finding joy and contentment in one's home, however imperfect it might be.

*It's Mine—A Greedy Book*. Crosby Bonsall. New York: Harper and Row, 1964. This simple story tells of a young boy and girl who refuse to share their special toys, and how in the end they discover sharing can be fun.

*The King, the Mice and the Cheese*. Nancy Gurney. New York: Beginner Books, 1965. A humorous tale for young children, about how a king comes to understand that sharing his cheese with the mice isn't so bad after all.

"The Feast." In *The Kings Drum and Other African Stories*. Harold Courlander. New York: Harcourt, Brace, 1950. When each guest at the chief's feast pours a calabash of water into the chief's wine pot instead of the palm wine requested, they learn an important lesson.

*The Last Butterfly*. Michael Jacot. Indianapolis: Bobbs-Merrill, 1974. A moving collection of poems written by children in one of the Nazi concentration camps. The last verse of one, called "Birdsong" reads: "Try to open up your heart to beauty; go to the woods someday and weave a wreath of memory there. Then if the tears obscure your way, you'll know how wonderful it is to be alive."

*The Legend of the Bluebonnet*. Tomi De Paolo. New York: Putnam, 1983. A girl gives up her most valuable possession, her doll, to the rain gods because there is a drought and the only way to get the rain to return is for the people to be less selfish.

*Molly's Pilgrim*. Barbara Cohen. New York: Lothrop, Lee & Shepard Books, 1983. When Molly is given the assignment to make a pilgrim doll for the Thanksgiving display, her mother makes a doll of herself when she came to this country. The other children laugh at Molly and her doll but they end up learning an important lesson about the wonder of each person.

*The Monkey and the Wild, Wild Wind*. Ryerson Johnson. New York: Aberlard-Schuman, 1963. A little monkey helps a group of animals find a better way of life in spite of their great physical differences.

*Move Over Twerp*. Martha Alexander. New York: Dial, 1989. In this short story, a boy creatively handles bullies on the bus, showing the use of humor in defusing conflict.

*Music, Music for Everyone*. Vera B. Williams. New York: Greenwillow, 1985. Rosa and her friends form the Oak Street Band to help raise money for the expenses of Rosa's sick grandmother, with several joyful results.

*My Shalom, My Peace: Paintings and Poems by Jewish and Arab Children*. Jacob Zim. New York: McGraw Hill, 1975. A moving collection of paintings and poems on the themes of peace.

"Old Joe and the Carpenter." Pleasant DeSpain. *Mother Earth News*, January-February 1984. Old Joe hires a carpenter to build a fence right on top of the creek that separates his and his ex-friend's land. Instead, the carpenter builds a bridge. Before Joe has the chance to be mad about it, his friend comes walking across the bridge with his hands outstretched in thanks for Joe's seeing through their argument.

*On the Other Side of the River.* Joanne Oppenheim. New York: Franklin Watts, 1972. The people who live on separate banks of a river have argued for years, but when the bridge that spans the river collapses, they realize how much they need each other.

*Once the Hoja and Once the Mulla.* Alice Geer Kelsey. New York: Longmans Green, 1943 and 1954. These stories about the character of Nasredine are packed full of wisdom about life. Nasredine was a real-life religious teacher who taught by making a fool of himself and others so that all might see the truth. Another book of these tales is The Incomparable Exploits of Nasredine Hoja, by Idries Shah.

*Once a Mouse.* Marcia Brown. New York: Charles Scribner's Sons, 1961. A story from India about how growing big and powerful often brings us to forget our humble past.

*Peace Be With You.* Cornelius Lehn. Newton, KS: Faith and Life, 1980. Stories of nonviolent peace heroes from the first century to the present, from a Christian perspective. There are stories appropriate for most age groups.

"The People Could Fly." In *The People Could Fly: American Black Folktales.* Virginia Hamilton. New York: Knopf, 1985. In this legend, passed down by southern blacks, the slaves of one African tribe flew away when things got too bad.

*Poor Elephants.* Yukio Tauchiya. Tokyo: Kinno Hoshi Sha, Japan, n.d. A sad, true story of how the zoo keepers of the Tokyo zoo were forced to starve the zoo's three greatly loved elephants to death, so that in case of a bombing, the elephants would not escape and harm anyone. With the last elephant dead in their arms, the grieving zoo people yell to the roaring planes, "Stop the war . . . Stop the war!"

*Potatoes, Potatoes.* Anita Lobel. New York: Harper and Row, 1967. Two sons go off and become generals of opposing armies. When the armies run low on food, they both converge on their mother's home to find potatoes. A great battle takes place, until the brothers find their mother seemingly dead. The battle is stopped, and only then does the mother arise with potatoes for all.

"The Power of Light." In *Stories for Children.* Isaac Bashevis Singer. New York: Farrar, Straus, Giroux, 1984. The story of how two children escaped from the Warsaw ghetto and the Nazis with the strength they found in a Hanukkah candle. (Many of the stories in this book and Isaac Bashevis Singer's other books relate to peace and justice issues.)

*The Princess and the Admiral.* Charlotte Pomerantz. Reading, MA: Addison-Wesley, 1974. Based on an old Vietnamese legend, this is the tale of a tiny kingdom about to celebrate one hundred years of peace when a warship appears, and how the princess outwits the admiral and averts war.

"The Princess Who Wanted to See God." In *Who Knows Ten?* Molly Cone. New York: Union of American Hebrew Congregations, 1965. A young princess for the first time learns compassion when, in her search to see God, she meets a crippled girl.

*Sadako and the Thousand Paper Cranes*. Eleanor Coerr. New York: G.P. Putnam's Sons, 1977. The moving true story of a young Japanese girl's struggle against the "atom bomb sickness" (leukemia), ten years after the bomb was dropped on her town of Hiroshima. One of the most sensitive books dealing with the tragedy of nuclear war and hopes for a world of peace. This is a long story, but can and has been adapted for telling.

"Silent Bianca." In *The Girl Who Cried Flowers*. Jane Yolen. New York: Schocken Books, 1981. Bianca averts a battle through imitating the cries of wives and mothers. A beautiful and wise story.

*The Singing Tree*. Kate Seredy. New York: Viking, 1940. The story of a farm family in Hungary during World War I. This book contains the story of "The Singing Tree," an incident that occurred on the battlefield.

*Sneetches*. Dr Seuss. New York: Random House, 1961. Several wonderful stories: themes of conflict resolution, the absurdity of discrimination, being afraid of the dark, prejudging people and situations, and more.

"The Strong One." In *A Treasury of African Folklore*. Harold Courlander. New York: Crown, 1975. The strongest man in the world is downed by a feather from a great bird, and saved by a woman. Power is not necessarily what you think it is.

*The Third Gift*. Jan Carew, Boston: Little, Brown, 1974. A story based on African folklore about a tribe of people who, after receiving two gifts of work and beauty, were given the most important gift of all.

*The Tiger's Whisker*. Harold Courlander. New York: Harcourt Brace, 1959. A Korean tale about a woman whose husband returned from a war, harsh and angry—and how a wise sage taught her to reach him once again.

"To a Siberian Woodsman." In *Openings*. Wendell Berry. New York: Harcourt, Brace, Jovanovich, Inc. 1968. In this touching poem Berry writes as if he were writing to a Siberian woodsman trying to understand all that they have in common: "Who has imagined that I would not speak familiarly with you . . ."

*Twenty-two Splendid Tales to Tell, Volumes 1 and 2*. Pleasant de Spain. Seattle: Merrill Court, 1990. These two books are full of tellable tales. Many of them could be considered tales of peace and justice.

"The Theft of Smell." A poor man is brought to court for stealing the smells from a stingy baker's bakery. The judge rules that payment shall be the sound of the poor man's coins clinking together.

"The Wisdom of Solomon." A tiny bee helps King Solomon distinguish the real pot of flowers from a perfect replica.

*Where the Sidewalk Ends*. Shel Silverstein. New York: Harper and Row, 1974. This book of well-loved poems contains several appropriate to peace, justice, and environmental themes.

"The Generals." A poem about two generals who decide they'd rather play at the beach then fight, but end up fighting anyway.

"I Won't Hatch." A poem about a chick who refuses to hatch, because it hears about all of the world's problems.

*Zen Flesh, Zen Bones*. Paul Rep. Garden City, New York: Doubleday Anchor, n.d., and *Zen Buddhism*. Mount Vernon, New York: Peter Pauper, 1959. Two short teaching tales appear in both of these books.

"A Parable." The story of a traveler who finds himself hanging from a vine over the edge of a cliff. Two hungry tigers wait above. Two mice begin to chew the vine above his head. In the midst of this dilemma, he sees a strawberry growing out of the cliffside. He tastes the strawberry: "Ah, how delicious!"

"Muddy Road." The story of a young monk who, having sworn to have no contact with women, chastises an old monk who carries a woman in a silk kimono across a muddy road. The old monk responds, "I left her way back down the road. Are you still carrying her?"

## Environmental Stories

*Annie and the Old One*. Miska Miles. Boston: Little Brown, 1971. In this touching story about a young girl's attempts to stop her grandmother's death, Annie learns the wonder of nature's life and death cycles.

"Coyote at the Movies." Tim McNulty. In *Coyote's Journal*. Edited by James Koller, 'Gogosge,' Carroll Arnett, Steve Nemirow and Peter Blue Cloud. Wingbow, 1982. When Coyote gets hold of a Georgia Pacific forestry promo film, he knows immediately what to do with it. He invites all his animal friends and shows the film backwards to the absolute delight of his displaced animal friends (especially when the "shaman" waves his magic wand and makes the trees jump back on their stumps).

*The Education of Little Tree*. Forest Carter. Albuquerque: University of New Mexico Press, 1976. A touching story about a Cherokee boy growing up with his grandparents in the hills of Tennessee in the 1930's. The story touches on Native American lifestyles and philosophy, and has an environmentally sensitive way of looking at the earth. It can be read as a complete story or small stories can be extracted from it for telling.

"Elsie Piddock Skips in Her Sleep." In *Martin Pippin in the Daisy-field*. Eleanor Farjeon. New York: Lippincott, 1937. Elsie learns to skip rope from the fairies and with her special skill she saves her town's precious land from development.

*A Good Morning's Work*. Nathan Zimelman. Austin, TX: Steck-Vaughn, 1968. In a day's work clearing and hoeing a field, a boy leaves many spots of grass to protect their little inhabitants, such as a spider's web, a frog puddle, and flowers for the bees. A warm story about appreciating nature.

*The Great Kapok Tree*. Lynne Cherry. New York: Harcourt Brace Jovanovich, 1990. Thanks to the community of animals that live in the kapok tree, a man makes an important decision about how he sees the rainforest.

*How the People Sang the Mountains Up: How and Why Stories*. Maria Leach. New York: Viking Press, 1967. An excellent collection of stories from all over the world about how and why things came to be the way the are.

"An Interview With a Lemming." James Thurber. In *Zoo, 2000*. Jane Yolen. New York: Seabury, 1972. A scientist who has been studying lemmings meets a lemming who has been studying humans. When the scientist asks why lemmings drown themselves in the sea, the lemming replies, "That's curious—the one thing I don't understand is why you human beings don't."

*The Invisible Hunter or Los Cazadore Invisible*. Harriet Rohmer. San Francisco: Children's Book Press, 1987. A rainforest legend from the Miskito Indians of Nicaragua tells of what happens to a group of hunters who abuse their powers and overhunt a certain region using modern weaponry.

"Island of the Endangered." Dale Ferguson. In *Zoo, 2000*. Jane Yolen. New York: Seabury, 1972. A bittersweet tale of the future about how the only remaining male bison is united with a female of his species on the Island of the Endangered, where humans put the last of each species.

"Justice." In *The Devil's Other Story Book*. Natalie Babbit. New York: Farrar, Straus, Giroux, 1987. A hunter who poached all kinds of species during his lifetime is sentenced at the gate of hell to catch a rhinoceros with a net. But instead of catching the rhino he ends up being chased by it through eternity.

*Keepers of the Earth: Native American Stories and Environmental Activities for Children*. Michael J. Caduto and Joseph Bruchac. Golden, CO: Fulcrum, 1988. An excellent book of stories and activities that teach about the environment.

*Last Panther in Eastern Kentucky*. Sy Kahn. On "Ancient Creek," a June Appal recording. A great hunter wants to kill the last panther in Eastern Kentucky. He asks an old woman to lead him to it, but he gets a surprise.

*The Loudest Noise in the World*. Benjamin Elkin. New York: The Viking Press, 1954. A city is transformed in a most delightful way from being the loudest city in the world (and loving it), to being the softest city in the world (so they can hear the birds singing and the wind blowing through the branches of the trees). The story is also about the importance of each individual.

*The Lorax*. Dr. Seuss. New York: Random House, 1971. A marvelous story that shows how important each individual is in solving environmental problems. "Unless someone like you cares a whole awful lot, nothing's going to get better, it's not. So catch! Don't let them fall, they're trufula seeds, the last ones of all . . . ."

*The Magic Listening Cap*. Yoshiko Uchida. New York: Harcourt Brace Jovanovich, 1955. A healing story in which a magic cap gives an old man the ability to understand what the animals and plants are saying.

"The Man Who Planted Hope and Grew Happiness." Jean Giono. In *Sharing the Joy of Nature*. Joseph Cornell. Nevada City, CA: Dawn, 1989. A powerful true story of a man who spent the last forty years of his life planting trees and single-handedly reforesting a section of southern France. He worked through two world wars, restoring the region to life and living.

*The Other Way to Listen*. Byrd Baylor and Peter Parnall. New York: Charles Scribner's Sons, 1978. A simple tale, told from the perspective of a child, about being at one with creation. You can hear rocks murmur and hills sing, if you learn to listen and become at peace with the world around you.

*The Snow Goose*. Paul Gallico. New York: Knopf, 1972. This is a beautiful love story between a grotesquely formed reclusive man and a young woman. Their love grows around their caring for a stray, crippled snow goose. This tale is long, but can be edited to make it tellable.

*Where the Forest Meets the Sea*. Jeannie Baker. New York: Greenwillow Books, 1987. A boy visits the rainforest of Australia with his father and wonders if the rainforest will still be there if they travel there again.

*Who Speaks for Wolf?* Paula Underwood Spencer. Austin: Tribe of Two Press (P.O. Box 1763, Austin, TX, 78767), 1983. A tribe moves to a new area before consulting with their member Wolf's Brother who knows the ways of the wolf. Their homesite disrupts the living patterns of wolves and impacts their own lives as well.

"Why Men Have To Work." In *Black Folktales*. Julius Lester. New York: Grove-Weidenfeld, 1970. A story that brings to mind our waste problems. The sky used to be close to the earth and feed the people all their food, until it got tired of people using more sky than they needed. So the sky moved far away and the people had to pick up a rake and hoe and start working.

## Storytelling Books and Indexes

*Bookfinder*. Sharon Spredemann-Dreyer. Circle Pines, MA: American Guidance Service, 1985. A well-organized index that helps locate recent children's books on various topics.

*Just Enough to Make a Story: A Sourcebook for Storytelling*. Nancy Schimmel. Berkeley, CA: Sisters' Choice Press, Revised second edition, 1987. A fine book of stories to tell and how to tell them.

Multicultural Storytelling List. Arts In Progress, 11 Green Street, Jamaica Plain, MA 02130. (617) 524-1160. A sixteen-page bibliography of tellable stories from different countries around the world.

*The Storyteller's Sourcebook*. Margret Read MacDonald. Detroit, MI: Gale, 1982. An index for locating folk and fairy tales by title, subject, author or motif.

*Tell Me Another*. Bob Barton. Portsmouth, NH: Heinemann Educational Books, Inc., 1986. A fine book on how to creatively tell and read stories.

*The Way of the Storyteller*. Ruth Sawyer. Baltimore: Penguin, 1977. One of the classic books on storytelling: from history to how-to.

## Activity Resource Books

There are many wonderful books of activities and games that can be used to create preparation and follow-up activities for a story. Many of the books we are familiar with have been listed in relevant chapters of this book. You'll find the most inclusive lists at the ends of:

- "Stories: The Teaching Tool," page 11;
- "Chew Your Rock Candy," page 25;
- "The Snowflake Story," page 59;

- "A Tree Planting In South Africa," page 181;
- "What Now, Cloacina?," page 217;
- "Talking Without Words," page 255.

Other resources we like are:

*Children's Songs for a Friendly Planet.* Compiled by Evelyn Weiss, Priscilla Prutzman, and Nancy Silber. Nyack, NY: Children's Creative Response to Conflict, 1986. A great little songbook of topical songs. CCRC's address is in the Organizations section below.

*Creative Conflict Resolution: More than 200 Activities for Keeping Peace in the Classroom K-6.* William J. Kreidler. Glenview, IL: Good Year Books, 1984.

*50 Simple Things You Can Do To Save the Earth* and *50 Simple Things Kids Can Do To Save the Earth.* The Earth Works Group. Berkeley, CA: Earthworks Press, 1989. Excellent, accessible books on what each of us can do to support the earth.

*Helping Kids Learn Multi-Cultural Concepts: A Handbook of Strategies.* Michael G. Pasternak. Champaign, IL: Research Press, 1979. (2612 N. Mattis Avenue, Champaign, IL 61820). A book full of activities and exercises for the classroom. Includes a bibliography for multicultural materials for the class.

*Keepers of the Earth: Native American Stories and Environmental Activities for Children.* Michael J. Caduto and Joseph Bruchac. Golden, CO: Fulcrum, 1988. An excellent book of stories and activities that teach about the environment.

*Recyclopedia: Games, Science Equipment, and Crafts from Recycled Materials.* Robin Simons. Boston: Houghton-Mifflin, 1976. How to recycle in your own house or classroom.

*Rise Up Singing.* Edited by Peter Blood-Patterson. Philadelphia: Sing Out, 1988. A wide-ranging source for songs of all kinds. From funny songs to songs of freedom. Songs by lots of folks: from Pete Seeger to the Beatles.

*White Awareness: Handbook for Anti-racism Training.* Judy Katz. Norman, OK: University of Oklahoma Press, 1978. A book of teacher-training activities on understanding racism in many manifestations.

## Organizations

There are many organizations doing top quality work on issues of peace, justice, and the environment. Here is a list of some of those that are specifically focused towards storytelling, the arts in general, education, or parenting.

**Children's Creative Response to Conflict**, Box 271, 523 North Broadway, Nyack, NY 10960. (914) 358-4601. Resources and workshops for students, teachers and others on creatively dealing with conflict.

**Children's Music Network**, P.O. Box 307, Montvale, NJ 07645. Supports and promotes quality educational music for children.

**The Children's Rainforest**, P.O. Box 936, Lewiston, ME 04240. (207) 784-1069. Promotes awareness of and education about rainforests, and channels donated funds to preserve undisturbed tropical rainforest in Costa Rica.

**Educators for Social Responsibility**, 23 Garden Street, Cambridge, MA 02139. (617) 492-1764. Organized nationally and locally to help teachers, school administrators and parents respond positively, through education, to students' concerns about issues of peace, justice, and the environment.

**Hitchcock Center for the Environment**, 525 South Pleasant Street, Amherst, MA 01002. (413) 256-6006. Environmental curriculum development resources for teachers.

**Jane Addams Peace Association Inc.**, Jane Addams Children's Book Award, 777 United Nations Plaza, New York, NY 10017. Sponsors and finances educational programs of the Women's International League for Peace and Freedom. Send self-addressed stamped envelope for a bibliography of Jane Addams Children's Book Award winners.

**The Lion and the Lamb Peace Arts Center**, Bluffton College, Bluffton, OH 45817. (401) 358-8015. Promotes peace through the arts and literature for children.

**National Association for the Preservation and Perpetuation of Storytelling (NAPPS)**, P.O. Box 309, Jonesborough, TN 37659. (615) 753-2171. Contact for regional and local storytelling organizations. Publishes Yarnspinner (a storytelling magazine), a catalogue of storytelling books and resources, and a national directory of storytellers. Sponsors storytelling events and workshops.

**National Association of Mediation in Education**, 425 Amity Street, Amherst, MA 01002. (413) 545-2462. Mediation trainings and information for students, teachers, and others.

**The National Network for Environmental Education**, 10751 Ambassador Drive, Suite 201, Manassas, VA 22110. (703) 335-1025. Information and resources about environmental education nationwide.

**National Parenting for Peace and Justice Network**, Institute for Peace and Justice, 4144 Lindell #400, St. Louis, MO 63108. (314) 533-4445. Newsletter and resources on parenting as it relates to the many issues of peace and justice. Send $2 and a self-addressed stamped envelope for a bibliography of peace stories.

**New Society Publishers**, New Society Educational Foundation, P.O Box 582, Santa Cruz, CA 95061-0582. (800) 333-9093. Publishes books to build a new society, including some excellent books on education.

**People's Music Network for Songs of Freedom and Struggle**, P.O. Box 26004, Alexandria, VA 22313. Supports and promotes topical songs and music of all kinds.

**Stories For World Change Network**, c/o Ed Brody, 661 Green Street, Cambridge, MA 02139. Editors of this book. Exchanges resources and ideas and supports people in finding ways to create a healthier world through the sharing of stories and the art of storytelling.

**Yellow Moon Press**, P.O. Box 1316, Cambridge, MA 02238. (617) 628-7894. A full catalogue of storytelling-related books, tapes, and videos.

# Additions to the Bibliography for the Second Edition

Here are some additional resources that have appeared or been reissued since *Spinning Tales* was first published.

## Anthologies of Peace, Justice, and Environmental Tales

*Doorways to the Soul: 52 Wisdom Tales from Around the World.* Elisa Davy Pearmain. Pilgrim Press, 1998. A delightful collection of wisdom tales, parables, and anecdotes from around the world.

*Earthcare: World Folktales to Talk About.* Margaret Read MacDonald. Linnet Books, 1999. Forty-one tales, fables, poems, stories and numerous proverbs (from 30 countries) that talk about human and ecological themes.

*The Hungry Tigress: Buddhist Legends and Jataka Tales.* Rafe Martin. Yellow Moon Press, 1999. Combining themes of wisdom, nonviolence, environmental awareness, and compassion for all living things, these tales unite an ancient story tradition with contemporary humanity.

*I Dream of Peace: Images of War by Children of Former Yugoslavia.* UNICEF/HarperCollins, 1994. Children's drawings and statements about their experiences.

*Peace Be With You.* Cornelia Lehn. Faith and Life Press, 1980. A chronological arrangement of stories dealing with peace themes. Good to use with children.

*Peace Tales: World Folktales to Talk About.* Margaret Read MacDonald. Linnet Books, 1992. Thirty-four folktales and a wealth of proverbs from all over the world that get people to think and talk about which things lead to war and which lead to peace.

*Who's Afraid...? Facing Children's Fears with Folktales.* Norma J. Livo. Teacher Ideas Press, 1994. Use the magic of stories to transform children's fears into understanding and acceptance.

*Wisdom Tales from Around the World.* Heather Forest. August House Publishers, 1996. Fifty gems of story and wisdom from such diverse traditions as Sufi, Zen, Taoist, Christian, Jewish, Buddhist, African and Native American.

## Stories

*The Bracelet.* Yoshiko Uchida. Philomel, 1993. A book about one Japanese-American girl's friendship with a white girl, and her experience in an internment camp during World War II.

"Old Joe and the Carpenter." In *Peace Tales.* Margaret Read MacDonald. Linnet Books, 1992. Old Joe hires a carpenter to build a fence right on top of the creek that separates his and his ex-friend's land. Instead, the carpenter builds a bridge. Before Joe has the chance to be mad about it, his friend comes walking across the bridge with his hands outstretched in thanks for Joe having seen through their argument.

*Secret of the Peaceful Warrior.* Dan Millman. H.J. Kramer, 1991. A boy learns to confront and overpower a bully and then become his friend.

*Seven Blind Mice.* Ed Young. Scholastic, 1992. A retelling of "The Blind Men and the Elephant" that reinforces cooperative learning.

"The Lion's Whisker." In *Peace Tales*. Margaret Read MacDonald. Linnet Books, 1992. A tale about a woman whose new son-in-law is harsh and angry at her loving gesture, and how a wise sage teaches her to approach him.

## Activity Resource Books

*Education by Design: Level 1 and 2 Coaching Kits*. Wendy Mobila, The Critical Skills Program, Antioch New England Graduate School, 1999. Education by Design offers a cohesive framework for developing rich K-12 learning environments based on the principles of an experiential, problem-based, collaborative, and standards-driven learning framework.

*ESR Conflict Resolution Workshop and Implementation Manual*. Educators for Social Responsibility, 1995.

*Elementary Perspectives 1, Teaching Concepts of Peace and Conflict*. William J. Kriedler. Educators for Social Responsibility, 1990.

*How to Teach Peace to Children*. Lorne J. Peachey. Herald Press, 1981. Practical suggestions to build peacemaking skills within the home and family.

*Human Rights for Children: A Curriculum for Teaching Human Rights to Children, Ages 3-12*. Human Rights for Children Committee. Hunter House, 1992.

*Parenting for Peace and Justice: Ten Years Later*. James and Kathleen McGinnis. Orbis Books, 1990. How can we act for justice without sacrificing our children? How can we build a family community without isolating ourselves from the world? How do we practice living simply in a society that becomes more materialistic every day? How can we promote nonviolence? A book for families to treasure!

*Peacemaking: Family Activities for Justice and Peace*. Jacqueline Haessly. Paulist Press, 1980. A book to help the family learn to live together in peace and justice, at home, with society, and with the world.

*Sing Your Peace Songbook*. Compiled by the Unitarian Universalist Peace Network, 1990. A book of peace songs compiled from numerous sources and original compositions.

## Organizations

**League for the Advancement of New England Storytelling (LANES)**, 411A Highland Avenue #351, Somerville, MA 02144. Phone: (617) 499-9662; Email: lanes@lanes.org; Website: www.lanes.org. Promotes storytelling in the New England area. Publishes *The New England Directory of Storytelling* and a fine members' publication: *The Museletter*. Produces "Sharing the Fire," a top-notch annual conference on the art of storytelling.

**The National Storytelling Association (NSA)**, 116 West Main Street, Jonesborough, TN 37659. Phone: (423) 753-2171 or (800) 525-4514. Contact NSA for regional and local storytelling organizations. Publishes *Storytelling Magazine*, the *National Storytelling Directory*, plus other storytelling books and resources. Sponsors story telling events, workshops, and an annual conference.

**Yellow Moon Press**, P.O. Box 381316, Cambridge, MA 02238. Phone: (617) 776-2230; Website: www.yellowmoon.com. Catalog order and store. The storefront is located at 689 Somerville Avenue, Somerville, MA 02143 and features a comprehensive selection of books, audio tapes, and CDs for storytellers, educators, and story-lovers. Visit their website for more information.

# Age Suitability Index

The following is an index of the stories in this book classified into the age groups to which each story is easily suitable. Of course, stories can be molded and adapted to fit other age groups, and many of the stories in this book have follow-up activities which address the needs of different ages. This index is merely meant as a guide—if there is a story you love, tell it to anyone you choose!

# Thematic Index

This index is a guide to help you locate stories which address a variety of themes. Some of the themes are addressed in indirect ways in other stories in the book.

## Environment

## Fantasy

## Friendship

## Fun

## Healing

## Individuals Make a Difference

## Insight

## Love

## Materialism

## Music

## Myth

## Old Age

## Pollution

## Power

## Racism

## Real Life ("True Stories")

## Recycling

## Responsibility

## Self-Esteem

## Struggle

## Trees

## War and Peace

## Water

## Women

# Directory of Contributors

This is a list of addresses and telephone numbers for the people whose stories are in this book. Please feel free to get in touch with them to share your experiences with these stories, or if you want to hire them to perform or give workshops.

We heartily encourage the telling and dissemination of these stories in the oral tradition. **All the storytellers who have contributed to this book have given permission for any storyteller to tell these stories to a live audience.** (You should contact them for copyright permission if you want to reprint or record the material in this book.)

**David Albert**
1717 18th Court NE
Olympia, WA 98506
Phone: (360) 352-0506
Email: shantinik@earthlink.net
Website: www.skylarksings.com

**Peter Amidon**
20 Willow Street
Brattleboro, VT 05301
Phone: (802) 257-1006
Email: info@amidonmusic.com
Website: www.amidonmusic.com

**Beauty and the Beast Storytellers**
954 Coddington Road
Ithaca, NY 14850
Phone: (607) 277-0016
Email: bnb@clarityconnect.com
Website: www.clarityconnect.com/webpages3/bnb

**Lahri Bond**
Heartswork Graphics
44 McClellan Street
Amherst, MA 01002
Phone: (413) 253-4722
Email: Lahri@javanet.com
Website: www.heartsworkgraphics.com

**Ed Brody**
661 Green Street
Cambridge, MA 02139
Phone: (617) 497-6858
Email: ed_brody@post.harvard.edu

**Joseph Bruchac**
2 Middle Grove Road
P.O. Box 308
Greenfield Center, NY 12833
Phone: (518) 584-1728
Email: nudatlog@earthlink.net
Website: www.josephbruchac.com

**Diane Edgecomb**
P.O. Box 16
Boston, MA 02130
Phone: (617) 522-4335
Email: dedge@livingmyth.com
Website: www.livingmyth.com

**Michael Evans**
4895 Earl Young Road
Bloomington, IN 47408
Phone: (812) 331-1479
Email: mirevans@indiana.edu

**Heather Forest**
Story Arts Inc.
P.O. Box 354
Huntington, NY 11743
Phone: (631) 271-2511
Email: heather@storyarts.org
Website: www.storyarts.org

**Hanna Bandes Geshelin**
P.O. Box 20363
Worcester, MA 01602-0363
Phone: (508) 791-3982
Email: info@geshelin.com
Website: www.geshelin.com

**Jay Goldspinner**
125 Chapman Street
Greenfield, MA 01301
Phone: (413) 773-8033

**Katie Green**
P.O. Box 12
Princeton, MA 01541
Phone: (978) 464-5146
Email: KTStories@aol.com

**Gavin Harrison**
c/o Shambala Publications
P.O. Box 308
300 Massachusetts Avenue
Boston, MA 02115

**Gail Neary Herman**
166 Lodge Circle
Swanton, MD 21561
Phone: (301) 387-9199
Email: gnherman@mail2.gcnet.net
Website: www.gcnet.net/storyteller

**Dr. Hugh Morgan Hill (Brother Blue)**
P.O. Box 381315
Cambridge, MA 02238-1315
Phone: (617) 491-8399
Email: r_hill@radcliffe.edu

**Marcia Lane**
462 Amsterdam Avenue
New York, NY 10024
Phone: (212) 799-1196

**Tracy Leavitt**
16 Lawrence Road
Accord, NY 12404
Phone: (845) 626-2546
Email: TALeavitt@aol.com

**Rona Leventhal**
P.O. Box 495
Hadley, MA 01035
Phone: (413) 586-0624
Email: ronatales@mindspring.com
Website: www.ronatales.com

**Barbara Lipke**
799 Commonwealth Avenue
Newton Center, MA 02459
Phone: (617) 244-5606
Email: bliptales@earthlink.net

**Doug Lipman**
P.O. Box 441195
West Somerville, MA 02144
Phone: (781) 391-3672
Email: doug@storydynamics.com
Website: www.storydynamics.com

**Medicine Story**
Mettanokit Outreach
Route 123
Greenville, NH 03048
Phone: (603) 878-2310
Website: www.avaloncity.com/
MedicineStory

**Jay O'Callahan**
P.O. Box 1054
Marshfield, MA 02050
Phone: (800) 626-5356
Email: jay@ocallahan.com
Website: www.ocallahan.com

**Papa Joe**
16 Sunny Lane
Fremont, NH 03044-3564
Phone: (603) 642-5880
Email: papajoe@storyteller.net
Website: http://travel.to/papajoes

**Michael Parent**
15 East Kidder Street
Portland, ME 04103
Phone: (207) 879-0401
Email: miklparent@junocom

**Sarah Pirtle**
63 Main Street
Shelburne Falls, MA 01370
Phone: (413) 625-2355
Email: discover@mtdata.com

**John Porcino**
120 Pulpit Hill Road
Amherst, MA 01002
Phone: (413) 549-5448
Email: john.porcino@cohousing.com
Website: www.johnporcino.com

**Michael Punzak**
23 Donnell Street
Cambridge, MA 02138-1305
Phone: (617) 876-5387

**Cheryl Savageau**
7 Rockland Street
Nashua, NH 03064
Phone: (603) 595-8339
Email: Chersav@aol.com

**Nancy Schimmel**
1639 Channing Way
Berkeley, CA 94703
Phone: (510) 843-0533
Email: nancy@sisterschoice.com
Website: www.sisterschoice.com

**Peninnah Schram**
525 West End Avenue-8C
New York, NY 10024
Phone: (212) 787-0626
Email: peninnah1@aol.com

**Susan Tobin**
12 Winch Park Road
Framingham, MA 01701
Phone: (508) 788-0194

111000

If you have enjoyed *Spinning Tales, Weaving Hope,*
you might enjoy other

# BOOKS TO BUILD A NEW SOCIETY

Our books provide positive solutions for people who
want to make a difference. We specialize in:

**Educational and Parenting Resources • Nonviolence**

**Sustainable Living • Ecological Design and Planning**

**Natural Building & Appropriate Technology • New Forestry**

**Environment and Justice • Conscientious Commerce**

**Progressive Leadership • Resistance and Community**

New Society Publishers aims to publish books for
fundamental social change through nonviolent action.
We focus especially on sustainable living, progressive leadership,
and educational and parenting resources.

Our full list of books can be browsed,
and purchased securely, on the worldwide web at:

## www.newsociety.com

or call **1-800-567-6772**

## NEW SOCIETY PUBLISHERS